Summer afternoon—summer afternoon;
to me those have always been the two most
beautiful words in the English language.

Henry James

Favourite Summer Stories from

Front Porch Al

SELECTED
AND
INTRODUCED
BY

ALAN MAITLAND

VIKING

VIKING
Published by the Penguin Group
Penguin Books Canada Ltd, 10 Alcorn Avenue, Toronto, Ontario M4V 3B2
Penguin Books Ltd, 27 Wrights Lane, London W8 5TZ, England
Viking Penguin, a division of Penguin Books USA Inc., 375 Hudson Street,
New York, New York 10014, U.S.A.
Penguin Books Australia Ltd, Ringwood, Victoria, Australia
Penguin Books (NZ) Ltd, 182–190 Wairau Road, Auckland 10, New Zealand

Penguin Books Ltd, Registered Offices: Harmondsworth, Middlesex, England

First published 1995
10 9 8 7 6 5 4 3 2 1

Introductions, Notes and Selection Copyright © Alan Maitland, 1995

Printed and bound in Canada on acid-free paper ∞

Canadian Cataloguing in Publication Data

Main entry under title:

Favourite summer stories from Front Porch Al

ISBN: 0-670-86134-0

1. Short stories, Canadian (English).* 2. Short stories, American. 3. Short
stories, English. 4. Canadian fiction (English)—20th century.* 5. American
fiction—20th century. 6. English fiction—19th century. 7. English fiction—
20th century. I. Maitland, Alan.

PS8321.F38 1995   C813'.010836   C94-932638-0
PR9197.32.F38 1995

This storybook is dedicated to all the "As It Happens"
Front Porch Al listeners who have heard these
stories and now want to read them.

And to my father, who, without knowing it,
passed along to me his love of reading—reading
for pleasure on your own front porch.

Acknowledgments

I am in debt to CBC's Mark Starowicz for starting the stories on "As It Happens," and of course to those who continued them. To Barbara Frum who dubbed me Fireside Al. To Jackie Kaiser of Penguin for transferring them from tape to the written page. It's exciting to see them collected in print. To George Jamieson and Don Mason for doing much of the early work. And to the many who have enjoyed the stories over the years on CBC radio. Now you can read them for yourselves. Enjoy!

Front Porch Al

INTRODUCTION

The August sky was clear and bright last night. My dog Gretzky and I were sitting outside enjoying the fresh evening air. I began to think of a wonderful story I had just finished reading about a little boy who looks up at the night sky and sees the moon sitting in a willow tree. I looked up. There was the moon. The old tree out back was bending against the sky. I tried the angles. How small was the boy? How big was the tree?

When I was a small boy growing up in the Ottawa Valley I used to look up at the summer sky and dream for hours. Summer seemed to be that one moment when time stood perfectly still. I remember camping out by Otter Lake and the stillness of the water as we paddled along the shoreline. Of course, in those days camping meant roughing it in a tent, not transporting all the comforts of home to the woods. One year my parents rented a rustic old cabin by the lakeside. It was an old, falling-down sort of place with mossy walls, an old wood stove and boughs growing up against the eaves. We quickly established a routine of lying about the porch in the afternoons when the weather got too warm, sipping iced tea or lemonade, eating fresh berries and jam sandwiches, and reading whatever was at hand. Pretty soon one or another of us would slip into a doze, lulled to sleep by the chirping of the cicadas.

One day the man from the neighbouring cottage dropped by for a visit. For a few moments we were all so glued to our books that we didn't even notice him. Finally, scratching his beard, a twinkle in his eye, he got up his courage and asked, "What's this, the public library? The reading club of Otter Lake?" I looked about and there we all were, like beached walruses basking ourselves in the August heat, a book cradled in our arms.

Summer's like that still, and though I seem to have less time now, and the world often seems altogether too busy for my liking, I still enjoy lying about on a warm summer afternoon, escaping into distant worlds from the pages of some book.

So here we are. The stories in this collection are stories of different times and places: of blood-red oranges in the gardens of Algiers and boating by the Seine; of cottage country and summer camp; the beach at noon, the prairie farmer; of childhood summers spent fishing and playing baseball, or of a sunny stream wandering through the fields of the Ukraine. Some are quiet, simple stories of childhood told on sunny afternoons; others are more deeply coloured, like a darkening field beneath a summer's storm; others are more fanciful still, like little fairy tales written for a warm summer evening's enjoyment.

This morning the sky is a brilliant blue. My little garden plot out back looks ragged and dusty—the tomatoes bending heavily to the ground. The old vine is still flowering on its tangled trellis, and climbing over everything. So now, if you'll excuse me, I'll leave you to enjoy these stories at your leisure. As for me, I'd better tend to my garden while the sun continues to shine.

TABLE OF CONTENTS

Poaching with *My Old Guy*

by
PAUL QUARRINGTON
(1953–   )

"Poaching with My Old Guy" is a kind of travelogue written for the obsessive angler. The story first appeared in Harrowsmith *magazine, and has that sort of* Harrowsmith *feel about it that I like so much—a rambling, shaggy-dog sort of story, characterized by odd, unexpected insights and asides. A fun, tumbling read from a writer who takes on new colours with each new work.*   ·

My parents own a beautiful piece of land in eastern Ontario. About two miles to the south of it lies Lake Ontario, and the lake and the land are connected by a stream. The stream is rather ambitious near the big water, pushing through farmers' fields with a certain amount of stateliness, but by the time it arrives at my parents' place it could more properly be called a rill. I am not even sure what a rill is, exactly, but it suits this: a small creek so meandering as to seem lost and confused. Still, the rill holds a few trout, and I am a fisherman (I speak not of skill but of devotion to the Art of the Angle) because of that rill.

Occasionally, I have run off poachers. I am alerted by strange sounds coming from the hills—poachers sneaking down to plunder the rill. I come upon them with stern words and foul language. I screw up my eyeballs to suggest advanced lunacy. Most simply turn back when asked to leave, sometimes blinking and looking around as if they had been somnambulating and are as surprised as anyone to find themselves standing in an alien wood. A few argue, claiming there were no signs (which is usually true, as they have torn them down) or expanding on some arcane bit of law.

A fellow once informed me that since one could not *own* waterways, he was therefore entitled to any fish he could pull out of them. I countered that the statute did not apply to rills, which did not satisfy him. All of this leads to my big solution to the problem. I borrow my sister-in-law's dog Jessie from time to time. Jessie is enormous and does not like interlopers. She will cock her head briefly, rush off with a series of stentorian heralds, and the surrounding hills will suddenly come alive with furious scurrying.

One of the fine things about the Art of the Angle is that proselytes need initiation and guidance. I have a theory about the transitional nature of a human life, how one needs someone to facilitate passage, how this is often accomplished by an elder under the pretence of imparting the minutiae of some art or craft. When one decides upon fishing as a hobby, one has elected a lifetime of education. Some anglers, near the end of their days, have acquired vast knowledge, which they then share with the young ones. Fishing is an area that can, even in this decidedly unmagical day and age, still produce magi. I call them *old guys*.

The term "old guy" is not intended to be disrespectful. I first heard it from the lips of Chris Korich, who at the time was competing in the North American Casting Championships, finishing second that year to his archrival and longtime friend, Steve Rajeff. I asked Chris how he learned his art. He described his first fly rod, which he found discarded on the bank of some rill, and how he had attached split shot to the end in order to make a cast. This aberrant behaviour—the heavy shot would travel dangerously fast—was noticed by some old guys who took young Korich under their wings and showed him how to work the thing properly. These old guys were actually master casters at San Francisco's famous Golden Gate Casting & Angling Club.

My old guy's name is Gordon. (Gordon is not that old, by the way, 50-something, but I hope you see that age has little to do with it.) Gordon is a world-class fly caster, a maker of rods, a tier of flies, a lover of nature. And when I say "lover of nature," I mean to raise the ante on that particular term. I never met a man who was so attuned to nature. In a way, he does not exist on the same planet as the rest of us. Gordon has an ability to disregard buildings and hydro towers, to simply not see them, with Mr. Magoo's blessed innocence. At the same time, he will spot things that might elude the notice of a team of binoculared scientists.

Here is the sort of thing Gordon does. We were driving along somewhere north of Toronto, having spent the morning fishing a small creek, um, somewhere north of Toronto. (I am not being secretive here. Gordon's favoured time of departure for fishing trips is several minutes after I have managed to get to sleep. I am usually too groggy to remember much beyond general direction.) Gordon will drive—a huge American motoring sedan, a great-finned land shark, which Gordon pilots as if it were a Jeep or four-by-four, blithely driving off the road and into the wilderness—staring straight ahead.

He will point out things that we pass by. There are big things, things that even I notice. Fields, for example. Gordon adores huge, empty, flat fields, which has to do with his casting practice. Tournament casting has six distance events, and when you start wielding a 30-foot salmon rod over your head, you need a little elbowroom.

Gordon also likes streams. "There's a good one!" he will exclaim. Often they appear to me to be nothing more than rills, but Gordon will go on at some length. In the time it takes him to drive by, and without turning his head, Gordon will note any number of features: felled trees, undercuts, small burns, all places that hold fish.

Gordon remarks on every stream and field that we pass by, which, if you happen to be driving all the way to Cincinnati with him, can become a little annoying. I did happen to be driving all the way to Cincinnati with him (for a casting tournament) and at one point remarked acidly on his predilection. "I like fields, and I like streams," he acknowledged. "And boy, I love that magazine."

But I have committed a huge writerly faux pas, leaping from a car somewhere north of Toronto to a car heading down to Cincinnati. It was the same car, but that is no excuse. So there are these large observations Gordon makes; then there is this sort: "Did you see that fox?"

Fox? Sometimes it takes me a moment to locate whatever *field* Gordon is referring to. During my car trips with Gordon, we have driven by every creature, great and small, that abides in this fair land. I have seen none of them; Gordon has noticed all of them, without turning his head. Gordon claims to possess exceptional peripheral vision, and it is true that he is a hard guy to sneak up on. (I often try to disprove his claim.)

You are probably asking yourselves, how do you know he is not lying? I do not, really, except that from time to time, Gordon will notice something that makes him slam on the brakes, stopping his huge motor sedan somewhere near the soft shoulder. This could be one of two things. It could be a road-kill, which Gordon will gleefully scrape up and toss into the trunk of his motoring sedan. What he wants, you understand, is the fur or feathers (which the owner no longer needs) to use as fly-tying materials.

The other thing that will cause Gordon to stop is the sighting of food. (There have been a few ghastly occasions when the line between the two got a little blurry, but I will not go into it now.) Gordon believes that much of the world is edible. To be fair, what Gordon believes is that there are things to eat out there, delicious and free, which most people drive by without noticing. (He has written quite a good book on the subject, although he does suggest a few things that I think might have had even Euell Gibbons, noted forager, he of *Stalking the Wild Asparagus*, scurrying for the flounder box.)

Let me illustrate by returning to somewhere north of Toronto. I am sitting (groggily) not noticing anything; Gordon has remarked on hawks, hairy toads, lemurs and leopards (or something like that). Suddenly, he throws on the brakes and pulls the car into geographical proximity of the soft shoulder.

"Look!" he says, pointing at a field. "Puffballs!"

I manage to spot the field—the white fence was a giveaway—and am willing to accept that there are puffballs in it. I am not willing to leap the fence and claim them—Gordon is—

particularly when two large mastiffs run up and defend their side of the fence with bared teeth and maniacal ululations. Gordon starts climbing.

"Don't worry about them," he says. "Look at their tails."

Their tails have a vague wagging motion, almost imperceptible, likely the result of a small breeze. But when Gordon drops into their midst, the dogs look at each other in bewilderment. The barking and fang-baring have always done the trick before. Having exhausted their repertoire, the hounds turn away dejectedly and Gordon pulls puffballs.

So we see, in my old guy, certain characteristics, including a unique relationship with the natural world and (I am sure this did not go unnoticed) something of a disregard for the concept of private property.

Now it came to pass one summer's day that Gordon and I went fishing. "I'll see you here at five o'clock," he said, meaning his house, meaning in the morning. Gordon himself goes to bed around eight. He does not understand night owls like me who might like to stay up and see what Peter Mansbridge has to report. I managed to make it to his house by five, although I arrived heavy-lidded, confused and unable to form complete sentences. The good thing about Gordon's earth boat is that it is spacious and comfy, so as soon as we pulled out of the drive, I drifted off.

I awoke what I suppose was about two hours later, and I awoke for this reason: Gordon had blithely turned the car off the road. He did not turn off the freeway onto a two-lane, or off a two-lane onto a dirt road; no, he turned off a dirt road onto unadulterated topography. When he does this sort of thing, he affects the air of a person out for a Sunday drive, drumming his fingers on the steering wheel, whistling tunelessly.

He stopped at the edge of a gorge, and we climbed out of the car and looked at the river. I suppose I could name it, but for some reason, I am reluctant to. It is a good river, well known. Where it is crossed by the Macdonald-Cartier Freeway (which the highway accomplishes via a bridge of great length), the river is wide and violent, all white water and concrete abutments. Farther north, it turns quiet. Where Gordon and I stood, the river was perhaps 20 feet across. We stood at an elbow, where time had made the water shallow and formed a sandbar. Standing on the sandbar and looking farther north still, we saw that the river made itself even smaller and wandered into the shadowy woods.

We followed it there, but not before putting on our stuff. One of the auxiliary pleasures of the Art of the Angle is the putting on of stuff. My own stuff was fairly new: I had scientifically advanced neoprene hip waders, Polaroid sunglasses and a fishing vest that was, for all intents and purposes, one of those stylish multipocketed photojournalist's jackets, except for a little patch of fuzz to stick flies on and a few extra pockets.

Gordon's own hip waders were rendered out of whatever was used before they discovered rubber. His fishing vest was weathered (I have just been to the thesaurus and am disappointed to find that there are no words like "typhooned" or "hurricaned" to employ in this case). It was zipperless and may or may not have retained some buttons; it was impossible to tell, because Gordon wore the contents of a Canadian Tire franchise on it. From the shoulders streamed long pieces of twine with split shot clamped on, which somehow lent Gordon a quasi-military aspect. Dangling from the vest were some tools: knives, nail-clippers, hook removers, pliers, a thick piece of rubber for straightening leaders. Oh, that's right, he also wore leaders on his vest, tiny loops of line filed in some manner; the vest was also bedecked with a multitude of tiny flies, and in case there was not the precise one needed, some of the pockets were filled with fur and feathers so that Gordon could whip it up streamside. Other pockets were crammed with hooks, lures, floats, swivels, weights, line and spare reel parts.

And Gordon wore a hat, an old Andy Capp thing, that made him look as if he had a road-kill balanced on top of his head.

The sky was empty, the sun had been awakened early, the day was already toasty. If we had been observed by alien eyes—I often have this thought, "What would a Venusian think?"—I am sure we would have added to humankind's already eccentric reputation. "There it was, 35 degrees Celsius, these guys dressed up in *rubber*."

I will tell you how Gordon fishes a river: on tiptoe. He inches his way along and spends very little time actually putting line to water. Gordon will simply judge a piece of river and quickly decide where the fish are likely to be. Now as a rule of thumb, I can report that fish are likeliest to be where it is difficult, if not impossible, to place a fly or lure. This is where it comes in pretty handy being the North American Masters Casting Champion, which Gordon has been for many years now.

Gordon also benefits from some practice at a pastime called Arrenburg, which is a European casting game designed to test streamside skills. Casts are made underhanded, from the side, just as they must be when the angler is confined and constricted by brush. So while Gordon tiptoed and cast with breathtaking precision, I plodded along behind, still half-asleep, distributing terminal tackle in various branches, a fact I mention because I suppose at some point during the initial stages of the fishing, Gordon and I went over, under or through some manner of barricade, boundary or fence.

We came to a little crook in the river, edging toward it as if the river itself were a skittish deer and likely to bolt at any time. Gordon saw something that cracked his face apart with a smile. He pulled me back, well out of the water's earshot, and gesticulated wildly.

"The tree, the tree," he whispered.

A tree had fallen, keeled over head-first like a drunk at dawn, and lay half in and half out of the water. These were trout digs if ever there were trout digs, and Gordon was offering me first crack at it. Gordon always offered me first crack. I usually offered it right back, especially if the preamble went anything like, "Can you see the undercut just behind that gnarly mass of briar all of which is obscured from view by this enormous weeping willow? Cast there."

However, I had a chance at this felled tree. And, I should mention, precisely that—a single chance. I was casting a tiny Mepps lure, and my first and only cast would either (a) convince the fish that a large and juicy bug had tumbled from a branch*, or (b) announce the arrival of yet another clumsy angler. (*Here is one of Gordon's tips, offered just in case you hoped you might learn anything about fishing by reading this story: Remove that little bit of red tubing that Mepps puts on the shank of the hook, because it destroys the tumblebug illusion.) At any rate, I remembered as well as I could Gordon's various instructions—he was, after all, my old guy—and managed a neat little flick that plopped musically near the felled tree, and I saw the fish drift out to investigate.

They say, you know, that Ted Williams could see the seams on a baseball as it came at him in the batter's box, and I seem to have acquired something of this preternatural visual ability, seeing things with astounding clarity and in slow motion, for I saw the fish look at the lure and decide, "Oh-oh, stupid fishermen..." I gave the line a little twitch then, and the lure jerked in the fish's face; the fish said, "Hold on here," and ate that tumbling bug in a flash. Then it lit out for the territories.

One often sees fishermen following their fish downstream or upstream, quivering rods held out in front like dowsing sticks. These nimrods tramp through the water, screaming, "Fish, on!" to other anglers (which is to say, "Clear out of the way!"), acting as if their trout were part St. Bernard and in need of its daily perambulation. Gordon views this with a fair measure of disdain, his thinking being that if one is willing to follow the fish long enough, one is likely to claim it. Gordon is nothing if not sporting, and for that reason, he stands his ground, refusing to budge, and if he is your old guy, that is the sort of thing that is expected.

The fish on the other end of the line was not a behemoth, please do not misunderstand, but it was a three-pound rainbow trout, and its fury bent my rod over sharply. My first thought was that if I could walk it down to Lake Ontario, it might give up out of boredom. Gordon touched my arm, staying me on the bank, and fastened his eyes to the water. Like many fine anglers, Gordon has the ability to see into water, to correct optically for the refraction and reflection, and he gave me the somewhat alarming news that the fish was headed for a submerged tree stump as gnarly with roots as Medusa's head. Gordon was giggling as he gave me this news, delighted with my good fortune.

'Lower your rod," he advised urgently—it is hard to sound urgent and giggle at the same time, but Gordon managed it—and then he gently guided my rod down until it lay perpendicular to the horizon, still wowed and aquiver, and in this manner was the fish dissuaded from the stump, its escape coming to naught. In some minutes, the fish joined Gordon and me—by now, we were both giggling—on the shore. We stopped giggling in order to dispatch the fish, which we did with both celerity and solemnity.

It was then that the hound from hell made its appearance. It seems to me that the cur must have been hanging in the trees while all this was going on. All I know is that it dropped into our midst with raised hackles, bared teeth and flashing eyes. Its tail was not wagging, not even the slightest bit. It did not bark, other than a single, eloquent yawp that razored through my innards. I am not sure of Gordon's reaction—I was too busy watching my life flash before my eyes—but I suspect that he remained placid, seeing at once the poetry of his existence being snuffed out by a slobbering mastiff.

We were spared by its master's voice—"Bob!"—but I suspected we were still in deep trouble, not trusting anyone who would name his dog Bob. And when the man appeared—was he, too, hanging from the trees, just waiting to pounce?—my suspicions were confirmed. He was enormous, for one thing, with unruly hair and dark grey eyes. He advanced on us evenly, each footfall heavy and ominous. OBSCURE WRITER AND HIS OLD GUY, the headlines would read, perhaps not on the front page, MURDERED BY SERIAL KILLER.

"Hey!" he barked—I think it was him; it may have been the dog. "What have you got behind your back?"

"Oh, nothing," said I.

"Good morning, sir, and a wonderful morning it is!" Gordon piped up.

"What is it?" the man demanded of me once more. "Is it a fish?"

"Oh, say, yes, it is a fish!"

"*Poachers*," the man snarled. I believe he may have added an adjective or two.

"Are we on your land?" asked Gordon with a large dollop of stagy innocence.

"It's my land," said he, "and my fish." He held out his hand, and I meekly tendered the catch, which nestled with frightening ease in the palm.

Gordon removed his road-kill cap and scratched at his head. "We must have got lost in the woods," he suggested.

"I don't believe you got lost in the woods," said the man, "but you're going to get lost now. *Bob...*"

So get lost we did, at a world-record pace, and soon the two of us were hiking along a country road, fishing rods slung over our shoulders. The red-winged blackbirds perched on their bulrushes and seemed to taunt us as we walked by. Gordon was grinning. I was red-faced and fuming.

"I can't believe it," I muttered. "I can't believe I'm a poacher."

"Poaching," said my old guy, "has a long and honourable history."

I stopped and wondered what Gordon meant by that. And suddenly I understood. I do not think I would have understood on a day that was not so gorgeous. There was a stillness, except for Gordon and me tramping down a road, roasting under the sun in our rubberwear. The world was wide awake but curiously lazy and still—the world had hung a sign where its business shingle should have been: GONE FISHING. Gordon and I had been forced off one tiny piece of the planet, but it was a beautiful planet and very, very large. I understood then why Gordon grinned all the time, because I found myself grinning. This story is about learning that from my old guy.

So I understood his statement totally, utterly, but only for that wonderful while. I have not turned into an anarchic angler. I abide by the law. But these days when I hear the sounds coming from the woods at my parents' place—they are giggles, mostly—I usually go indoors and read a book for an hour or two. When I come back out, all is silent once more.

The *Little White Girl*

by
JOYCE MARSHALL
(1913–   )

I first came across the story of "The Little White Girl" a couple of years ago in a collection called Any Time At All. *I hadn't heard of Joyce Marshall before, and couldn't remember when I was last so quietly and unexpectedly impressed by a story. As Timothy Findley has it, "Joyce Marshall is one of a handful—and a handful only—of writers whose stories consistently bear re-reading."*

We were not liked in the village, or in any of the villages where we spent our summers. That could be a story in itself but I think it's part of this. I was eight years old that year, used, I believe, to being disliked—in an inclusive way, simply for being. I no longer puzzled over this or questioned it especially. It was just something I'd learned and knew. We looked wrong. Did not wear black dresses—I'm speaking of myself and my sisters; our parents' garments were equally out of line, my strong gay father in white tennis-flannels, my pretty mother's skirts showing her knees—but trailed along the curve of that village street in our cotton bathing-suits, long and limp and purply-blue when they were new, gradually shrinking in to our bodies and bleaching to driftwood grey. We didn't have pointy features or black, glossy eyes. Our hair too was peculiar—not dark and straight, sliced off at the mid-point of the ear, but an unstable mixture of blond and brown and red, mop-like by fall, trimmed before we left the city into what our mother, who despised hair-brushing, called "nice close crops, so lovely for swimming." (I'm sorry to give the impression I thought all the little girls in the village looked exactly alike. But until I saw the one particular little white girl, who gave that walk its mystery and its intensity, I honestly thought they did. When your glance meets only hostility or a twitter to a companion in a secret language, you don't look for very long.) Above all, we weren't pale. We didn't spend our days indoors or creaking sedately in the shade on wooden swings. Our mother was a fresh-air fiend, a sun fiend.

And, of course, we spoke English. I don't know whether I saw our speech as a graver flaw in village eyes than the lack of stockings and black dresses to cover us decently from toes to wrists. The two went together. By that summer I was over the worst of my terror of French. I'd heard my father speak it, which he did well. I myself would learn when I started grade three in the fall. (I expected French to come by a miracle, as reading had: one minute the sounds all loose—bbb, aaa—and the next joining to form words, so that I ran home, calling out every sign, picked up books and newspapers, could read anything.) I was used, at least, to living among sounds that seemed to me empty. I had a flashback to that early terror when, fully grown up, I got off the plane in Copenhagen and was lost amid mouthings that meant nothing; I was two years old again, shrieking, "But what are they saying?" I don't think it ever occurred to me that those little village girls, who looked at us briefly and turned away, might also be veterans of two-year-old terror.

So there we were, my two younger sisters and I, having to run that gauntlet of dislike four times almost every day from May till November. I think it was the longest gauntlet we ever had to run—from one end of that curved village street to the other. Though we rented a house just outside the city on what Montrealers called the lakeshore every summer, my parents never got organized in time to find one that had enough bedrooms, was properly furnished—or anywhere near the beach. We summered in some curious houses—gloomy with horsehair and funeral wreaths, their kitchens full of interesting smells. We children liked the excitement of not knowing how hot the upstairs would be or what would leak or where, but every autumn my mother vowed she'd never submit to this again. We'd stay in Montreal like a reasonable family and go for two weeks to Old Orchard, where she'd once spent a magic holiday with her mother; she pitied her own poor children who'd never seen the ocean, just the old dreary St. Lawrence River widening out and pretending to be a lake. But every year, in March or April, my parents drove the few miles to the lakeshore and scoured us up another house.

But even when we had to sleep crowded as we were that year, all three, into a stuffy little room with torn green netting at the tiny window, we had marvellous summers. Absolutely free. Swimming and tumbling about till we were drunk from the water, our finger-tips puckered, our lips blue. I still think it was worth being disliked as we were to be so free. Considerably freer than children are today. And certainly freer than any of our friends. Magnificent swimmers themselves, our parents assumed that once a child was swimming, not just bluffing with an occasional foot on the bottom, she was as much, and as wary, a creature of water as any fish or frog. The summer I was eight, two of us were swimmers so we could walk through the village alone to spend the whole morning, and later the whole afternoon, at our little shallow sandy-bottomed swimming-cove. There were usually other people there, and Mother came most days at three o'clock to coach us for a while, then set off for a long swim in the deep water. I wish now that I knew what those solitary journeys meant to her. I can think myself back to the moment of her turning from us, her clear beautiful eyes lit with something like exultation, then all I can see is her bobbing rubber-capped head and the diminishing spray from her quick but seemingly tireless overarm side-stroke as I wondered whether this time she'd reach Nuns' Island—a green smudge whose very name suggested peril—and never come back to us again.

When I was a little older I had a spell of feeling shamed by all this freedom, saw it as a sign we were not loved. But where my parents saw danger, they were cautious. Maddeningly so; I started when I was three to pray for a bicycle and to wish, for good measure, on every white horse and every nun I saw, but wasn't given one till I was twelve. And though traffic through that village was limited to a car, a delivery cart or a buggy every ten minutes or so, we had to cross the road in front of our house, with Mother directing from the gallery. We were thus also spared the hazards of crossing St. John's Road, a hilly track that came down into the middle of the village, bringing occasional farmers in their buggies—rigs we called them—drawn by nobbly horses that tended to get skittish at the sight, even careful on the wooden sidewalk, of English children in their cotton bathing-suits. But I'd have faced dozens of such horses and hundreds of cars rather than the village people on their galleries four times almost every day.

These galleries, which were unrailed and rather shallow, were seldom more than a foot or so from the sidewalk, and here people sat side by side in wooden rocking-chairs, contemplating the life on the street. Not whole families in the day-time—just the old black-clad men and women and a few careful little girls. And though this was our second summer in that village, no-one gave any hint of knowing us or even smiled. Not that we wanted them to. To us they were scented with danger, being connected with nuns—mounds of black cloth surrounding tiny, cross-looking faces, menacing creatures eager to snatch up little Protestant girls and put them in convents, where they'd have to keep out of the sun and worship holy pictures instead of dreaming through long, broody Anglican services like those we were dragged to once or twice a year. Luckily for my nerves as nominal custodian of our little group, there were no nuns in the village. Nor do I remember seeing any priests, whom I still believed were married to the nuns, the fathers of those gaggles of children I'd seen being shepherded about the streets in Montreal. If there'd been a chance of meeting any of those dark parents, all anxious to add to the size of their families, I don't think I'd have been able to make the walk.

Then at some point in that summer—we were tanned, I know, the hems of our bathing-suits no longer chafed our knees when dry—I saw the little white girl. She was just suddenly there, on a gallery that had been empty. I was impressed first by the chair she sat in. It was large and square and not a rock-er, upholstered in the same brown faded-flowery plush as the chairs at my grandparents', which were also angular, impossi-ble to snuggle into and clearly made for bigger people. Hers had a sort of foot-rest, though she was very small and, even with a cushion behind her, couldn't as much as bend her legs. She wore one of the usual black dresses with a crimped white edging at the neck, thick creamy stockings, rumpled at the ankles, and party-shoes—round-toed patent-leather slippers with a strap. I noticed that their soles were clean, with scarcely a scratch. Also her hair was curly and not chopped straight off, as light a brown as mine though not as unruly as mine became the moment it grew in.

But it was chiefly her face that made her distinct from the other village children. It laughed, it was always changing expression, it sparkled. I had never seen such joy on a human face. And seldom since, though I've seen transient joy capture the faces of friends and strangers. And even roused it a few times. The little girl's joy wasn't transient. And what I could see of her—her face and her hands—was most exquisitely white. I had never seen such whiteness before. Like her joy, it seemed to set her apart from ordinary people. Apart especially from tanning little girls trudging home from swimming with scabs on their knees—or ooze, because they could never resist lifting the edge of a scab to see if it was healed. I knew there could be no scabs under those white stockings. She was perfect.

And she was loved. I could see that, for she was always sur-rounded by four or five children. Her sisters? It was possible. Their sizes shaded into one another's, unlike ours with our clear, two-and-a-half years' jump between. I remember them as always on their feet gathered around her, though surely they must sometimes have been sitting. Laughing with her, twitter-ing with her in that mysterious language. Sometimes a plump, aproned lady came out and leaned over her to comb her hair or lift her to another part of the chair or just stand for a while and laugh. I found it all astonishing. I envied it. Envied her, because I could see she was the centre and the source; the joy wouldn't have existed without her.

I took to walking slowly as we passed that house. The others would yank at me, "Marty, come on," for it was a myth that I was in charge of my sisters; I, to my disgrace and sometimes sorrow, was dreamy—"moony," according to my mother—and they would never have obeyed an order from me even if I'd thought of one to give. When I could manage it, I'd stop—just before we came to the chair and the circle of children. I didn't dare go any closer. I'd pretend I had to shake grit from my sandals and thus gain a few seconds to look more carefully and wonderingly at the little white girl. She never seemed to see me. She was too surrounded. I wouldn't have expected her to see me. But my seeing her became the most important part of my day—of every day except those few when we didn't go to the beach. Now and then we'd be invited to a birthday party by one of the other city children. Mother would make a wild attempt to pretty us up, attaching bows to our cropped heads, speaking reproachfully (and rather unfairly) of the lovely ringlets worn by other little girls, running up pink organdy dresses on her old treadle machine. Or she'd have one of her furies of preserving and we'd have to stay home mornings to pick over currants or clip heads and tails from gooseberries. Missing a swim to "help" became unbearable punishment. "You're so mean, I hate you," I'd scream, comparing my own clumsiness, my inability to behave properly even when I could decide how that was (a failing not as exclusive to me as I believed) with the gaiety and joy that enclosed the little white girl. She was my first secret—she herself and my need to look at her, marvel at her, and wonder about her.

Do we as adults remember how few of the things that are read to them children confide? Their whole life is a struggle to keep secrets, gain a little space. They've come late, they see, into a world where their parents have lived forever and, at a time when they themselves are always changing, they must wrest a small area of their own from adults who are immutable. They must also survive. And as this survival demands a constant jockeying for place and particularity in the hearts of their parents, they're afraid to reveal themselves to one another. If my mother noticed that I no longer nagged to be let stay home and read on rainy days, she probably imagined that the wholesome outdoor habits she was determined to root in me were finally taking hold. Reading was all very well—we were expected to read, read anything from the adult shelves that caught our attention—but only when some form of vigorous physical activity wasn't to be had. So we would be packed off to swim in teeming rain.

Somewhere towards the end of that summer, when the village was becoming increasingly dusty, our bathing-suits were tight at the crotch, and weeds had poked up between the splintery boards of the sidewalk, I discovered that the chair in which the little girl sat wasn't only a chair. The step her feet never reached could be drawn up and then the chair became a bed. A most unusual square bed, rather like a brown plush crib, in which the little girl now lay, a pillow under her head so that I could see her as clearly as ever, a knitted coverlet hiding most of her black dress. I was fascinated. She still laughed, her eyes still shone with joy. She moved her head a great deal, turning to one or other of her sisters, the rest of her motionless. She hadn't moved her body to any extent even when she sat. I didn't find this strange. It was just another part of her and, if I thought of it at all, I probably felt that she didn't need to move. Why should she? Everything was given to her. But now that she lay instead of sitting, I saw that she was not much longer than the younger of my sisters. And not anything like as wide. Yet I felt that she was closer to my own age. I'm almost sure it never occurred to me that there was anything wrong with the little white girl. I knew about illness. My own father had lain for three months in bed in our Montreal house with typhoid—horribly flushed at first when I defied orders and peeked, just as horribly yellowish when we were allowed at last into his room. But he had nurses. And bowls. There was a great and ominous flurry. The house stank of medicine. Even without these trappings, I might have guessed, if the little white girl had looked sad. Or fretful. But her joy was real. I knew that. It lasted even when she was alone.

As I saw her only once, a day or two before we were to move back to the city. I was also alone. My mother had sent me to the store just before supper. I think I offered to go, which astonished her, since I usually made use of my free moments after swimming to sneak off somewhere with a book. The little girl was still encircled by her sisters when I went down. Alone when I came back. It was late, the beginning of a September twilight; the village looked strange and rather threatening, deserted chairs on galleries all set to start rocking by themselves. I realized vaguely that the little girl's sisters had gone in to set the table or some other girl-y thing. She lay there, not exactly laughing, which would have been absurd since no-one was with her, but her eyes alight the way they always were. I stopped in front of her, my mother's old cloth shopping-bag clutched to my side, ready to flee if she didn't like my being there. An enemy, after all. We looked at each other. For the first time I saw the little cross she wore, that alien symbol, mark of the nuns. Mostly I noticed the soft yet glinting darkness of her eyes. She laughed. Not only that, she spoke, just a twitter or so but as if she expected me to understand and answer. "Hello," I said. She went on laughing, as if I'd been delightfully comic. I laughed too and tried to think of some way of bypassing words, using my hands or my face. It may have been only a few seconds but as I stood there, very conscious of my wrongness, awkwardness, brownness, scabs, it seemed to me that she was trying to tell me something and that I almost caught it. But then I saw the shadow of her mother at the door and took to my heels.

We went back to Montreal soon after that. It was a fairly ordinary winter. We were all sick, first with mumps, then with chicken pox. Just after the last placard came down, we had a new baby, our fourth girl. My tan faded but my skin didn't become really white. In my intervals at school I had a French lesson every morning. I thought often about the little white girl and about learning something to say to her. In the meantime I practised what the others described as a simpering smile. My mother, who was beginning to fear I might grow up to be eccentric or morbid, and thus doomed to be unhappy, started me on dancing lessons to cut down on my reading—and its companion in my case, brooding. Spring came and I wanted to keep the hair that had grown raggedly to my shoulders; a discussion of whether I could look after it myself went suddenly awry, one of us said the wrong thing, my wish became a challenge. In the ensuing battle of wills, I lost. My mother lifted me into the barber's chair and held me there while I screamed, "I hate you, Mother, I'll always hate you. And when I grow up, I'll never do anything you say. I'll read all day. I'll never go out of the house. Not ever." I sobbed all night, humiliated by my own behaviour and by hers. I suppose she was also ashamed though neither of us apologized. We were both pigheaded, particularly with one another. We'd battled only mildly until then; I was beginning to have more to fight with, we were at odds about almost everything from then on and I even won a few times. She died when I was still quite young and before anything was really settled between us—I had not yet escaped the boundaries (rather good boundaries but not mine) that she was trying to set for me or discovered my own space. But that's another story and much longer—a story I imagine I'm still living and will always live.

Meanwhile, though there'd been no miracle and I'd given up expecting that there would be, I'd been learning French. I would see the little white girl and—sing "*Frère Jacques?*" Or, more appropriate for one on her way to or from the beach, "*Vive l'eau?*" Perhaps I could base something on our endless classroom examination of the picture of *la famille Labranche* that Mademoiselle, a drawling, always tired-looking Swiss woman, rolled down with a clack each morning at ten o'clock.

"*La classe, qu'est-ce que Marie fait?*"

"*Marie joue avec une poupée.*"

So…"*Qu'est-ce que vous faites?*" I might say.

"*Je joue avec…*" But she didn't play. Well, perhaps she'd answer in some of the words I knew.

What with the new baby, our parents were even more dilatory than usual about finding us a house for the summer. This year's was the pokiest and least convenient—a derelict farmhouse a long way back from the village on St. John's Road. My mother mourned being tied down with an infant and not even within sight of the water. She talked a great deal about Old

Orchard and the frustration of being married to a man who preferred dull, flat old Lake St. Louis to the ocean. For us children, trips to the beach now began with a hilly trudge down a dirt road, leaps every now and then across ditches to avoid farmers in their rigs, but daily miracles along our way—devil's paintbrushes, chicory and vetch, and once, overnight, a whole broad field of quivering blue-eyed grass. We didn't mind in the least and stoutly said that we had no interest in Old Orchard.

It took me many weeks to realize I wasn't going to see the little white girl. When her gallery was empty, I waited for sunnier days, then for real summer. But summer became as real as it would ever be and still she didn't appear. I didn't even see her sisters. At least not there. I probably wouldn't have known them if I'd seen them anywhere else. I hoped for a long time, hoped daily and then gradually lost the expectation of seeing her, though I still thought about her in the same wondering way. Because I'd never mentioned her to anyone, I didn't ask about her now. My parents probably wouldn't have been able to tell me where she'd gone. But before the end of that summer—the last of the three we spent in the village—the curve of that road round to the beach wrote itself into my feet and from my feet into whatever part of ourselves it is that invents the language of our dreams.

For a long time, however, I didn't know it was the lakeshore curve of my dreams—of the one particular dream I've had again and again since I was not far out of my teens. It has always come at rather long intervals and the strange thing is that I never wake straight out of it as one does from ordinary dreams. But it leaves a mood, a sense of clarity and rightness, and at some point during the next few days I find myself thinking: I'm glad I found it, it's still there just where I knew it ought to be. And I realize I've been on that road again. I always reach it by some complicated, even terrifying journey, never the same way twice. I shuttle back and forth on trains, missing my station, arguing with conductors who refuse to let me off, or I have many miles to walk and fences to climb with people rising up to bar my path or stubbornly give wrong directions. Once, I remember, I travelled by ship through the Great Lakes and was sailing down the Mississippi before I got headed in the right way. But eventually I'm there and it was only recently, when I chanced to think about the little white girl, that I knew what road it was. Because the houses and their galleries, the butcher's and the grocer's have all gone and the road curves now beside the lake. It's a very slow curve, matched to eight-year-old feet, and the road with its scattering of trees reflected in the water, which is green with that special green of the St. Lawrence, alters only slightly as I walk. I am coming from the beach, the water to my left. The houses on the other side of the road are also gone, replaced by tall pines, beautifully spaced and scented, not at all scrubby, an ideal wood. At some point, which I recognize as being right, I cross the road and go in among the trees. For a while, as I strike in more deeply, I don't hear it. Then all at once I do. The sound of a waterfall, tumbling in the distance. Or at least that's what I thought it was, though lately I've wondered whether it might not be laughter. For in my dream I never reach the source of that delicate light sound. I may not even wish to reach it since that might mean going too far and too dangerously into what has been for some time now a darkening wood. It seems enough to be just where I am, knowing it's still there and still ahead, the clear single answer to everything, and that however late it gets, by some means and always, I can find my way back to it.

The
Rooted Lover

by
LAURENCE HOUSMAN
(1865–1959)

*Laurence Housman is like one of those rare Victorian trea-
sure-troves: a little dusty perhaps—hidden for long decades in
some dark attic—but full of a wondrous curiosity and peculiar innocence. "The Rooted Lover" is a fanciful, magical tale
told with a Cinderella-like charm. Like many late Victorians,
Laurence Housman seemed to want to live forever—living on
until the ripe old age of 94. Here, then, is a story from a forgotten world, from an age of darkening innocence.*

Morning and evening a ploughboy went driving his team through a lane at the back of the palace garden. Over the hedge the wind came sweet with the scents of a thousand flowers, and through the hedge shot glimpses of all the colours of the rainbow, while now and then went the sheen of silver and gold tissue when the Princess herself paced by with her maidens. Also above all the crying and calling of the blackbirds and thrushes that filled the gardens with song, came now and then an airy exquisite voice flooding from bower to field; and that was the voice of the Princess Fleur-de-lis herself singing.

When she sang all the birds grew silent; new flowers came into bud to hear her and into blossom to look at her; apples and pears ripened and dropped down at her feet; her voice sang the bees home as if it were evening; and the ploughboy as he passed stuck his face into the thorny hedge, and feasted his eyes and ears with the sight and sound of her beauty.

He was a red-faced boy, red with the wind and the sun: over his face his hair rose like a fair flame, but his eyes were black and bold, and for love he had the heart of a true gentleman.

Yet he was but a ploughboy, rough-shod and poorly clad in

a coat of frieze, and great horses went at a word from him. But no word from him might move the heart of that great Princess; she never noticed the sound of his team as it jingled by, nor saw the dark eyes and the bronzed red face wedged into the thorn hedge for love of her.

"Ah! Princess," sighed the ploughboy to himself, as the thorns pricked into his flesh, "were it but a thorn-hedge which had to be trampled down, you should be my bride to-morrow!" But shut off by the thorns, he was not a whit further from winning her than if he had been kneeling at her feet.

He had no wealth in all the world, only a poor hut with poppies growing at the door; no mother or father, and his own living to get. To think at all of the Princess was the sign either of a knave or a fool.

No knave, but perhaps a fool, he thought himself to be. "I will go," he said at last, "to the wise woman who tells fortunes and works strange cures, and ask her to help me."

So he took all the money that he had in the world and went to the wise woman in her house by the dark pool, and said, "Show me how I may win Princess Fleur-de-lis to be my wife, and I will give you everything I possess."

"That is a hard thing you ask," said the wise woman; "how much dare you risk for it?"

"Anything you can name," said he.

"Your life?" said she.

"With all my heart," he replied, "for without her I shall but end by dying."

"Then," said the wise woman, "give me your money, and you shall take your own risk."

Then he gave her all.

"Now," said she, "you have but to choose any flower you like, and I will turn you into it; then, in the night I will take you and plant you in the palace garden; and if before you die the Princess touches you with her lips and lays you as a flower in her bosom, you shall become a man again and win her love, but if not, when the flower dies you will die too and be no more. So if that seems to you a good bargain, you have but to name your flower, and the thing is done."

"Agreed, with all my heart!" cried the ploughboy. "Only make me into some flower that is like me, for I would have the Princess to know what sort of man I am, so that she shall not be deceived when she takes me to her bosom."

He looked himself up and he looked himself down in the pool which was before the wise woman's home; at his rough frieze coat with its frayed edges, his long supple limbs, and his red face with its black eyes, and hair gleaming at the top.

"I am altogether like a poppy," he said, "what with my red head, and my rough coat, and my life among fields which the plough turns to furrow. Make a poppy of me, and put me in the palace garden, and I will be content."

Then she stroked him down with her wand full couthly, and muttered her wise saws over him, for she was a wonderful witch-woman; and he turned before her very eyes into a great red poppy, and his coat of frieze became green and hairy all over him, and his feet ran down into the ground like roots.

The wise woman got a big flower-pot and a spade; and she dug him up out of the ground and planted him in the pot, and having watered him well, waited till it was quite dark.

As soon as the pole-star had hung out its light she got across her besom, tucked the flower-pot under her arm, and sailed away over hedge and ditch till she came to the palace garden.

There she dug a hole in a border by one of the walks, shook the plough-boy out of his flower-pot, and planted him with his feet deep down in the soil. Then giving a wink all round, and a wink up to the stars, she set her cap to the east, mounted her besom, and rode away into thin space.

But the poppy stood up where she had left him taking care of his petals, so as to be ready to show them off to the Princess the next morning. He did not go fast asleep, but just dozed the time away, and found it quite pleasant to be a flower, the night being warm. Now and then small insects ran up his stalks, or a mole passed under his roots, reminding him of the mice at home. But the poppy's chief thought was for the morning to return; for then would come the Princess walking straight up to where he stood, and would reach out a hand and gather him, and lay her lips to his and his head upon her bosom, so that in the shaking of a breath he could turn again to his right shape, and her love would be won for ever.

Morning came, and gardeners with their brooms and barrows went all about, sweeping up the leaves, and polishing off the slugs from the gravel-paths. The head gardener came and looked at the poppy. "Who has been putting this weed here?" he cried. And at that the poppy felt a shiver of red ruin go through him for what if the gardener were to weed him up so that he could never see the Princess again?

All the other gardeners came and considered him, twisting wry faces at him. But they said, "Perhaps it is a whim of the Princess's. It's none of our planting." So after all they let him be.

The sun rose higher and higher, and the gardeners went carrying away their barrows and brooms; but the poppy stood waiting with his black eye turned the way by which the Princess should come.

It was a long waiting, for princesses do not rise with the lark, and the poppy began to think his petals would be all shrivelled and old before she came. But at last he saw slim white feet under the green boughs and heard voices and shawm-like laughter and knew that it was the Princess coming to him.

Down the long walks he watched her go, pausing here and there to taste a fruit that fell or to look at a flower that opened. To him she would come shortly, and so bravely would he woo her with his red face, that she would at once bend down and press her lips to his, and lift him softly to her bosom. Yes, surely she would do this.

She came; she stopped full and began looking at him: he burned under her gaze. "That is very beautiful!" she said at last. "Why have I not seen that flower before? Is it so rare, then, that there is no other?" But, "Oh, it is too common!" cried all her maids in a chorus, "It is only a common poppy such as grows wild in the fields."

"Yet it is very beautiful," said the Princess; and she looked at it long before she passed on. She half bent to it. "Surely now," said the poppy, "her lips to mine!"

"Has it a sweet smell," she asked. But one of her maids said, "No, only a poor little stuffy smell, not nice at all!" and the Princess drew back.

"Alas, alas," murmured the poor poppy in his heart, as he watched her departing, "why did I forget to choose a flower with a sweet smell then surely at this moment she would have been mine." He felt as if his one chance were gone, and death already overtaking him. But he remained brave: "At least," he said, "I will die looking at her; I will not faint or wither, till I have no life left in me. And after all there is to-morrow." So he went to sleep hoping much, and slept late into the morning of the next day.

Opening his eyes he was aware of a great blaze of red in a border to his right. Ears had been attentive to the words of Princess Fleur-de-lis, and a whole bed of poppies had been planted to gratify her latest fancy. There they were, in a thick mass, burning the air around them with their beauty. Alas! against their hundreds what chance had he?

And the Princess came and stood by them, lost in admiration, while the poppy turned to her his love-sick eye, trying to look braver than them all. And she being gracious, and not forgetful of what first had given her pleasure, came and looked at him also, but not very long; and as for her lips, there was no chance for him there now. Yet for the delight of those few moments he was almost contented with the fate he had chosen—to be a flower, and to die as a flower as soon as his petals fell.

Days came and went; they were all alike now, save that the Princess stayed less often to look at him or the other poppies which had stolen his last chance from him. He saw autumn changes coming over the garden: flowers sickened and fell, and were removed, and the nights began to get cold.

Beside him the other poppies were losing their leaves, and their flaming tops had grown scantier; but for a little while he would hold out still: so long as he had life his eye should stay open to look at the Princess as she passed by.

The sweet-smelling flowers were gone, but the loss of their

fragrant rivalry gave him no greater hopes: one by one every gorgeous colour dropped away; only when a late evening primrose hung her lamp beside him in the dusk did he feel that there was anything left as bright as himself to the eye. And now death was taking hold of him, each night twisting and shrivelling his leaves; but still he held up his head, determined that, though but for one more day, his eye should be blessed by a sight of his Princess. If he could keep looking at her he believed he should dream of her when dead.

At length he could see that he was the very last of all the poppies, the only spot of flame in a garden that had gone grey. In the cold dewy mornings cobwebs hung their silvery hammocks about the leaves, and the sun came through mist, making them sparkle. And beautiful they were, but to him they looked like the winding-sheet of his dead hopes.

Now it happened just about this time that the Prince of a neighbouring country was coming to the Court to ask Princess Fleur-de-lis' hand in marriage. The fame of his manners and of his good looks had gone before him, and the Princess being bred to the understanding that princesses must marry for the good of nations according to the bidding of their parents, was willing, since the King her father wished it, to look upon his suit with favour. All that she looked for was to be wooed with sufficient ardour, and to be allowed time for a becoming hesitancy before yielding.

A great ball was prepared to welcome the Prince on his arrival; and when the day came, Princess Fleur-de-lis went into the garden to find some flower that she might wear as an adornment of her loveliness. But almost everything had died of frost, and the only flower that retained its full beauty was the poor bewitched poppy, kept alive for love of her.

"How wonderfully that red flower has lasted!" she said to one of her maidens. "Gather it for me, and I will wear it with my dress to-night."

The poppy, not knowing that he was about to meet a much more dangerous rival than any flower, thrilled and almost fainted for bliss as the maid picked him from the stalk and carried him in.

He lay upon Princess Fleur-de-lis' toilet-table and watched the putting on of her ballroom array. "If she puts me in her breast," he thought, "she must some time touch me with her lips; and then!"

And then, when the maid was giving soft finishing touches to the Princess's hair, the beloved one herself took up the poppy and arranged it in the meshes of gold. "Alas!" thought the poppy, even while he nestled blissfully in its warm depths, "I shall never reach her lips from here; but I shall dream of her when dead; and for a ploughboy, that surely is enough of happiness."

So he went down with her to the ball, and could feel the soft throbbing of her temples, for she had not yet seen this Prince who was to be her lover, and her head was full of gentle agitation and excitement to know what he would be like. Very soon he was presented to her in state. Certainly he was extremely passable: he was tall and fine and had a pair of splendid mustachios that stuck out under his nostrils like walrus-tusks, and curled themselves like ram's horns. Beyond a slight fear that these might sweep her away when he tried to kiss her, she favoured his looks sufficiently to be prepared to accept his hand when he offered it.

Then music called to them invitingly, and she was led away to the dance.

As they danced the Prince said: "I cannot tell how it is, I feel as if someone were looking at me."

"Half the world is looking at you," said the Princess in slight mockery. "Do you not know you are dancing with Princess Fleur-de-lis?"

"Beautiful Princess," said the Prince, "can I ever forget it? But it is not in that way I feel myself looked at. I could swear I have seen somewhere a man with a sunburnt face and a bold black eye looking at me."

"There is no such here," said the Princess; and they danced on.

When the dance was over the Prince led her to a seat screened from view by rich hangings of silken tapestry; and the Princess Fleur-de-lis knew that the time for the wooing was come.

She looked at him; quite clearly she meant to say "yes." Without being glad, she was not sorry. If he wooed well she would have him.

"It is strange," said the Prince, "I certainly feel that I am being looked at."

The Princess was offended. "I am not looking at you in the least," she said slightingly.

"Ah!" replied the other, "if you did, I should lose at once any less pleasant sensation; for when your eyes are upon me I know only that I love you—you, Princess, who are the most beautiful, the most radiant, the most accomplished, the most charming of your sex! Why should I waste time in laying my heart bare before you? It is here; it is yours. Take it!"

"Truly," thought the Princess, "this is very pretty wooing, and by no means ill done." She bent down her head, and she toyed and she coyed, but she would not say "yes" yet.

But the poppy, when he heard the Prince's words, first went all of a tremble, and then giving a great jump fell down at the Princess's feet. And she, toying and coying, and not wishing to say "yes" yet, bent down and taking up the poppy from where it had fallen, brushed it gently to and fro over her lips to conceal her smiles, and then tucking her chin down into the dimples of her neck began to arrange the flower in the bosom of her gown.

As she did so, all of a sudden a startled look came over her face. "Oh! I am afraid!" she cried. "The man, the man with the red face, and the strong black eyes!"

"What is the matter!" demanded the Prince, bending over her in the greatest concern.

"No, no!" she cried, "go away! Don't touch me! I can't and I won't marry you! Oh, dear! Oh, dear! What is going to become of me?" And she jumped up and ran right away out of the ballroom, and up the great staircase, where she let the poppy fall, and right into her own room, where she barred and bolted herself in.

In the palace there was the greatest confusion: everybody was running about and shaking heads at everybody else.

"Heads and tails! has it come to this?" cried the King, as he saw a party of serving men turning out a ploughboy who by some unheard-of means had found his way into the palace. Then he went up to interview his daughter as to her strange and sudden refusal of the Prince.

The Princess wrung her hands and cried: she didn't know why, but she couldn't help herself: nothing on earth should induce her to marry him.

Then the King was full of wrath, and declared that if she were not ready to obey him in three days' time, she should be turned out into the world like a beggar to find a living for herself.

So for three days the Princess was locked up and kept on nothing but bread and water; and every day she cried less, and was more determined than ever not to marry the Prince.

"Whom do you suppose you are going to marry then?" demanded the King in a fury.

"I don't know," said the Princess, "I only know he is a dear; and has got a beautiful tanned face and bold black eyes."

The King felt inclined to have all the tanned faces and bold black eyes in his kingdom put to death: but as the Princess's obstinacy showed no signs of abating he ended by venting all his anger upon her. So on the third day she was clothed in rags, and had all her jewelry taken off her, and was turned out of the palace to find her way through the world alone.

And as she went on and on, crying and wondering what would become of her, she suddenly saw by the side of the road a charming cottage with poppies growing at the door. And in the doorway stood a beautiful man, with a tanned face and bold black eyes, looking as like a poppy as it was possible for a man to look.

Then he opened his arms: and the Princess opened her arms: and he ran, and she ran. And they ran and they ran and they ran, till they were locked in each other's arms, and lived happily ever after.

Shellfish for Monsieur Chabre

by
EMILE ZOLA
(1840–1904)

"Shellfish for Monsieur Chabre" is a story seasoned heavily by the sea and the sand and the sky. Set in the old French town of Piriac, along the Breton coast, the ramparts of the old town seem to glimmer in the sun beneath a blur of flowering vines. Below lies the sea—and a story of indiscretion played out on the sands of comic intrigue.

Monsieur Chabre had one great sorrow: he was childless. He had married a Mademoiselle Estelle Catinot (of the firm of Desvignes and Catinot). She was tall, beautiful and blonde, only eighteen years of age; but for the last four years he had been anxiously waiting, with growing dismay and wounded pride at the failure of his efforts.

Monsieur Chabre was a retired corn-merchant and a very wealthy man. Despite having lived continently, as befitted a solid middle-class business man bent on becoming a millionaire, he walked with the heavy tread of an old man, although he was only forty-five. His face, prematurely lined with financial cares, was as dull as ditchwater. And he was in despair, for a man who enjoys an investment income of fifty thousand francs a year has the right to feel surprised when he discovers that it is more difficult to become a father than to become rich.

Madame Chabre was twenty-two years old and beautiful. With her peach-like complexion and golden blonde hair curling in ringlets over her neck, she was quite adorable. Her blue-green eyes were like slumbering pools hiding depths difficult to plumb. When her husband complained of their childlessness, she would arch her supple body, emphasizing the

curves of her hips and bosom, and her wry half-smile plainly
said: 'Is it any fault of mine?' It must be added that in her circle of friends and acquaintances, Madame Chabre was
acknowledged as a young woman of perfect breeding, ade-
quately pious and incapable of giving rise to the slightest
breath of scandal, brought up, indeed, in the soundest of middle-class principles by a strict mother. Only the nostrils of her
little white nose would give an occasional nervous twitch
which might have given some cause for concern to anyone but
a retired corn-merchant.

Meanwhile the family doctor, Dr Guiraud, a large, shrewd,
smiling man, had already been called in for a number of private consultations with Monsieur Chabre. He had explained to
him how backward science was: you can't plant a child as
you'd plant an oak, dear me no! However, not wishing to leave
anyone entirely without hope, he had promised to give
thought to the case. So, one July morning he called on
Monsieur Chabre and said:

'You ought to go on a holiday to the sea and do some
bathing. It's an excellent thing. And above all, eat shellfish, lots
of shellfish. Nothing but shellfish.'

Monsieur Chabre's hopes rose.

'Shellfish, doctor?' he asked eagerly. 'Do you think that
shellfish...?'

'Yes, I do indeed! There's strong evidence of the success of
that treatment. So you must understand, every day you eat
oysters, mussels, clams, sea-urchins, not forgetting crayfish
and lobsters!'

Then, just as he was standing in the doorway ready to leave,
he added casually:

'Don't bury yourself in some out-of-the-way place. Madame
Chabre is young and needs entertainment... Go to Trouville,
it's full of ozone.'

Three days later, the couple were on their way. However,
the ex-corn-merchant had thought it pointless to go to
Trouville, where he'd have to spend money hand-over-fist. You
can eat shellfish anywhere, indeed, in an out-of-the-way resort
the shellfish would be more plentiful and far cheaper. As for

entertainment, there's always too much of that. After all, they weren't travelling for pleasure.

A friend had recommended the tiny resort of Pouliguen, close to Saint Nazaire, a new town with its modern, dead-straight streets still full of building sites. They visited the harbour and loitered round the streets where the shops hesitated between being tiny, gloomy village stores and large luxury grocers. At Pouliguen there was not one single house left unlet. The little timber and plaster houses, looking like garish fairground shacks, which stretched round the bay, had all been invaded by the English and rich Nantes tradesmen. Estelle pulled a wry face when she saw the queer structures in which middle-class architects had given free rein to their imagination.

The travellers were advised to spend the night in Guérande. It was a Sunday. When they arrived just before noon, even Monsieur Chabre, although not naturally a poetic person, was at first struck with admiration by this little jewel of a medieval town, so well-preserved with its ramparts and deep gateways with battlements. Estelle looked at the drowsy little town, surrounded by its esplanades shaded by tall trees, and its charm brought a gleam into the dreamy pools of her eyes. Their carriage drove in through one of the gateways and clattered at a trot over the cobblestones of the narrow streets. The Chabres had not exchanged a word.

'What a dump!' the ex-corn-merchant muttered finally. 'The villages round Paris are far better built.'

Their carriage halted in front of the Hôtel du Commerce, in the centre of the town, next to the church, and as they were getting out, Mass was just ending. While her husband was seeing to their luggage, Estelle was intrigued to see the congregation coming out of church, many of whom were dressed in quaint costumes. Some of the men were wearing white smocks and baggy breeches; these were those who lived and worked in the vast, desolate salt-marshes which stretch between Guérande and Le Croisic. Then there were the share-croppers, a completely different species, who wore short woollen jackets and round broad-brimmed hats. But Estelle was particularly excited by the ornate costume worn by one girl. Her headdress fitted tightly round the temples and rose up to a point. Over her red bodice with wide-cuffed sleeves, she had a silk front brocaded with brightly coloured flowers. Her triple, tight-pleated, blue woollen skirt was held by a belt embroidered in gold and silver, while a long orange-coloured apron hung down, revealing her red woollen stockings and dainty yellow slippers.

'How can they allow that sort of thing!' exclaimed Monsieur Chabre. 'You only see that kind of circus get-up in Brittany.'

Estelle made no reply. A tall young man, about twenty years of age, was coming out of the church, giving his arm to an old lady... He had a very pale complexion and honey-coloured hair; he looked very self-possessed and was something of a giant, with broad shoulders and muscular arms, despite his youth. Yet he had a delicate, gentle expression which, combined with his pink complexion and smooth skin, gave him a girlish appearance. As Estelle was staring at him, struck by his good looks, he turned his head and his eyes rested on her for a second. Then he blushed to the roots of his hair.

'Well there's someone at least who looks human. He'll make a fine cavalry officer,' said Monsieur Chabre.

'That's Monsieur Hector Plougastel with his mother,' said the hotel maid, hearing this remark. 'He's such a kind, well-behaved boy.'

While the Chabres were taking lunch, a lively argument arose at their table d'hôte. The registrar of mortgages, who took his meals at the Hôtel du Commerce, was speaking approvingly of Guérande's patriarchal way of life and particularly of the high moral standards of the young people. He claimed that it was their religious upbringing which was responsible for their good behaviour. However, a commercial traveller, who had arrived that morning with a stock of false jewellery, recounted with a grin how he'd seen young men and girls kissing behind the hedgerows as he was driving along the road. He would have liked to see what the lads of the town would have done if given the chance to meet a few attractive friendly ladies. And he went on to poke fun at religion, priests and nuns until the outraged registrar of mortgages flung down his napkin and stamped out of the room. The Chabres had gone on eating without saying a word, with the husband furious at the sort of conversation you have to listen to at a table d'hôte while his wife sat with a placid smile on her face as if she didn't understand a word of what they were talking about.

The Chabres spent the afternoon visiting Guérande. The church of St Aubin was deliciously cool and as they walked slowly around inside, they looked up at the arched vaulting supported on slender columns which shot upwards like stone rockets, stopping to admire the strange carved capitals depicting torturers sawing their victims in two and roasting them on grills, using large bellows to fan the flames. Then they strolled round the five or six main streets of Guérande and Monsieur Chabre was confirmed in his view: it was nothing but a dump, with no trade to speak of, just one more of those antiquated medieval towns so many of which had already been knocked down. The streets were deserted, with their rows of gabled houses piled up side by side like so many tired old women. The pointed roofs, the slate-covered pepper-pots and corner turrets and the weather-worn sculptures made some of the quiet back streets of the town seem like museums drowsing in the sun. At the sight of all the leadlighted windows, a dreamy look came into Estelle's eyes; since her marriage she had taken to reading novels and she was thinking of Walter Scott.

But when the Chabres went outside the town and walked all round it, they found themselves nodding their heads appreciatively. They had to admit that it really was charming. The granite walls which completely encircled the town had weathered to a rich honey colour and were as intact as when they had been built, though ivy and honeysuckle now draped the battlements. Shrubs had grown on the towers flanking the ramparts and their brightly coloured flowers, golden gorse and flaming gilly-flower, glowed under the clear blue sky. Grassy walks under shady age-old oaks extended all around the town. They picked their way carefully, as though stepping on a carpet, as they walked along beside the former moat, partly filled in and further on turning into weed-covered stagnant pools in whose mysteriously glinting surface were mirrored the white trunks of birch trees growing close up to the walls amongst the wispy green undergrowth. Rays of light shone through the trees lighting up hidden nooks and crannies, and deep-set posterns where the peace of centuries was disturbed only by the sudden leaps of frightened frogs.

'There are ten towers, I've just been counting them,' exclaimed Monsieur Chabre when they had come round to their starting point.

He had been particularly struck by the four gateways with their long narrow entrances through which only one carriage could pass at a time. Wasn't it quite absurd to keep yourself shut in like that in the nineteenth century? If he'd been in charge he'd have knocked down the fortress-like gateways, with their useless loopholes and such thick walls that you could have built a couple of six-storey dwellings on their sites.

'Not to mention all the building materials you'd get from demolishing the ramparts,' he added.

They were standing in the Mall, a spacious raised esplanade which curved in a quarter-circle from the eastern to the southern gateways. Estelle was gazing pensively over the striking panorama which spread out for miles beyond the roofs of the suburbs. First of all there came a dense, dark green belt of gnarled shrubs and pine trees leaning sideways from the force of the winds coming in from the ocean. Then followed the immense plain of desolate salt-marshes, flat and bare, with their square patches of seawater gleaming like mirrors beside the little heaps of salt which shone white against the grey expanse of sand. Further on, at the skyline, she could make out the deep blue of the Atlantic on which three tiny sails looked like white swallows.

'There's the young man we saw this morning,' said Monsieur Chabre suddenly. 'Doesn't he remind you of Lavière's son? If he had a humpback, he'd look exactly like him.'

Estelle turned slowly round but Hector, standing at the edge of the Mall and equally absorbed in watching the sea on the distant horizon, did not seem to notice that he was being observed. The young woman started walking slowly on again. She was using her long sunshade as a walking stick but she had barely taken a dozen steps before its bow came loose. The

Chabres heard a voice behind them.

'Excuse me, madame...'

Hector had retrieved the bow.

'Thank you very much indeed,' said Estelle with her quiet smile.

He really was a nice, well-mannered young man. Monsieur Chabre took to him at once and explained to him the problem facing them of finding a suitable resort, and even asked for Hector's advice.

Hector was very shy.

'I don't think you'll find the sort of place you're looking for either at Le Croisic or Le Batz,' he said, pointing to the church spires of these two little towns on the horizon. 'I think your best plan would be to go to Piriac.'

He gave them some details: Piriac was about seven miles away; he had an uncle living on the outskirts. Finally, in reply to questions by Monsieur Chabre, he said that there were plenty of shellfish to be found there.

The young woman was poking the point of her sunshade into the short turf. The young man kept his eyes averted as though embarrassed to look her in the face.

'Guérande is an extremely pretty place,' she said finally in her soft voice.

'Oh yes, extremely,' stammered Hector, suddenly devouring her with his eyes.

2

One morning, three days after settling in at Piriac, Monsieur Chabre was standing on the platform at the end of the seawall protecting the tiny harbour, stolidly keeping watch over Estelle who was bathing. At the moment she was floating on her back. The sun was already very hot and, decorously dressed in black frock-coat and felt hat, he was warding off its rays by means of a sunshade with a green lining. He looked every inch the holiday visitor.

'Is the water warm?' he enquired, feigning interest in his wife's bathing.

'Lovely!' she replied, turning on to her front.

Monsieur Chabre was terrified of the water and never ventured into it. He would explain that his doctors had explicitly forbidden him to bathe in the sea. When a wave so much as came towards his shoes on the beach, he would start back in alarm as if he were being faced by some vicious animal baring its teeth. In any case, seawater would have disturbed his decorum; he looked on it as dirty and disgusting.

'So it really is warm?' he enquired again, his head swimming from the heat. He felt both drowsy and uncomfortable standing at the end of the seawall.

Estelle did not bother to reply: she was busy swimming a dog-paddle. In the water, she was as fearless as a boy and would swim for hours, to the dismay of her husband who felt it incumbent on him to wait at the water's edge. At Piriac Estelle had found the sort of bathing she liked; she despised gently shelving beaches where you have to walk a long way out before the water comes up to your waist. She would go to the end of the seawall wrapped in her flannel bathrobe, slip it off and take a header without a second thought. She used to say that she needed fifteen feet of water to avoid striking her head on the rocky bottom. Her skirtless one-piece bathing costume clung to her tall figure and the long blue belt tied round her waist emphasized the graceful curve of her firm, full hips. Moving through the clear water, with her hair caught up in a rubber bathing cap from which a few strands of blonde curls were escaping, she looked like some sleek agile dolphin with a disconcertingly pink woman's face.

Monsieur Chabre had been standing in the sweltering hot sun for a good quarter of an hour. He had already consulted his watch three times. Finally he risked a timid comment:

'You've been a long time, my dear. Oughtn't you to come out? You'll get tired, bathing so long.'

'But I've only just gone in,' the young woman replied. 'I'm as warm as toast.'

Then, turning on her back again, she added:

'If you're bored, you needn't stay. I don't need you.'

He objected with a shake of his head, pointing out how quickly a danger could arise; Estelle smiled at the thought; her husband would be a fat lot of good if she were suddenly attacked by cramp. But at this moment her attention was drawn to another side of the seawall, towards the bay that lay to the left of the village.

'Good gracious!' she exclaimed. 'What's happening over there? I'm going to have a look.'

And she swam off with a long, powerful breast-stroke.

'Estelle, come back!' shouted Monsieur Chabre. 'You know I can't bear it when you take risks!'

But Estelle was not listening and he had to possess himself in patience. Standing on tiptoe to watch the white speck of his wife's straw hat, he merely transferred his sunshade to the other hand; he was finding the stifling heat more and more unbearable.

'What on earth has she seen?' he muttered to himself. 'Oh, it's that thing floating over there… A bit of rubbish, I expect. A bunch of seaweed, perhaps? Or a barrel. No, it can't be, it's moving.'

Then he suddenly recognized what it was:

'It's a man swimming!'

However, after a few strokes, Estelle had also recognized perfectly well that it was a man. She therefore stopped swimming straight towards him, since that seemed hardly the proper thing. But she mischievously decided not to swim back to the seawall and continued to make for the open sea, pleased to be able to show how bold she was. She pursued her course, pretending not to notice the other swimmer, who was now gradually coming up towards her, as if being carried by the current. Thus, when she turned round to swim back to the seawall, their paths crossed, apparently quite fortuitously.

'I hope you are well, madame?' the young man enquired politely.

'Oh, it's you!' Estelle exclaimed brightly.

And she added with a smile: ·

'What a small world it is, isn't it?'

It was young Hector de Plougastel. He was still very shy, very well built and looked very pink in the water. For a moment they swam without speaking, maintaining a decent distance between each other. In order to converse, they had to raise their voices. However, Estelle felt that she ought to be polite.

'We're very grateful to you for having told us about Piriac... My husband is delighted with it.'

'Isn't that your husband standing by himself on the seawall?' asked Hector.

'Yes,' she replied.

Silence fell again. They were watching her husband who looked like a tiny black insect above the sea. Very intrigued, Monsieur Chabre was craning his neck even more and wondering who the man was whose acquaintance his wife had just made in the middle of the sea. There was no doubt about it, his wife was definitely chatting with him. It must be one of their Paris friends. But running his mind over the list of their friends, he could not think of one bold enough to swim so far out. And so he waited, aimlessly twirling his sunshade round in his hand.

'Yes,' Hector was explaining to the attractive Madame Chabre, 'I've come over to spend a few days in my uncle's château which you can see over there, halfway up the hill. So for my daily swim, I set off from that piece of land jutting out opposite the terrace and swim to the seawall and back. Just over a mile in all. It's wonderful exercise... But you're a very daring swimmer, I don't think I've ever met such a daring lady swimmer.'

'Oh I've been splashing about in the water ever since I was a little girl,' said Estelle. 'Water doesn't have any secrets for me, we're old friends.'

To avoid having to talk so loudly, they were gradually drawing closer to each other. On this beautiful warm morning, the sea was like one vast piece of watered silk, drowsing in the sun. Parts were as smooth as satin, separated by narrow bands of shimmering water, stretching out into the distance, currents looking like creases in a cloth. Once they were closer to each other, their conversation took a more intimate turn.

'What a superb day!' And Hector began to point out several landmarks along the coast. That village over there, less than a mile away, was Port aux Loups; opposite was the Morbihan, with its white cliffs standing out sharply as in some water-colour; and finally, in the other direction, towards the open sea, the island of Dumet could be seen as a grey speck set in the blue sea. Each time Hector pointed, Estelle stopped swimming for a second, charmed to see these distant sights from sea-level against the infinite backdrop of the limpid sky. When she looked towards the sun, her eyes were dazzled and the sea seemed as though transformed into a boundless Sahara, with the blinding sunlight bleaching the immense stretch of sandy beach.

'Isn't it lovely,' she murmured. 'Isn't it really gorgeous!'

She turned over and relaxed, lying back motionless in the water with her arms stretched out sideways. Her gleaming white thighs and arms floated on the surface.

'So you were born in Guérande?' she asked.

'Yes,' he replied. 'I've only been once as far as Nantes.'

In order to talk more comfortably, Hector now also turned over on to his back. He gave details of his upbringing, for which his mother had been responsible: a narrow devout woman whose values had been the traditional ones of the old aristocracy. He had had a priest as tutor who had taught him more or less what he would have learned in a private school, plus large amounts of catechism and heraldry. He rode, fenced and took a great deal of exercise. And with all this, he seemed as innocent as a babe in arms. He went to Mass every week, never read novels and when he reached his majority, would be marrying a very plain cousin.

'Goodness me! So you're only just twenty,' exclaimed Estelle, casting an astonished glance at this young colossus. Her maternal instincts were aroused; this fine specimen of the Breton race intrigued her. But as they continued floating on their backs, lost in contemplation of the transparent blue sky and quite oblivious of land, they drifted so close together that he slightly knocked against her.

'Oh, I'm sorry,' he said.

And dived and came to the surface five yards away. She burst into laughter and began to swim again.

'You boarded me!' she cried.

He was very red in the face. He swam nearer again, watching her slyly. Under her broad-brimmed straw hat, she seemed to him delightful. He could see nothing but her face and her dimpled chin clipping into the water. A few drops of water dripped from the blonde curls escaping from beneath her bathing cap, and glistened like pearls on the down of her cheeks. He could imagine nothing more charming than the smile and pretty face of this young woman swimming ahead of him, gently splashing and leaving behind her merely a silvery trail.

When he noticed that Estelle realized that she was being watched and was amused at the odd figure he was certainly cutting, Hector blushed an even deeper red. He tried to find something to say:

'Your husband seems to be getting impatient.'

'Oh, I don't think so,' she replied calmly. 'He's used to being kept waiting when I'm having a swim.'

In fact, Monsieur Chabre was becoming restless. He kept taking four steps forward, turning round and taking four steps backward, twirling his sunshade even more vigorously in an endeavour to cool himself.

It suddenly occurred to Estelle that perhaps her husband hadn't recognized Hector.

'I'll call out and tell him it's you,' she said.

And as soon as she was in earshot of the seawall, she shouted: 'It's the gentleman we met in Guérande who was so helpful.'

'Oh good!' Monsieur Chabre shouted back. He raised his hat and said politely:

'Is the water warm?'

'Very pleasant, thank you,' Hector replied.

Their bathe continued under the eye of the husband who could now hardly complain, even though his feet were excruciatingly hot from having to stand on the scorching stones. At the end of the seawall, the water was wonderfully transparent and you could see the fine sandy bottom some two or three fathoms down, speckled here and there with pale or dark pebbles amidst waving tendrils of seaweed rising perpendicularly towards the surface. Estelle was fascinated by the clearness of the water as she swam gently along in order not to ruffle the surface, bending her head forward until the water came up to her nose and watching the sand and the pebbles stretched out in the mysterious depths below. She was especially fascinated by the clumps of green seaweed that seemed almost like living creatures with their swaying jagged leaves resembling hundreds of crabs' claws, some of them short and sturdy growing between the rocks and others long and flexible like snakes. She kept uttering little cries each time she discovered something new:

'Oh what a big stone! It looks as if it's moving... Oh, there's a tree, a real tree with branches! Oh, there's a fish! It's darting away!'

Then suddenly she exclaimed:

'What on earth is that? It's a wedding bouquet! Do you think there really are wedding bouquets in the sea? Look, wouldn't you say that they're like orange blossoms? Oh, it's so pretty!'

Hector immediately dived and came up with a fistful of whitish seaweed which drooped and faded as soon as it left the water.

'Oh, thank you so much,' said Estelle. 'You shouldn't have bothered... Here you are, keep that for me, will you?' she added, throwing the bunch of seaweed at her husband's feet. For a few moments the young couple continued their swim. The air was filled with spray from their flailing arms and then, suddenly, they relaxed and glided through the water, in a circle of ripples which spread out and died away; and the surging water around them filled them with a private sensual pleasure all their own. Hector was trying to glide along in the wake of Estelle's body as it slid through the water and he could feel the warmth left by the movement of her limbs. All around, the sea had become even calmer and its pale blue had taken on a touch of pink.

'You'll be getting cold, my dear,' urged Monsieur Chabre, who was dripping with sweat himself.

'All right, I'm coming out,' she replied.

And so she did, pulling herself up quickly with the help of a chain hanging down the sloping side of the seawall. Hector must have been watching for her to climb out; but when he raised his head on hearing the spatter of drops she left behind, she was already on the platform and wrapped in her bathing robe. He looked so surprised and disconcerted that she had to smile as she gave a little shiver; and she gave a little shiver because she knew that she was charming when she did so, draped in her bathrobe with her tall figure standing out against the sky.

The young man reluctantly took his leave.

'We hope to see you again,' the husband said.

And while Estelle ran back along the seawall, watching Hector's head disappearing over the water as he swam back across the bay, Monsieur Chabre walked after her with the bunch of seaweed gathered by the young man solemnly held out in order to avoid wetting his frock coat.

3

In Piriac the Chabres had rented the first floor of a large house overlooking the sea. As the village had no decent restaurants, they had had to take on a local woman to cook for them. And a queer sort of cook she was, producing roasts burnt to a cinder and such peculiar-looking sauces that Estelle preferred to stick to bread. But as Monsieur kept pointing out, they hadn't come to enjoy the pleasures of the table. In any case, he hardly touched either the roasts or the sauces for he was stuffing himself, morning, noon and night, on shellfish of every description, with the determination of someone taking medicine. The unfortunate thing was that he loathed these strange, oddly shaped creatures, having been brought up on a typical middle-class diet of insipid hygienic food, and retained his childish predilection for sweet things. The queer flavour and salty fieriness of shellfish burnt his tongue and made him pull a face every time he swallowed them; but in his eagerness to become a father, he would have swallowed the shells themselves.

'Estelle, you're not eating any,' he would exclaim, for he insisted that she should eat as many as he and when Estelle pointed out that Dr Guiraud hadn't mentioned her, Monsieur Chabre replied that, logically, they should both submit to the same treatment. Estelle pursed her lips, let her bright eyes rest for a moment on her husband's pasty paunch and could not repress a slight smile which deepened the dimples on her cheek. She made no comment, for she did not like hurting people's feelings. Having discovered that there was a local oyster bed, she even consented to eat a dozen of them at every meal, not because she, personally, needed oysters; but she adored them.

Life in Piriac was monotonous and soporific. There were only three families of holiday-makers: a wholesale grocer from Nantes, a former lawyer from Guérande, as naive as he was deaf, and a couple from Angers who spent all day waist-deep in the sea, fishing. The restricted company would hardly be described as boisterous. They would greet each other each time they met but made no attempt to further their acquaintance. The greatest excitement was provided by the occasional dogfight on the deserted quayside.

Accustomed to the noise and bustle of Paris, Estelle would have been bored to death had Hector not taken to calling every day. After going for a walk with Monsieur Chabre along the coast, he had become a firm friend of the older man who in an expansive moment had confided to him the purpose of his trip, in the discreetest possible terms, in order not to shock the modest young man's delicate sensibilities. When he mentioned the scientific reason for eating such vast quantities of shellfish, Hector was so amazed that he forgot to blush and looked him up and down without even bothering to conceal his surprise that a man might need to submit to such a diet. Nevertheless, the following morning he presented him with a small basketful of clams which the ex-corn-merchant accepted with obvious gratitude. Since then, being a highly competent all-round fisherman and familiar with every rock in the bay, Hector had never come to the house without bringing some shellfish: superb mussels which he had gathered at low tide; sea-urchins which he cut open and cleaned, pricking his fingers in the process; and limpets which he prised off the rocks with the tip of his knife; in a word, every kind of shellfish, often bearing barbarous names, and which he would never have dreamt of eating himself. No longer having to spend a penny on his diet, Monsieur Chabre was profuse in his thanks.

Hector now had a permanent pretext to come to the

Chabres' flat. Every time he arrived carrying his little basket, he would make the same remark when he saw Estelle:

'I'm bringing your husband some shellfish.'

And the couple would exchange a smile with a glint in their half-closed eyes; they found Monsieur Chabre's shellfish rather funny.

Estelle now discovered that Piriac was full of charm. Every day after her bathe, she would go for a walk with Hector; her husband lumbered along, heavy-footed, some distance behind; they often went too fast for him. Hector would point out examples of Piriac's more elegant past, remains of sculpture and delicately worked ornamental doors and windows. By now, what used to be a town had become merely a remote village with its narrow streets blocked by dung heaps and lined with gloomy hovels. But Estelle found the stillness and isolation so charming that she was quite prepared to step over the foul-smelling pools of liquid seeping from the middens, intrigued by every quaint old-world corner and peering inquisitively at the miserable gim-crackery lying about the mud floors of the local inhabitants' poverty-stricken houses. Hector would stop and show her the superb fig trees in the gardens, with their broad, furry, leathery leaves overhanging the low fences. They went into the narrowest little streets and leaned over the banks of the wells to look at their smiling faces mirrored in the clear shining water below, while behind them Monsieur Chabre was busy digesting his shellfish in the shade of the green-lined sunshade which never left his grip.

One of Estelle's great joys was to see the groups of pigs and geese roaming freely round the village. At first she had been terribly frightened of the pigs because the unpredictable movements of their fat sturdy bodies supported on such puny little feet made her continually apprehensive of being knocked into and tipped over; and they were filthy, too; with their bellies covered in black mud, they kept grunting all the time as they grubbed in the ground with their dirty snouts. But Hector assured her that pigs were the nicest sort of animals and now she was amused to see how they dashed wildly up to be fed and she loved their fresh pink skin looking like a silky evening gown, after the rain had washed them clean. The geese fascinated her, too. Two gaggles of them would often meet at the end of a lane beside a holeful of dung, coming from opposite directions. They seemed to greet each other with a click of their beaks and then joined forces to pick over the vegetable peelings floating on the surface. One of them would climb majestically on to the top of the pile, stretching out his neck and opening his eyes wide; he seemed almost to be strutting as he fluffed out the down on his breast; with his prominent yellow nose, he looked like a real king of the castle. Meanwhile the others bent their necks to peck at the ground, quacking in unison as they did so. Then, suddenly, the big goose would come squawking down from the top and the geese belonging to his group would follow him away, all poking out their necks in the same direction and waddling in time, as if they all had a limp. If a dog appeared, they would stretch their necks out even more and start hissing. At this, Estelle would clap her hands and follow the solemn procession of the two companies of geese as they made their way home like highly respectable people intent on important business. Another of her entertainments was to see both pigs and geese going down to the beach in the afternoon, just like human beings.

On her first Sunday in Piriac, Estelle felt that she ought to go to Mass, something which she never did in Paris. But in the country, Mass was a way of passing the time, and a chance to dress up and see people. Indeed, she met Hector there, reading out of an enormous prayerbook whose binding was coming unstuck. He did not take his eyes off her, peeping over the top of his book while still reading religiously; but the glint in his eye hinted that he was smiling inwardly. As they were leaving the church, he offered his arm to Estelle as they were passing through the churchyard. In the afternoon, after Vespers, there was another spectacle, a procession to a Calvary at the other end of the village. A peasant led the way carrying a purple silk banner embroidered in gold and attached to a red shaft. Then followed two straggling lines of women. The priests were in the middle; the parish priest with his curate and the local squire's tutor were all singing at the tops of their voices. Bringing up the rear, behind a white banner carried by a brawny girl with tanned arms, there came the congregation, tramping along in their heavy clogs like a disorderly flock of sheep. As the procession passed beside the harbour, the banner and the white headdresses of the women stood out against the bright blue sea and in the sunlight, the slow procession suddenly took on a simple grandeur.

The little churchyard made Estelle feel all sentimental, although normally she didn't like sad things. On the day she had arrived, she had shuddered at the sight of all those graves underneath her window. The church was not far from the sea and the arms of the crosses all around it stretched out towards the immense sky and sea; on windy nights, the moisture-laden sea breeze seemed to be weeping on this forest of dark wooden posts. But she quickly became accustomed to this mournful sight, for the tiny churchyard had something gentle and even cheerful about it. The dead seemed to be smiling in the midst of the living, who were almost rubbing elbows with them. As the cemetery was enclosed by a low wall and thus blocked the way through the centre of Piriac, people did not think twice about stepping over the wall and following the paths which were almost invisible in the tall grass. Children used to play there, scampering about all over the granite flagstones. Cats would suddenly leap out from under the bushes and chase each other; you could often hear their amorous caterwauling and see their dark shapes with fur bristling and long tails waving in the air. It was a delightful corner covered with weeds and enormous fennel plants with broad yellow flowers; on a warm day, their heady perfume would come wafting up from the graves, filling the whole of Piriac with a scent of aniseed. And at night, how still and gentle the green graveyard was! The peace of Piriac itself seemed to be emanating from the cemetery. The darkness hid the crosses and people taking a late evening stroll would sit down on the granite benches against the wall and watch the waves rolling in almost at their feet, enjoying the salty tang of the sea carried in on the evening breeze.

One evening as Estelle was going home on Hector's arm she felt a sudden desire to go through the deserted graveyard.

Monsieur Chabre thought it was a romantic whim and showed his protest by himself going along the quayside. The path was so narrow that Estelle was obliged to let go of Hector's arm. In the tall grass her skirt made a long swishing sound. The scent of fennel was so overpowering that the lovelorn cats did not run away but remained lying languidly in the undergrowth. As they came into the shadow of the church, she felt Hector's hand touch her waist. She gave a startled cry.

'How stupid!' she exclaimed as they came out of the shadow. 'I thought I was being carried off by a ghost.'

Hector laughed and offered his own explanation:

'It must have been the fennel brushing against your skirt.'

They stopped to look at the crosses all around them and the profound stillness of the dead lying beneath their feet filled them with a strange tenderness. They moved on, full of suppressed emotion.

'You were scared; I heard you,' said Monsieur Chabre. 'It serves you right!'

At high tide, they would amuse themselves by going down to watch the arrival of the sardine boats; Hector would tell the Chabres when a sail was seen making for the harbour. But after seeing a few boats come in, Monsieur Chabre announced that it was always the same thing. Estelle on the other hand never seemed to weary of the scene and enjoyed going out on to the seawall more and more. They often had to run. She would leap over the uneven stones, her skirts flying in the air, and she would catch hold of them to avoid tripping over. When she arrived, she was quite puffed and, putting her hand on her chest, she would throw her head back to regain her breath. With her dishevelled hair and devil-may-care boyish air, Hector found her adorable. Meanwhile the boat had tied up and the fishermen were carrying up their baskets of sardines which glistened in the sun like silver with blue and sapphire, pink and pale ruby-red tints. The young man always provided the same information: a basket contained a thousand sardines which would fetch a price fixed every morning according to the size of the catch; the fishermen would share the proceeds of the sale after handing over one-third to the owner of the boat. Then the sardines would be salted straightaway in wooden boxes with holes to allow the brine to drip away. However, Estelle and her companion gradually came to neglect the sardines. They would still go and see; but they didn't look. They would hurry down to the harbour and then return in silence, lazily gazing at the sea.

'Was it a good catch?' Monsieur Chabre would enquire each time they returned.

'Yes, very good,' they would reply.

And every Sunday evening Piriac put on an open-air dance. The young men and girls of the district would join hands and dance round in a circle for hours on end, droning out the same strongly accentuated refrain, and as these harsh voices boomed out in the half-light, they gradually took on a kind of barbaric charm. As she sat on the beach with Hector lying at her feet, Estelle was soon sunk in daydreams. The sea came lapping in, gently but boldly; as it broke on the sand, it seemed like a voice full of passion suddenly stilled as the sound died away and the water receded with a plaintive murmur like a love that had now been tamed. And Estelle would sit dreaming of being loved by a giant who she had succeeded in turning into a little boy.

'You must be bored in Piriac, my dear,' Monsieur Chabre would occasionally say, in an enquiring tone, to his wife.

And she would hasten to reply:

'Oh no, not at all, I promise you.'

She was, in fact, enjoying her stay in this remote, dead-and-alive little place. The geese and pigs and sardines had assumed great importance; even the little churchyard was a cheerful spot. This drowsy, unsociable sort of life in a village inhabited only by the grocer from Nantes and the deaf lawyer from Guérande seemed more exciting than the bustling existence of the fashionable resorts. After a fortnight, bored to tears, Monsieur Chabre would willingly have returned home to Paris. Surely the shellfish must have produced their effect by now, he said. But she protested:

'Oh no, my dear, you haven't had enough yet... I'm quite sure you need still more.'

4

One morning Hector said to the couple:

'Tomorrow there's an exceptionally low tide. We could go shrimping.'

Estelle was delighted by the suggestion. Oh yes, they certainly must go and catch shrimps! She'd been looking forward to this excursion for ages! But Monsieur Chabre had objections. First of all, you never catch anything... Furthermore, it was much simpler to go and buy a franc's worth of shrimps from a local fisherman, without having to get wet up to your middle and scrape the skin off your feet. But in the face of his wife's enthusiasm, he was forced to give way.

There were elaborate preparations. Hector undertook to provide the nets. Despite his dislike of cold water, Monsieur Chabre had expressed his willingness to participate and, once having agreed, he was determined to do the job properly. On the morning of the expedition, he had a pair of boots dubbined; he then dressed himself in white twill from top to toe; but his wife could not persuade him to forgo his bow tie, the ends of which he fluffed out as if he were going to a wedding. The bow tie was his protest, as a respectable member of society, against the slovenliness of the Atlantic. As for Estelle, she merely slipped a shift over her bathing costume. Hector was also wearing a bathing costume.

The three of them set off at about two o'clock in the afternoon with their nets over their shoulders. It was more than a mile across sand and seaweed to reach the rock where Hector had promised they would find plenty of shrimps. He piloted the couple towards their goal, taking them in a bee-line through all the rock pools and calmly ignoring the hazards on the way. Estelle followed intrepidly, cheerfully paddling over the cool wet sand. Bringing up the rear, Monsieur Chabre could see no need to get his boots wet before they reached the shrimping grounds. He conscientiously skirted every pool, jumping over the channels of water left behind by the ebbing tide and cautiously picking his way over the dry spots like a true Parisian balancing himself on the tops of the paving-sets on a muddy day in the Rue Vivienne. He was already out of breath and kept asking:

'Is it still a long way? Why can't we start shrimping here? I'm positive I can see some... Anyway, they're all over the place in the sea, aren't they? I bet you only need to push your net through the sand.'

'Go ahead and push, Monsieur Chabre,' replied Hector each time.

So in order to recover his breath, Monsieur Chabre would push his net along the bottom of a pool not much larger than a pocket handkerchief and as empty of shrimps as it was transparent. So he caught nothing, not even seaweed. Then he would set off again, pursing his lips and looking dignified, but as he lost ground each time he insisted on proving that there were shrimps everywhere, he ended up by dropping a long way behind.

The tide was still going out, retreating almost a mile from the coast. As far as the eye could see, the rocky, pebbly sea-bed was emptying out, leaving a vast, wet, uneven and desolate wilderness, like some storm-ravaged plain. In the distance the only visible thing was the green fringe of the still receding sea, as if being swallowed up by the land, while long, narrow bands of dark rock slowly emerged like promontories stretching out in the stagnant water. Estelle stopped to look at this immense, bare expanse.

'Isn't it big!' she murmured.

Hector pointed to a number of greenish rocks worn smooth by the waves.

'Those are only uncovered twice a month,' he explained. 'People go there to collect mussels. Can you see that brown spot over there? That's the Red Cow rocks, the best place to catch lobsters. You can't see them except at the two lowest tides of the year. But we must get a move on. We're going to those rocks over there whose tops are just beginning to show.'

When they started to go into the sea, Estelle could hardly restrain her excitement. She kept lifting her feet high in the air and bringing them down with a splash, laughing as the spray shot up. Then, when the sea came up to her knees, she strode along, delighted to feel the water pressing hard against her thighs and surging between them.

'Don't be scared,' said Hector, 'You'll be getting into water up to your waist but it becomes shallower after that. We're nearly there.'

And after crossing a narrow channel, they waded out of the water and climbed up on to a wide rocky platform uncovered by the tide. When the young woman looked round, she uttered a cry of surprise at seeing how far she had come from the shore. The houses of Piriac were just a line of tiny white spots stretching out along the shore, dominated by the square tower of its green-shuttered church. Never had she seen such a vast expanse, with the strip of sand gleaming in the bright sunlight and the dark green seaweed and brilliantly coloured rocks glistening with water. It was as if the earth had reached its uttermost limit in a heap of ruins on the brink of empty space.

Estelle and Hector were just about to start shrimping when they heard a plaintive call. It was Monsieur Chabre stuck in the middle of the channel and wanting to know which way to go. 'How do I get across?' he was shouting. 'Do I keep straight on?'

'Go to your left,' called Hector.

He went to his left but the shock of finding himself in still deeper water again brought him to a halt. He did not dare even to retrace his steps.

'Come and help me,' he wailed. 'I'm sure there are holes round here. I can feel them...'

'Keep to your right, Monsieur Chabre, to your right!' shouted Hector.

And the poor man looked so funny in the middle of the water, with his net over his shoulder and his splendid bow tie, that Estelle and Hector could not refrain from sniggering. In the end he managed to find a way through but he arrived in a very nervous state and snapped angrily:

'I can't swim, you know.'

He now began to worry about how to get back. When the young man explained to him how important it was not to be caught on the rock by the rising tide, he started becoming anxious again:

'You will warn me, won't you?'

'Don't worry, I'll look after you.'

They all three started shrimping, probing the holes with their narrow nets. Estelle showed a feminine enthusiasm and it was she who caught the first shrimps, three large red ones which leapt about wildly in her net. She called out to Hector to help her because she was rather scared by their lively behaviour; but when she saw that they stopped moving as soon as you caught hold of them by their heads, she became bolder and had no trouble in slipping them herself into the little basket which she was carrying slung over her shoulder. Sometimes she netted a whole bunch of seaweed and had to rummage through it each time a sound like the fluttering of wings warned her that shrimps were hidden there. She sorted carefully through the seaweed, picking it up gingerly between finger and thumb, rather uneasy at the strange tangle of fronds, soft and slimy like dead fish. Now and again, she would peep impatiently into her basket, keen to fill it.

'How odd,' Monsieur Chabre kept exclaiming. 'I haven't caught a single one.'

Being afraid of venturing between the gaps in the rocks and greatly hampered also by his boots which had become water-logged, he was pushing his net along the sandy beach and thereby catching nothing but crabs, half-a-dozen or even up to ten of them at a time. Every so often he would turn anxiously round to see if the tide was still ebbing.

'You're sure it's still going out?' he kept asking.

Hector merely nodded; he was shrimping with all the assurance of a man who knows exactly where to go and as a result he was catching great handfuls of them with each sweep of his net. Whenever he found himself working beside Estelle, he would tip his catch into her basket while she kept laughing and giving a wink in the direction of her husband, with her finger to her lips. She looked most attractive as she bent forward over the long wooden handle of her net or else leaning her blonde curly head over it as she eagerly peered to examine her catch. There was a breeze blowing and the water dripping from her net soaked her bathing costume with spray and made it cling to her, revealing every contour of her youthful body.

They had been shrimping like this for some two hours

when she stopped for a rest, quite out of breath and with her honey-coloured curls damp with perspiration. The immense deserted seascape still spread out, peaceful and magnificent; only the sea could be seen shimmering in the distance, creating a murmur that seemed to be growing louder. The sun was blazing in the fiery sky; it was now four o'clock and its pale blue had turned almost grey; but this leaden, torrid heat was tempered and dispersed by the coolness of the water, and a gentle haze dimmed the harsh glare. Estelle was particularly charmed by the sight of a whole host of little black dots standing out very clearly on the horizon; they were shrimpers like themselves, incredibly delicate in outline and no larger than ants, ridiculous in their insignificance in the vast immensity; yet you could distinguish their every gesture, their shoulders hunched over their nets and their arms reaching out and gesticulating feverishly, like trapped flies, as they sorted out their catch, wrestling with the seaweed and the crabs.

'I assure you the tide's coming in,' Monsieur Chabre called anxiously. 'Look over there, that rock was uncovered a moment ago.'

'Of course it's coming in,' Hector retorted impatiently at last, 'and that's exactly the time when you catch most shrimps.'

But Monsieur Chabre was beginning to panic. At his last attempt he had just caught a strange fish, an angler-fish, whose freakish-looking head had terrified him. He had had enough.

'Come on, let's go. We must be going!' he kept repeating. 'It's stupid to take risks.'

'But we've just been telling you it's the best time when the tide's starting to come in,' his wife replied.

'And it's coming in with a vengeance!' Hector added in an undertone, with a mischievous glint in his eyes.

The waves were indeed beginning to roll in, booming as they swallowed up the rocks; a whole spit of sand would suddenly disappear, swamped by the sea. The breakers were triumphantly retaking possession of their age-old domain, foot by foot. Estelle had discovered a pool the bottom of which was covered in long fronds of seaweed, swirling round like strands of hair, and she was catching enormous shrimps, ploughing up long furrows with her net and leaving behind large swathes, like a reaper. She was thrashing around and determined not to be dragged away.

'All right then,' Monsieur Chabre exclaimed in a tearful voice, 'there's nothing to be done, I'm off. There's no sense in us all being cut off.'

So he went off first, sounding the depth of the holes with the long handle of his shrimping net. When he had gone two or three hundred yards, Hector at last prevailed on Estelle to follow his example.

'We're going to be up to our shoulders,' he said with a smile. 'Monsieur Chabre's going to get a thorough wetting. Look how deep he is already.'

Ever since the start of the outing, Hector had had the slightly furtive and preoccupied look of a young man in love and promising himself to declare his feelings; but he had not been able to pluck up courage to do so. As he had slipped his shrimps into Estelle's basket, he had indeed endeavoured to touch her fingers but it was plain that he was furious with himself for being so timorous. He would have been delighted to see Monsieur Chabre fall into a hole and drown, because, for the first time, he was finding the husband's presence a hindrance.

'I tell you what,' he said suddenly, 'you must climb up on my back and I'll give you a lift. Otherwise you're going to get soaked through. How about it? Up you get!'

He offered her his back but she blushed and declined, looking embarrassed. He, however, refused to take no for an answer, arguing that he was responsible for her safety. Eventually, she clambered up, placing her two hands on his shoulders. He stood as firm as a rock, straightened his back and set off, carrying her as lightly as a feather, telling her to hang on tight as he strode through the water.

'We've got to go right, haven't we?' Monsieur Chabre called out to Hector in a plaintive voice. The water was already up to his hips.

'That's it, keep going right,' the young man called back.

Then, as the husband turned to go on, shivering with fright when he felt the water coming up to his armpits, Hector, greatly daring, kissed one of the tiny hands resting on his shoulder. Estelle tried to draw it away but Hector warned her to keep quite still or else he could not be responsible for what would happen. He started kissing her hand again: it was cool and salty and seemed to be offering all the bitter delights of the Ocean.

'Will you please stop doing that,' Estelle kept protesting, trying to sound cross. 'You're taking advantage of me. If you don't stop, I'll jump off.'

He didn't stop, nor did she jump off. He was keeping a tight hold on her ankles while covering her hands with kisses, not saying a word but also keeping a close eye on Monsieur Chabre's back or at least all that could be seen of his pathetic back, now threatening to disappear beneath the waves at every step.

'Did you say keep to the right?' the husband called imploringly.

'Go left if you like!'

Monsieur Chabre took a step to his left and gave a cry. The water had come up to his neck, submerging his bow tie. Hector gratefully accepted the opportunity of making his declaration:

'I love you...'

'You're not to say that, I forbid it!'

'I love you... I adore you... I haven't had the courage to tell you so up till now because I was afraid of offending you.'

He could not turn his head to look at her and continued to stride along with water up to his chest. Estelle could not refrain from laughing out loud at the absurdity of the situation.

'You must stop talking like that,' she went on, adopting a motherly tone and giving him a slap on his shoulder. 'Now, be a good boy and above all, mind you don't miss your step.'

Feeling the slap on his shoulder, Hector was filled with joy: it was the seal of approval! And as poor Monsieur Chabre was still in trouble, Hector gave a cheerful shout:

'Keep straight on now!'

When they reached the beach, Monsieur Chabre attempted to give an explanation:

"Pon my word, I was nearly caught. It's my boots,' he stammered.

But Estelle opened her basket and showed him it, full of shrimps.

'Did you catch all those?' he exclaimed in amazement. 'You certainly are a good shrimper!'

'Oh,' she replied with a smile, 'this gentleman showed me the way.'

5

The Chabres had only two days left in Piriac. Hector seemed dismayed and furious, yet humble. As for Monsieur Chabre, he reviewed his health every morning and seemed puzzled.

'You can't possibly leave without visiting the Castelli rocks,' Hector said one evening. 'Let's organize an excursion for tomorrow.'

He explained that the rocks were less than a mile away. They had been undermined by the waves and hollowed out into caves which extended for a mile and a half along the coast. According to him, they were completely unspoilt and wild.

'All right, we'll go tomorrow,' said Estelle in the end. 'Are they difficult to get at?'

'No, there are just a couple of spots where you have to wade through some shallow water, that's all.'

But Monsieur Chabre did not want even to get his feet wet. Ever since his experience of almost going under during the shrimping expedition, he had harboured a grudge against the sea and so he expressed considerable opposition to Hector's suggestion. It was absurd to take risks like that: in the first place, he was not going to climb down to those rocks and risk breaking his leg jumping around like a goat; if he were absolutely compelled to, he would accompany them on the cliff path above and even that he would be doing only as a favour.

To make him relent, Hector had a sudden inspiration.

'I tell you what,' he said, 'you'll be going past the Castelli semaphore station. Well, you can call in there and buy some shellfish from the crew. They always have superb shellfish which they practically give away.'

The ex-corn-merchant perked up. 'That's a good idea,' he replied. 'I'll take a little basket with me and I'll be able to have a final feast of shellfish.'

And turning to his wife, he said with a leer: 'Perhaps that'll do the trick.'

Next day, they had to wait for low tide before they set off and, as Estelle was not ready in time, they in fact did not leave until five o'clock. However, Hector assured them that they would not be caught by the tide. The young woman was wearing cloth bootees over her bare feet and a very short and slightly raffish-looking grey linen dress which exposed a slim pair of ankles. As for Monsieur Chabre, he was dressed, most correctly, in a pair of white trousers and a long alpaca coat. He had brought his sunshade and a little basket; he had the appearance of a respectable middle-class Paris gentleman setting off on a shopping expedition.

Reaching the first of the rocks was awkward: they had to walk for some distance over quicksands in which their feet sank. The ex-corn-merchant was soon puffing and blowing.

'All right then, I'll let you go on and I'll go up,' he gasped at last.

'That's right, take that path there,' Hector replied. 'If you come any further, there's no way up. Would you like some help?'

They watched him climb to the top of the cliff. Once there, he opened his sunshade and, swinging his basket in the other hand, called down:

'I've done it, it's much better up here. Now, don't do anything rash, will you? Anyway, I'll be able to keep an eye on you from up here.'

Hector and Estelle began walking over the rocks. The young man led the way, leaping from boulder to boulder in his high boots with the grace and agility of a mountaineer. Estelle followed intrepidly on the same stones and when he turned to ask:

'Shall I give you a hand?' she replied:

'Certainly not! Do you take me for a grandmother?'

They had now reached a vast floor of granite worn down by

the sea and hollowed out into deep crevasses. It was like the skeleton of some sea monster whose dislocated vertebrae were protruding from the sand. In the hollows there was flowing water and dark seaweed was dangling like strands of hair. They continued to leap from stone to stone, pausing now and then to recover their balance and laughing each time they dislodged a boulder.

'They're rather tame, your rocks,' said Estelle with a smile. They wouldn't be out of place in a drawing-room!'

'Just you wait,' retorted Hector. 'You'll see in a minute.'

They had reached a narrow passage, a sort of gap between two enormous blocks of stone, and the way through was barred by a rock-pool, a hole full of water.

'I'll never get across that!' the young woman exclaimed.

He suggested carrying her but she shook her head: she was not going to let herself be carried again. He then started looking round for some rocks big enough to make stepping-stones; but they kept slipping and sinking to the bottom. Finally, losing patience, she said:

'Give me your hand, I'm going to jump.'

She jumped short and one foot went into the water and this made them laugh again. Then, when they had gone through the passage, she stopped and exclaimed out loud in admiration.

In front of her lay a large round bay full of gigantic tumbled rocks, enormous blocks of stone standing like sentries keeping guard over the waves. All along the foot of the cliffs the land had been eroded by storms, leaving behind vast masses of bare granite, with creeks and promontories, unexpected inlets forming deep caverns and beaches littered with blackish slabs of marble looking like large stranded fish. It was like some Cyclopean town, battered and ravaged by the sea, with its battlements knocked down, its towers half demolished and its buildings toppled and lying in heaps of ruins. Hector showed Estelle every nook and cranny of these storm-wrecked ruins. She walked over sand as fine and yellow as gold dust, with pebbles speckled with mica glinting in the sun. She clambered over fallen rocks where she had, at times, to hang on with both hands to prevent herself from slipping into the crevasses.

She went through natural porticos and triumphal archways curved like those in Romanesque churches or soaring pointed arches like those of Gothic cathedrals. She scrambled down into cool deserted hollows a good dozen yards square, charmed by the blue thistles and dark green succulent plants standing out in contrast to the dark grey walls of the rockface on which they grew and delighted by the friendly little brown seabirds fluttering within her reach as they repeated their chirpy little calls. And what amazed her most was that, each time she turned round, she could see the ever-present blue line of the Atlantic stretching out, majestic and calm, between every block of rock.

'Ah, there you are!' cried Monsieur Chabre from the top of the cliff. "I was worried because I had lost sight of you... Aren't these heights terrifying?'

He was standing a good six yards back from the edge, shading himself under his parasol with his little basket hitched over his arm. He added:

'It's coming in fast, be careful!'

'There's plenty of time, never fear,' replied Hector.

Meanwhile, Estelle had sat down and was gazing, speechless with admiration, at the vast horizon. In front of her three round pillars of granite, made smooth by the waves, were standing like the giant columns of a ruined temple. Behind them, bathed in the golden half-light of the evening, the open sea spread out, a royal blue speckled with gold. In the far distance she could see a brilliant white dot, a tiny sail skimming like a seagull over the surface of the water. The calm of evening was already reaching out over the pale blue sky. Never had she felt so overpowered by such an all-pervading tenderness and exquisitely voluptuous delight.

'Let's go,' said Hector, gently touching her arm.

She gave a start and stood up, full of languor and acquiescence.

'That little house with the mast is the semaphore, isn't it?' called Monsieur Chabre. 'I'm going to get some shellfish, I'll catch you up in a minute.'

Then, in an attempt to shake off the listlessness that had

overtaken her, Estelle set off running like a child, leaping over the puddles as she made towards the sea, seized by a sudden whim to climb to the top of a heap of rocks which would be completely surrounded by water at high tide. And when, after scrambling laboriously through the gaps in the rocks, she finally reached the top, she hoisted herself on to the highest point and was delighted to see that she could dominate the whole sweep of the tragically devastated coastline. She stood outlined in the pure sea air, her skirt fluttering like a flag in the breeze.

As she came down, she peered into every little crevice as she passed. In the smallest cranny, she could see tiny slumbering pools whose limpid surfaces were reflecting the sky like shining mirrors. On the bottom, emerald-green seaweed was growing, like some romantic forest. The only living creatures were large black crabs which leapt up like frogs before disappearing without even stirring up the water. The young woman had a dreamy look in her eyes as if she had been granted a glimpse into secret regions of a vast, mysterious and happy land.

When they had come back to the foot of the cliff, she noticed that her companion had filled his handkerchief with some limpets.

'They're for your husband,' he said. 'I'll take them up to him.'

At that very moment, a disconsolate Monsieur Chabre came into sight.

'They hadn't even got a mussel at the semaphore,' he shouted down to them. 'You see, I was right not to want to come.'

But on seeing Hector's limpets, he cheered up; and he was staggered at the young man's agility as he clambered up by a track known only to himself, over a cliff-face that seemed completely smooth rock. His descent was even more impressive.

'It's nothing, really,' Hector said. 'It's as easy as going upstairs once you know where the steps are.'

Monsieur Chabre now suggested turning back: the sea was beginning to look threatening. So he begged his wife at least to find an easy way up to the top of the cliff. Hector laughed and replied that there was no way suitable for ladies; they would now have to go on to the end. In any case, they hadn't yet visited the caves. Monsieur Chabre was compelled to continue along the top of the cliffs by himself. As the sun was now much lower in the sky, he closed his parasol and used it as a walking-stick. In his other hand, he held his basketful of limpets.

'Are you feeling tired?' Hector asked Estelle gently.

'A little bit,' she replied and took hold of the arm which he offered. However, she was not tired; but her delicious feeling of languor was slowly spreading through her whole body and the emotion she had felt at seeing the young man hanging from the cliff-face had left her trembling inwardly. They were walking slowly over a beach composed of broken shells which crunched under their feet like a gravel garden path. Both had again fallen silent. He showed her two wide openings in the rock: the Monk's Hole and the Cat's Grotto. As they walked on over another beach of fine sand, they looked at each other, still without exchanging a word, and smiled. The tide was now coming in, rippling gently over the sand; but they did not hear it. Up above, Monsieur Chabre had started calling to them; but they did not hear him either.

'It's sheer madness!' the ex-corn-merchant was shouting, waving his sunshade and swinging his basket of limpets. 'Estelle! Monsieur Hector! Listen to me! You're going to be cut off! Your feet are already getting wet.'

But they did not feel the cool water lapping round their feet.

'What's the matter with him?' the young woman muttered at last.

'Oh, it's you, Monsieur Chabre,' Hector called out. 'There's no need to worry. We've only got the Lady's Cave to look at now.'

Monsieur Chabre made a despairing gesture and repeated:

'It's sheer madness! You'll both be drowned.'

They were no longer paying attention... To avoid the rising tide, they went along the foot of the cliff and finally came to the Lady's Cave. It was a grotto hollowed out of a vast block of granite that jutted out towards the sea. Its roof, extremely high and wide, was shaped like a dome. Storms had polished its walls until they shone like agate and the pink and blue veins in the dark rock formed magnificent patterns of arabesques like the barbaric handiwork of primitive artists decorating a grandiose bathroom for a sea-goddess. The gravelly floor of the cave, still wet, was glittering like a bed of precious stones while at the far end there was a softer bed of dry yellow sand, so pale as to be almost white.

It was here that Estelle sat down to inspect the grotto.

'It's the sort of place you could live in,' she murmured.

But now Hector at last seemed to become aware of the tide and his face assumed a look of dismay.

'Oh my goodness, we're caught! The sea's cut us off! We're going to have to wait for two hours...'

He went out and looked up at Monsieur Chabre who was standing on top of the cliff, just above the grotto. He told him that they were cut off.

'What did I tell you?' Monsieur Chabre cried triumphantly. 'But you refused to listen to me, didn't you? Is there any danger?'

'None at all,' Hector replied. 'The tide only comes fifteen or twenty feet into the cave. The only thing is that we shall have to wait a couple of hours before we can get out. There's nothing to be alarmed at.'

Monsieur Chabre was annoyed: so they wouldn't be back by dinner-time and he was already feeling hungry! It really was a mad sort of outing! Then he sat down, grumbling, on the short grass, placing his sunshade on his left and his basket of limpets on his right.

'Well, I'm going to have to wait, then,' he called. 'Go back to my wife and make sure she doesn't catch cold.'

Back in the cave, Hector sat down beside Estelle. After a moment, silently, he ventured to reach out and take hold of her hand; she did not try to draw it away. She sat looking into the distance. Dusk was falling and the light of the dying sun was veiled by a gentle haze. On the horizon, the sky was taking on a tender tinge of deepest red and the sea grew slowly darker, stretching out with not a soul in sight. The tide crept gently into the cave, quietly lapping over the glittering shingle and murmuring a promise of exquisite sea-pleasures with its disturbing salty tang of desire.

'I love you, Estelle,' Hector said, smothering her hands in kisses.

Choking with emotion, she made no reply, as though uplifted on the rising tide. She was by now half-lying on the bed of fine sand, looking like some sea-nymph, caught unawares and already at his mercy.

Monsieur Chabre's voice abruptly broke in, faint and hollow:

'Aren't you hungry? I'm ravenous! Fortunately I've got my penknife, so I'll have a first installment of my limpets.'

'I love you, Estelle,' said Hector again, taking her in his arms.

The night was dark and the pale sea lit up the sky. At the mouth of the grotto, a plaintive murmur was rising from the water while a last gleam of light deserted the top of the domed roof. The sea rippled and a scent of fruitfulness was hanging in the air. Slowly Estelle's head sank on to Hector's shoulder and on the evening air the breeze carried away a murmur of delight.

Up above, by the light of the stars, Monsieur Chabre was methodically chewing away at his limpets and giving himself indigestion as he ate the whole lot, without any bread.

6

Nine months after her return to Paris, the lovely Madame Chabre gave birth to a bouncing boy. A delighted Monsieur Chabre took Dr Guiraud aside and said proudly:

'It was the limpets that did the trick, I'm absolutely convinced of it! I ate a whole basketful of them one evening, in very peculiar circumstances, by the way. Anyway, never mind the details, doctor, but I never thought shellfish could have such remarkable effects.'

The Thrill
of the Grass

by
W. P. KINSELLA
(1935–   )

The playing field as political metaphor. A quiet revolution taking place under cover of night. W. P. Kinsella's "The Thrill of the Grass" has quickly become a benchmark in baseball mythology—of a golden era before strikes, lock-outs and the introduction of artificial turf.

1 981: the summer the baseball players went on strike. The dull weeks drag by, the summer deepens, the strike is nearly a month old. Outside the city the corn rustles and ripens in the sun. Summer without baseball: a disruption to the psyche. An unexplainable aimlessness engulfs me. I stay later and later each evening in the small office at the rear of my shop. Now, driving home after work, the worst of the rush hour traffic over, it is the time of evening I would normally be heading for the stadium.

I enjoy arriving an hour early, parking in a far corner of the lot, walking slowly toward the stadium, rays of sun dropping softly over my shoulders like tangerine ropes, my shadow gliding with me, black as an umbrella. I like to watch young families beside their campers, the mothers in shorts, grilling hamburgers, their men drinking beer. I enjoy seeing little boys dressed in the home team uniform, barely toddling, clutching hotdogs in upraised hands.

I am a failed shortstop. As a young man, I saw myself diving to my left, graceful as a toppling tree, fielding high grounders like a cat leaping for butterflies, bracing my right foot and tossing to first, the throw true as if a steel ribbon connected my hand and the first baseman's glove. I dreamed of leading the American League in hitting—being inducted into the Hall of Fame. I batted .217 in my senior year of high school and averaged 1.3 errors per nine innings.

I know the stadium will be deserted; nevertheless I wheel my car down off the freeway, park, and walk across the silent lot, my footsteps rasping and mournful. Strangle-grass and creeping charlie are already inching up through the gravel, surreptitious, surprised at their own ease. Faded bottle caps, rusted bits of chrome, an occasional paper clip, recede into the earth. I circle a ticket booth, sun-faded, empty, the door closed by an oversized padlock. I walk beside the tall, machinery-green, board fence. A half mile away a few cars hiss along the freeway; overhead a single-engine plane fizzes lazily. The whole place is silent as an empty classroom, like a house suddenly without children.

It is then that I spot the door-shape. I have to check twice to be sure it is there: a door cut in the deep green boards of the fence, more the promise of a door than the real thing, the kind of door, as children, we cut in the sides of cardboard boxes with our mother's paring knives. As I move closer, a golden circle of lock, like an acrimonious eye, establishes its certainty.

I stand, my nose so close to the door I can smell the faint odour of paint, the golden eye of a lock inches from my own eyes. My desire to be inside the ballpark is so great that for the first time in my life I commit a criminal act. I have been a locksmith for over forty years. I take the small tools from the pocket of my jacket, and in less time than it would take a speedy runner to circle the bases I am inside the stadium. Though the ballpark is open-air, it smells of abandonment; the walkways and seating areas are cold as basements. I breathe the odours of rancid popcorn and wilted cardboard.

The maintenance staff were laid off when the strike began. Synthetic grass does not need to be cut or watered. I stare down at the ball diamond, where just to the right of the pitcher's mound, a single weed, perhaps two inches high, stands defiant in the rain-pocked dirt.

The field sits breathless in the orangy glow of the evening

sun. I stare at the potato-coloured earth of the infield, that wide, dun arc, surrounded by plastic grass. As I contemplate the prickly turf, which scorches the thighs and buttocks of a sliding player as if he were being seared by hot steel, it stares back in its uniform ugliness. The seams that send routinely hit ground balls veering at tortuous angles, are vivid, grey as scars.

I remember the ballfields of my childhood, the outfields full of soft hummocks and brown-eyed gopher holes.

I stride down from the stands and walk out to the middle of the field. I touch the stubble that is called grass, take off my shoes, but find it is like walking on a row of toothbrushes. It was an evil day when they stripped the sod from this ballpark, cut it into yard-wide swathes, rolled it, memories and all, into great green-and-black cinnamonroll shapes, trucked it away. Nature temporarily defeated. But Nature is patient.

Over the next few days an idea forms within me, ripening, swelling, pushing everything else into a corner. It is like knowing a new, wonderful joke and not being able to share. I need an accomplice.

I go to see a man I don't know personally, though I have seen his face peering at me from the financial pages of the local newspaper, and the *Wall Street Journal*, and I have been watching his profile at the baseball stadium, two boxes to the right of me, for several years. He is a fan. Really a fan. When the weather is intemperate, or the game not close, the people around us disappear like flowers closing at sunset, but we are always there until the last pitch. I know he is a man who attends because of the beauty and mystery of the game, a man who can sit during the last of the ninth with the game decided innings ago, and draw joy from watching the first baseman adjust the angle of his glove as the pitcher goes into his windup.

He, like me, is a first-base-side fan. I've always watched baseball from behind first base. The positions fans choose at sporting events are like politics, religion, or philosophy: a view of the world, a way of seeing the universe. They make no sense to anyone, have no basis in anything but stubbornness.

I brought up my daughters to watch baseball from the first-base side. One lives in Japan and sends me box scores from Japanese newspapers, and Japanese baseball magazines with pictures of superstars politely bowing to one another. She has a season ticket in Yokohama; on the first-base side.

"Tell him a baseball fan is here to see him," is all I will say to his secretary. His office is in a skyscraper, from which he can look out over the city to where the prairie rolls green as mountain water to the limits of the eye. I wait all afternoon in the artificially cool, glassy reception area with its yellow and mauve chairs, chrome and glass coffee tables. Finally, in the late afternoon, my message is passed along.

"I've seen you at the baseball stadium," I say, not introducing myself.

"Yes," he says. "I recognize you. Three rows back, about eight seats to my left. You have a red scorebook and you often bring your daughter..."

"Granddaughter. Yes, she goes to sleep in my lap in the late innings, but she knows how to calculate an ERA and she's only in Grade 2."

"One of my greatest regrets," says this tall man, whose moustache and carefully styled hair are polar-bear white, "is that my grandchildren all live over a thousand miles away. You're very lucky. Now, what can I do for you?"

"I have an idea," I say. "One that's been creeping toward me like a first baseman when the bunt sign is on. What do you think about artificial turf?"

"Hmmmf," he snorts, "that's what the strike should be about. Baseball is meant to be played on summer evenings and Sunday afternoons, on grass just cut by a horse-drawn mower," and we smile as our eyes meet.

"I've discovered the ballpark is open, to me anyway," I go on. "There's no one there while the strike is on. The wind blows through the high top of the grandstand, whining until the pigeons in the rafters flutter. It's lonely as a ghost town."

"And what is it you do there, alone with the pigeons?"

"I dream."

"And where do I come in?"

"You've always struck me as a man who dreams. I think we have things in common. I think you might like to come with me. I could show you what I dream, paint you pictures, suggest what might happen..."

He studies me carefully for a moment, like a pitcher trying to decide if he can trust the sign his catcher has just given him.

"Tonight?" he says. "Would tonight be too soon?"

"Park in the northwest corner of the lot about 1:00 a.m. There is a door about fifty yards to the right of the main gate. I'll open it when I hear you."

He nods.

I turn and leave.

The night is clear and cotton warm when he arrives. "Oh, my," he says, staring at the stadium turned chrome-blue by a full moon. "Oh, my," he says again, breathing in the faint odours of baseball, the reminder of fans and players not long gone.

"Let's go down to the field," I say. I am carrying a cardboard pizza box, holding it on the upturned palms of my hands, like an offering.

When we reach the field, he first stands on the mound, makes an awkward attempt at a windup, then does a little sprint from first to about half-way to second. "I think I know what you've brought," he says, gesturing toward the box, "but let me see anyway."

I open the box in which rests a square foot of sod, the grass smooth and pure, cool as a swatch of satin, fragile as baby's hair.

"Ohhh," the man says, reaching out a finger to test the moistness of it. "Oh, I see."

We walk across the field, the harsh, prickly turf making the bottoms of my feet tingle, to the left-field corner where, in the angle formed by the foul line and the warning track, I lay down the square foot of sod. "That's beautiful," my friend says, kneeling beside me, placing his hand, fingers spread wide, on the verdant square, leaving a print faint as a veronica.

I take from my belt a sickle-shaped blade, the kind used for cutting carpet. I measure along the edge of the sod, dig the point in and pull carefully toward me. There is a ripping sound, like tearing an old bed sheet. I hold up the square of artificial turf like something freshly killed, while all the time digging the sharp point into the packed earth I have exposed. I replace the sod lovingly, covering the newly bared surface.

"A protest," I say.

"But it could be more," the man replies.

"I hoped you'd say that. It could be. If you'd like to come back…"

"Tomorrow night?"

"Tomorrow night would be fine. But there will be an admission charge."

"A square of sod?"

"A square of sod two inches thick…"

"Of the same grass?"

"Of the same grass. But there's more."

"I suspected as much."

"You must have a friend…"

"Who would join us?"

"Yes."

"I have two. Would that be all right?"

"I trust your judgement."

"My father. He's over eighty," my friend says. "You might have seen him with me once or twice. He lives over fifty miles from here, but if I call him he'll come. And my friend…"

"If they pay their admission they'll be welcome…"

"And they may have friends…"

"Indeed they may. But what will we do with this?" I say, holding up the sticky-backed square of turf, which smells of glue and fabric.

"We could mail them anonymously to baseball executives, politicians, clergymen."

"Gentle reminders not to tamper with Nature."

We dance toward the exit, rampant with excitement.

"You will come back? You'll bring others?"

"Count on it," says my friend.

They do come, those trusted friends, and friends of friends, each making a live, green deposit. At first, a tiny row of sod squares begins to inch along toward left-centre field. The next night even more people arrive, the following night more again, and the night after there is positively a crowd. Those who come once seem always to return accompanied by friends, occasionally a son or young brother, but mostly men my age or older, for we are the ones who remember the grass.

Night after night the pilgrimage continues. The first night I stand inside the deep green door, listening. I hear a vehicle stop; hear a car door close with a snug thud. I open the door when the sound of soft soled shoes on gravel tells me it is time. The door swings silent as a snake. We nod curt greetings to each other. Two men pass me, each carrying a grasshopper-legged sprinkler. Later, each sprinkler will sizzle like frying onions as it wheels, a silver sparkler in the moonlight.

During the nights that follow, I stand sentinel-like at the top of the grandstand, watching as my cohorts arrive. Old men walking across a parking lot in a row, in the dark, carrying coiled hoses, looking like the many wheels of a locomotive, old men who have slipped away from their homes, skulked down their sturdy sidewalks, breathing the cool, grassy, after-midnight air. They have left behind their sleeping, grey-haired women, their immaculate bungalows, their manicured lawns. They continue to walk across the parking lot, while occasionally a soft wheeze, a nibbling, breathy sound like an old horse might make, divulges their humanity. They move methodically toward the baseball stadium which hulks against the moon-blue sky like a small mountain. Beneath the tint of starlight, the tall light standards which rise above the fences and grandstand glow purple, necks bent forward, like sunflowers heavy with seed.

My other daughter lives in this city, is married to a fan, but one who watches baseball from behind third base. And like marrying outside the faith, she has been converted to the third-base side. They have their own season tickets, twelve rows up just to the outfield side of third base. I love her, but I don't trust her enough to let her in on my secret.

I could trust my granddaughter, but she is too young. At her age she shouldn't have to face such responsibility. I remember my own daughter, the one who lives in Japan, remember her at nine, all knees, elbows and missing teeth—remember peering in her room, seeing her asleep, a shower of well-thumbed baseball cards scattered over her chest and pillow.

I haven't been able to tell my wife—it is like my compatriots and I are involved in a ritual for true believers only. Maggie, who knew me when I still dreamed of playing professionally myself—Maggie, after over half a lifetime together, comes and sits in my lap in the comfortable easy chair which has adjusted through the years to my thickening shape, just as she has. I love to hold the lightness of her, her tongue exploring my mouth, gently as a baby's finger.

"Where do you go?" she asks sleepily when I crawl into bed at dawn.

I mumble a reply. I know she doesn't sleep well when I'm gone. I can feel her body rhythms change as I slip out of bed after midnight.

"Aren't you too old to be having a change of life," she says, placing her toast-warm hand on my cold thigh.

I am not the only one with this problem.

"I'm developing a reputation," whispers an affable man at the ballpark. "I imagine any number of private investigators following any number of cars across the city. I imagine them creeping about the parking lot, shining pen-lights on licence plates, trying to guess what we're up to. Think of the reports they must prepare. I wonder if our wives are disappointed that we're not out discoing with frizzy-haired teenagers?"

Night after night, virtually no words are spoken. Each man seems to know his assignment. Not all bring sod. Some carry rakes, some hoes, some hoses, which, when joined together, snake across infield and outfield, dispensing the blessing of water. Others, cradle in their arms bags of earth for building up the infield to meet the thick, living sod.

I often remain high in the stadium, looking down on the men moving over the earth, dark as ants, each sodding, cutting, watering, shaping. Occasionally the moon finds a knife blade as it trims the sod or slices away a chunk of artificial turf, and tosses the reflection skyward like a bright ball. My body tingles. There should be symphony music playing. Everyone should be humming "America The Beautiful."

Toward dawn, I watch the men walking away in groups, like small patrols of soldiers, carrying instead of arms, the tools and utensils which breathe life back into the arid battle-field.

Row by row, night by night, we lay the little squares of sod, moist as chocolate cake with green icing. Where did all the sod come from? I picture many men, in many parts of the city, surreptitiously cutting chunks out of their own lawns in the leafy midnight darkness, listening to the uncomprehending protests of their wives the next day—pretending to know nothing of it—pretending to have called the police to investigate.

When the strike is over I know we will all be here to watch the workouts, to hear the recalcitrant joints crackling like twigs after the forced inactivity. We will sit in our regular seats, scattered like popcorn throughout the stadium, and we'll nod as we pass on the way to the exits, exchange secret smiles, proud as new fathers.

For me, the best part of all will be the surprise. I feel like a magician who has gestured hypnotically and produced an elephant from thin air. I know I am not alone in my wonder. I know that rockets shoot off in half-a-hundred chests, the excitement of birthday mornings, Christmas eves, and home-town doubleheaders, boils within each of my conspirators. Our secret rites have been performed with love, like delivering a valentine to a sweetheart's door in that blue-steel span of morning just before dawn.

Players and management are meeting round the clock. A settlement is imminent. I have watched the stadium covered square foot by square foot until it looks like green graph paper. I have stood and felt the cool odours of the grass rise up and touch my face. I have studied the lines between each small square, watched those lines fade until they were visible to my eyes alone, then not even to them.

What will the players think, as they straggle into the stadium and find the miracle we have created? The old-timers will raise their heads like ponies, as far away as the parking lot, when the thrill of the grass reaches their nostrils. And, as they dress, they'll recall sprawling in the lush outfields of childhood, the grass as cool as a mother's hand on a forehead.

"Goodbye, goodbye," we say at the gate, the smell of water, of sod, of sweat, small perfumes in the air. Our secrets are safe with each other. We go our separate ways.

Alone in the stadium in the last chill darkness before dawn, I drop to my hands and knees in the centre of the outfield. My palms are sodden. Water touches the skin between my spread fingers. I lower my face to the silvered grass, which, wonder of wonders, already has the ephemeral odours of baseball about it.

Storm Glass

by
JANE URQUHART
(1949–   )

Jane Urquhart gathers glimpses of a past like rounded pieces of glass along the shore—"inert and beautiful after being tossed and rubbed by the real weather of the world." Urquhart has that rare ability to evoke past worlds through a glimmer of the senses—the touch, the scent, the colour of a stone, or a piece of broken glass upon the shoreline.

From where she lay she could see the lake. It seemed to her to be heading east, as if it had a definite destination in mind and would someday be gone altogether from the place where it was now. But it was going nowhere; though diminished by sun, replenished by rain and pushed around by strong winds, it was always a lake. And always there. God knows it had its twentieth-century problems; its illnesses, its weaknesses. Some had even said it was dying. But she knew better. She was dying, and although she felt as close as a cousin to the lake, she did not sense that it shared with her this strong, this irreversible decline. It would always be a lake, and always there, long after she had gone somewhere else. Alone.

She was alone in the room now. As alone as she would be a few months later when the brightness of the last breath closed on the dark, forever. She had imagined the voyage in that dark—her thoughts speaking in an alien tongue—textural black landscape—non-visual—swimming towards the change. And then she had hoped that she would be blessed with some profound last words, some small amount of theatre to verify the end of things. But somehow she sensed it would be more of a letting go, slipping right through the centre of the concentric circles that are the world and into a private and inarticulate focus, and then...

The shore had changed again and again since her first summers there. One year there had been unexpected sand for her babies to play in. She remembered fine grains clinging to their soggy diapers, and their flat sturdy footprints which had existed for seconds only before the lake gathered them up. But a storm the following winter had altered the patterns of the water and the next year her small children had staggered over beach stones to the edge. In subsequent weeks their bare feet had toughened, allowing them to run over rocks and pebbles without pain. Her own feet had resisted the beach stones summer after summer, forcing her to wear some kind of shoes until she left the land for the smooth softness of the water.

Her husband, larger, more stubborn, less willing to admit to weaknesses than she, would brave the distance of the beach, like the children, barefoot. But his feet had never toughened, and standing, as she sometimes had, on the screened veranda, she had watched the pain move through his stiffened legs and up his back until, like a large performing animal, he had fallen, backwards and laughing, into the lake.

He was not there now, unwilling to admit to this, her last, most impossible weakness.

Yet he came and went, mostly at mealtimes, when a hired woman came to cook for them. He came in heavy with the smell of the farm where he had worked and worked, making things come to be; a field of corn, a litter of pigs, or even a basket of smooth, brown eggs. The farm took all of his time now, as if, as she moved down this isolated tunnel towards that change, it was even more important that he make things come to be. And though this small summer cottage was only minutes away from the earth that he worked, the fact of her lying there had made it a distance too great for him to travel except for the uncontrollable and predictable necessities of hunger and of sleep.

The beach was smaller this year, and higher. Strong spring winds had urged the lake to push the stones into several banks, like large steps, up to the grass. These elevations curved in a regular way around the shoreline as if a natural amphitheatre had been mysteriously provided so that audiences of pilgrims might come and sit and watch the miracle of the lake. They never arrived, of course, but she sometimes found it fun to conjure the image of the beach filled with spectators, row on row, cheering on the glide of a wave, the leap of a fish, the flash of a white sail on the horizon. In her imagination she could see their backs, an array of colourful shirts, covering the usual solid grey of the stones.

And yet, even without the imaginary spectators, the grey was not entirely solid. Here and there a white stone shone amongst the others, the result of some pre-Cambrian magic. In other years the children had collected these and old honey pails full of them still lined the windowsills on the porch. The children had changed, had left, had disappeared into adulthood, lost to cities and success. And yet they too came and went with smiles and gifts and offers of obscure and indefinite forms of help. She remembered mending things for them; a toy, a scratch on the skin, a piece of clothing, and she understood their helpless, inarticulate desire to pretend that now they could somehow mend her.

In her room there were two windows. One faced the lake, the other the weather, which always seemed to come in from the east. In the mornings when the sun shone, a golden rectangle appeared like an extra blanket placed on the bed by some anonymous benevolent hand. On those days her eyes moved from the small flame of her opal ring to the millions of diamonds scattered on the lake and she wished that she could lie out there among them, rolling slightly with the current until the sun moved to the other side of the sky. During the heat of all those summers she had never strayed far from the water, teaching her children to swim or swimming herself in long graceful strokes, covering the distance from one point of land to another, until she knew by heart the shoreline and the horizon visible from the small bay where the cottage was situated. And many times she had laughed and called until at last, with a certain reluctance, her husband had stumbled over the stones to join her.

He seldom swam now, and if he did it was early in the morning before she was awake. Perhaps he did not wish to illustrate to her his mobility, and her lack of it. Or perhaps, growing older, he wished his battle with the lake to be entirely private. In other times she had laughed at him for his method of attacking the lake, back bent, shoulders drawn forward, like a determined prize fighter, while she slipped effortlessly by, as fluid as the water, and as relaxed. His moments in the lake were tense, and quickly finished; a kind of enforced pleasure, containing more comedy than surrender.

But sometimes lately she had awakened to see him, shivering and bent, scrambling into his overalls in some far corner of the room and knowing he had been swimming, she would ask the customary questions about the lake. 'Was it cold? Was there much of an undertow?' and he had replied with the customary answers. 'Not bad, not really, once you are in, once you get used to it.'

That morning he had left early, without swimming. The woman had made her bed, bathed her and abandoned her to the warm wind that drifted in one window and the vision of the beach and the lake that occupied the other. Her eyes scanned the stones beyond the glass trying to remember the objects that, in the past, she had found among them. Trying to remember, for instance, the look and then the texture of the clean dry bones of seagulls; more delicate than the dried stems of chrysanthemums and more pleasing to her than that flower in full bloom. These precise working parts of once animate things were so whole in themselves that they left no evidence of the final breakdown of flesh and feather. They were suspended somewhere between being and non-being like the documentation of an important event and their presence somehow justified the absence of all that had gone before.

But then, instead of bone, she caught sight of a minuscule edge of colour, blue-green, a dusty shine, an irregular shape surrounded by rounded rocks—so small she ought not to have seen it, she ought to have overlooked it altogether.

'Storm glass,' she whispered to herself, and then she laughed

realizing that she had made use of her husband's words without thinking, without allowing the pause of reason to interrupt
her response as it so often did. When they spoke together she
sometimes tried expressly to avoid his words, to be in possession of her own, hard thoughts. Those words and thoughts,
she believed, were entirely her own. They were among the few
things he had no ability to control with either his force or his
tenderness.

It must have been at least fifteen summers before, when the
children, bored and sullen in the clutches of early adolescence,
had sat day after day like ominous boulders on the beach,
until she, remembering the honey pails on the windowsills,
had suggested that they collect the small pieces of worn glass
that were sometimes scattered throughout the stones. Perhaps,
she had remarked, they could do something with them; build
a small patio or path, or fill glass mason jars to decorate their
bedrooms. It would be better, at least, than sitting at the
water's edge wondering what to do with the endless summer
days that stretched before them.

The three children had begun their search almost immediately; their thin backs brown and shining in the hot sun. Most
of the pieces they found were a dark ochre colour, beer bottles
no doubt, thrown into the lake by campers from the provincial
park fifteen miles down the road. But occasionally they would
come across a rarer commodity, a kind of soft turquoise glass
similar to the colour of bottles they had seen in antique shops
with their mother. These fragments sometimes caused disputes
over who had spotted them first but, as often as not, there
were enough pieces to go fairly around. Still rarer and smaller
were the particles of emerald green and navy blue, to be found
among the tiny damp pebbles at the very edge of the shore,
the remnants of bottles even more advanced in age than those
that were available in the shops. But the children had seen
these intact as well, locked behind the glass of display cases in
the county museum. Often the word poison or a skull and
crossbones would be visible in raised relief across the surface
of this older, darker glassware. Their mother knew that the
bottles had held cleaning fluid, which was as toxic now in its

cheerful tin and plastic containers as it had been then housed in dark glass, but the children associated it with dire and passionate plots, perhaps involving pirates, and they held it up to their parents as the most important prize of all.

The combing of the beach had lasted two days, maybe three, and had become, for a while, the topic of family conversations. But one evening, she remembered, when they were all seated at the table, her husband had argued with her, insisting as he often did on his own personal form of definition—even in the realm of the activities of the children.

'It's really storm glass,' he had announced to the children who had been calling it by a variety of different names, 'that's what I always called it.'

'But,' she had responded, 'I remember a storm glass from high school, from physics, something to do with predicting weather, I don't know just what. But that's what it is, not the glass out there on the beach.'

'No,' he had continued, 'storms make it with waves and stones. That wears down the edges. You can't take the edge off a piece of glass that lies at the bottom of a bird bath. Storms make it, it's storm glass.'

'Well, we always called it beach glass, or sometimes water glass when we were children, and the storm glass came later when we were in high school.'

'It is storm glass,' he said, with the kind of grave finality she had come to know; a statement you don't retract, a place you don't return from.

It was after these small, really insignificant, disputes that they would turn silently away from each other for a while; she holding fiercely, quietly, to her own privacy, her own person. To him it seemed she refused out of stubbornness to accept his simplified sense of the order of things, that she wished to confuse him by leaning towards the completeness of alternatives. He was not a man of great intellect. Almost every issue that he had questioned had settled into fact and belief in early manhood. He clung to the predictability of these preordained facts with such tenacity that when she became ill the very enormity of the impending disorder frightened him beyond words and into the privacy of his own belief that it was not so, could not be happening to her, or, perhaps more importantly, to him. They did not speak of it but turned instead quietly from each other, she not wishing to defend her own tragedy, and he not wishing to submit to any reference to such monumental change.

But fifteen years before, in the small matter of the glass, the children had submitted easily, as children will, to the sound of his authority; and storm glass it had become. Within a week, however, their project had been abandoned in favour of boredom and neither path nor patio had appeared. Nevertheless, the glass itself appeared year after year among the stones on the beach and, try as she might, she could never quite control the impulse to pick it up. The desire to collect it was with her even now, creating an invisible tension, like a slim, taut wire, from her eyes to her hands to the beach as she lay confined within her room. It was, after all, a small treasure, an enigma; broken glass robbed by time of one of its more important qualities, the ability to cut. And though she could no longer rub it between her palms she knew it would be as firm and as strong as ever. And as gentle.

From where she lay she could see the lake and she knew that this was good; to be able to see the land and the end of the land, to be able to see the vast indefinite bowl of the lake. And she was pleased that she had seen the storm glass. She felt she understood the evolution of its story. What had once been a shattered dangerous substance now lay upon the beach, harmless, inert and beautiful after being tossed and rubbed by the real weather of the world. It had, with time, become a pastel memory of a useful vessel, to be carried, perhaps in a back pocket, and brought out and examined now and then. It was a relic of that special moment when the memory and the edge of the break softened and combined in order to allow preservation.

How long, she wondered, did it take, from the break on the rocks, through the storms of different seasons, to the change? When did the edges cease to cut?

That night he came in tired and heavy, followed by the smell of making things come to be. He spoke of problems with the farm, of obstinate machinery that refused to function or of crops with inexplicable malformations—events that, even in the power of his stubbornness, he could never hope to control. And when he turned to look at her his eyes were like fresh broken glass: sharp, dangerous, alive. She answered him with kindness, though, knowing the storm ahead and then the softening of edges yet to come.

'There's storm glass on the beach,' she said.

Mouche
Reminiscences of a Rowing Man

by
GUY DE MAUPASSANT
(1850–1893)

*What a wonderful name—Mouche. I've always liked this
story. It reminds me of the Renoir painting of the boaters by
the Seine—the cocked hats and colourful costumes, their faces
flushed with wine. Past summers seem rose-coloured from a
distance, though the darker moments of "Mouche" still res-
onate beneath the boater's memories like discordant echoes—
creasing the surface of a youthful summer's dream.*

This is what he told us:

'I saw some funny things and some funny girls in those days, when I used to go boating on the river. Many's the time I've felt like writing a little book called *On the Seine*, describing that carefree athletic life, a life of poverty and gaiety, of noisy, rollicking fun, that I led in my twenties.

'I was a penniless clerk at the time; now I'm a successful man who can throw away huge sums to gratify a passing whim. I had a thousand modest, unattainable desires in my heart which gilded my existence with fantastic hopes. Today, I really can't think of anything that would induce me to get out of the armchair where I sit dozing. Though life could be hard, how simple and enjoyable it was to live like that, between the office in Paris and the river and Argenteuil. For ten years my great, my only, my absorbing passion was the Seine, that lovely, calm, varied, stinking river, full of mirages and filth. I think I loved it so much because it gave me the feeling of being alive. Oh, those strolls along the flower-covered banks, with my friends the frogs dreamily cooling their bellies on water-lily leaves, and the frail, dainty lilies among the tall grasses, which parted suddenly to reveal a scene from a Japanese album as a kingfisher darted past me like a blue flame! How I loved all that, with an instinctive passion of the eyes which spread through my whole body in a feeling of deep and natural joy!

'Just as others remember nights of passion, I cherish memories of sunrises on misty mornings, with floating, drifting vapours, white as ghosts before the dawn, and then, as the first ray of sunshine touched the meadows, lit with a lovely rosy glow; and I cherish memories too of the moon silvering the rippling surface of the water with a radiance which brought all my dreams to life.

'And all that, that symbol of everlasting illusion, was born for me on the foul water which swept all the refuse of Paris down to the sea.

'Besides, what a gay life we led! There were five of us, a small group of friends who are pillars of the community today. As none of us had any money we had set up an indescribable sort of club in a frightful pothouse at Argenteuil, renting a single dormitory bedroom where I spent what were the maddest nights of my life. We thought about nothing but having fun and rowing, for all of us, with one exception, regarded rowing as a religion. I remember adventures those five rascals had, and pranks they thought up, which were so fantastic that nobody could possibly believe them today. Nobody behaves like that any more, even on the Seine, because the crazy fun which was the breath of life to us means nothing to people nowadays.

'The five of us owned a single boat between us, which had cost us enormous trouble to buy and which gave us far more fun than we shall ever have again. It was a yawl, broad in the beam and rather heavy, but solid, roomy and comfortable. I won't try to describe my friends to you. One of them was a mischievous little chap nicknamed Petit Bleu, and another a tall, wild-looking fellow with grey eyes and black hair whom we called Tomahawk. Then there was a lazy, witty character we nicknamed La Tôque, the only one who never touched an oar, on the pretext that he would be sure to capsize the boat; a slim, elegant, very well-groomed fellow we called N'a-qu'un-Oeil after a recently published novel by Cladel, and also because he wore a monocle; and lastly myself, whom the others had baptized Joseph Prunier. We lived in perfect harmony, our only regret being that we hadn't a girl to take the tiller. A woman is an indispensable adjunct to a boat like ours—indispensable because she keeps minds and hearts awake, because she provides excitement, amusement and distraction, and because she gives a spice to life and, with a red parasol gliding past green banks, decoration too. But an ordinary coxwoman was no use to us five, who could scarcely be described as ordinary people. We needed somebody unusual, odd, ready for anything, in short almost impossible to find. We had tried a good many without success—girls who just played at being helmswomen, stupid creatures who were more interested in the light wine that went to their heads than in the water that kept them afloat. We kept them for a single Sunday and then sent them packing in disgust.

'But then one Saturday evening N'a-qu'un-Oeil brought along a lively, skinny little thing who was always hopping and skipping around, a young tease who was full of that skittishness which passes for wit among the street arabs of both sexes who have grown up on the pavements of Paris. She was a sweet girl but not really pretty, a rough sketch of a woman with a little of everything in her, one of those silhouettes which artists draw in three strokes on a tablecloth in a café after dinner, between a glass of brandy and a cigarette. Nature sometimes turns out creatures like that.

'On that first evening she astonished and amused us, and was so unpredictable that none of us could make up our minds about her. Landing in the midst of a bunch of men who were ready to get up to any kind of prank, she was soon in command of the situation, and by the next day she had conquered us completely.

'She was absolutely crazy into the bargain. She told us that she had been born with a glass of absinthe in her belly, which her mother had drunk just before giving birth to her, and she had never sobered up since, because, she said, her nurse used to keep her strength up with tots of rum. She herself always called the bottles lined up on bar-room shelves "my Holy Family."

'I don't know which of us christened her "Mouche," nor why that name was given her. But it suited her perfectly, and it stuck to her. So every week our yawl, which was called Feuille-à-l'Envers, would travel along the Seine between Asnières and Maisons-Laffitte with a load of five light-hearted strapping young fellows, steered by a lively, scatter-brained creature under a parasol of painted paper, who treated us as if we were slaves charged with the duty of taking her for a row, and whom we all adored.

'We adored her, first of all for a variety of reasons, and then for one in particular. She was a sort of little word-mill in the stern of our boat, chatting away in the wind blowing over the water. She bubbled incessantly with the continuous sound of those winged toys that spin in the breeze, trotting out the most unexpected, amusing and astonishing things. In that mind of hers, which seemed like a patchwork of rags of all kinds and colours, not sewn together but only tacked, there was a fairy-tale fantasy, bawdy, immodesty, impudence, jokes and surprises, and a sense of fresh air and scenery such as you would get travelling in a balloon.

'We used to ask her questions just to hear the far-fetched answers she would produce. The one we fired at her most often was: "Why are you called Mouche?"

'She thought up such fantastic reasons that we would stop rowing to laugh at them.

'She appealed to us as a woman too and La Tôque, who never did any rowing but spent the whole day sitting beside her in the helmsman's seat, once said in reply to the traditional question "Why are you call Mouche?": "Because she's a little Spanish fly."

'And that is exactly what she was: a little buzzing, exciting Spanish fly, not the classic poisonous cantharides, shiny and hooded, but a little red-winged Spanish fly who was beginning to have an oddly disturbing effect on the whole crew of the Feuille-à-l'Envers.

'What stupid jokes we made about that Leaf on which our

Fly had alighted!

'Ever since Mouche had joined our crew N'a-qu'un-Oeil had taken up a superior, preponderant role among us, the role of a gentleman who has a woman, compared with four others who have not. He sometimes abused this privilege to the point of exasperating us by kissing Mouche in front of us, perching her on his knees after meals, and assuming all kinds of humiliating and irritating prerogatives.

'We had fitted up a curtain in the dormitory to isolate them from the rest of us.

'But I soon noticed that my companions were thinking along the same lines as myself, and asking themselves: "Why, under what exceptional law, by virtue of what inadmissible principle, should Mouche, who seems uninhibited by any principles, be faithful to her lover when women of higher social standing are not faithful to their husbands?"

'Our assessment of the situation was accurate, as we soon discovered. Our only regret was that we hadn't made it earlier and so wasted precious time. Mouche was unfaithful to N'a-qu'un-Oeil with all the other sailors of the Feuille-à-l'Envers.

'She did this without any difficulty, without any resistance, the first time each of us asked.

'Heavens, how shocking prudish folk are going to find this! But why? Is there a single fashionable courtesan without a dozen lovers, and is there a single one of those lovers stupid enough not to know it? Isn't it the done thing to have a regular evening with some famous, much-sought-after woman, just as one has a regular evening at the Opera, the Théâtre-Français, or the Odéon, now that they are putting on the minor classics? A dozen men club together to keep a cocotte who finds it difficult to make a fair distribution of her time, just as a dozen men will club together to buy a racehorse ridden by a single jockey—the perfect symbol of the real lover.

'For reasons of delicacy we left Mouche to N'a-qu'un-Oeil from Saturday evening to Monday morning. The days on the river were his. We deceived him only during the week, in Paris, far from the Seine, which for boating men like us was almost tantamount to not deceiving him at all.

'The odd thing about the situation was that the four men filching Mouche's favours knew all about the sharing of those favours, talked about it among themselves, and even made veiled allusions to it in her presence which made her roar with laughter. Only N'a-qu'un-Oeil seemed to know nothing about it, and his ignorance of the situation produced a sort of awkwardness between him and us; it seemed to set him apart, isolate him, and destroy our former trust and intimacy. It gave him in our eyes a difficult and rather ridiculous part to play, the part of a deceived lover, almost that of a husband.

'However, as he was extremely intelligent, and had a dry sense of humour, we sometimes wondered, rather uneasily, whether he might not have his suspicions.

'He took care to enlighten us in a way which was painful for us. We were on our way to Bougival for lunch and we were rowing hard when La Tôque, who had the triumphant look of a contented man that morning, and, seated beside the helmswoman, seemed to be pressing up against her rather too freely for our liking, suddenly called out: "Stop!"

'The eight oars rose out of the water.

'Then, turning to his neighbour, he asked: "Why are you called Mouche?"

'Before she could answer, N'a-qu'un-Oeil, who was sitting on the bows, said drily: "Because she settles on all sorts of carrion."

'At first there was an embarrassed silence, followed by a general inclination to laugh. Even Mouche was dumbfounded.

'Then La Tôque gave the order: "All together."

'The boat moved forward again.

'The matter was closed, the mystery cleared up.

'This little incident changed nothing in our habits. Its only result was to restore cordial relations between N'a-qu'un-Oeil and ourselves. He became once more the privileged possessor of Mouche from Saturday evening until Monday morning, his superiority over the rest of us having been firmly established by this definition, which incidentally put a stop to all questions about the name Mouche. From then on we contented ourselves with the secondary role of grateful and attentive friends who took discreet advantage of weekdays without there being any sense of rivalry between us.

'Everything went very well for about three months. Then, all of a sudden, Mouche began to behave strangely with us all. She was less high-spirited and became edgy, ill-at-ease, almost irritable.

'We kept asking her: "What's the matter with you?"

'She would answer: "Nothing, leave me alone."

'We learned the truth from N'a-qu'un-Oeil one Saturday evening. We had just sat down at table in the little dining-room which Barbichon, the proprietor of our pothouse, reserved for us in his establishment, and after finishing our soup we were waiting for the fried fish when our friend, who also looked a little worried, took Mouche's hand, and then began speaking.

'"My dear friends," he said, "I have something very serious to tell you which may lead to some lengthy discussion. But we'll have time for that between courses. Poor Mouche has given me a disastrous piece of news which she has asked me to pass on to you.

'"She is pregnant.

'"I have only two things to add. This is no time to leave her in the lurch, and any attempt to find out who's the father is forbidden."

'The first effect of this news was utter amazement, a sense of disaster. We looked at one another as if we wanted to accuse somebody. But whom? Yes, whom? I have never felt as keenly as I did at that moment the unfairness of that cruel jest of Nature's which never allows a man to know for certain whether he is the father of his child.

'Then, little by little, we came to experience a comforting sense of consolation, born, oddly enough, of a vague feeling of solidarity.

'Tomahawk, who hardly ever spoke, expressed this growing serenity in the following words: "Well, it can't be helped, and union is strength."

'A boy came in from the kitchen with the gudgeon. We didn't pitch into it as we usually did, because when all was said and done we were rather upset.

'N'a-qu'un-Oeil went on: "In these circumstances she has been good enough to make a full confession to me. We are all equally guilty. Let's shake hands on it and adopt the child."

'This proposal was unanimously accepted. We raised our arms above the dish of fried fish and swore a solemn oath: "We'll adopt it."

'Then, suddenly realizing that she was saved, and relieved of the horrible weight of anxiety which had been burdening her for a month, that sweet, crazy victim of love exclaimed: "Oh, my dear friends! You're so kind, so very, very kind... Thank you all!"

'And for the first time in our presence she burst into tears.

'From then on we would talk about the child in the boat as if it had already been born, and each of us showed an exaggerated degree of interest in the slow but regular swelling of our helmswoman's waist.

'We would stop rowing and ask: "Mouche?"

'She would reply: "Present!"

'"Boy or girl?"

'"Boy."

'"What will he be?"

'Then she would give free rein to her imagination in the most fantastic way, telling us endless stories, astonishing accounts of the child's life from the day of his birth to his final triumph. He was everything, that child, in the innocent, passionate, touching dreams of that extraordinary little creature who now lived chastely among the five men she called her "five papas." She saw and described him as a sailor discovering a new world bigger than America; as a general winning back Alsace and Lorraine for France; as an emperor founding a dynasty of wise and generous sovereigns who would give our country lasting happiness; as a scientist finding first the secret of making gold and then that of eternal life; and as an aeronaut devising a method of travelling to the stars and turning the infinite reaches of space into a vast promenade for mankind—thus making all men's most improbable and magnificent dreams come true.

'Heavens, how sweet and amusing the poor thing was until the end of the summer!

'It was on the twentieth of September that her dream was destroyed. We were rowing back after lunch at Maisons-Laffitte, and we were passing Saint-Germain when she said that she was thirsty and asked us to stop at Le Pecq.

'For some time past she had been growing heavy and this annoyed her dreadfully. She could no longer skip around as before, or leap from the boat to the bank as she was used to doing. But she still tried to, in spite of all we said or did to stop her, and she would have fallen a score of times if our arms had not been waiting to catch her.

'That day she was rash enough to try to leave the boat while it was still moving, in one of those displays of bravado which sometimes prove fatal to sick or tired athletes.

'Just as we were coming alongside, before we could guess what she was going to do or stop her, she stood up, took a spring, and tried to jump on to the quay.

'But she was not strong enough to reach it and just touched the stone edging with one foot. She slipped, struck her belly against the sharp corner, and with a loud cry disappeared into the water.

'All five of us dived in together, and brought out a poor fainting creature, deathly pale and already suffering terrible pain.

'We carried her as quickly as we could to the nearest inn and then sent for a doctor.

'During the ten hours her miscarriage lasted she bore the appalling agony with heroic courage. We stood around miserably, sick with worry and fear.

'Finally she was delivered of a dead child, and for a few more days we had serious fears for her life.

'At last the doctor told us one morning: "I think she's over the worst. That girl must be made of iron!" And we all went into her room together, our hearts bursting with relief.

'Speaking for us all, N'a-qu'un-Oeil said to her: "You're out of danger, Mouche dear, and we're all delighted!"

'Then for the second time we saw her cry. With her eyes

swimming with tears, she stammered: "Oh, if you only knew, if you only knew.... I'm so unhappy, so unhappy.... I'll never get over it."

"'Over what, Mouche dear?"

"'Killing him, of course, for I did kill him! Oh, I know I didn't mean to, but I'm so unhappy all the same...."

'She burst out sobbing. We stood around her, deeply moved, not knowing what to say.

'She went on: "Did you see him?"

'With one voice we answered: "Yes."

"'It was a boy, wasn't it?"

"'Yes."

"'And beautiful?"

'We hesitated. Petit-Bleu, who had fewer scruples than the rest of us, made up his mind what to say.

"'Very beautiful."

'This was unwise of him, for she started moaning, almost howling with despair.

'Then N'a-qu'un-Oeil, who perhaps loved her more than any of us, hit on a wonderful idea to calm her down. Kissing her tear-dimmed eyes, he said: "Cheer up, Mouche dear, cheer up. We'll make you another one."

'The sense of humour which was in her very bones suddenly came alive, and half convinced, half laughing, with tears still in her eyes and her heart full of pain, she looked around at us all and asked: "Honest?"

'And we answered as one man: "Honest.'"

Shoo-fly Dyck

by
JOHN KOOISTRA
(1953–   )

"Shoo-fly Dyck" is what John Kooistra calls the "baseball book-ends" of a novel in progress about a Mennonite farmer turned relief pitcher for the pennant-winning Blue Jays. I think it's the odd angles of this story that first seduced me, the slightly off-centre energy of the story—like an oddly thrown slider.

I t is the ninth inning of the seventh game, and all through the Big City's brand-new baseball playpen men, women and children scream as if the salvation of every individual soul is at stake. For doubters, the Toronto Blue Jays and all of Canada are in the midst of Armageddon and damnation. For the hopelessly optimistic, the Toronto Blue Jays and all of Canada are on the eve of a Golden Age which will release every average summer-time Canadian from the Stigma of Inadequacy—the Stigma of the Great Canadian Choke—*one more time.*

No more than a manger's worth of human beings at SkyDome manage to keep their distance from the emotional turbine, from the maelstrom of sound and fury. One of these is a baby, miraculously asleep in her father's arms. A television camera zooms in from the bleachers in the east and blesses the child with five seconds of international exposure. The spectatoring universe welcomes this momentary respite from the overwhelming tension of the real trial of real men.

"The innocent, the foolish, and the holy shall ever mock the sound and fury of the princes and the powers of the air," thinks a TV-bound man of the cloth, Pastor Dieter Dyck of

Virgil, Southern Ontario, in the process of hoisting his seventh bottle of Blue Light to parched lips.

Few Canadians within the broadcasting sphere of this Beer and Baseball Empire have managed, all spring, summer and autumn long, to stay clear of the Cult of the Blue Jays. One group, clearly guilty of the Sin of Omission, simply does not care about baseball.

There are also the out-and-out heretics, those who hate Toronto. A victory today would mean that the Bay Street, smug Ontario, American-loving WASP mentality was about to gain a new ascendance in the Great White North through its bat-wielding minions. On the other claw, in the Haters' vulture-sharp view, a Blue Jay loss in the Establishment's own "Hogtown Corral" would bring both joy to their spiritual Mudvilles and a *shot-in-the-arm* for Canadian unity.

The Blue Jays carry a 3-2 lead into the top half of the ninth inning of the seventh game of the World Series. The deciding blow has been Sylvio Biancanello's inside-the-park two-run home-run in the bottom of the seventh. Part of the beauty and the depth of the tension now is that second-baseman Biancanello is Canadian. From Saskatchewan—what did the heretics make of this? A Canadian from Moose Jaw stands to win the World Series for Canada.

The first batter for the Los Angeles Dodgers strikes out to one of the Four Horsemen of the Apocalypse, the media's oft-repeated term for the four relief pitchers who have spelled misery for opposing batters in the last month of the season. Three of them earn much more than a million dollars each, but the fourth, a recent signing, works for minimum wage.

Strangely, without the fourth man, the power of the pitching staff would never have been revealed. The first three began to pitch "like hairy thunder," in the words of a true believer, after the rookie had signed his contract.

Millionaire reliever number one is indeed relieved to get the strikeout. He knows, all too well, that he does not have his good stuff. The next batter slams a double to left-centre field, the ball surfing on air laden with the perfume of six-dollar cups of beer and then bouncing in a clean straight line on the perfect, plastic, magic-marker-green grass all the way to the wall.

Millionaire number two has an overcooked noodle for an arm from a long stint in the previous game, so the third Horseman of the Apocalypse is called in. He walks the first batter he faces, intentionally. This is supposed to set up a double play, so that a ground ball will lead to two quick outs and instantaneous glory.

The next batter makes a close study of five pitches without swinging his bat. Four of those pitches are balls—a horrifying mistake. The bases are loaded now, and another walk or a lazy fly ball could tie the game, since the runner on third base would simply tag up and trot home. One cheap little single could put the Dodgers into the lead.

Worst of all, the Dodgers' clean-up man, a monstrously muscled right-handed batter, is due up. Far off in the distance, away from the artificial grass and the man-made dome, long low thunder rumbles across the troubled waters of Lake Ontario.

The manager of the Jays, Harris Burden, breaks for the mound. A fresh, right-handed pitcher is necessary in this situation.

Burden walks as slowly as he can, head down, and the fans read these signs and know that a change is about to be made. The brilliant rookie, the man known as the Saviour of the Jays, the man just recently christened the "Fourth Horseman," surely this man is about to be given the call.

From the outfield bleachers in two waves that collide in the super-rich seats behind home plate and then roll back out through the whole stadium, a thunderous, desperate, wildly joyful sound convulses the spectators.

The sound, the chanting of a player's nickname, echoes and reverberates in wavelets through clutches of Blue Jay believers behind the large-screen television sets in half a million restaurants and bars. Even solitary men and women, swept away by the rhythmic fever, fail to hear themselves shouting their lonely prayer at the two-dimensional images on TV.

The focus of the faith is the second full-blooded Canadian

on the team, still warming up in the bullpen. When the manager orders the young rookie sensation onto the field and into the game, the cry for salvation reaches its crescendo—"SHOO-FLY! SHOO-FLY! SHOO-FLY!..."

Richard Dyck his name was, son of Harold, scion of a wandering Mennonite tribe renowned through eleven generations in seven nations for its prowess in ploughing, land drainage, pie-making and cherry-picking.

In casual conversation, he was often heard to say, "Call me Richard," but most folks didn't like the sound of it, nor did they like Rich, Rick, Ricky, Tricky or Dick Dyck. Not only that, but there were several other Richard Dycks and a lot of Dyck families in the Living Waters Church of Virgil in Southern Ontario.

So, everyone who knew these Dycks at all knew that Richard was called Shoo-fly Dyck, or Shoo-fly Junior. Harold, or Shoo-fly Senior, was the source of the moniker because of his long-term manic craving for a Swiss-branch Mennonite delicacy called shoo-fly pie. Folks knew the whole family as the Shoo-fly Dycks, a *wunderbar* advance in linguistic technology which kept these Dycks distinct from the Porcelain Dycks, the Salesman Dycks, the Chicken Dycks and the Holy Dycks.

Now, what does all this have to do with the man who came to be known as the greatest Canadian baseball player, maybe the greatest in the Americas, who ever lived? You could even say the greatest in the world. Why not? That would light a Roman Candle under the behinds of those idolatrous, bragging Amerikaners and their so-called *World* Series.

World Series? World? Has Sadaharu Oh ever led his Toyota Giants or whatever they're called onto the field at Yankee Stadium to challenge our brain-cramp that a World Series means Champion of The World? And don't tell me that "World" means a dead New York news-rag—when we speak it, we mean the whole, wide world.

I repeat, what does all this have to do with the name of Shoo-fly Dyck? Well, with any other name Shoo-fly Dyck the Younger would never have got his break in the majors.

The last thing Shoo-fly Junior ever wanted to do was to play adult baseball.

He *did* want, even at age twenty-one, any kind of work that was simple, tiring, long, and well-paying enough to let him stay in Virgil, his home town. "By the sweat of his brow shall man earn his bread"—this was not a curse to Shoo-fly, but a formula for happiness. Without labour, without sweat, without body-aching races against the dying sun to get a solid day's work done, food tasted like cancer, the mind was besieged with grave doubts about what was good in living, and everything, for Shoo-fly, got kind of pink, fleshy, soft, sickly—like Babylon and Gomorrah.

Shoo-fly's friend Jonah Neufeld came over to the Dyck farm one night toward the end of a June that had been heavenly for baseball players, nightmarishly dry for farmers. A full moon on the eastern front rested uneasily within a tangle of peach tree branches. Jonah was trying, for the third time that year, to get Shoo-fly out to the game. The game was between the Niagara Fall Mariners, Jonah's team, and the Toronto Maple Leafs.

"I can't," said Shoo-fly.

"You can't live on work alone," said Jonah. "Give yourself a couple of hours."

Shoo-fly's father ran the farm, and Shoo-fly helped with that and ran a landscaping company to fill in the slack hours. Words that filled the father with delight but the son with anxious disgust were, "Let's take a break," or "Take five," or "I think we really ought to take a day off."

"Been meaning to put this fence up since early spring," said Shoo-fly.

Said Jonah, "You've been putting up walls against everything since you first got peach-fuzz under your nose."

"So say you," said Shoo-fly, "and so be it if you mean I try not to waste time on…"

"On what?"

Jonah stopped to look up at a catbird in the front-yard apple tree. The bird was singing its critically suspect imitations of bluejays and orioles and cardinals. Shoo-fly thought about the fence. It was needed to spruce up that corner of the lot that he used as home-base for his landscaping business. He ought to set his own ragged mess of a yard in order. Physician, heal thyself. Shoemaker, fix your heels. Landscaper, weed your garden.

Jonah tried again. "Othelia should be there."

"Why is that?" asked Shoo-fly.

"What do you mean, 'Why is that'? Maybe she likes baseball." Jonah said more. "And maybe she's there to see Johnny Martens."

Shoo-fly said, "I meant, why does it matter that Othelia Funk is at a baseball game?"

Jonah turned to go. "I see all the beautiful work you do, Richard. You and your father have a beautiful farm. Where can I find a weed? You made beautiful gardens for Salesman Dyck and Bill Katzman and Mr. Fedorowich, which I see because they're all on my street. And you made beauty, you made one fantastic rock garden for Gabriel Funk for almost no profit. But you never see what your friends can do."

The bird, silent now, flew over to a perch on the run-down split-cedar fence. Jonah kept on: "Say, you know Freddy Giesbrecht is the other Mennonite on the team. What were all the guys talking about before Church last Sunday? Freddy's grand slam, that's what."

Shoo-fly Dyck Junior scratched his snow-white, sun-bleached hair and smiled. "I know I should know this—but what's a grand slam?"

Harris "Crawdaddy" Burden, manager of the Toronto Blue Jays, had three relief pitchers worth, on average, $2,666,000 US annually. Translated into Canadian English at the current, late-June rate of exchange, that meant more than three million per arm. As far as total assets were concerned, each man was capable of paying a small third world country's debt to the World Bank.

The Jays had gone into the seventh inning with a 5-2 lead. That was when million-dollar fireman number one came in. It was now the top of the ninth. Two out. 5-4. Someone was at second base on a walk and a wild pitch. The Yankee at bat hit a bloop single into centre field to tie the game.

The Blue Jays paid this particular pitcher, when you averaged all the numbers out, approximately a thousand bucks *per pitch*.

Shoo-fly Dyck took Jonah Neufeld's baseball and glove. "I haven't tried this in years. How far is it again from the pitcher to the catcher's box?"

"About 60 feet and a bit," said Jonah.

The two young men measured 60 feet from the side of the barn. "Let's mark a square for the strike zone," Jonah said. "I'll take three throws, and you take three. If I hit the zone more than you, then you have to come to the game tonight."

"No fair. You play all the time."

"Yeah? So how come, like, every single game, from the right field bleacher, I hear this old fart say, 'Hey, Neufie—you couldn't hit the broad side of a barn'?"

Jimmy Blue, scout for the Chicago Cubs, called up his old buddy, Jenkinson Kilgus. Jenkie, till this point, has been the greatest Canadian major leaguer of all time. He had seven 20-game winning seasons, and was now, among scores of other activities, an administrator and good-will ambassador for the Inter-County League of Southern Ontario.

"Say Jenkie," said Jimmy, long distance from Flint, Michigan. "Is there anyone I should be looking at in that fun league of yours?"

"Yeah, there's a handful of really good kids. Real sharp, real strong," said Kilgus: "No word of a lie."

"Name one," said hawk-eyed Mr. Blue, naturally mistrustful of everything, but especially so of non-Americans' ability to evaluate talent, even when they were friends—and former Major League all-stars.

"Fred Giesbrecht. Hit his third grand slam of the year against one of the best pitchers in the league last week."

"Okay. What's his overall average, Jenkie?"

"Around .250, .270, I guess."

"Come on, Jenk," said Jimmy Blue. "That translates to maybe a .120 in Chicago. Anyone else?"

"Your turn," Jonah said. "You've got to get two out of three to beat me."

Shoo-fly Dyck rolled the ball around at the tip of his fingers. He thought about the fence he was going to erect. He thought about Othelia Funk, and Johnny Martens. He thought about how Ricky Dyck used to play baseball, how well he used to throw—when he was 9, only, he beat the Youth Group teenagers in a throwing contest at the church picnic. Shoo-fly thought about the square marked on the inch thick siding on the wooden barn.

He threw the ball as hard as he could, and it sailed over the barn by about 10 feet and carried on for about 50 yards into a strawberry patch. Jonah got a second, hacked-up ball from his ancient Dodge Barracuda. "Shoo-fly, you couldn't hit the broad side of a...of a whale. If you miss this time, you have to come to the game."

Shoo-fly Dyck rolled the second ball around in his fingers. He thought about the fence, Othelia, Johnny. He thought about his father's $600,000 debt.

He switched all that off, and concentrated on the strike zone. He whipped the ball right into the heart of the marked box.

"Beginner's luck," laughed Jonah, but he had been impressed by the speed of the ball. "This is your last throw. You have to make it. Do or die, Shoo-fly baby."

Shoo-fly seemed to take the threat literally. The next pitch had a kind of scared ferocity, and again it struck the heart of the box, this time shattering the wood.

Five pigs inside the barn watched a white orb land in the oozing pay-dirt in the middle of their sty. They nosed it out of the mud, making positive, neutral and negative comments like a wallow of sportwriters assessing a rookie.

"OK, Jonah," said Shoo-fly Dyck. "I won. But I'll join you just this once."

Jonah Neufeld could not speak. The last throw was awesome. The last time a pitch impressed him that much was years ago, when he had seen "Goose" Gossage still not too far on the sunset side of his prime.

Othelia Funk was brushing her hair, and counting. "Oh, this is *merde*," she said aloud. Her golden tresses were half groomed to death. No make-up will be put on tonight, either, she pronounced silently.

She shocked herself, thinking this. It was a pleasant shock, the beginning of a behavioural and spiritual revolution in the silence of her mother's exquisitely appointed powder-blue bathroom. Yes, that would be the first line of her novel, a *bildungsroman* about the rise of an extremely intelligent superwoman to an awfully impressive Somewhere.

"*Quelle* shit," she said aloud.

Johnny Martens would be by soon with Freddy Giesbrecht and Mack McCollick and the usual crew.

She imagined a new person in the car with them. Someone from a distance; someone inscrutable, a cause of pure excitement.

Life in the confines of the Virgil Corral was good, but The Good Life was certainly in some other sphere.

Jonah looked at his friend, and tried to think of something. What do you say when you think you've seen what might be an angel, or a unicorn, or the phoenix itself rising out of black ash, and all of your other senses and the world assure you that you've actually seen nothing but the usual goose egg.

Shoo-fly Dyck was nothing but the white-haired son of a farmer who liked shoo-fly pie. Shoo-fly Dyck was a farmer himself and a part-time landscaper whose muscles had ballooned to bursting, like udders at milking time. Shoo-fly Dyck loved shovels and dirt and privet hedges more than he liked people, so it seemed, and that's why Jonah was trying to get his friend's nose out of the topsoil and into the nightlights of a baseball game.

The wood in the strike zone was probably rotten.

Othelia Funk, Johnny Martens, and the Virgil gang were in the right-field stands, having made the 10-mile drive to the Honeymoon Capital of the World. Mack McCollick was telling some old favourites in a Snagglepuss accent: "Why do they smear garbage on the walls at a Mennonite wedding?... To keep the flies off the bride, obviously!"

Jokes like this never stuck to Othelia, for one, because—with her ample breasts, ballerina legs, grain-gold tresses and angelic features (a little too ethereal, perhaps)—she was one of the most beautiful girls ever to grace the Oakes Park bleachers in Niagara Falls. In this way, in a letter to a friend, did Jonah Neufeld, the budding novelist, once describe Othelia.

The non-Mennonite McCollick came back with all the zest of an outlander: "How do you tell the bride at a Mennonite wedding?... Ah, but she's the one with the braided armpits."

"How do you tell the groom?" asked Johnny Martens.

"He's da one—I'm surprised at you, Mr. Martens—Yah! Da vun *mit der* clean bowling shirt."

Somewhere near them in the stands sat Murphy DuMaurier, veteran reporter for the *Niagara Falls Review*. Someone told him that the loud kids were Mennonites, most of them. Mennonites! This required investigation. Mennonites were sourpusses in funeral clothes driving black horse-drawn buggies, and were definitely not supposed to be hoisting mickeys of gin.

"Hey Neufie," shouted Grape Queen Wiebe. Jonah Neufeld, walking into the park with Shoo-fly, waved to Monika Wiebe (runner-up years ago in a Grape Festival contest) and to the rest of his friends.

"What gives?" said Johnny Martens. "Richard Dyck is not digging ditches tonight?"

As Shoo-fly came over, Othelia transfixed him with her mellifluous voice: "Shoo-fly, that's a very nice bowling shirt."

Shoo-fly could only hear *her* words for the next five seconds, and he felt good—her words were like joyful laughter slopping around in his chest. Then he heard the others laughing, and felt the blood rush round his ears.

At that moment, his ragged brown hair streaming out behind him, Jonah came running from the dressing room to the stands. "Shoo-fly, Johnny—come on over here. Yeah, now."

Half the Mariners had eaten at Calypso's Steak House, and five were suffering badly from food poisoning. They wouldn't be able to set sail, so to speak, for another couple of days, and so these five players would also probably miss the following night's game, a Saturday gig against the Stratford Hillers. Manager Parsons could do nothing about bolstering his crew this evening against Toronto—all players had to be signed at least 24 hours before the start of a game. But he wanted to sign up 2 or 3 extra players immediately, to be sure of a full bench for the game against Stratford.

Jonah didn't really know why he called Shoo-fly Dyck to the dressing room: maybe a half-notion that the big baby or little frankenstein might be convinced to take its first step. Johnny Martens was an obvious choice—he was average, a late cut from the Mariners during spring training.

Whatever else Jonah was thinking or not thinking, he must have sensed that Shoo-fly could actually play the game. As a reserve outfielder, maybe, or a relief pitcher in a game the Mariners were losing by 10 or more runs.

In the confusion that frazzled the dressing room, Knobby Parsons had one look at the side of beef that barely fit through the door and thought, "That man is either a baseball player or a linebacker for the Argonauts." Adding his half-decibel of noise to the general pandemonium, he thrust a player contract in front of Shoo-fly Dyck and demanded that he fill it out as fast as he could write.

Two hours earlier, Shoo-fly had promised himself to put up a fence. Now, for the following night, he had promised to forsake the digging of holes in the good earth and to ride the waves of applause as a Niagara Falls Mariner.

That was the beginning. The other salient baseball facts are these.... Richard Dyck shines in the Inter-County League—professional scouts take heed. On the very day of his signing with Toronto, a catastrophic accident and drug scandal involving a third of the Jays' pitching staff lands Shoo-fly on the mound at SkyDome. He reveals, on national television, that he can throw 105 miles per hour—with both arms. He also reveals huge gaps in his knowledge of the game, and is sent down to "the farm" to complete his education as a major leaguer. He arises from Syracuse in September to rejoin a team that wins the pennant, the American League semi-finals, and the American League Championship....

And now, ladies and gentlemen, it is the seventh game of the World Series. It is Sunday, October the 24th. The Blue Jays carry a 3-2 lead into the top half of the ninth inning against the Los Angeles Dodgers.

Centrefielder Jerry Bimm hits a one-out double. The next two Dodgers, Axworthy and Santana, are walked—the first intentionally, the second mistakenly. Worst of all, the Dodgers' clean-up man, a right-handed batter, the red-hot, indomitable Juan Cerbantes, is due up. Far off in the distance, long, low thunder rumbles across the troubled waters of Lake Ontario.

Manager Burden breaks for the mound, thinking, "I'm going to bring the kid in and leave him in, until we win—even if it takes another nine innings—or until we die." The fans' anxious, ecstatic prayer reaches its crescendo—"SHOO-FLY! SHOO-FLY! SHOO-FLY!..."

The manager is remarkably calm: "Obviously we need strikeouts in this situation, but keep an eye on that jackrabbit at third. And remember what we talked about the other day, what Knobby said. If you have to throw to any base, Richard, use your right hand." Burden is the first manager in World Series history to advise choice of throwing arm.

The Blue Jay infielders catch all or part of the conference—third-baseman Jack Hume, short-stop Manny Menendez, catcher Sly Cooder and first baseman Moose Mansour. They take up their positions again, a little less nervous than they were before, bracing themselves to respond quickly, confidently, intelligently to whatever fate will throw their way.

Shoo-fly takes his nine warm-ups, and deliberately throws one of them in the dirt and one very high and wide. Knobby told him to do that every warm-up—but Richard doesn't think Cerbantes can be intimidated. Cooder stops one wild pitch, and watches the other hiss toward the back-stop.

Cerbantes steps in, taking a good 15 seconds to plant himself in the batter's box, making sure his distance from the plate is just right, juggling his jock, spitting twice, and—despite his skepticism—crossing himself: Father, Son and Holy Ghost.

While his former team-mate on the Syracuse Chiefs goes through his ritual, Shoo-fly steps off the mound and gathers himself in. It is so much more difficult now, because he cares. He wants to do well, to please his fans, please the ghost of Mr. Parsons, please his father, his team-mates on three different teams, Othelia Funk, and most of all "Grape Queen" Wiebe, the one and only woman he's ever necked with, and that just a week ago.

But he shuts them all out. He says—despite qualms about mixing baseball and religion—"for my life and the good earth, thank you God!"

He focuses on the field beside him and behind him, and he brands the strike zone on his mind like the mark of the just. He ascends the mound just as Juan Cerbantes packs his luggage one last time.

Shoo-fly stares at the jackrabbit on the third base, taking a lead at least two feet longer than he had before. Jack Hume is also a lot closer to the bag, guarding the line with the bases drunk.

Shoo-fly reads the sign, and fires a strike, knee-high, inside corner....

The next pitch is called a ball, outside. NBC announcer Townsend Crichton comments to a billion, transfixed viewers: "On the replay, Whitey, that looked a lot like a strike. Umpire Saywell might be havin' trouble seein' those hummers comin' in."

"Unbelievable, Townsend," says Whitey Cash, manager of the Detroit Tigers turned colour commentator. "Speed gun says 103 M.P.H.! And Cooder seems fit to be tied up in knots, too. I'm wondering, did Harris Burden consider the wild pitch? The passed ball?"

Shoo-fly reads the sign again. He pauses—then wheels toward second base, throwing a thunderbolt to Manny Menendez, who brush-tags a stunned Franklin Axworthy—he had strayed far too far from the safety of the bag, and to *this day* cannot believe that Toronto *dared* a pick off move.

The Blue Jay faithful go berserk with joy—one more out for salvation!

An outwardly calm Harris Burden quivers with anxiety. Cooder made a good call, but Dyck is out there to throw strikeouts, not go Dodger-picking.

Burden stays put, and flashes confident thumbs-up signs to Cooder and Menendez. Dyck has breathing room now. The bases are not loaded. This is the time for a strikeout, Richard.

Jerry Bimm is thinking of the seven times he has stolen home in his career, and takes the same dangerously long lead. Bimm reads the green light signal from the dugout. One mistake by Shoo-fly, and he was going for it.

Mustafa Mansour has come in again to cover first base, with second base open. Santana might go—he's been caught just once in 47 tries this year.

Shoo-fly goes into motion, and throws an off-speed slider. Cerbantes, looking for the fast-ball, swings early. The crushed ball sails down the line towards the left-field stands. Jerry Howarth has to do his professional duty, and sound excited, but the veteran radio announcer is in agony: "Hit to left field! Long drive! Deep drive! But it's hooking, hooking... it misses the foul pole in left field by inches! Whoa, Nelly—that ball was 50 feet up, folks, and just wide of the pole." Tom Cheek jumps in: "Man ohhh man...Cerbantes just let a prize fish slip out of the net on that one!"

Shoo-fly's next pitch is his 106 mile an hour heater—it looks like a strike, but Saywell calls it a ball. Cerbantes thinks: "I should have swung. This guy is too simple, too stupid to waste any pitches."

Shoo-fly reads the new sign, then stares at Bimm. He fakes a throw to third—then wheels around and throws a strike at first base. Santana gets back safely, although experts all over the broadcast world, for the third time that inning, disagree with the umpires and call him out.

At the very moment the ball leaves Richard's hand toward first, Jerry Bimm breaks for home. Mansour fires at Sly

Cooder, high and wide to the third-base side. Cooder leaps, catches the ball, and sprawls rear-first on the streaking Dodger, stopping a yard short of the plate.

Ah, but the ball pops out of Cooder's glove. Bimm stretches an injured hand for home, like a desperate Adam reaching for God. He does not slap synthetic rubber: he slaps the real leather glove of a diving Shoo-fly, who has backed up his catcher exactly as Knobby Parsons first taught him.

Richard Shoo-fly Dyck is the prime mover in a 1-3-2-1 put-out to save the game and the World Series!

Toronto fans raise a joyful noise unto the Dome; the Blue Jay players rush off the bench to mob Cooder, Dyck and each other; and masses of grimly happy security people rush into place to prevent civilized Torontonians from ripping Labatt property—players and stadium—to shreds.

Shoo-fly squirms out of the scrum, and backs away from the mob scene, horrified. He'd expected to shake hands, and do a lot of hugging, but not this orgiastic rolling and tumbling over everybody. He backs into Juan Cerbantes, still staring at home plate, feeling emasculated. Cerbantes catches the pitcher's eyes in his own evil stare.

Shoo-fly speaks, but Cerbantes cannot hear. Shoo-fly yells into his ear, "Sure glad I didn't have to PITCH another one to YOU!"

Cerbantes spits, "What are you talking about?"

Shoo-fly shouts back, "Looked like you were picking peaches, man!"

Juan smiles. The two men shake hands, and Shoo-fly retreats into the dressing room, escaping two hours later drenched in beer and champagne, although he hasn't willingly put a single drop past his lips. It isn't a matter of principle. He is simply too happy, too full of the spirit to bother tipping bottle-neck into his mouth.

The next day, there is a parade downtown, and Richard stands in a car with Sylvio Biancanello. All along the route, multicultural Toronto is waving its uniform Blue Jay banners, and the shouting at the two Canadians is sometimes "Ca-na-da! Ca-na-da!" and sometimes "Italia! Italia!" and sometimes the first names of the magnificent duo.

In Nathan Phillips Square, 70,000 people roar approval as each player steps forward on a makeshift podium to hear a congratulatory line from Mayor Dinah McLung, receive a set of keys to the city, and then make a little speech of their own if they so choose. SkyDome itself could not be used for the celebration, since the World Wrestling Federation was setting up a show featuring the predestined demise of an overweight, over-aged Undertaker. The show is entitled, "Autumn Slam—Burial of the Western Empire."

As Richard Dyck steps forward, Mayor McLung's voice is drowned out, and a speech from Richard is not possible. In a chant that rocks the concave sides of City Hall, reverberates down the cash-rich avenues of inner Toronto, and rolls on up to rattle windows at the tower-tops of Toronto Dominion and the Royal Bank of Canada, joyful fanatics bellow their favourite word, "SHOO-FLY! SHOO-FLY! SHOO-FLY!"

The *Book* of *Beasts*

by
E. NESBIT
(1858–1924)

I never actually read E. Nesbit as a child, at least not that I can remember. "The Book of Beasts" is just a wonderfully beastly book. I could read it over and over. Nesbit's books have become known as children's classics, but this seems to me a peculiarly adult story. Besides, where would we all be without Dragons and flying Hippogriffs and sleepy Manticora creatures?

He happened to be building a Palace when the news came, and he left all the bricks kicking about the floor for Nurse to clear up—but then the news was rather remarkable news. You see, there was a knock at the front door and voices talking downstairs, and Lionel thought it was the man come to see about the gas which had not been allowed to be lighted since the day when Lionel made a swing by tying his skipping-rope to the gas-bracket.

And then, quite suddenly, Nurse came in, and said, 'Master Lionel, dear, they've come to fetch you to go and be King.'

Then she made haste to change his smock and to wash his face and hands and brush his hair, and all the time she was doing it Lionel kept wriggling and fidgeting and saying, 'Oh, don't, Nurse,' and, 'I'm sure my ears are quite clean,' or, 'Never mind my hair, it's all right,' and 'That'll do.'

'You're going on as if you was going to be an eel instead of a King,' said Nurse.

The minute Nurse let go for a moment Lionel bolted off without waiting for his clean handkerchief, and in the draw-ing-room there were two very grave-looking gentlemen in red robes with fur, and gold coronets with velvet sticking up out of the middle like the cream in the very expensive jam tarts.

They bowed low to Lionel, and the gravest one said:

'Sire, your great-great-great-great-great-grandfather, the King of this country, is dead, and now you have got to come and be King.'

'Yes, please, sir,' said Lionel; 'when does it begin?'

'You will be crowned this afternoon,' said the grave gentleman who was not quite so grave-looking as the other.

'Would you like me to bring Nurse, or what time would you like me to be fetched, and hadn't I better put on my velvet suit with the lace collar?' said Lionel, who had often been out to tea.

'Your Nurse will be removed to the Palace later. No, never mind about changing your suit; the Royal robes will cover all that up.'

The grave gentleman led the way to a coach with eight white horses, which was drawn up in front of the house where Lionel lived. It was No. 7, on the left-hand side of the street as you go up.

Lionel ran upstairs at the last minute, and he kissed Nurse and said:

'Thank you for washing me. I wish I'd let you do the other ear. No—there's no time now. Give me the hanky. Good-bye, Nurse.'

'Good-bye, ducky,' said Nurse; 'be a good little King now, and say "please" and "thank you," and remember to pass the cake to the little girls, and don't have any more than two helps of anything.'

So off went Lionel to be made a King. He had never expected to be a King any more than you have, so it was all quite new to him—so new that he had never even thought of it. And as the coach went through the town he had to bite his tongue to be quite sure it was real, because if his tongue was real it showed he wasn't dreaming. Half an hour before he had been building with bricks in the nursery; and now—the streets were all fluttering with flags; every window was crowded with people waving handkerchiefs and scattering flowers; there were scarlet soldiers everywhere along the pavements, and all the bells of all the churches were ringing like mad, and like a great song to the music of their ringing he heard thousands of people shouting, 'Long live Lionel! Long live our little King!'

He was a little sorry at first that he had not put on his best clothes, but he soon forgot to think about that. If he had been a girl he would very likely have bothered about it the whole time.

As they went along, the grave gentlemen, who were the Chancellor and the Prime Minister, explained the things which Lionel did not understand.

'I thought we were a Republic,' said Lionel. 'I'm sure there hasn't been a King for some time.'

'Sire, your great-great-great-great-great-grandfather's death happened when my grandfather was a little boy,' said the Prime Minister, 'and since then your loyal people have been saving up to buy you a crown—so much a week, you know, according to people's means—sixpence a week from those who have first-rate pocket-money, down to a halfpenny a week for those who haven't so much. You know it's the rule that the crown must be paid for by the people.'

'But hadn't my great-great-however-much-it-is-grandfather a crown?'

'Yes, but he sent it to be tinned over, for fear of vanity, and he had had all the jewels taken out, and sold them to buy books. He was a strange man; a very good King he was, but he had his faults—he was fond of books. Almost with his latest breath he sent the crown to be tinned—and he never lived to pay the tinsmith's bill.'

Here the Prime Minister wiped away a tear, and just then the carriage stopped and Lionel was taken out of the carriage to be crowned. Being crowned is much more tiring work than you would suppose, and by the time it was over, and Lionel had worn the Royal robes for an hour or two and had had his hand kissed by everybody whose business it was to do it, he was quite worn out, and was very glad to get into the Palace nursery.

Nurse was there, and tea was ready; seedy cake and plummy

cake, and jam and hot buttered toast, and the prettiest china with red and gold and blue flowers on it, and real tea, and as many cups of it as you liked. After tea Lionel said:

'I think I should like a book. Will you get me one, Nurse?'

'Bless the child,' said Nurse, 'you don't suppose you've lost the use of your legs with just being a King? Run along, do, and get your books yourself.'

So Lionel went down into the library. The Prime Minister and the Chancellor were there, and when Lionel came in they bowed very low, and were beginning to ask Lionel most politely what on earth he was coming bothering for now—when Lionel cried out:

'Oh, what a worldful of books! Are they yours?'

'They are yours, your Majesty,' answered the Chancellor. 'They were the property of the late King, your great-great—'

'Yes, I know,' Lionel interrupted. 'Well, I shall read them all. I love to read. I am so glad I learned to read.'

'If I might venture to advise your Majesty,' said the Prime Minister, 'I should *not* read these books. Your great—'

'Yes?' said Lionel, quickly.

'He was a very good King—oh, yes, really a very superior King in his way, but he was a little—well, strange.'

'Mad?' asked Lionel, cheerfully.

'No, no'—both the gentlemen were sincerely shocked. 'Not mad; but if I may express it so, he was—er—too clever by half. And I should not like a little King of mine to have anything to do with his books.'

Lionel looked puzzled.

'The fact is,' the Chancellor went on, twisting his red beard in an agitated way, 'your great—'

'Go on,' said Lionel.

'Was *called* a wizard.'

'But he wasn't?'

'Of course not—a most worthy King was your great—'

'I see.'

'But I wouldn't touch his books.'

'Just this one,' cried Lionel, laying his hands on the cover of a great brown book that lay on the study table. It had gold patterns on the brown leather, and gold clasps with turquoises and rubies in the twists of them, and gold corners, so that the leather should not wear out too quickly.

'I must look at this one,' Lionel said, for on the back in big letters he read: 'The Book of Beasts.'

The Chancellor said, 'Don't be a silly little King.'

But Lionel had got the gold clasps undone, and he opened the first page, and there was a beautiful Butterfly all red, and brown, and yellow, and blue, so beautifully painted that it looked as if it were alive.

'There,' said Lionel, 'isn't that lovely? Why—'

But as he spoke the beautiful Butterfly fluttered its many-coloured wings on the yellow old page of the book, and flew up and out of the window.

'Well!' said the Prime Minister, as soon as he could speak for the lump of wonder that had got into his throat and tried to choke him, 'that's magic, that is.'

But before he had spoken the King had turned the next page, and there was a shining bird complete and beautiful in every blue feather of him. Under him was written, 'Blue Bird of Paradise,' and while the King gazed enchanted at the charming picture the Blue Bird fluttered his wings on the yellow page and spread them and flew out of the book.

Then the Prime Minister snatched the book away from the King and shut it up on the blank page where the bird had been, and put it on a very high shelf. And the Chancellor gave the King a good shaking, and said:

'You're a naughty, disobedient little King,' and was very angry indeed.

'I don't see that I've done any harm,' said Lionel. He hated being shaken, as all boys do; he would much rather have been slapped.

'No harm?' said the Chancellor. 'Ah—but what do you know about it? That's the question. How do you know what might have been on the next page—a snake or a worm, or a centipede or a revolutionist, or something like that.'

'Well, I'm sorry if I've vexed you, said Lionel. 'Come, let's kiss and be friends.' So he kissed the Prime Minister, and they settled down for a nice quiet game of noughts and crosses, while the Chancellor went to add up his accounts.

But when Lionel was in bed he could not sleep for thinking of the book, and when the full moon was shining with all her might and light he got up and crept down to the library and climbed up and got 'The Book of Beasts.'

He took it outside on to the terrace, where the moonlight was as bright as day, and he opened the book, and saw the empty pages with 'Butterfly' and 'Blue Bird of Paradise' underneath, and then he turned the next page. There was some sort of red thing sitting under a palm tree, and under it was written 'Dragon.' The Dragon did not move, and the King shut up the book rather quickly and went back to bed.

But the next day he wanted another look, so he got the book out into the garden, and when he undid the clasps with rubies and turquoises, the book opened all by itself at the picture with 'Dragon' underneath, and the sun shone full on the page. And then, quite suddenly, a great Red Dragon came out of the book, and spread vast scarlet wings and flew away across the garden to the far hills, and Lionel was left with the empty page before him, for the page was quite empty except for the green palm tree and the yellow desert, and the little streaks of red where the paint brush had gone outside the pencil outline of the Red Dragon.

And then Lionel felt that he had indeed done it. He had not been King twenty-four hours, and already he had let loose a Red Dragon to worry his faithful subjects' lives out. And they had been saving up so long to buy him a crown, and everything!

Lionel began to cry.

Then the Chancellor and the Prime Minister and the Nurse all came running to see what was the matter. And when they saw the book they understood, and the Chancellor said:

'You naughty little King! Put him to bed, Nurse, and let him think over what he's done.'

'Perhaps, my Lord,' said the Prime Minister, 'we'd better first find out just exactly what he *has* done.'

Then Lionel, in floods of tears, said:

'It's a Red Dragon, and it's gone flying away to the hills, and I *am* so sorry, and, oh, do forgive me!'

But the Prime Minister and the Chancellor had other things to think of than forgiving Lionel. They hurried off to consult the police and see what could be done. Everyone did what they could. They sat on committees and stood on guard, and lay in wait for the Dragon but he stayed up in the hills, and there was nothing more to *be* done. The faithful Nurse, meanwhile, did not neglect her duty. Perhaps she did more than anyone else, for she slapped the King and put him to bed without his tea, and when it got dark she would not give him a candle to read by.

'You are a naughty little King,' she said, 'and nobody will love you.'

Next day the Dragon was still quiet, though the more poetic of Lionel's subjects could see the redness of the Dragon shining through the green trees quite plainly. So Lionel put on his crown and sat on his throne and said he wanted to make some laws.

And I need hardly say that though the Prime Minister and the Chancellor and the Nurse might have the very poorest opinion of Lionel's private judgement, and might even slap him and send him to bed, the minute he got on his throne and set his crown on his head, he became infallible—which means that everything he said was right, and that he couldn't possibly make a mistake. So when he said:

'There is to be a law forbidding people to open books in schools or elsewhere'—he had the support of at least half of his subjects, and the other half—the grown-up half—pretended to think he was quite right.

Then he made a law that everyone should always have enough to eat. And this pleased everyone except the ones who had always had too much.

And when several other nice new laws were made and written down he went home and made mud-houses and was very happy. And he said to his Nurse:

'People will love me now I've made such a lot of pretty new laws for them.'

But Nurse said: 'Don't count your chickens, my dear. You haven't seen the last of that Dragon yet.'

Now the next day was Saturday. And in the afternoon the Dragon suddenly swooped down upon the common in all his hideous redness, and carried off the Football Players, umpires, goal-posts, football, and all.

Then the people were very angry indeed, and they said:

'We might as well be a Republic. After saving up all these years to get his crown, and everything!'

And wise people shook their heads, and foretold a decline in the National Love of Sport. And, indeed, football was not at all popular for some time afterwards.

Lionel did his best to be a good King during the week, and the people were beginning to forgive him for letting the Dragon out of the book. 'After all,' they said, 'football is a dangerous game, and perhaps it is wise to discourage it.'

Popular opinion held that the Football Players, being rough and hard, had disagreed with the Dragon so much that he had gone away to some place where they only play cats' cradle and games that do not make you hard and tough.

All the same, Parliament met on the Saturday afternoon, a convenient time, when most of the Members would be free to attend, to consider the Dragon. But unfortunately the Dragon, who had only been asleep, woke up because it was Saturday, and he considered the Parliament, and afterwards there were not any Members left, so they tried to make a new Parliament, but being an M.P. had somehow grown as unpopular as football playing, and no one would consent to be elected, so they had to do without a Parliament. When the next Saturday came round everyone was a little nervous, but the Red Dragon was pretty quiet that day and only ate an Orphanage.

Lionel was very, very unhappy. He felt that it was his disobedience that had brought this trouble on the Parliament and the Orphanage and the Football Players, and he felt that it was his duty to try and do something. The question was, what?

The Blue Bird that had come out of the book used to sing very nicely in the Palace rose-garden, and the Butterfly was very tame, and would perch on his shoulder when he walked among the tall lilies: so Lionel saw that *all* the creatures in the Book of Beasts could not be wicked, like the Dragon, and he thought:

'Suppose I could get another Beast out who would fight the Dragon?'

So he took the Book of Beasts out into the rose-garden and opened the page next to the one where the Dragon had been just a tiny bit to see what the name was. He could only see 'cora,' but he felt the middle of the page swelling up thick with the creature that was trying to come out, and it was only by putting the book down and sitting on it suddenly, very hard, that he managed to get it shut. Then he fastened the clasps with the rubies and turquoises in them and sent for the Chancellor, who had been ill on Saturday week, and so had not been eaten with the rest of the Parliament, and he said:

'What animal ends in "cora"?'

The Chancellor answered:

'The Manticora, of course.'

'What is he like?' asked the King.

'He is the sworn foe of the Dragons,' said the Chancellor. 'He drinks their blood. He is yellow, with the body of a lion and the face of a man. I wish we had a few Manticoras here now. But the last died hundreds of hears ago—worse luck!'

Then the King ran and opened the book at the page that had 'cora' on it, and there was the picture-Manticora, all yellow, with a lion's body and a man's face, just as the Chancellor had said. And under the picture was written 'Manticora.'

And in a few minutes the Manticora came sleepily out of the book, rubbing its eyes with its hands and mewing piteously. It seemed very stupid, and when Lionel gave it a push and said, 'Go along and fight the Dragon, do,' it put its tail between its legs and fairly ran away. It went and hid behind the Town Hall, and at night when the people were asleep it went round and ate all the pussy-cats in the town. And then it mewed more than ever. And on the Saturday morning, when people were a little timid about going out, because the Dragon had no regular hour of calling, the Manticora went up and down the streets and drank all the milk that was left in the cans at the doors for people's teas, and it ate the cans as well.

And just when it had finished the very last little ha'porth, which was short measure, the Red Dragon came down the street looking for the Manticora. It edged off when it saw him coming, for it was not at all the Dragon-fighting kind; and, seeing no other door open, the poor, hunted creature took refuge in the General Post Office, and there the Dragon found it, trying to conceal itself among the ten o'clock mail. The Dragon fell on the Manticora at once, and the mail was no defence. The mewings were heard all over the town. All the pussies and the milk the Manticora had had seemed to have strengthened its mew wonderfully. Then there was a sad silence, and presently the people whose windows looked that way saw the Dragon come walking down the steps of the General Post Office spitting fire and smoke, together with tufts of Manticora fur, and the fragments of the registered letters. Things were growing very serious. However popular the King might become during the week, the Dragon was sure to do something on Saturday to upset the people's loyalty.

The Dragon was a perfect nuisance for the whole of Saturday, except during the hour of noon, and then he had to rest under a tree or he would have caught fire from the heat of the sun. You see, he was very hot to begin with.

At last came a Saturday when the Dragon actually walked into the Royal nursery and carried off the King's own pet Rocking-Horse. Then the King cried for six days, and on the seventh he was so tired that he had to stop. Then he heard the Blue Bird singing among the roses and saw the Butterfly fluttering among the lilies, and he said:

'Nurse, wipe my face, please. I am not going to cry any more.'

Nurse washed his face, and told him not to be a silly little King. 'Crying,' said she, 'never did anyone any good yet.'

'I don't know,' said the little King. 'I seem to see better, and to hear better now that I've cried for a week. Now, Nurse, dear, I know I'm right, so kiss me in case I never come back. I *must* try if I can't save the people.'

'Well, if you must, you must,' said Nurse; 'but don't tear

your clothes or get your feet wet.'

So off he went.

The Blue Bird sang more sweetly than ever, and the Butterfly shone more brightly, as Lionel once more carried the Book of Beasts out into the rose-garden, and opened it—very quickly, so that he might not be afraid and change his mind. The book fell open wide, almost in the middle, and there was written at the bottom of the page, 'The Hippogriff,' and before Lionel had time to see what the picture was, there was a fluttering of great wings and a stamping of hoofs, and a sweet, soft, friendly neighing; and there came out of the book a beautiful white horse with a long, long white mane and a long, long white tail, and he had great wings like swan's wings, and the softest, kindest eyes in the world, and he stood there among the roses.

The Hippogriff rubbed its silky-soft, milky-white nose against the little King's shoulder, and the little King thought: 'But for the wings you are very like my poor, dear, lost Rocking-Horse.' And the Blue Bird's song was very loud and sweet.

Then suddenly the King saw coming through the sky the great straggling, sprawling, wicked shape of the Red Dragon. And he knew at once what he must do. He caught up the Book of Beasts and jumped on the back of the gentle, beautiful Hippogriff, and leaning down he whispered in the sharp white ear:

'Fly, dear Hippogriff, fly your very fastest to the Pebbly Waste.'

And when the Dragon saw them start, he turned and flew after them, with his great wings flapping like clouds at sunset, and the Hippogriff's wide wings were snowy as clouds at the moon-rising.

When the people in the town saw the Dragon fly off after the Hippogriff and the King they all came out of their houses to look, and when they saw the two disappear they made up their minds to the worst, and began to think what would be worn for Court mourning.

But the Dragon could not catch the Hippogriff. The red

wings were bigger than the white ones, but they were not so strong, and so the white-winged horse flew away and away and away, with the Dragon pursuing, till he reached the very middle of the Pebbly Waste.

Now, the Pebbly Waste is just like the parts of the seaside where there is no sand—all round, loose, shifting stones, and there is no grass there and no tree within a hundred miles of it.

Lionel jumped off the white horse's back in the very middle of the Pebbly Waste, and he hurriedly unclasped the Book of Beasts and laid it open on the pebbles. Then he clattered among the pebbles in his haste to get back on his white horse, and had just jumped on when up came the Dragon. He was flying very feebly, and looking round everywhere for a tree, for it was just on the stroke of twelve, the sun was shining like a gold guinea in the blue sky, and there was not a tree for a hundred miles.

The white-winged horse flew round and round the Dragon as he writhed on the dry pebbles. He was getting very hot: indeed, parts of him even had begun to smoke. He knew that he must certainly catch fire in another minute unless he could get under a tree. He made a snatch with his red claws at the King and Hippogriff, but he was too feeble to reach them, and besides, he did not dare to over-exert himself for fear he should get any hotter.

It was then that he saw the Book of Beasts lying on the pebbles, open at the page with 'Dragon' written at the bottom. He looked and he hesitated, and he looked again, and then, with one last squirm of rage, the Dragon wriggled himself back into the picture, and sat down under the palm tree, and the page was a little singed as he went in.

As soon as Lionel saw that the Dragon had really been obliged to go and sit under his own palm tree because it was the only tree there, he jumped off his horse and shut the book with a bang.

'Oh, hurrah!' he cried. 'Now we really have *done* it.'

And he clasped the book very tight with the turquoise and ruby clasps.

'Oh, my precious Hippogriff,' he cried, 'you are the bravest, dearest, most beautiful—'

'Hush,' whispered the Hippogriff, modestly. 'Don't you see that we are not alone?'

And indeed there was quite a crowd round them on the Pebbly Waste: the Prime Minister and the Parliament and the Football Players and the Orphanage and the Manticora and the Rocking-Horse, and indeed everyone who had been eaten by the Dragon. You see, it was impossible for the Dragon to take them into the book with him—it was a tight fit even for one Dragon—so, of course, he had to leave them outside.

They all got home somehow, and all lived happy ever after.

When the King asked the Manticora where he would like to live he begged to be allowed to go back into the book. 'I do not care for public life,' he said.

Of course he knew his way on to his own page, so there was no danger of his opening the book at the wrong page and letting out a Dragon or anything. So he got back into his picture, and has never come out since: that is why you will never see a Manticora as long as you live, except in a picture-book. And of course he left the pussies outside, because there was no room for them in the book—and the milk-cans too.

Then the Rocking-Horse begged to be allowed to go and live on the Hippogriff's page of the book. 'I should like,' he said, 'to live somewhere where Dragons can't get at me.'

So the beautiful, white-winged Hippogriff showed him the way in, and there he stayed till the King had him taken out for his great-great-great-great-grandchildren to play with.

As for the Hippogriff, he accepted the position of the King's Own Rocking-Horse—a situation left vacant by the retirement of the wooden one. And the Blue Bird and the Butterfly sing and flutter among the lilies and roses of the Palace garden to this very day.

The
Country

by
IVAN TURGENEV
(1818–1883)

Late in his life Ivan Turgenev wrote a series of idyllic sketches called Poems in Prose. *Delicately observed glimpses of Russian life in the middle nineteenth century, these "poems" have remained with me for decades. "The Country" is the opening sketch, and recalls a Russia rarely remembered—an idealized Russia deeply coloured by the fond memories of Turgenev's youth.*

The last day of July; for a thousands versts around, Russia, our native land.

An unbroken blue flooding the whole sky; a single cloudlet upon it, half floating, half fading away. Windlessness, warmth...air like new milk!

Larks are trilling; pouter-pigeons cooing; noiselessly the swallows dart to and fro; horses are neighing and munching; the dogs do not bark and stand peaceably wagging their tails.

A smell of smoke and of hay, and a little of tar, too, and a little of hides. The hemp, now in full bloom, sheds its heavy, pleasant fragrance.

A deep but sloping ravine. Along its sides willows in rows, with big heads above, trunks cleft below. Through the ravine runs a brook; the tiny pebbles at its bottom are all aquiver through its clear eddies. In the distance, on the border-line between earth and heaven, the bluish streak of a great river.

Along the ravine, on one side, tidy barns, little storehouses with close-shut doors; on the other side, five or six pinewood huts with boarded roofs. Above each roof, the high pole of a pigeon-house; over each entry a little short-maned horse of wrought iron. The window-panes of faulty glass shine with all the colours of the rainbow. Jugs of flowers are painted on the shutters. Before each door, a little bench stands prim and neat; on the mounds of earth, cats are basking, their transparent ears pricked up alert; beyond the high door-sills, is the cool dark of the outer rooms.

I lie on the very edge of the ravine, on an outspread horse-cloth; all about are whole stacks of fresh-cut hay, oppressively fragrant. The sagacious husbandmen have flung the hay about before the huts; let it get a bit drier in the baking sunshine; and then into the barn with it. It will be first-rate sleeping on it.

Curly, childish heads are sticking out of every haycock; crested hens are looking in the hay for flies and little beetles, and a white-lipped pup is rolling among the tangled stalks.

Flaxen-headed lads in clean smocks, belted low, in heavy boots, leaning over an unharnessed wagon, fling each other smart volleys of banter, with broad grins showing their white teeth.

A round-faced young woman peeps out of a window; laughs at their words or at the romps of the children in the mounds of hay.

Another young woman with powerful arms draws a great wet bucket out of the well… The bucket quivers and shakes, spilling long, glistening drops.

Before me stands an old woman in a new striped petticoat and new shoes.

Fat hollow beads are wound in three rows about her dark thin neck, her grey head is tied up in a yellow kerchief with red spots; it hangs low over her failing eyes.

But there is a smile of welcome in the aged eyes; a smile all over the wrinkled face. The old woman has reached, I dare say, her seventieth year…and even now one can see she has been a beauty in her day.

With a twirl of her sunburnt finger, she holds in her right hand a bowl of cold milk, with the cream on it, fresh from the cellar; the sides of the bowl are covered with drops, like strings of pearls. In the palm of her left hand the old woman brings me a huge hunch of warm bread, as though to say, 'Eat, and welcome, passing guest!'

A cock suddenly crows and fussily flaps his wings; he is slowly answered by the low of a calf, shut up in the stall.

'My word, what oats!' I hear my coachman saying... Oh, the content, the quiet, the plenty of the Russian open country! Oh, the deep peace and well-being!

And the thought comes to me: what is it all to us here, the cross on the cupola of St. Sophia in Constantinople and all the rest that we are struggling for, we men of the town?

Dulse

by
ALICE MUNRO
(1931–   )

I never quite know how to say what I want to say about Alice Munro. "Dulse" is an old favourite, not so much for any particular incident or characteristic as for the dulse itself—the dark salty seaweed that flavours the story throughout. Pungent and darkly lingering, Munro's "Dulse" is a story quietly unravelling on the rim of a summer's storm.

At the end of the summer Lydia took a boat to an island off the southern coast of New Brunswick, where she was going to stay overnight. She had just a few days left until she had to be back in Ontario. She worked as an editor, for a publisher in Toronto. She was also a poet, but she did not refer to that unless it was something people already knew. For the past eighteen months she had been living with a man in Kingston. As far as she could see, that was over.

She had noticed something about herself, on this trip to the Maritimes. It was that people were no longer interested in getting to know her. It wasn't that she had created such a stir, before, but something had been there that she could rely on. She was forty-five, and had been divorced for nine years. Her two children had started on their own lives, though there were still retreats and confusions. She hadn't got fatter or thinner, her looks had not deteriorated in any alarming way, but nevertheless she had stopped being one sort of woman and had become another, and she had noticed it on this trip. She was not surprised because she was in a new, strange condition at the time. She made efforts, one after the other. She set little blocks on top of one another and she had a day. Sometimes she almost could not do this. At other times the very deliberateness, the seeming arbitrariness, of what she was doing, the way she was living, exhilarated her.

She found a guest-house overlooking the docks, with their stacks of lobster traps, and the few scattered stores and houses that made up the village. A woman of about her own age was cooking dinner. This woman took her to a cheap, old-fashioned room upstairs. There were no other guests around, though the room next door was open and seemed to be occupied, perhaps by a child. Whoever it was had left several comic books on the floor beside the bed.

She went for a walk up the steep lane behind the guesthouse. She occupied herself by naming shrubs and weeds. The goldenrod and wild aster were in bloom, and Japanese boxwood, a rarity in Ontario, seemed commonplace here. The grass was long and coarse and the trees were small. The Atlantic coast, which she had never seen before, was just as she had expected it to be. The bending grass; the bare houses; the sea light. She started wondering what it would be like to live there, whether the houses were still cheap or if people from the outside had started to buy them up. Often on this trip she had busied herself with calculations of this kind, and also with ideas of how she could make a living in some new way, cut off from everything she had done before. She did not think of making a living writing poetry, not only because the income would be so low but because she thought, as she had thought innumerable times in her life, that probably she would not write any more poems. She was thinking that she could not cook well enough to do it for pay but she could clean. There was at least one other guest-house besides the one where she was staying, and she had seen a sign advertising a motel. How many hours' cleaning could she get if she cleaned all three places, and how much an hour did cleaning pay?

There were four small tables in the dining room, but only one man was sitting there, drinking tomato juice. He did not look at her. A man who was probably the husband of the woman she had met earlier came in from the kitchen. He had a grayish-blond beard, and a downcast look. He asked Lydia's name and took her to the table where the man was sitting. The man stood up, stiffly, and Lydia was introduced. The man's name was Mr. Stanley and Lydia took him to be about sixty. Politely, he asked her to sit down.

Three men in work clothes came in and sat down at another table. They were not noisy in any self-important or offensive way, but just coming in and disposing themselves around the table, they created an enjoyable commotion. That is, they enjoyed it, and looked as if they expected others to. Mr. Stanley bowed in their direction. It really was a little bow, not just a nod of the head. He said good evening. They asked him what there was for supper, and he said he believed it was scallops, with pumpkin pie for dessert.

"These gentlemen work for the New Brunswick Telephone Company," he said to Lydia. "They are laying a cable to one of the smaller islands, and they stay here during the week."

He was older than she had thought at first. It did not show in his voice, which was precise and American, or in the movements of his hands, but in his small separate, brownish teeth, and in his eyes, which had a delicate milky skin over the light-brown iris.

The husband brought their food, and spoke to the workmen. He was an efficient waiter, but rather stiff and remote, rather like a sleep-walker, in fact, as if he did not perform this job in his real life. The vegetables were served in large bowls, from which they helped themselves. Lydia was glad to see so much food: broccoli, mashed turnips, potatoes, corn. The American took small helpings of everything and began to eat in a very deliberate way, giving the impression that the order in which he lifted forkfuls of food to his mouth was not haphazard, that there was a reason for the turnip to follow the potatoes, and for the deep-fried scallops, which were not large, to be cut neatly in half. He looked up a couple of times as if he thought of saying something, but he did not do it. The workmen were quiet now, too, laying into the food.

Mr. Stanley spoke at last. He said, "Are you familiar with the writer Willa Cather?"

"Yes." Lydia was startled, because she had not seen anybody reading a book for the past two weeks; she had not even noticed any paperback racks.

"Do you know, then, that she spent every summer here?"

"Here?"

"On this island. She had her summer home here. Not more than a mile away from where we are sitting now. She came here for eighteen years, and she wrote many of her books here. She wrote in a room that had a view of the sea, but now the trees have grown up and blocked it. She was with her great friend, Edith Lewis. Have you read *A Lost Lady*?"

Lydia said that she had.

"It is my favorite of all her books. She wrote it here. At least, she wrote a great part of it here."

Lydia was aware of the workmen listening, although they did not glance up from their food. She felt that even without looking at Mr. Stanley or each other they might manage to communicate an indulgent contempt. She thought she did not care whether or not she was included in this contempt, but perhaps it was for that reason that she did not find anything much to say about Willa Cather, or tell Mr. Stanley that she worked for a publisher, let alone that she was any sort of writer herself. Or it could have been just that Mr. Stanley did not give her much of a chance.

"I have been her admirer for over sixty years," he said. He paused, holding his knife and fork over his plate. "I read and reread her, and my admiration grows. It simply grows. There are people here who remember her. Tonight, I am going to see a woman, a woman who knew Willa, and had conversations with her. She is eighty-eight years old but they say she has not forgotten. The people here are beginning to learn of my interest and they will remember someone like this and put me in touch.

"It is a great delight to me," he said solemnly.

All the time he was talking, Lydia was trying to think what his conversational style reminded her of. It didn't remind her of any special person, though she might have had one or two teachers at college who talked like that. What it made her think of was a time when a few people, just a few people, had never concerned themselves with being democratic, or ingratiating, in their speech; they spoke in formal, well-thought-out, slightly self-congratulating sentences, though they lived in a country where their formality, their pedantry, could bring them nothing but mockery. No, that was not the whole truth. It brought mockery, and an uncomfortable admiration. What he made Lydia think of, really, was the old-fashioned culture of provincial cities long ago (something she of course had never known, but sensed from books); the high-mindedness, the propriety; hard plush concert seats and hushed libraries. And his adoration of the chosen writer was of a piece with this; it was just as out-of-date as his speech. She thought that he could not be a teacher; such worship was not in style for teachers, even of his age.

"Do you teach literature?"

"No. Oh, no. I have not had that privilege. No. I have not even studied literature. I went to work when I was sixteen. In my day there was not so much choice. I have worked on newspapers."

She thought of some absurdly discreet and conservative New England paper with a fusty prose style.

"Oh. Which paper?" she said, then realized her inquisitiveness must seem quite rude, to anyone so circumspect.

"Not a paper you would have heard of. Just the daily paper of an industrial town. Other papers in the earlier years. That was my life."

"And now, would you like to do a book on Willa Cather?" This question seemed not so out of place to her, because she was always talking to people who wanted to do books about something.

"No," he said austerely. "My eyes do not permit me to do any reading or writing beyond what is necessary."

That was why he was so deliberate about his eating.

"No," he went on, "I don't say that at one time I might not have thought of that, doing a book on Willa. I would have written something just about her life here on the island. Biographies have been done, but not so much on that phase of her life. Now I have given up the idea. I do my investigating just for my own pleasure. I take a camp chair up there, so I can sit underneath the window where she wrote and looked at the sea. There is never anybody there."

"It isn't being kept up? It isn't any sort of memorial?"

"Oh, no indeed. It isn't kept up at all. The people here, you know, while they were very impressed with Willa, and some of them recognized her genius—I mean the genius of her personality, for they would not be able to recognize the genius of her work—others of them thought her unfriendly and did not like her. They took offense because she was unsociable, as she had to be, to do her writing."

"It could be a project," Lydia said. "Perhaps they could get some money from the government. The Canadian government and the Americans too. They could preserve the house."

"Well, that isn't for me to say." He smiled; he shook his head. "I don't think so. No."

He did not want any other worshippers coming to disturb him in his camp chair. She should have known that. What would this private pilgrimage of his be worth if other people got into the act, and signs were put up, leaflets printed; if this guest-house, which was now called Sea-View, had to be renamed Shadows on the Rock? He would let the house fall down and the grass grow over it, sooner than see that.

After Lydia's last attempt to call Duncan, the man she had been living with in Kingston, she had walked along the street in Toronto, knowing that she had to get to the bank, she had to buy some food, she had to get on the subway. She had to remember directions, and the order in which to do things: to open her checkbook, to move forward when it was her turn in line, to choose one kind of bread over another, to drop a token in the slot. These seemed to be the most difficult things she had ever done. She had immense difficulty reading the names of the subway stations, and getting off at the right one, so that she could go to the apartment where she was staying. She would have found it hard to describe this difficulty. She knew perfectly well which was the right stop, she knew which stop it came after; she knew where she was. But she could not make the connection between herself and things outside herself, so that getting up and leaving the car, going up the steps, going along the street, all seemed to involve a bizarre effort. She thought afterwards that she had been seized up, as machines are said to be. Even at the time she had an image of herself. She saw herself as something like an egg carton, hollowed out in back.

When she reached the apartment she sat down on a chair in the hall. She sat for an hour or so, then she went to the bathroom, undressed, put on her nightgown, and got into bed. In bed she felt triumph and relief, that she had managed all the difficulties and got herself to where she was supposed to be and would not have to remember anything more.

She didn't feel at all like committing suicide. She couldn't have managed the implements, or aids, she couldn't even have thought which to use. It amazed her to think that she had chosen the loaf of bread and the cheese, which were now lying on the floor in the hall. How had she imagined she was going to chew and swallow them?

After dinner Lydia sat out on the verandah with the woman who had cooked the meal. The woman's husband did the cleaning up.

"Well, of course we have a dishwasher," the woman said. "We have two freezers and an oversize refrigerator. You have to make an investment. You get the crews staying with you, you have to feed them. This place soaks up money like a sponge. We're going to put in a swimming pool next year. We need more attractions. You have to run to stay in the same place. People think what an easy nice life. Boy."

She had a strong, lined face, and long straight hair. She wore jeans and an embroidered smock and a man's sweater.

"Ten years ago I was living in a commune in the States. Now I'm here. I work sometimes eighteen hours a day. I have to pack the crew's lunch yet tonight. I cook and bake, cook and bake. John does the rest."

"Do you have someone to clean?"

"We can't afford to hire anybody. John does it. He does the laundry—everything. We had to buy a mangle for the sheets. We had to put in a new furnace. We got a bank loan. I thought that was funny, because I used to be married to a bank manager. I left him."

"I'm on my own now, too."

"Are you? You can't be on your own forever. I met John, and he was in the same boat."

"I was living with a man in Kingston, in Ontario."

"Were you? John and I are extremely happy. He used to be a minister. But when I met him he was doing carpentry. We both had sort of dropped out. Did you talk to Mr. Stanley?"

"Yes."

"Had you ever heard of Willa Cather?"

"Yes."

"That'd make him happy. I don't read hardly at all, it doesn't mean anything to me. I'm a visual person. But I think he's a wonderful character, old Mr. Stanley. He'a real old scholar."

"Has he been coming here for a long time?"

"No, he hasn't. This is just his third year. He says he's wanted to come here all his life. But he couldn't. He had to wait till some relative died, that he was looking after. Not a wife. A brother maybe. Anyway he had to wait. How old do you think he is?"

"Seventy? Seventy-five?"

"That man is eighty-one. Isn't that amazing? I really admire people like that. I really do. I admire people that keep going."

"The man I was living with—that is, the man I used to live with, in Kingston," said Lydia, "was putting some boxes of papers in the trunk of his car once, this was out in the country, at an old farmhouse, and he felt something nudge him and he glanced down. It was about dusk, on a pretty dark day. So he thought this was a big friendly dog, a big black dog giving him a nudge, and he didn't pay much attention. He just said go on, now, boy, go away now, good boy. Then when he got the boxes arranged he turned around. And he saw it was a bear. It was a black bear."

She was telling this later that same evening, in the kitchen.

"So what did he do then?" said Lawrence, who was the boss of the telephone work crew. Lawrence and Lydia and Eugene and Vincent were playing cards.

Lydia laughed. "He said, *excuse me*. That's what he claims he said."

"Papers all he had in the boxes? Nothing to eat?"

"He's a writer. He writes historical books. This was some material he needed for his work. Sometimes he has to go and scout out material from people who are very strange. That bear hadn't come out of the bush. It was a pet, actually, that had been let off its chain, for a joke. There were two old brothers there, that he got the papers from, and they just let it off its chain to give him a scare."

"That's what he does, collects old stuff and writes about it?" Lawrence said. "I guess that's interesting."

She immediately regretted having told this story. She had brought it up because the men were talking about bears. But there wasn't much point to it unless Duncan told it. He could show you himself, large and benign and civilized, with his courtly apologies to the bear. He could make you see the devilish old men behind their tattered curtains.

"You'd have to know Duncan," was what she almost said. And hadn't she told this simply to establish that she had known Duncan—that she had recently had a man, and an interesting man, an amusing and adventurous man? She wanted to assure them that she was not always alone, going on her aimless travels. She had to show herself attached. A mistake. They were not likely to think a man adventurous who collected old papers from misers and eccentrics, so that he could write books about things that had happened a hundred years ago. She shouldn't even have said that Duncan was a man she had lived with. All that could mean, to them, was that she was a woman who had slept with a man she was not married to.

Lawrence the boss was not yet forty, but he was successful. He was glad to tell about himself. He was a free-lance labor contractor and owned two houses in St. Stephen. He had two cars and a truck and a boat. His wife taught school. Lawrence was getting a thick waist, a trucker's belly, but he still looked alert and vigorous. You could see that he would be shrewd enough, in most situations, for his purposes; sure enough, ruthless enough. Dressed up, he might turn flashy. And certain places and people might be capable of making him gloomy, uncertain, contentious.

Lawrence said it wasn't all true—all the stuff they wrote about the Maritimes. He said there was plenty of work for people who weren't afraid to work. Men or women. He said he was not against women's lib, but the fact was, and always would be, that there was work men did better than women and work women did better than men, and if they would both settle down and realize that they'd be happier.

His kids were cheeky, he said. They had it too soft. They got everything—that was the way nowadays, and what could you do? The other kids got everything, too. Clothes, bikes, education, records. He hadn't had anything handed to him. He had got out and worked, driven trucks. He had got to Ontario, got as far as Saskatchewan. He had only got to grade ten in school but he hadn't let that hold him back. Sometimes he wished, though, that he did have more of an education.

Eugene and Vincent, who worked for Lawrence, said they had never got past grade eight, when that was as far as you could go in the country schools. Eugene was twenty-five and Vincent was fifty-two. Eugene was French-Canadian from northern New Brunswick. He looked younger than his age. He had a rosy color, a downy, dreamy, look—a masculine beauty that was nevertheless soft-edged, sweet-tempered, bashful. Hardly any men or boys have that look nowadays. Sometimes you see it in an old photograph—of a bridegroom, a basketball player: the thick water-combed hair, the blooming boy's face on the new man's body. Eugene was not very bright, or perhaps not very competitive. He lost money at the game they were playing. It was a card game that the men called Skat. Lydia remembered playing it when she was a child, and calling it Thirty-one. They played for a quarter a game.

Eugene permitted Vincent and Lawrence to tease him about losing at cards, about getting lost in Saint John, about women he liked, and about being French-Canadian. Lawrence's teasing amounted to bullying. Lawrence wore a carefully good-natured expression, but he looked as if something hard and heavy had settled inside him—a load of self-esteem that weighed him down instead of buoying him up. Vincent had no such extra weight, and though he too was relentless in his teasing—he teased Lawrence as well as Eugene—there was no sense of cruelty or danger. You could see that his natural tone was one of rumbling, easy mockery. He was sharp and sly but not insistent; he would always be able to say the most pessimistic things and not sound unhappy.

Vincent had a farm—it was his family's farm, where he had grown up, near St. Stephen. He said you couldn't make enough to keep you nowadays, just from farming. Last year he put in a potato crop. There was frost in June, snow in September. Too short a season by a long shot. You never knew, he said, when you might get it like that. And the market is all controlled now, it is all run by the big fellows, the big interests. Everybody does what he can, rather than trust to farming. Vincent's wife works too. She took a course and learned to do hair. His sons are not hardworking like their parents. All they want to do is roar around in cars. They get married and the first thing their wives want is a new stove. They want a stove that practically cooks the dinner by itself and puts it on the table.

It didn't use to be that way. The first time Vincent ever had boots of his own—new boots that hadn't been worn by anybody before him—was when he joined the army. He was so pleased he walked backwards in the dirt to see the prints they made, fresh and whole. Later on, after the war, he went to Saint John to look for work. He had been working at home on the farm for a while and he had worn out his army clothes— he had just one pair of decent pants left. In a beer parlor in Saint John a man said to him, "You want to pick up a good pair of pants cheap?" Vincent said yes, and the man said, "Follow me." So Vincent did. And where did they end up? At the undertaker's! For the fact was that the family of a dead man usually bring in a suit of clothes to dress him in, and he only needs to be dressed from the waist up, that's all that shows in the coffin. The undertaker sold the pants. That was true. The army gave Vincent his first pair of new boots and a corpse donated the best pair of pants he ever wore, up to that time.

Vincent had no teeth. This was immediately apparent, but it did not make him look unattractive; it simply deepened his look of secrecy and humor. His face was long and his chin tucked in, his glance unchallenging but unfooled. He was a lean man, with useful muscles, and graying black hair. You could see all the years of hard work on him, and some years of it ahead, and the body just equal to it, until he turned into a ropy-armed old man, shrunken, uncomplaining, hanging on to a few jokes.

While they played Skat the talk was boisterous and interrupted all the time by exclamations, joking threats to do with the game, laughter. Afterwards it became more serious and personal. They had been drinking a local beer called Moose, but when the game was over Lawrence went out to the truck and brought in some Ontario beer, thought to be better. They called it "the imported stuff." The couple who owned the guest-house had long ago gone to bed, but the workmen and Lydia sat on in the kitchen, just as if it belonged to one of them, drinking beer and eating dulse, which Vincent had brought down from his room. Dulse was a kind of seaweed, greenish-brown, salty and fishy-tasting.

Vincent said it was what he ate last thing at night and first thing in the morning—nothing could beat it. Now that they had found out it was so good for you, they sold it in the stores, done up in little wee packages at a criminal price.

The next day was Friday, and the men would be leaving the island for the mainland. They talked about trying to get the two-thirty boat instead of the one they usually caught, at five-thirty, because the forecast was for rough weather; the tail end of one of the tropical hurricanes was due to hit the Bay of Fundy before night.

"But the ferries won't run if it's too rough, will they?" said Lydia. "They won't run if it's dangerous?" She thought that she would not mind being cut off, she wouldn't mind not having to travel again in the morning.

"Well, there's a lot of fellows waiting to get off the island on a Friday night," Vincent said.

"Wanting to get home to their wives," said Lawrence sardonically. "There's always crews working over here, always men away from home." Then he began to talk in an unhurried but insistent way about sex. He talked about what he called the immorality on the island. He said that at one time the authorities had been going to put a quarantine around the whole island, on account of the V.D. Crews came over here to work and stayed at the motel, the Ocean Wave, and there'd be parties there all night every night, with drinking and young girls turning up offering themselves for sale. Girls fourteen and fifteen—oh, thirteen years of age. On the island, he said, it was getting so a woman of twenty-five could practically be a grandmother. The place was famous. Those girls would do anything for a price, sometimes for a beer.

"And sometimes for nothing," said Lawrence. He luxuriated in the telling.

They heard the front door open.

"Your old boyfriend," Lawrence said to Lydia.

She was bewildered for a moment, thinking of Duncan.

"The old fellow at the table," said Vincent.

Mr. Stanley did not come into the kitchen. He crossed the living room and climbed the stairs.

"Hey? Been down to the Ocean Wave?" said Lawrence softly, raising his head as if to call through the ceiling. "Old bugger wouldn't know what to do with it," he said. "Wouldn't've known fifty years ago any better than now. I don't let any of my crews go near that place. Do I, Eugene?"

Eugene blushed. He put on a solemn expression, as if he was being badgered by a teacher at school.

"Eugene, now, he don't have to," Vincent said.

"Isn't it true what I'm saying?" said Lawrence urgently, as if somebody had been disputing with him. "It's true, isn't it?"

He looked at Vincent, and Vincent said, "Yeah. Yeah." He did not seem to relish the subject as much as Lawrence did.

"You'd think it was all so innocent here," said Lawrence to Lydia. "Innocent! Oh, boy!"

Lydia went upstairs to get a quarter that she owed Lawrence from the last game. When she came out of her room into the dark hall, Eugene was standing there, looking out the window.

"I hope it don't storm too bad," he said.

Lydia stood beside him, looking out. The moon was visible, but misty.

"You didn't grow up near the water?" she said.

"No, I didn't."

"But if you get the two-thirty boat it'll be all right, won't it?"

"I sure hope so." He was quite childlike and unembarrassed about his fear. "One thing I don't like the idea of is getting drownded."

Lydia remembered that as a child she had said "drownded." Most of the adults and all the children she knew then said that.

"You won't," she said, in a firm, maternal way. She went downstairs and paid her quarter.

"Where's Eugene?" Lawrence said. "He upstairs?"

"He's looking out the window. He's worried about the storm."

Lawrence laughed. "You tell him to go to bed and forget about it. He's right in the room next to you. I just thought you ought to know in case he hollers in his sleep."

Lydia had first seen Duncan in a bookstore, where her friend Warren worked. She was waiting for Warren to go out to lunch with her. He had gone to get his coat. A man asked Shirley, the other clerk in the store, if she could find him a copy of *The Persian Letters*. That was Duncan. Shirley walked ahead of him to where the book was kept, and in the quiet store Lydia heard him saying that it must be difficult to know where to shelve *The Persian Letters*. Should it be classed as fiction or as a political essay? Lydia felt that he revealed something, saying this. He revealed a need that she supposed was common to customers in the bookstore, a need to distinguish himself, appear knowledgeable. Later on she would look back on this moment and try to imagine him again so powerless, slightly ingratiating, showing a bit of neediness. Warren came back with his coat on, greeted Duncan, and as he and Lydia went outside Warren said under his breath, "The Tin Woodman." Warren and Shirley livened up their days with nicknames for customers: Lydia had already heard of Marble-Mouth, and Chickpea and the Colonial Duchess. Duncan was the Tin Woodman. Lydia thought they must call him that because of the smooth gray overcoat he wore, and his hair, a bright gray which had obviously once been blond. He was not thin or angular and he did not look as if he would be creaky in the joints. He was supple and well-fleshed and dignified and pleasant; fair-skinned, freshly groomed, glistening.

She never told him about that name. She never told him that she had seen him in the bookstore. A week or so later she met him at a publisher's party. He did not remember ever seeing her before, and she supposed he had not seen her, being occupied with chatting to Shirley.

Lydia trusts what she can make of things, usually. She trusts what she thinks about her friend Warren, or his friend Shirley, and about chance acquaintances, like the couple who run the guest-house, and Mr. Stanley, and the men she has been playing cards with. She thinks she knows why people behave as they do, and she puts more stock than she will admit in her own unproved theories and unjustified suspicions. But she is stupid and helpless when contemplating the collision of herself and Duncan. She has plenty to say about it, given the chance, because explanation is her habit, but she doesn't trust what she says, even to herself; it doesn't help her. She might just as well cover her head and sit wailing on the ground.

She asks herself what gave him his power? She knows who did. But she asks what, and when—when did the transfer take place, when was the abdication of all pride and sense?

She read for half an hour after getting into bed. Then she went down the hall to the bathroom. It was after midnight. The rest of the house was in darkness. She had left the door ajar, and coming back to her room, she did not turn on the hall light.

The door of Eugene's room was also ajar, and as she was passing she heard a low, careful sound. It was like a moan, and
also like a whisper. She remembered Lawrence saying Eugene
hollered in his sleep, but this sound was not being made in
sleep. She knew he was awake. He was watching from the bed
in his dark room and he was inviting her. The invitation was
amorous and direct and helpless-sounding as his confession of
fear when he stood by the window. She went on into her own
room and shut the door and hooked it. Even as she did this,
she knew she didn't have to. He would never try to get in;
there was no bullying spirit in him.

Then she lay awake. Things had changed for her; she
refused adventures. She could have gone to Eugene, and earlier in the evening she could have given a sign to Lawrence. In
the past she might have done it. She might, or she might not
have done it, depending on how she felt. Now it seemed not
possible. She felt as if she were muffled up, wrapped in layers
and layers of dull knowledge, well protected. It wasn't altogether a bad thing—it left your mind unclouded. Speculation
can be more gentle, can take its time, when it is not driven by
desire.

She thought about what those men would have been like, as
lovers. It was Lawrence who would have been her reasonable
choice. He was nearest to her own age, and predictable, and
probably well used to the discreet encounter. His approach
was vulgar, but that would not necessarily have put her off. He
would be cheerful, hearty, prudent, perhaps a bit self-congrat-
ulatory, attentive in a businesslike way, and he would manage
in the middle of his attentions to slip in a warning: a joke, a
friendly insult, a reminder of how things stood.

Eugene would never feel the need to do that, though he
would have a shorter memory even than Lawrence (much
shorter, for Lawrence, though not turning down opportunities,
would carry afterward the thought of some bad consequence,
for which he must keep ready a sharp line of defense). Eugene
would be no less experienced than Lawrence; for years, girls
and women must have been answering the kind of plea Lydia
had heard, the artless confession. Eugene would be generous,

she thought. He would be a grateful, self-forgetful lover, show-ing his women such kindness that when he left they would never make trouble. They would not try to trap him; they wouldn't whine after him. Women do that to the men who have held back, who have contradicted themselves, promised, lied, mocked. These are the men women get pregnant by, send desperate letters to, preach their own superior love to, take their revenge on. Eugene would go free, he would be an inno-cent, happy prodigy of love, until he decided it was time to get married. Then he would marry a rather plain, maternal sort of girl, perhaps a bit older than himself, a bit shrewder. He would be faithful, and good to her, and she would manage things; they would raise a large, Catholic family.

What about Vincent? Lydia could not imagine him as she easily imagined the others: their noises and movements and bare shoulders and pleasing warm skin; their power, their exertions, their moments of helplessness. She was shy of thinking any such things about him. Yet he was the only one whom she could think of now with real interest. She thought of his courtesy and reticence and humor, his inability to better his luck. She liked him for the very things that made him dif-ferent from Lawrence and ensured that all his life he would be working for Lawrence—or for somebody like Lawrence—never the other way around. She liked him also for the things that made him different from Eugene: the irony, the patience, the self-containment. He was the sort of man she had known when she was a child living on a farm not so different from his, the sort of man who must have been in her family for hundreds of years. She knew his life. With him she could fore-see doors opening, to what she knew and had forgotten; rooms and landscapes opening; *there*. The rainy evenings, a country with creeks and graveyards, and chokecherry and finches in the fence-corners. She had to wonder if this was what happened, after the years of appetite and greed—did you drift back into tender-hearted fantasies? Or was it just the truth about what she needed and wanted; should she have fallen in love with, and married, a man like Vincent, years ago; should she have concentrated on the part of her that would have been content with such an arrangement, and forgotten about the rest?

That is, should she have stayed in the place where love is managed for you, not gone where you have to invent it, and reinvent it, and never know if these efforts will be enough?

Duncan spoke about his former girlfriends. Efficient Ruth, pert Judy, vivacious Diane, elegant Dolores, wifely Maxine, Lorraine the golden-haired, full-breasted beauty; Marian the multilingual; Caroline the neurotic; Rosalie who was wild and gypsy-like; gifted, melancholy Louise; serene socialite Jane. What description would now do for Lydia? Lydia the poet. Morose, messy, unsatisfactory Lydia. The unsatisfactory poet.

One Sunday, when they were driving in the hills around Peterborough, he talked about the effects of Lorraine's beauty. Perhaps the voluptuous countryside reminded him. It was almost like a joke, he said. It was almost silly. He stopped for gas in a little town and Lydia went across the street to a discount store that was open Sundays. She bought makeup in tubes off a rack. In the cold and dirty toilet of the gas station she attempted a transformation, slapping buff-colored liquid over her face and rubbing green paste on her eyelids.

"What have you done to your face?" he said when she came back to the car.

"Makeup. I put some makeup on so I'd look more cheerful."

"You can see where the line stops, on your neck."

At such times she felt strangled. It was frustration, she said to the doctor later. The gap between what she wanted and what she could get. She believed that Duncan's love—love for her—was somewhere inside him, and that by gigantic efforts to please, or fits of distress which obliterated all those efforts, or tricks of indifference, she could claw or lure it out.

What gave her such an idea? He did. At least he indicated that he could love her, that they could be happy, if she could honor his privacy, make no demands upon him, and try to alter those things about her person and behavior which he did not like. He listed these things precisely. Some were very intimate in nature and she howled with shame and covered her ears and begged him to take them back or to say no more.

"There is no way to have a discussion with you," he said. He said he hated hysterics, emotional displays, beyond anything, yet she thought she saw a quiver of satisfaction, a deep thrill of relief, that ran through him when she finally broke under the weight of his calm and detailed objections.

"Could that be?" she said to the doctor. "Could it be that he wants a woman close but is so frightened of it he has to try to wreck her? Is that oversimplified?" she said anxiously.

"What about you?" said the doctor. "What do you want?"

"For him to love me?"

"Not for you to love him?"

She thought about Duncan's apartment. There were no curtains; he was higher than the surrounding buildings. No attempt had been made to arrange things to make a setting; nothing was in relation to anything else. Various special requirements had been attended to. A certain sculpture was in a corner behind some filing cabinets because he liked to lie on the floor and look at it in shadow. Books were in piles beside the bed, which was crossways in the room in order to catch the breeze from the window. All disorder was actually order, carefully thought out and not to be interfered with. There was a beautiful little rug at the end of the hall, where he sat and listened to music. There was one great, ugly armchair, a masterpiece of engineering, with all its attachments for the head and limbs. Lydia asked about his guests—how were they accommodated? He replied that he did not have any. The apartment was for himself. He was a popular guest, witty and personable, but not a host, and this seemed reasonable to him, since social life was other people's requirement and invention.

Lydia brought flowers and there was nowhere to put them except in a jar on the floor by the bed. She brought presents from her trips to Toronto: records, books, cheese. She learned pathways around the apartment and found places where she could sit. She discouraged old friends, or any friends, from phoning or coming to see her, because there was too much she couldn't explain. They saw Duncan's friends sometimes, and she was nervous with them, thinking they were adding her to a list, speculating. She didn't like to see how much he gave them of that store of presents—anecdotes, parodies, flattering wit—which were also used to delight her. He could not bear dullness. She felt that he despised people who were not witty. You needed to be quick to keep up with him, in conversation, you needed energy. Lydia saw herself as a dancer on her toes, trembling delicately all over, afraid of letting him down on the next turn.

"Do you mean you think I don't love him?" she said to the doctor.

"How do you know you do?"

"Because I suffer so when he's fed up with me. I want to be wiped off the earth. It's true. I want to hide. I go out on the streets and every face I look at seems to despise me for my failure."

"Your failure to make him love you."

Now Lydia must accuse herself. Her self-absorption equals Duncan's, but is more artfully concealed. She is in competition with him, as to who can love best. She is in competition with all other women, even when it is ludicrous for her to be so. She cannot stand to hear them praised or know they are well remembered. Like many women of her generation she has an idea of love which is ruinous but not serious in some way, not respectful. She is greedy. She talks intelligently and ironically and in this way covers up her indefensible expectations. The sacrifices she made with Duncan—in living arrangements, in the matter of friends, as well as in the rhythm of sex and the tone of conversations—were violations, committed not seriously but flagrantly. That is what was not respectful, that was what was indecent. She made him a present of such power, then complained relentlessly to herself and finally to him, that he had got it. She was out to defeat him.

That is what she says to the doctor. But is it the truth?

"The worst thing is not knowing what is true about any of this. I spend all my waking hours trying to figure out about him and me and I get nowhere. I make wishes. I even pray. I throw money into those wishing wells. I think that there's something in him that's an absolute holdout. There's something in him that has to get rid of me, so he'll find reasons. But he says that's rubbish, he says if I could stop over-reacting we'd be happy. I have to think maybe he's right, maybe it is all me."

"When are you happy?"

"When he's pleased with me. When he's joking and enjoying himself. No. No. I'm never happy. What I am is relieved, it's as if I'd overcome a challenge, it's more triumphant than happy. But he can always pull the rug out."

"So, why are you with somebody who can always pull the rug out?"

"Isn't there always somebody? When I was married it was me. Do you think it helps to ask these questions? Suppose it's just pride? I don't want to be alone. I want everybody to think I've got such a desirable man? Suppose it's the humiliation, I want to be humiliated? What good will it do me to know that?"

"I don't know. What do you think?"

"I think these conversations are fine when you're mildly troubled and interested but not when you're desperate."

"You're desperate?"

She felt suddenly tired, almost too tired to speak. The room where she and the doctor were talking had a dark-blue carpet, blue-and-green-striped upholstery. There was a picture of boats and fishermen on the wall. Collusion somewhere, Lydia felt. Fake reassurance, provisional comfort, earnest deceptions.

"No."

It seemed to her that she and Duncan were monsters with a lot of heads, in those days. Out of the mouth of one head could come insult and accusation, hot and cold, out of another false apologies and slimy pleas, out of another just mealy, reasonable, true-and-false chat as she had practised with the doctor. Not a mouth would open that had a useful thing to say, not a mouth would have the sense to shut up. At the same time she believed—though she didn't know she believed it— that these monster heads with their cruel and silly and wasteful talk could all be drawn in again, could curl up and go to sleep. Never mind what they'd said; never mind. Then she and Duncan with hope and trust and blank memories could reintroduce themselves, they could pick up the undamaged delight with which they'd started, before they began to put each other to other uses.

When she had been in Toronto a day she tried to retrieve Duncan, by phone, and found that he had acted quickly. He had changed to an unlisted number. He wrote to her in care of her employer, that he would pack and send her things.

Lydia had breakfast with Mr. Stanley. The telephone crew had eaten and gone off to work before daylight.

She asked Mr. Stanley about his visit with the woman who had known Willa Cather.

"Ah," said Mr. Stanley, and wiped a corner of his mouth after a bite of poached egg. "She was a woman who used to run a little restaurant down by the dock. She was a good cook, she said. She must have been, because Willa and Edith used to get their dinners from her. She would send it up with her brother, in his car. But sometimes Willa would not be pleased with the dinner—perhaps it would not be quite what she wanted, or she would think it was not cooked as well as it might be—and she would send it back. She would ask for another dinner to be sent." He smiled, and said in a confidential way, "Willa could be imperious. Oh, yes. She was not perfect. All people of great abilities are apt to be a bit impatient in daily matters."

Rubbish, Lydia wanted to say, she sounds a proper bitch.

Sometimes waking up was all right, and sometimes it was very bad. This morning she had wakened with the cold conviction of a mistake—something avoidable and irreparable.

"But sometimes she and Edith would come down to the café," Mr. Stanley continued. "If they felt they wanted some company, they would have dinner there. On one of these occasions Willa had a long talk with the woman I was visiting. They talked for over an hour. The woman was considering marriage. She had to consider whether to make a marriage that she gave me to understand was something of a business proposition. Companionship. There was no question of romance, she and the gentleman were not young and foolish. Willa talked to her for over an hour. Of course she did not advise her directly to do one thing or the other, she talked to her in general terms very sensibly and kindly and the woman still remembers it vividly. I was happy to hear that but I was not surprised."

"What would she know about it, anyway?" Lydia said.

Mr. Stanley lifted his eyes from his plate and looked at her in grieved amazement.

"Willa Cather lived with a woman," Lydia said.

When Mr. Stanley answered he sounded flustered, and mildly upbraiding.

"They were devoted," he said.

"She never lived with a man."

"She knew things as an artist knows them. Not necessarily by experience."

"But what if they don't know them?" Lydia persisted. "What if they don't?"

He went back to eating his egg as if he had not heard that. Finally he said, "The woman considered Willa's conversation was very helpful to her."

Lydia made a sound of doubtful assent. She knew she had been rude, even cruel. She knew she would have to apologize. She went to the sideboard and poured herself another cup of coffee.

The woman of the house came in from the kitchen.

"Is it keeping hot? I think I'll have a cup, too. Are you really going today? Sometimes I think I'd like to get on a boat and go too. It's lovely here and I love it but you know how you get."

They drank their coffee standing by the sideboard. Lydia did not want to go back to the table, but knew that she would have to. Mr. Stanley looked frail and solitary, with his narrow shoulders, his neat bald head, his brown checked sports jacket which was slightly too large. He took the trouble to be clean and tidy, and it must have been a trouble, with his eyesight. Of all people he did not deserve rudeness.

"Oh, I forgot," the woman said.

She went into the kitchen and came back with a large brown-paper bag.

"Vincent left you this. He said you liked it. Do you?"

Lydia opened the bag and saw long, dark, ragged leaves of dulse, oily-looking even when dry.

"Well," she said.

The woman laughed. "I know. You have to be born here to have the taste."

"No, I do like it," said Lydia. "I was getting to like it."

"You must have made a hit."

Lydia took the bag back to the table and showed it to Mr. Stanley. She tried a conciliatory joke.

"I wonder if Willa Cather ever ate dulse?"

"Dulse," said Mr. Stanley thoughtfully. He reached into the bag and pulled out some leaves and looked at them. Lydia knew he was seeing what Willa Cather might have seen. "She would most certainly have known about it. She would have known."

But was she lucky or was she not, and was it all right with that woman? How did she live? That was what Lydia wanted to say. Would Mr. Stanley have known what she was talking about? If she had asked how did Willa Cather live, would he not have replied that she did not have to find a way to live, as other people did, that she was Willa Cather?

What a lovely, durable shelter he had made for himself. He could carry it everywhere and nobody could interfere with it. The day may come when Lydia will count herself lucky to do the same. In the meantime, she'll be up and down. "Up and down," they used to say in her childhood, talking of the health of people who weren't going to recover. "Ah. She's up and down."

Yet look how this present slyly warmed her, from a distance.

The
Selfish Giant

by
OSCAR WILDE
(1854–1900)

Oscar Wilde is always charming, but especially so in this little parable of a selfish Giant's sin and redemption. It is a story of the changing seasons—of a long-suffered Winter that gives way in the end to the coming of Spring, and to the fruits of the Summer and Autumn that follow.

very afternoon, as they were coming from school, the children used to go and play in the Giant's garden.

It was a large lovely garden, with soft green grass. Here and there over the grass stood beautiful flowers like stars, and there were twelve peach-trees that in the spring-time broke out into delicate blossoms of pink and pearl, and in the autumn bore rich fruit. The birds sat on the trees and sang so sweetly that the children used to stop their games in order to listen to them. 'How happy we are here!' they cried to each other.

One day the Giant came back. He had been to visit his friend the Cornish ogre, and had stayed with him for seven years. After the seven years were over he had said all that he had to say, for his conversation was limited, and he determined to return to his own castle. When he arrived he saw the children playing in his garden.

'What are you doing there?' he cried in a very gruff voice, and the children ran away.

'My own garden is my own garden,' said the Giant; 'any one can understand that, and I will allow nobody to play in it but myself.' So he built a high wall all round it, and put up a notice-board.

**TRESPASSERS
WILL BE
PROSECUTED**

He was a very selfish Giant.

The poor children had now nowhere to play. They tried to play on the road, but the road was very dusty and full of hard stones, and they did not like it. They used to wander round the high wall when their lessons were over, and talk about the beautiful garden inside. 'How happy we were there,' they said to each other.

Then the Spring came, and all over the country there were little blossoms and little birds. Only in the garden of the Selfish Giant it was still winter. The birds did not care to sing in it as there were no children, and the trees forgot to blossom. Once a beautiful flower put its head out from the grass, but when it saw the notice-board it was so sorry for the children that it slipped back into the ground again, and went off to sleep. The only people who were pleased were the Snow and the Frost. 'Spring has forgotten this garden,' they cried, 'so we will live here all the year round.' The Snow covered up the grass with her great white cloak, and the Frost painted all the trees silver. Then they invited the North Wind to stay with them, and he came. He was wrapped in furs, and he roared all day about the garden, and blew the chimney-pots down. 'This is a delightful spot,' he said, 'we must ask the Hail on a visit.' So the Hail came. Every day for three hours he rattled on the roof of the castle till he broke most of the slates, and then he ran round and round the garden as fast as he could go. He was dressed in grey, and his breath was like ice.

'I cannot understand why the Spring is so late in coming,' said the Selfish Giant, as he sat at the window and looked out at his cold white garden; 'I hope there will be a change in the weather.'

But the Spring never came, nor the Summer. The Autumn

gave golden fruit to every garden, but to the Giant's garden she gave none. 'He is too selfish,' she said. So it was always Winter there, and the North Wind and the Hail, and the Frost, and the Snow danced about through the trees.

One morning the Giant was lying awake in bed when he heard some lovely music. It sounded so sweet to his ears that he thought it must be the King's musicians passing by. It was really only a little linnet singing outside his window, but it was so long since he had heard a bird sing in his garden that it seemed to him to be the most beautiful music in the world. Then the Hail stopped dancing over his head, and the North Wind ceased roaring, and a delicious perfume came to him through the open casement. 'I believe the Spring has come at last,' said the Giant; and he jumped out of bed and looked out.

What did he see?

He saw a most wonderful sight. Through a little hole in the wall the children had crept in, and they were sitting in the branches of the trees. In every tree that he could see there was a little child. And the trees were so glad to have the children back again that they had covered themselves with blossoms, and were waving their arms gently above the children's heads. The birds were flying about and twittering with delight, and the flowers were looking up through the green grass and laughing. It was a lovely scene, only in one corner it was still winter. It was the farthest corner of the garden, and in it was standing a little boy. He was so small that he could not reach up to the branches of the tree, and he was wandering all round it, crying bitterly. The poor tree was still quite covered with frost and snow, and the North Wind was blowing and roaring above it. 'Climb up! little boy,' said the Tree, and it bent its branches down as low as it could; but the boy was too tiny.

And the Giant's heart melted as he looked out. 'How selfish I have been!' he said; 'now I know why the Spring would not come here. I will put that poor little boy on the top of the tree, and then I will knock down the wall, and my garden shall be the children's playground for ever and ever!' He was really very sorry for what he had done.

So he crept downstairs and opened the front door quite softly, and went out into the garden. But when the children saw him they were so frightened that they all ran away, and the garden became winter again. Only the little boy did not run, for his eyes were so full of tears that he did not see the Giant coming. And the Giant stole up behind him and took him gently in his hand, and put him up into the tree. And the tree broke at once into blossom, and the birds came and sang on it, and the little boy stretched out his two arms and flung them round the Giant's neck, and kissed him. And the other children, when they saw that the Giant was not wicked any longer, came running back, and with them came the Spring. 'It is your garden now, little children,' said the Giant, and he took a great axe and knocked down the wall. And when the people were going to market at twelve o'clock they found the Giant playing with the children in the most beautiful garden they had ever seen.

All day long they played, and in the evening they came to the Giant to bid him good-bye.

'But where is your little companion?' he said: 'the boy I put into the tree.' The Giant loved him the best because he had kissed him.

'We don't know,' answered the children; 'he has gone away.'

'You must tell him to be sure and come here to-morrow,' said the Giant. But the children said that they did not know where he lived, and had never seen him before; and the Giant felt very sad.

Every afternoon, when school was over, the children came and played with the Giant. But the little boy whom the Giant loved was never seen again. The Giant was very kind to all the children, yet he longed for his first little friend, and often spoke of him. 'How I would like to see him!' he used to say.

Years went over, and the Giant grew very old and feeble. He could not play about any more, so he sat in a huge armchair, and watched the children at their games, and admired his garden. 'I have many beautiful flowers,' he said; 'but the children are the most beautiful flowers of all.'

One winter morning he looked out of his window as he was

dressing. He did not hate the Winter now, for he knew that it was merely the Spring asleep, and that the flowers were resting.

Suddenly he rubbed his eyes in wonder, and looked and looked. It certainly was a marvellous sight. In the farthest corner of the garden was a tree quite covered with lovely white blossoms. Its branches were all golden, and silver fruit hung down from them, and underneath it stood the little boy he had loved.

Downstairs ran the Giant in great joy, and out into the garden. He hastened across the grass, and came near to the child. And when he came quite close his face grew red with anger, and he said, 'Who hath dared to wound thee?' For on the palms of the child's hands were the prints of two nails, and the prints of two nails were on the little feet.

'Who hath dared to wound thee?' cried the Giant; 'tell me, that I may take my big sword and slay him.'

'Nay!' answered the child; 'but these are the wounds of Love.'

'Who art thou?' said the Giant, and a strange awe fell on him, and he knelt before the little child.

And the child smiled on the Giant, and said to him, 'You let me play once in your garden, to-day you shall come with me to my garden, which is Paradise.'

And when the children ran in that afternoon, they found the Giant lying dead under the tree, all covered with white blossoms.

Viper's Bugloss

by
JANICE KULYK KEEFER
(1953–)

The return to the summer cottage somehow marks a return to a former self. The lake is the same, the woods the same, and yet the lives of the returning cottagers have inevitably changed and moved on. "Viper's Bugloss" is a story of personal progression and loss—of denial and recognition seen through the richly textured landscape of a long-lost summer's memory.

The first thing he remembered was the jack pine in stiff shock against the fence: it was still there, still there, a pledge that everything else would be waiting for him, just as it once had been. "Look, Sally— Jerome, do you see? That goddamned beautiful bald tree—it hasn't changed at all!" They didn't see, and besides, Sally didn't feel like putting herself out for one jack pine among the hundred she'd already seen on the drive up: she was conjecturing the size of the cabin, judging that Nick had exaggerated its spaciousness just to lure her up into the bush for a week. It had been hard enough to take time off from the offices—his and hers—and Jerome would be missing the first week of the summer school they'd decided to invest in for him—the kid needed some stimulation: as Nick kept on complaining, he had no imagination. A week up here, without Pac-Man or video cassettes, just the wash of the Lake and the stretch of the sand. She had had her doubts. Turning around to look at him she found the child obstinate as ever, stretched out on the back seat and staring up at the upholstery of the car roof, not even caring to pretend to be asleep.

Five minutes later they were out of the car, their arms full of suitcases, beach towels, books and groceries and inflatable rafts. It was only a dash from the car to the porch, but Nick's keys wouldn't open the front door and by the time they'd discovered the back one, the mosquitoes had had their feast. Then, going up the concrete steps, Jerome managed to drop the one bottle of Off!; as Nick bent down to clear up the glass he identified the weeds sprouting all along the path they'd just negotiated as poison ivy.

"Hot water and soap, hot water and soap and we'll be just fine," he kept singing into Sally's ears: she was ready to wash out his mouth with the stuff, except that of all the things to have left behind, they'd forgotten the soap. Still, some ten minutes later Nick had a kettle steaming and was lathering their shins with some detergent he'd discovered below the sink. Then they dumped their gear in the bedrooms, turned on whatever lights were working and, shivering into bathing-suits, picked their way down the steep slope of sand to the lake.

He knew better than to exult: he let that water and this sky sing out for him. Jerome had run headlong into the lake and was swimming strongly out: not bad for a ten year old, thought Nick, trying to remember what distance he'd been able to make at that age. With his brother and sister he'd raced between the Fairlie cottage and Elephant Rock, a good half mile; using a steady crawl stroke, too, none of this changing-over every couple of yards. He watched the wake his son had left behind: just a slight snag on the water. You couldn't believe the stillness and completeness: even the air seemed to have its arms full of everything there was in the world to be caught and held onto. A moment or an hour later there was the sound of water being poured from the glass pitcher: Sally, entering the lake at last. Her bathing-suit was black: it made him think of a mourner's armband on a white shirt-sleeve. Too thin and too pale; she worked too hard although there was no need, now that his business was taking off at last. But that was the way she wanted it—and he had hardly known her any heavier: even when eight months pregnant with Jerome, she'd been addressed as "Miss" in stores—or so she had boasted. And Jerome, now, swimming free of them both: you would never believe that they had made him out of one careless embrace. Feeling comfortably sentimental, Nick settled down on a driftwood log and let his memory out with his stomach: twenty, twenty-two years since he'd last seen this place. When his mother had died the three children had decided to sell the cabin, the half-acreage of forest and the strip of beach that had made up the property. His older brother had handled the sale—badly, as it turned out, for the buyer had got rid of the place at three times the price they'd asked, just five years later.

The Fairlie place was still standing, though who could tell if it had remained in the family: perhaps tomorrow he'd walk over there. If any of them were still there—what was the daughter's name, she'd been about his age—they would surely remember him. They could get together, have a drink; it would be pleasant to have someone to talk to. Annie—her name had been Annie. Still is, he corrected himself: daft to assume she'd dropped out of existence just because he'd forgotten her. Daft was one of her words—Annie's—the family had emigrated from some place in the north of Scotland, he remembered: there had been nine of them altogether. And his family had been five: why was it that people had so few children, nowadays, or none at all?

Sally was waving to him from the sandbar: her voice tumbled gently into the still air, giving a tenderness to tired words: "Come on in, it's as warm as soup!" Still bobbing among memories, he recalled the packages of instant soup-mix he'd carried in from the car. His mother had simmered beef bones for them—they would have the marrow scraped over toast for a snack before supper, and listen to "Calling All Britons" over the radio: his mother had been a war bride, and had left her whole family behind her to come to Canada. She and Mrs. Fairlie would drink tea together in the afternoons while the kids played together on the sandhills, or explored the shoreline around Gulbransen's General Provisions, chewing on ropes of red licorice that you could buy for a penny. Gulbransen's was gone—the old man had died the same year his own father had, the last year they'd all been up at the cabin together. Still, there could be no harm in walking along the shore to where the shop had been—with Jerome. The kid was much too far out; Sally should have followed him: he stood up and cupped his hands and called out the boy's name, but though he was sure he'd been heard, Jerome kept on swimming away. There was nothing for it but to get into the water and bring him back, though he felt a peevish reluctance to get wet: it was too comfortable just sitting on that log, remembering things, alone. After all, the others couldn't feel the way he did—it was just a cabin by a lake to them, and he couldn't blame anyone for that but himself. They'd been fools to sell the place and lose all this.

The water was only slightly cooler than Sally had promised: it was like being extinguished, sliding in, or like turning transparent as an empty glass—no name or business or relation anymore, just a substance to be buoyed up. Then he began to swim, exuberantly: he'd always been a strong swimmer, with never a moment's fear of the water. His father had taught them all to swim before they could properly walk; the first thing he'd always do, coming up to join them here on weekends, would be to strip off his workclothes, race down to the water and swim a mile or more, even in the roughest waves. The poor bastard had never had more than a week at a stretch up here; if he'd taken longer holidays they'd never have had the money to keep the place on. And then, the first winter of his retirement, shovelling the walk one night, he'd slipped on a handspan of ice and burst one small blood vessel in his brain. He'd died still unconscious, two days later, in hospital.

Nick reached Jerome and gave him a tow back to the sandbar, the way you'd rescue an exhausted swimmer. He felt the child's arms on his shoulders and the strangeness of this: when was the last time he'd ever touched him? Again, he thought of his father, and the way the children had all ridden on his shoulders in the water. He swam faster, until it became too shallow: as the both of them stood up he reached for Jerome's hand to walk with him over the stones into shore, but the boy didn't know to wait, just hobbled in on his own. Sally was there with enormous towels for them: they rubbed themselves as dry as they could and started up the hill. "Listen—" Nick made them stop halfway up. You could hear water lap at each stone; somewhere in the distance a motorboat droned and a sandpiper gave odd little cries, to which it seemed to expect no response. The sand slid every which way under their feet, they had to push down hard to keep from slipping, helping one another till they reached the fence behind which the coarse grass began. Nick was the last one inside: standing on the porch, the doorhandle in his fingers, he stopped a moment and looked out between the jack pine's seedy boughs to the lake. "It's good to be here: good to be back," he spoke out loud. But he couldn't hang onto the words, they sank into the calm of the evening like a rounded stone into the sandy bottom of a pool. The only noise on the air came from the door as it snapped on its hinges, shut.

It couldn't have worked out otherwise: he had the luck to wake first that morning and, as Sally was huddled up against the wall with all the covers, he could slip into the bathroom with his clothes without waking her. In the narrow corridor he paused outside Jerome's room: the cedar walls didn't quite reach up to the ceiling, you could hear the merest toss or turn from one room to the next. The child was breathing softly, regularly, no doubt exhausted from the long drive and the evening's swim. Once in the bathroom Nick stumbled over a tin bucket that had been placed just inside the door: he started to curse, but ended by laughing, sitting on the edge of the window sill to rub his toe. So that leak in the ceiling was still there, the one his father had never got round to repairing. He looked up critically; if there were tools around perhaps he would fix it—not for the present owner's ease, but as something owed to his own father.

It was the cabin's only view of the lake, this short oblong cut into the bathroom wall: whoever first modernized the place ought to have designed it the other way around, with the parlour where the toilet was. His mother would pull a face, shrug shoulders: why else had they got it so cheap? They'd bought it from the nephew of two ancient spinsters—the Misses Spencer, he remembered—who'd practically been born in the cabin, and who'd told of having once spent a winter up here. A spew of blackish drops in the basin: this time he did curse: he'd cut his chin with the razor, wasn't used to one but had been damned if he was going to bring an electric shaver to this place. He peered into the shard of mirror tacked over the sink: deep enough, he'd have to put a bandage on. Sally would see and laugh at him, having told him this would happen while they were packing to come. But he had nothing to staunch the blood, the cut stung, he felt betrayed as well as wounded—until he discovered, tucked into the pocket of his shaving kit, a wad of bandaids: Sally, having the last laugh after all. He dabbed the blood, pressed on the bandage and managing to avoid more bloodshed as he finished shaving, even began to whistle under his breath. Think of it, good Christ: two thin-blooded spinsters—in their sixties—spending a god-damned winter up here: no insulation (you could see light splintering between mortar and logs) and an outdoor privy smack in the poison ivy. What had they done with them-selves all winter long besides shake and shiver and cajole a fire from the hearth? People had been different then, made of bet-ter stuff—think of his own parents, no hell of a life for them: never enough money, three kids to dress and feed and send to school, no holidays away from the kids (he and Sally usually spent their summer vacation at a lodge with Jerome, the kind of place where the kids have a separate playground and din-ing-room and all the bedrooms are soundproofed). Whatever had his own folks done, his father coming up from the hot, dank city, spending his two nights a week with his woman in a bed whose springs would sing out for miles around if they so much as rubbed shoulders? He thought of Sally, shivering in the satin baby-doll pyjamas she'd insisted on bringing, wrenching the covers away from him in the night: he felt a shallow stab of guilt—it wasn't a real holiday up here, having to cook for themselves and leave the place in reasonable order; there'd be no dancing after dinner, no tennis courts, no sail-boats or sundecks. But, then, at least it was a change—better still it was something real, the three of them together here with only each other for company and help. Why, he'd take Jerome into the woods that very afternoon, show him the place where you could find raspberries growing—

Shaved, washed, dressed, he strode into the kitchen, put the kettle on and looked over the shelves while the water came to a boil. Sally had arranged their own provisions on an empty shelf, but the other ledges were full of unfamiliar plates and cups, most of them chipped and cracked, none of a pattern: the usual cottage ware. He recognized a certain sparse and deliberate order in these shelves, painted a dead-white; narrow, bearing ancient and unused jars of split peas or pearl barley. They seemed all necessary and good: they had reason to be there, unlike most of the things on the tables and in the cabinets of their apartment in the city: expensive, time-saving electrical appliances; computerized games and gadgets; crystal and glass from the January sales; everything braying its cost and their success in meeting it. The kettle sent up clouds to divert him; into a coronation mug he spooned instant coffee and milk, then came the silver spurt from the kettle. Simple acts, simple objects—he felt absurdly happy.

He sat down with his second cup of coffee on an uncomfortable, overpadded sofa in the parlour: it had always been the darkest room in the place, with its low, slitted windows screened by leaves and twigs. This furniture was all unfamiliar—they might have left the old stuff there, it had all been part of the sale. He felt an unreasonable grudge against the owner, a man he knew only from an ad in the paper: "Charming heritage log-cabin for rent by week or month; a holiday the whole family won't forget: moderate terms." On a hunch Nick had dialed the number, heard a closer description and hadn't been able to resist a return to the old place, despite Sally's level suspiciousness and Jerome's indifference. Of course he'd had his qualms as they drove up and found, for miles around, the ordered suburban lots run up by developers: blank, glossy names like "Georgian Sands," "Hemlock Court," "Lakeside Manor"—the joke of it, driving for hours along a super highway only to find the same sweet home at the journey's end. But their own road was the same, the forest still virgin, so that they would be wakened by birds and not someone else's television every morning. It must have been by some negligent Providence that things here were so unchanged; if the place hadn't prospered much, neither had it suffered. Perhaps it was the ghost of his family life that had protected it, the influence of people whose relations with each other were direct and simple, day to day: husband and wife, parents and children. He looked for confirmation to the little niche hollowed out in the great stone chimney over the fireplace. It couldn't be—he never would have bet on it, but there it was, still sheltering inside, the little china figure his mother had won at a raffle—a cross between Charlie Chan and the Buddha. His mother had believed it brought them good luck, and perhaps it had. For looking at all things equally, who could have had a happier childhood? His parents had given him not only food and clothes and toys but this as well: a steady structure under his feet and all around—to every act, a genuine response, whether enlightened or not it scarcely seemed to matter, now. That things had fallen apart after their deaths was no-one's fault. His sister had moved out west, married a lawyer: she sent him a Christmas card every other year, with snapshots of her kids. He and his brother lived in the same city but only met for stilted family meals at New Year's and Easter: their wives didn't get along at all and Jerome was much younger than his cousins. Damn it, he'd phone his brother soon as he got back; he'd tell him about the cabin, persuade him to help buy it back—it had been the mistake of their lives ever to have lost this place. Sally would surely agree once she'd been here for a bit. He could hear her now, stumbling along the corridor, pouring coffee in the kitchen, cursing because there was no artificial sugar. What did it matter—she was his wife, no stranger: she would make allowances, and understand.

It had been a halcyon morning—he liked to use that phrase, it said so exactly what he felt and dignified it in the process. They'd gone down to the beach, swum, lain in the sun: he'd even coaxed Jerome to help build a fortress in the sand. At lunch the soup had been lumpy and the cheese dry, but he at least hadn't cared. He'd announced to Sally at the very end that he and Jerome would be going berry-picking, thinking the child would enjoy the surprise, the sudden conspiracy, and not having dared to risk an outright refusal by asking Jerome beforehand. What could he say now—of course he would go, silent or not. Sally had given them plastic containers with a wry face, as if to ask what the sudden father-son business was all about, but he had just smiled at her, cursing her inwardly for a suspicious bitch. Lovely Sally, slim as any of these saplings and about as sturdy: she hadn't wanted to breast-feed Jerome and didn't want another child, and that was that. Up till now he hadn't had any ammunition against her constant gibes: "What, you really want another? You hardly know what the one we've already got looks like, and you still want to play at being a father?" Well, he was refuting that now as he led the child, all unwilling, through the thicket to where the path began.

What was the matter with the boy, was he afraid of poison ivy—of him? No doubt he'd rather be back in the city, reading a comic book in front of the television. "Come on, don't drag your feet, you're turning this into a funeral." Weeds and brambles had gorged on the path—they had to fight their way along, and Nick himself got forearms and hands scratched while his eyes furred with mosquitoes and his ears thickened with their whine. If there were any berries, they had been eaten up long before. An enormous, rotting stump was now blocking their way: one second too late he recognized the drone of wasps rising within—and Jerome allergic to their sting. "Run, run!" he shouted, nearly kicking the boy ahead of him: if he got badly stung they would have to drive back right away and see a doctor. Sally should have reminded him, what sort of a mother was she to let her kid go off like this into the bush? They ran and ran, tripping over sapped branches and clumped stones but managing somehow to get back onto the main road, panting and sweating and ridiculous, with the little cartons all cracked now by their flight. Jerome seemed to have been crying and Nick, feeling responsible, wheeled furiously around, searching for something to justify the scare, to put a brighter face on things so that they could face Sally with some slight show of success. At the turn-off to the cabin he stopped willfully and stabbed with his hands into the undergrowth. By sheer luck he found something there. "Look, Jerome, what's this, what do you see?" The boy stared up into his father's eyes: twisting his mouth half into a pout, half into an accusation, he said nothing. And then, grabbing Jerome's T-shirt: "What the hell do you see— look, goddamn you, haven't you got eyes?" The child looked sullenly down into the clump of grass; stringing his father's patience, he at last mumbled out the one word: "Weeds."

Nick loosened his grip, let his hands hang at his sides. "Weeds? What kind of smart-ass answer is that? Is that what they teach you in science class? Why, when I was you age I knew the names of a hundred wildflowers—maybe more, Jesus Christ, kid. Why, my father and brother and sister and I would go out every Sunday morning here and just walk along the side of this road looking for them—Queen Anne's lace, chickory, buttercups. Look, it's Christ-bitten buttercup, didn't you even know that?" He stooped, ripped up the plant and thrust it into his son's face—and then relaxed his hand so that the flower fell brightly into the dust. He brought his hand slowly, unsurely, to the boy's head; he stroked the hair softly until he could no longer ignore the scowl on Jerome's face, then dropped his hand and stood stupidly at the roadside, admitting his fault, his utter failure, in the steady misery of the child's face before him. He felt like weeping, like howling—"Why my father and broth- er and sister and I...." And then Jerome touched his arm, quickly, and pointed over to a spar of brilliant blue. "What's that one called?" he challenged. His father, glad of the chance to change his face, walked over to where his son was pointing; parted the stems of grass and tilted the strange plant toward him. On an ugly, haired stalk a cup of violet and magenta and impossibly bright blue blared out. Its scent was strong, unpleasant even, but the flower was so curiously shaped, so outrageously coloured that it drew his eyes away from every- thing else. "What is it?" Jerome repeated, uneasily. "I can't remember," Nick at last replied, and then, sitting back on his haunches, he whistled. "Bugger if it isn't viper's bugloss. Viper's bugloss—I haven't seen this since I was your age—younger." "No, don't pick it." Jerome wailed as he watched his father twist at the stem. "It might be poisonous—it looks poisonous, I don't like it!" "Nonsense," Nick overrode him, working the stem away from the earth at last, staining his hands with its acrid-smelling juice. "No, you're thinking of belladonna—that's the deadly one." He held the flower straight up into the sun, admiring the sheer bright violence of it. "Let's take this home to your mother," he finished: "we'll put it in a jam-jar on the parlour table—quick now, let's hurry."

But the child had been right—if not precisely poisonous, it was a bringer of no good omen. As they hurried down to the water for their evening swim, the air seemed thicker than it had the night before; you could feel raindrops clinging together. They stayed too long in the water and came out chilled, Sally in a foul temper, having grazed her ankle on a rock. And as the clean sand sifted under their feet, making them lunge and strain to get up the hill, they heard the weird undulant cries of loons on the water, suddenly terrifying as the glint of a knife in a late-night subway car back in the city.

In the middle of that night it began to rain—Nick and Sally woke together, and Sally rolled over, groaning—"I knew this would happen—you just wait and see, it'll rain all week and then where will our holiday be?" He didn't answer her immediately, but ten minutes later reached for her and caught only a glide of satin as she shook off his hands. She was too tired, she said: she couldn't sleep on this rusty, lumpy excuse for a bed, anyway. She just didn't want to, she insisted, as Nick began to pull her toward him: and besides, the soap wasn't the only thing they'd managed to forget. Her pills were on the dresser back in the apartment. He let it go at that, but wouldn't let her settle back into sleep: "Would it be such a catastrophe if you conceived a child?" he spoke out to the rain.

"What?" She sat up in the slanting bed, clutching the sheet to her, looking to Nick like a prudish corpse. "Are you crazy? Don't you realize that Jerome can hear every word we're saying?"

"So, what's so shameful about having a family—it'd do the kid good to have a brother—sister."

"You're mad, Nick, just sheer, stupid, God—I don't know what! With a ten-year gap? I don't believe it. As if you'd be willing to give up your work and mind a baby. Well, would you, would you? You're not fair, you never have been. If you dare—oh, let's go back to sleep, you must be having a nightmare, and talking in your dreams—go to bed, goodnight: let's not wake Jerome."

He listened to her fake an even breathing and then, annoyed at paying even this attention, turned away from her and pretended, himself, to sleep. An hour later he groped his way to the kitchen, poured himself a scotch—that they hadn't managed to forget—and then went into the parlour. The Buddha was still there, gleaming blankly in the dark. He rubbed his hands over his face and sat for a long while. When at last he uncovered his eyes the first thing he saw was the viper's bugloss in its jar on the dinner table. He walked over to it, plucked it up from the water and twirled the hairy stem between his fingers. The flowers had shut fast, tight, in the blackness. "No," he said, "you're not poisonous; it's just us, Sally and me: whatever's between us—or whatever's not." All the same he couldn't sleep till he'd taken the flower, jar and all, and thrown the whole thing into the bush outside the kitchen door. The rain was still falling, making a noise like steel pins showering a glass floor. He locked the door, shut off the light in the kitchen and went to sleep on the green, over-upholstered sofa in the parlour.

In the morning it was worse: endless rain. They had brought books to read—Nick had been grandiose and taken only Shakespeare and the Bible: Sally settled down with Agatha Christie. The light in the parlour was bad; with this rain the dramatic gloom that sank the room on the sunniest of days turned merely dreary, dirtying everything—the maps on the wall, the farmer's daughter calendar-photos, the old-English prints of "Nature's Bounty" that Nick's mother had hung on the walls—cottages profuse with clematis and wisteria, with sentimental lovers in eighteenth-century costume, sighing together at a wishing-well. After 40 minutes Nick slammed *The Tempest* shut and began to rummage among the old, old *Life* magazines and yellowed *Maclean's* inside the buffet. After an hour he developed a headache: Jerome was stomping around, bored to death, and Sally had decided to do her nails, so that the reek of varnish drove little steel-heads of pain into his skull. The next morning they were on the road. Whenever Sally switched on the radio, the report was the same: showers through the week, clearing slightly Saturday: the high 68, the low—

Well, he'd had it, royally. It was the same jack pine beside the fence, the same cabin, even the same water: he wouldn't argue that. It was there, a rock for him to stand on, to survey the general, confused ruin of his adult life. His parents' deaths; selling the cottage and loosing the last ties with the family; marrying Sally, pretty, clever Sally; having Jerome and losing Jerome between all their business trips and overtime and weekend assignments.... All for the good life, soft and shiny: summers at a lodge and winters in Mexico with Jerome thrown to the mercy of housekeepers and what some ironist in PR had called the "home" computer. Clear as the weather report; he'd made his choices. But why, how? He could have stayed at the cottage, always; married Annie Fairlie; raised five kids and taught them all the names of wildflowers—

Daft. Idiot. Kill himself with work, as his father had, and all for nothing? Have his wife turn miserable and blowsy, raising children, simmering soup bones? How real could his own childhood have been, what fictions were his memories, for him to have thrown over every trace of them when it had come his turn to leave, marry, raise a child? Family love— strong and durable as some cooking-pot or kettle; or the coupled loneliness of his own marriage—which was the real, the only possibility? The car swerved over a greasy bit of road—it would be easy to have an accident in this rain, thinking such confusing things. He turned up the radio and shut off everything except the road and the shifting gears of Muzak.

Late that night, back in the neutral, calm décor of his apartment, his marriage, his life, he couldn't sleep. The same rain that had doused his holiday was rattling down the apartment windows. He lit the bedside lamp, saw the case of Sally's pills that she had remembered to take, this time. He turned his head to where she lay, crouched up against his body's heat, her face curiously soft and full. She had been right, of course: you didn't start things you knew you couldn't carry out. He eased himself as cautiously as he could out of their bed and covered her, as charitably as he would a stranger, with the blankets. He thought he should go check Jerome, but was terrified of finding him awake, so went instead to what they called his study—a large closet, really, in which were crammed the virgin upright piano, a reproduction antique desk on which an unframed photograph of Sally and Jerome curled helplessly, and the few books he'd not sold or given away on leaving university. He put back the Shakespeare he'd taken so extravagantly to the cottage, and pulled out *The Native Wildflowers of Central Canada*—a book, the flyleaf told him, which he'd won as a graduation prize on leaving high school, centuries ago.

Dithering through the index, he found at last the entry that he wanted:

Viper's Bugloss (Echium vulgare) Borage or Forget-Me-Not Family (Boraginaceae). A tall, erect, very rough, bristly, leafy plant, simple or branched. The lance-shaped, bristly pointed leaves are up to 41/2" long, progressively smaller and sessile upward. Strikingly showy purplish blue flowers are bell-shaped. June to September.

This was it, exactly. He found comfort in the finality bred by such precise detail, the Latin terms, the absence of alternative or choice. These things were as they were, could be no different; to question would be to undo them, entirely. He put his finger to the text and read aloud: "Habitat: Dry fields, waste places." But this wasn't right—wasn't fair: it read like a judgement, or a warning. He shut his eyes, trying to remember the feel, the look of that flower he'd tugged up: rough-haired, grotesquely brilliant, utterly unexpected, like a signal fire, a siren in his eyes. A book fell off the shelf behind him and he jumped as if a gun had gone off in his ears.

Not a book; or rather, a book knocked over by the boy, Jerome, standing there in his pyjama bottoms, his white skin looking so delicate it seemed as if the glare from the electric light would bruise it. He stood before Nick's chair, expectant, frozen, like a small animal in the headlights of an oncoming car.

"Jerome," began Nick, afraid to touch and startle him.

"I can't sleep."

"No. Me too. Jerome—" Words of one syllable; his name— begin at the beginning, not like the last time. But what now, with the child standing here in front of him, staring, wanting, silent—

"Look; come over here. Close enough so you can see this picture. Remember that weed—that flower we found in the woods? Maybe you've forgotten—"

"Viper's bugloss." Jerome lifted his long, awkward arms and folded them across his chest, as if to hug his pleasure in having remembered the name. And Nick, carefully as if he were transplanting some fragile plant, dangling its roots in a shock of rough, cold air, reached up and patted his son's shoulder.

"Smart kid. That's the way. Why, when I was your.... Look, Jerome, I know what we'll do. Tomorrow we'll go down the ravine out back—forget the summer school, it's not important—to the ravine, and find as many kinds of different wildflowers as we can—we'll take this book. If it rains? We'll go to the museum—they've got rooms and rooms of plants there— everything. Okay?"

"Sure, I guess. If you want. Okay."

Nick gently withdrew his hand from Jerome's shoulder, closed the book and pulled himself out of his chair.

"Now let's turn out the lights and go to bed. Lunatic, being up this late—it's past two o'clock. You can tuck yourself in? Of course you can, of course. Goodnight, then—don't wake your mother—don't forget, tomorrow morning—"

As Nick slid back into bed and stretched out toward sleep he thought, one last time, of the cabin. It didn't belong to him, anymore—it never really had. It was here, in the city, this apartment, that he had to stake out something, to make a start— with Jerome; with Sally, reaching out for him in sleep now, as she could never do, once woken. Here, now—he had to begin. His eyes closed over images, precise, detailed, as if he were dying, seeing for the last time the still, blank lake, the Buddha over the fireplace, the bald jack pine against the cabin fence. All the lightning glare of that intractable, bruise-coloured flower.

The *Town* of the *Little People*

by
SHOLOM ALEICHEM
(1859–1926)

"The Town of the Little People" is a real Front Porch Al type of story, what with its simple innocence, a lightly comic touch, and its sense of warmth and enduring humanity. Sholom Aleichem could write story after story about "The Town of the Little People" and I would be happy just listening on.

The town of the little people into which I shall now take you, dear reader, is exactly in the middle of that blessed Pale into which Jews have been packed as closely as herring in a barrel and told to increase and multiply. The name of the town is Kasrilevka. How did this name originate? I'll tell you:

Among us Jews poverty has many faces and many aspects. A poor man is an unlucky man, he is a pauper, a beggar, a *schnorrer*, a starveling, a tramp, or a plain failure. A different tone is used in speaking of each one, but all these names express human wretchedness. However, there is still another name—*kasril*, or *kasrilik*. That name is spoken in a different tone altogether, almost a bragging tone. For instance, "Oh, am I ever a *kasrilik*!" A *kasrilik* is not just an ordinary pauper, a failure in life. On the contrary, he is a man who has not allowed poverty to degrade him. He laughs at it. He is poor, but cheerful.

Stuck away in a corner of the world, isolated from the surrounding country, the town stands, orphaned, dreaming, bewitched, immersed in itself and remote from the noise and bustle, the confusion and tumult and greed, which men have created about them and have dignified with high-sounding names like Culture, Progress, Civilization. A proper person may take off his hat with respect to these things, but not these little people! Not only do they know nothing of automobiles, modern travel, airplanes—for a long time they refused to believe in the existence of the old, ordinary railroad train. "Such a thing cannot be," they said. "Why," they said, "it's a dream, a fairy tale. You might just as well talk of merry-go-rounds in heaven!"

But it happened once that a householder of Kasrilevka had to go to Moscow. When he came back he swore with many oaths that it was true. He himself had ridden in a train to Moscow, and it had taken him—he shrugged his shoulders— less than an hour. This the little people interpreted to mean that he had ridden less than an hour and then walked the rest of the way. But still the fact of the train remained. If a Jew and a householder of Kasrilevka swore to it, they could not deny that there was such a thing as a train. It had to be true. He could not have invented it out of thin air. He even explained to them the whole miracle of the train, and drew a diagram on paper. He showed them how the wheels turned, the smoke-stack whistled, the carriages flew, and people rode to Moscow. The little people of Kasrilevka listened and listened, nodded their heads solemnly, and deep in their hearts they laughed at him. "What a story! The wheels turn, the smokestack whistles, the carriages fly and people ride to Moscow—and then come back again!"

That's how they all are, these little people. None of them are gloomy, none of them are worried little men of affairs, but on the contrary they are known everywhere as jesters, storytellers, a cheerful, light-hearted breed of men. Poor but cheerful. It is hard to say what makes them so happy. Nothing—just sheer joy of living. Living? If you ask them, "How do you live?" they will answer, with a shrug and a laugh. "How do we live? Who knows? We live!" A remarkable thing—whenever you meet them they are scurrying like rabbits, this one here, that one there. They never have time to stop. "What are you hurrying for?" "What am I hurrying for? Well, it's like this. If we hurry we think we might run into something—earn a few pennies—provide for the Sabbath."

To provide for the Sabbath—that is their goal in life. All week they labor and sweat, wear themselves out, live without food or drink, just so there is something for the Sabbath. And when the holy Sabbath arrives, let Yehupetz perish, let Odessa be razed, let Paris itself sink into the earth! Kasrilevka lives! And this is a fact, that since Kasrilevka was founded, no Jew has gone hungry there on the Sabbath. Is it possible that there is a Jew who does not have fish for the Sabbath? If he has no fish, then he has meat. If he has no meat, then he has herring. If he has no herring, then he has white bread. If he has no white bread, then he has black bread and onions. If he has no black bread and onions, then he borrows some from his neighbor. Next week, the neighbor will borrow from him. "The world is a wheel and it keeps turning." The Kasrilevkite repeats this maxim and shows you with his hand how it turns. To him a maxim, a witty remark, is everything. For an apt remark he will forsake his mother and father, as the saying goes. The tales you hear about these little people sound fabulous, but you may be sure they are all true.

For instance, there is the story of the Kasrilevkite who got tired of starving in Kasrilevka and went out into the wide world to seek his fortune. He left the country, wandered far and wide, and finally reached Paris. There, naturally, he wanted to see Rothschild. For how can a Jew come to Paris and not visit Rothschild? But they didn't let him in. "What's the trouble?" he wants to know. "Your coat is torn," they tell him.

"You fool," says the Jew. "If I had a good coat, would I have gone to Paris?"

It looked hopeless. But a Kasrilevkite never gives up. He thought a while and said to the doorman: "Tell your master that it isn't an ordinary beggar who has come to his door, but a Jewish merchant, who has brought him a piece of goods such as you can't find in Paris for any amount of money."

Hearing this, Rothschild became curious and asked that the merchant be brought to him.

"*Sholom aleichem*," said Rothschild.

"*Aleichem sholom,*" said the merchant.

"Take a seat. And where do you come from?"

"I come from Kasrilevka."

"What good news do you bring?"

"Well, Mr. Rothschild, they say in our town that you are not so badly off. If I had only half of what you own, or only a third, you would still have enough left. And honors, I imagine, you don't lack either, for people always look up to a man of riches. Then what do you lack? One thing only—eternal life. That is what I have to sell you."

When Rothschild heard this he said, "Well, let's get down to business. What will it cost me?"

"It will cost you—" here the man stopped to consider—"it will cost you—three hundred rubles."

"Is that your best price?"

"My very best. I could have said a lot more than three hundred. But I said it, so it's final."

Rothschild said no more, but counted out three hundred rubles, one by one.

Our Kasrilevkite slipped the money into his pocket, and said to Rothschild: "If you want to live for ever, my advice to you is to leave this noisy, busy Paris, and move to our town of Kasrilevka. There you can never die, because since Kasrilevka has been a town, no rich man has ever died there."

And then there is the story of the man who got as far as America... But if I started to tell all the tales of these little people I'd have to sit with you for three days and three nights and talk and talk and talk. Instead, let us pass on to a description of the little town itself.

Shall I call it a beautiful little town? From a distance it looks—how shall I say it?—like a loaf of bread thickly studded with poppy seed. Some of the houses are built on the slope of a hill, the rest are huddled together at the base, one on top of the other, like the gravestones in an ancient cemetery. There are no streets to speak of because the houses are not built according to any plan, and besides, where is there room for such a thing? Why should there be vacant space when you can build something on it? It is written that the earth is to be inhabited, not merely to be gazed at.

Yet, don't be upset. There are some streets—big streets, little streets, back streets and alleys. What if they happen to twist and turn uphill and downhill and suddenly end up in a house or a cellar or just a hole in the ground? If you are a stranger, never go out alone at night without a lantern. As for the little people who live there, don't worry about them. A Kasrilevkite in Kasrilevka, among Kasrilevkites, will never get lost. Each one finds the way to his own house, to his wife and children, like a bird to its own nest.

And then in the center of the city there is a wide half-circle, or perhaps it is a square, where you find the stores, shops, market stands, stalls and tables. There every morning the peasants from the surrounding countryside congregate with their produce—fish and onions, horseradish, parsnips and other vegetables. They sell these things and buy from the little people other necessities of life, and from this the Kasrilevkites draw their livelihood. A meager one, but better than nothing. And in the square also lie all the town's goats, warming themselves in the sun.

There also stand the synagogues, the meeting houses, the chapels and schools of the town where Jewish children study the Holy Writ. The noise they and the rabbis make with their chanting is enough to deafen one. The baths where the women go to bathe are also there, and the poorhouse where the old men die, and other such public institutions. No, the Kasrilevkites have never heard of canals or water works or electricity or other such luxuries. But what does that matter? Everywhere people die the same death, and they are placed in the same earth, and are beaten down with the same spades. Thus my Rabbi, Reb Israel, used to say—when he was happiest, at a wedding or other celebration, after he had had a few glasses of wine and was ready to lift up the skirts of his long coat and dance a *kazatsky*...

But the real pride of Kasrilevka is her cemeteries. This lucky town has two rich cemeteries, the old and the new. The new one is old enough and rich enough in graves. Soon there will be no place to put anyone, especially if a pogrom should break out or any of the other misfortunes which befall us in these times.

But it is of the old cemetery that the people of Kasrilevka are especially proud. This old cemetery, though it is overgrown with grass and with bushes and has practically no upright headstones, they still value as they might a treasure, a rare gem, a piece of wealth, and guard it like the apple of their eye. For this is not only the place where their ancestors lie, rabbis, men of piety, learned ones, scholars and famous people, including the dead from the ancient massacres of Chmelnitski's time—but also the only piece of land of which they are the masters, the only bit of earth they own where a blade of grass can sprout and a tree can grow and the air is fresh and one can breathe freely.

You should see what goes on in this old cemetery a month before the New Year, during the "days of weeping." Men and women—mainly women—swarm up and down the paths to their ancestors' graves. From all the surrounding country they come to weep and to pour their hearts out at the holy graves. Believe me, there is no place where one can weep so freely and with such abandon as in "the field" of Kasrilevka. In the synagogue a person can weep pretty freely too, but the synagogue doesn't come up to the cemetery. The cemetery is a source of income for the Kasrilevkite stonecutters, innkeepers, cantors and sextons, and the month before the New Year is, for the paupers thereabouts and the old women and the cripples, the real harvest time.

"Have you been in 'our field' yet?" a Kasrilevkite will ask you cheerfully, as though he were asking if you had been in his father's vineyard. If you haven't been there, do him a kindness, and go down into "the field," read the old, half-obliterated inscriptions on the leaning tombstones and you will find in them the story of a whole people. And if you happen to be a man of feeling and imagination then you will look upon this poor little town with its rich cemeteries and repeat the old verses:

"How beautiful are your tents, O Jacob; how good are your resting places, O Israel."

Moon Prayer

by
ROCH CARRIER
(1937–   )

The boy, the willow, the moon. Here is a charming story of childish wonder—a simply told tale of trusting innocence and unanswered questions. Roch Carrier's "Moon Prayer" tells the story of a child's need to understand, and of the inevitable shortcomings and sorrows of everyday answers to his eternal questions.

Today, God, I'm going to pray in my bed instead of going to church. Thank You for the beautiful day You gave the Earth. I caught three big trouts in the Famine River, but I threw back a big carp. God, Your carp are really poor quality. They can't take the summer heat. Their flesh decomposes as if they were dead. But anyway, the bees and the butterflies seemed to be happy about everything. The day passed as quickly as the night does when you're asleep. I picked some strawberries, too. I brought home my trouts and a pailful of strawberries, already hulled. I'm not the kind of lazybones that picks strawberries and then doesn't hull them. But I think You could have made strawberries that don't have hulls. They'd be easier to pick.

Our mother sent me out to cord some wood. It's the beginning of July, and the sun's so hot you melt in your pants. But our father's getting ready for the winter. He's bought his wood, enough to heat every igloo at the North Pole and the polar ice cap, too. And we're the ones that have to cord it. Summer holidays would be the best time in my whole life if it wasn't for cording that wood. Sometimes when I look at the mountain of wood waiting for me, I wonder if I wouldn't be better off in school, learning lists of grammatical exceptions and how to make fishes plural.

It was really beautiful today. You should have seen Your sun, and the colour of the barley and the spruce trees. You should have heard Your birds singing and Your insects buzzing. You should have seen Your snakes baking their skins on piles of stones: You'd have been proud of Yourself. Days like that mean that the eternal goodness of Your Heaven overflowed onto Earth. I want to thank You, God, for the beautiful day. Even if tears are pouring out of my eyes, I'm really quite happy. It's dark in my room but You can see me. The tears are on account of our Uncle Marcel.

You're the only one that knows I'm bawling like a baby. When I cry I don't make any sound, I don't sniff or squawk. I suffer my sorrow in silence, as they say on the radio. If my brothers hear me crying they'll make fun of me and call me a baby. One sob and they'll be in my bed, landing on me with their feet and slapping me with their pillows. I'd rather keep my suffering inside for a while. My pillow's all wet. I really shouldn't be suffering like this after such a beautiful day.

Our Uncle Marcel is young and he's taller than me. He must be at least thirteen or twelve, our uncle. He's the one that holds the censer in the church procession. If you ask me, I think he'd rather be holding some girl's hand. Uncle Marcel smokes on the sly. That's a secret, but I can tell You because You've seen him. His mother, our grandmother, doesn't know. I think I'll tell her tomorrow. Uncle Marcel upset me a lot tonight. I know he smokes because he offered me his cigarette and he said:

"If you don't tell my mother, your grandmother, I'll let you take a puff."

I didn't take one puff, I took a dozen. All at once I felt like a man: I was dizzy and I wanted to throw up. My guts were squirming, my head was spinning. I still didn't say anything to Uncle Marcel's mother, our grandmother. Tomorrow, if You let me live long enough to open my eyes, I'm going to tell our grandmother on him because he upset me so much. I can't stand it when people laugh at me because I'm not as big as the others and because I'm younger.

Our Uncle Marcel is proud. He's always got a little mirror in one hand, and with the other hand he's always combing his hair. He wants the girls to think he's handsome. I'm going to tell our grandmother that he made me smoke. Then Uncle Marcel will be sentenced to stay in his room for quite a few nights. He'll have to go quite a few days without combing his hair because he'll have to go quite a few days without any girls seeing him. My pillow's all wet with tears, God, and I don't like going to sleep feeling sad.

Tonight our father said:

"The Moon's as full as a woman."

I didn't understand what he meant. I looked at the Moon. She was like a great big orange on a tablecloth, as blue as the sky, that had little holes like moth-holes in it, for the stars. The Moon also looked like the big head of a man, without any hair or a toupee or a body, but with eyes and a nose and a mouth. If the Moon was full, she was full of light. And I was looking up at her.

I wished I could reach up and touch Your Moon. I wished I could climb onto the Moon and scoop up a handful, like a handful of earth or a handful of snow. I wished I could see what it was made of. Is the Moon a ball of fire? Is the Moon just an explosion? Is the Moon solid like Earth? Is it a big diamond? Is it like a huge scoop of ice cream you can lick? Is it hot like fire? Is it cold like ice? Anyway, it's beautiful to look at. It's so far away from Earth that looking at it for a long time makes you dizzy, like when Uncle Marcel made me smoke a string cigarette. Our Uncle Marcel hasn't got any tobacco. He won't steal any from his father, our grandfather, because he says he's not a thief, so I bring him string from our father's store.

God, You hung the Moon so high up in the sky, it would take four hundred years to get there by train. That's what the nun at school told us. She didn't say how long it would take to build the railway. You'd have to know how long it took to build the railway that goes from one end of Canada to the other. And then calculate the distance between Earth and the Moon. Then divide that distance by the length of Canada. And then multiply the quotient obtained by the time needed to build the Canadian railway. The Moon's far, far away, farther than the end of our lives.

Nobody on the gallery outside our house dared to talk. We were all looking at the Moon. We were as quiet as if we were scared. It was a nice kind of fear, though. A gentle fear. The sleepy kind of fear when you don't understand something beautiful that you wish you could understand. It was as if the gallery had moved like a boat in the water. The men were smoking. The women were quiet, too. You could hear yourself breathe. That was the only sound our lives were making. The Moon was beautiful, round and yellow and shiny. There were a few stars, but you just knew that on this night, the sky was made for the Moon. It was really hard to believe that some of the stars were hundreds of times bigger than the Moon: they seemed to be hundreds of times smaller. The Moon was the queen of the stars, I tell You. Maybe the Moon isn't a star because it doesn't have points like a real star, but anyway, she was really shiny and far away up in the sky where the stars are, and where You are too, God. The sky You created on the first day of Creation is very beautiful; I wonder if it's become more beautiful since. You created it perfect, but if it's more beautiful now, it's Your fault. Thank You for beauty, God.

There were quite a lot of us out on the gallery. The men didn't dare smoke. The children were quiet. We felt as if we weren't exactly on the Earth: as if we'd floated a little on our gallery, between Earth and the Moon. And it felt as if Earth was flying in the sky.

There was practically a crowd of us out on the gallery: Monsieur Philippe from the elections and Roméo the ice-cream man and Juste and Madame Juste and Roland and Réal and Gaston who makes heels for ladies' shoes; there was Dorval who sells horses and all my brothers and sisters and the seminary student who's learning to read from a breviary and the thirteen Chabotte children. And then there were my friends Roger and Lapin. I'm pretty sure I've left out some but You saw them all, God, all sitting on the gallery and not talking.

Everybody was looking at the sky that had never been so bright. The sky was as blue as in the middle of the day. The sky above the village seemed as light as a curtain when the wind blows in. Behind the curtain, it was as if we could see You. It felt as if You were there. As we listened, it was as if we could hear You smoking Your pipe up in Heaven. But there wasn't any smoke; the sky was clean, without a cloud. In the cities, apparently, people never see the sky on account of the black clouds the factories make. I imagine people get out of the habit of looking at the sky, so they forget. Since people forget the things they don't see very often, they must forget You, too, God.

Our Uncle Marcel was sitting on the gallery too. He was quiet because if he'd said anything grandmother who was out there too, rocking, would have told him to go and make his noise somewhere else. He'd been quiet for a long time. Even though there weren't any girls to admire him, our Uncle Marcel's hair was combed better than anybody's; he looked really sharp. Uncle Marcel's the best player in any game; he's the fastest runner; he's got the worst temper. If there's girls around, it's Uncle Marcel they like best, and that makes me proud.

Our Uncle Marcel isn't one of those people who walks by you with his nose in the air so he can't smell you, as if you were a cat turd. He's practically twice as old as I am, but sometimes he plays with me as if he wasn't an uncle and he was the same age as me. Sometimes we even have fights. We roll in the grass like real enemies, but we laugh, and then we roll some more and we bang into each other and give each other wrist burns and we kick and rip each other's shirts and hit our heads on the grass and put our hands around each other's necks and choke, but we choke from laughing, too. Sometimes I cry because I'm smaller and because Uncle Marcel is better. But I'm proud of our uncle, even though I never win a fight with him. I don't know anybody else that's got an uncle who plays with him and rolls in the grass all the way from the road down to the vegetable garden. Everybody else with uncles has old uncles who are bald and scared they'll fall down and break their bones and kick a bucket. I'm really proud of our Uncle Marcel. Sometimes I try to comb my hair like him. When I'm grown up like him I'll be the best, like him, and I'll have the worst temper like him and I'll hit the ball as far as he does. The girls will know I'm the best.

Our Uncle Marcel was looking at the Moon, too, and he was quiet. But then all of a sudden he talked. Beside the house You planted a willow tree, an old, old one that was there long before the house. It's way higher than the house and its trunk is as wide as my bed. Four or five other trunks are growing out of the first one. Sitting on one of its branches is like climbing on the back of our father's horse.

The Earth had turned, or maybe the Moon had moved, and Uncle Marcel said in my ear, so he wouldn't interrupt the other people thinking:

"See that? The Moon's in the willow tree."

I looked with the eyes You gave me, God, and I saw the Moon in the willow tree, just like Uncle Marcel said.

"See? The Moon's up there on the biggest branch of the willow."

He said this in a whisper, and he was pointing at the Moon. Some of the people sitting on the gallery looked where his finger was pointing.

"Look, up there, leaning against the tip of the biggest branch: it's the Moon."

I stood up to get a better look. It was true. Uncle Marcel had noticed before any of the others that the Moon had stopped; she'd landed on the biggest branch, way up high above the roof of the house, higher than the chimney, almost as high as the church steeple, practically at the top of the willow.

"Yes, you're right," I said to our Uncle Marcel, "I can see the Moon perched at the very end of the biggest branch."

This time he spoke out loud:

"Want me to go up and get you a couple of handfuls of moon?"

"Yes," I told him, "I want three handfuls of moon, or four."

Everybody on the gallery heard our uncle, and they heard me answer. Everybody watched our uncle get out of his chair, walk down the gallery, go to the willow, jump up, and then, with his neatly combed hair and his nice clean clothes, start to climb that tree, as limber as a cat, without mussing his hair. Everybody was watching our uncle, especially that Clémence Chabotte who'd just arrived, she's the sister of Juste Chabotte's boys. I was really proud of our Uncle Marcel. I didn't know anybody else with an uncle like mine, that could climb a willow tree to bring down a handful of moon for his nephew. I stood up so I could watch him better. He was already high up; I could see the leaves stirring and tossing higher and higher. And then, all of a sudden, very high up, almost at the very end of the big branch, I saw our uncle right beside the Moon. I saw him touch the Moon. And then I saw him pull off a handful, two handfuls, three handfuls of moon; I saw him scoop up some moon the way you scoop up water in your hand. I was so happy! I was going to have some pieces of the Moon! I didn't know anybody else that had pieces of moon. I'd take them to show at school. No other uncle would dare to go up as high as our Uncle Marcel. I was proud, God, prouder than I'd ever been in my whole life.

Our uncle climbed back down as easily as he'd gone up. He came back to the gallery, slowly and carefully because he was carrying moon dust. It was fragile, I told myself. It could die and turn grey like ashes. It could scatter in the wind. Our Uncle Marcel was being careful. He was protecting his harvest. He was taking tiny little steps. He was hardly lifting his feet as he came towards us, with both hands closed around his catch that seemed to want to fly away like a bird. When he got really close to me, our Uncle Marcel said very loud:

"Still want a piece of moon?"

"Yes!"

I was so happy, I almost shouted.

Everybody came over quietly, like in church, to get a look at the piece of moon our Uncle Marcel had gone to get me in the sky, at the tip of the willow tree. He told me:

"Count to three. At three I'll open my hands…"

I was a little bit scared. I'd never touched moon before. Was it cold like ice? Was it hot like bread? I got my own hands ready to move fast.

He counted: "One, two…three…"

Our Uncle Marcel's hands were partly open and I caught the piece of moon. It was cool and wet. Everybody was looking at me. I was looking at the piece of moon. It wasn't shiny. It was wet. Crumpled. I looked more closely. It wasn't shiny. It wasn't ashes. It wasn't moon. It was a handful of leaves. So then I yelled:

"That isn't moon, it's willow leaves."

They all burst out laughing as if I'd made some funny joke. Everybody. Even our Uncle Marcel, who never laughs for fear of mussing his hair. Even Your seminary student. Even that Clémence Chabotte, who must think her Marcel's the best. I burst into tears like a bomb. Honest, God, I've never cried so hard in my whole life.

When I'm very old I'll still remember that Moon. It's so sad when grown-ups play tricks on you. I'm going to stop praying to You now, God, and I'm going to cry into my pillow because I still haven't cried out all my sorrow.

Patio Talk
and
Vines

by
LESLEY-ANNE BOURNE
(1964–   )

Here are two small enigmas from a recent book of poems by Lesley-Anne Bourne. I'll leave these two poems simply—without introduction—as curiously woven thoughts lying quietly on the page.

Patio Talk

Wrought iron chairs
a certain green
and a fringed umbrella tilted

over the bubbled glass.
Three straight days
without rain, warm afternoons
blazing nights.

Over coffee my neighbour
mentions again the emerald hedge
needs cutting, the rose

helped. Vines
through the trellis poke
their slender fans,

the middle of summer breezes
over us. Men from the past
lean everywhere. What was
I thinking? How could I have…

as if thoughts can finish.
Enough, she says
though I'm not sure of what.

Vines

Like the last time
(even the rain the same
and the dark as dark)
you turned to me.
Could've been that summer
when thunder started
far enough away. I thought
the usual—the storm
will miss us. Sometimes
whole fields lie drenched.
Others wait thirsty.
In the vineyard
the grapevines cling
to one particular night
when the rain came
warm and fast then
left them
wanting more.

Telemachus,
Friend

by
O. HENRY
(1867–1910)

*O. Henry has become a bit of an old friend. "Telemachus"
reads like an old movie of the American south. There is that
familiar old feeling of a bordertown past—of the honour of the
outlaw. The John Wayne-like character of the story is pre-
dictably on the side of decency and honour, though you always
have the feeling that with a toss of the coin a different, more
dangerous character might emerge.*

Returning from a hunting trip, I waited at the little town of Los Piños, in New Mexico, for the south-bound train, which was one hour late. I sat on the porch of the Summit House and discussed the functions of life with Telemachus Hicks, the hotel proprietor.

Perceiving that personalities were not out of order, I asked him what species of beast had long ago twisted and mutilated his left ear. Being a hunter, I was concerned in the evils that may befall one in the pursuit of game.

'That ear,' said Hicks, 'is the relic of true friendship.'

'An accident?' I persisted.

'No friendship is an accident,' said Telemachus; and I was silent.

'The only perfect case of true friendship I ever knew,' went on my host, 'was a cordial intent between a Connecticut man and a monkey. The monkey climbed palms in Barranquilla and threw down coconuts to the man. The man sawed them in two and made dippers, which he sold for two *reales* each and bought rum. The monkey drank the milk of the nuts. Through each being satisfied with his own share of the graft, they lived like brothers.

'But in the case of human beings, friendship is a transitory art, subject to discontinuance without further notice.

'I had a friend once, of the entitlement of Paisley Fish, that I imagined was sealed to me for an endless space of time. Side by side for seven years we had mined, ranched, sold patent churns, herded sheep, took photographs and other things, built wire fences, and picked prunes. Thinks I, neither homicide nor flattery nor riches nor sophistry nor drink can make trouble between me and Paisley Fish. We was friends an amount you could hardly guess at. We was friends in business, and we let our amicable qualities lap over and season our hours of recreation and folly. We certainly had days of Damon and nights of Pythias.

'One summer me and Paisley gallops down into these San Andrés mountains for the purpose of a month's surcease and levity, dressed in the natural store habiliments of man. We hit this town of Los Piños, which certainly was a roof-garden spot of the world, and flowing with condensed milk and honey. It had a street or two, and air, and hens, and a eating-house; and that was enough for us.

'We strikes the town after supper-time, and we concludes to sample whatever efficacy there is in this eating-house down by the railroad tracks. By the time we had set down and pried up our plates with a knife from the red oil-cloth, along intrudes Widow Jessup with the hot biscuit and the fried liver.

'Now, there was a woman that would have tempted an anchovy to forget his vows. She was not so small as she was large; and a kind of welcome air seemed to mitigate her vicinity. The pink of her face was the *in hoc signo* of a culinary temper and a warm disposition, and her smile would have brought out the dogwood blossoms in December.

'Widow Jessup talks to us a lot of garrulousness about the climate and history and Tennyson and prunes and the scarcity of mutton, and finally wants to know where we came from.

'"Spring Valley," says I.

'"Big Spring Valley," chips in Paisley, out of a lot of potatoes and knuckle-bone of ham in his mouth.

'That was the first sign I noticed that the old *fidus Diogenes* business between me and Paisley Fish was ended for ever. He knew how I hated a talkative person, and yet he stampedes into the conversation with his amendments and addendums of syntax. On the map it was Big Spring Valley; but I had heard Paisley himself call it Spring Valley a thousand times.

'Without saying any more, we went out after supper and set on the railroad track. We had been pardners too long not to know what was going on in each other's mind.

"'I reckon you understand," says Paisley, "that I've made up my mind to accrue that widow woman as part and parcel in and to my hereditaments for ever, both domestic, sociable, legal, and otherwise, until death do us part."

"'Why, yes," says I. "I read it between the lines, though you only spoke one. And I suppose you are aware," says I, "that I have a movement on foot that leads up to the widow's changing her name to Hicks, and leaves you writing to the society column to inquire whether the best man wears a japonica or seamless socks at the wedding!"

"'There'll be some hiatuses in your programme," says Paisley, chewing up a piece of a railroad tie. "I'd give in to you," says he, "in 'most any respect if it was secular affairs, but this is not so. The smiles of woman," goes on Paisley, "is the whirlpool of Squills and Chalybeates, into which vortex the good ship Friendship is often drawn and dismembered. I'd assault a bear that was annoying you," says Paisley, "Or I'd endorse your note, or rub the place between your shoulder-blades with opodeldoc the same as ever; but there my sense of etiquette ceases. In this fracas with Mrs Jessup we play it alone. I've notified you fair."

'And then I collaborates with myself, and offers the following resolutions and bye-laws—

"'Friendship between man and man," says I, "is an ancient historical virtue enacted in the days when men had to protect each other against lizards with eighty-foot tails and flying turtles. And they've kept up the habit to this day, and stand by each other till the bellboy comes up and tells them the animals are not really there. I've often heard," I says, "about ladies stepping in and breaking up a friendship between men. Why

should that be? I'll tell you, Paisley, the first sight and hot biscuit of Mrs Jessup appears to have inserted a oscillation into
each of our bosoms. Let the best man of us have her. I'll play
you a square game, and won't do any underhanded work. I'll
do all of my courting of her in your presence, so you will have
an equal opportunity. With that arrangement I don't see why
our steamboat of friendship should fall overboard in the medicinal whirlpools you speak of, whichever of us wins out."

"'Good old hoss!" says Paisley, shaking my hand. "And I'll
do the same," says he. "We'll court the lady synonymously, and
without any of the prudery and bloodshed usual to such occasions. And we'll be friends still, win or lose."

'At one side of Mrs Jessup's eating-house was a bench under
some trees where she used to sit in the breeze after the southbound had been fed and gone. And there me and Paisley used
to congregate after supper and made partial payments on our
respects to the lady of our choice. And we was so honorable
and circuitous in our calls that if one of us got there first we
waited for the other before beginning any gallivantery.

'The first evening that Mrs Jessup knew about our arrangement I got to the bench before Paisley did. Supper was just
over, and Mrs Jessup was out there with a fresh pink dress on,
and almost cool enough to handle.

'I sat down by her and made a few specifications about the
moral surface of nature as set forth by the landscape and the
contiguous perspective. That evening was surely a case in
point. The moon was attending to business in the section of
the sky where it belonged, and the trees was making shadows
on the ground according to science and nature, and there was
a kind of conspicuous hullabaloo going on in the bushes
between the bullbats and the orioles and the jack-rabbits and
other feathered insects of the forest. And the wind out of the
mountains was singing like a jew's harp in the pile of old
tomato cans by the railroad track.

'I felt a kind of sensation in my left side—something like
dough rising in a crock by the fire. Mrs Jessup had moved up
closer.

"'Oh, Mr Hicks," says she, "when one is alone in the world,

don't they feel it more aggravated on a beautiful night like this?"

'I rose up off of the bench at once.

'"Excuse me, ma'am," says I, "but I'll have to wait till Paisley comes before I can give a audible hearing to leading questions like that."

'And then I explained to her how we was friends cinctured by years of embarrassment and travel and complicity, and how we had agreed to take no advantage of each other in any of the more mushy walks of life, such as might be fomented by senti- ment and proximity. Mrs Jessup appears to think serious about the matter for a minute and then she breaks into a species of laughter that makes the wild-wood resound.

'In a few minutes Paisley drops around, with oil of bergamot on his hair, and sits on the other side of Mrs Jessup, and inau- gurates a sad tale of adventure in which him and Pieface Lumley has a skinning match of dead cows in '95 for a silver- mounted saddle in the Santa Rita valley during the nine months' drought.

'Now, from the start of that courtship I had Paisley Fish hobbled and tied to a post. Each one of us had a different sys- tem of reaching out for the easy places in the female heart. Paisley's scheme was to petrify 'em with wonderful relations of events that he had either come across personally or in large print. I think he must have got his idea of subjugation from one of Shakespeare's shows I see once called *Othello*. There is a colored man in it who acquires a duke's daughter by disburs- ing to her a mixture of the talk turned out by Rider Haggard, Lew Dockstader and Dr Parkhurst. But that style of courting don't work well off the stage.

'Now, I give you my own recipe for inveigling a woman into that state of affairs when she can be referred to as "née Jones." Learn how to pick up her hand and hold it, and she's yours. It ain't so easy. Some men grab at it so much like they was going to set a dislocation of the shoulder that you can smell the arni- ca and hear 'em tearing off bandages. Some take it up like a hot horseshoe, and hold it off at arm's length like a druggist pouring tincture of asafœtida in a bottle. And most of 'em catch hold of it and drag it right out before the lady's eyes like a boy finding a baseball in the grass, without giving her a chance to forget that the hand is growing on the end of her arm. Them ways are all wrong.

'I'll tell you the right way. Did you ever see a man sneak out in the back yard and pick up a rock to throw at a tom-cat that was sitting on a fence looking at him? He pretends he hasn't got a thing in his hand, and that the cat don't see him, and that he don't see the cat. That's the idea. Never drag her hand out where she'll have to take notice of it. Don't let her know that you think she knows you have the least idea she is aware you are holding her hand. That was my rule of tactics; and as far as Paisley's serenade about hostilities and misadventure went he might as well have been reading to her a timetable of the Sunday trains that stop at Ocean Grove, New Jersey.

'One night when I beat Paisley to the bench by one pipeful, my friendship gets subsidized for a minute, and I asks Mrs Jessup if she didn't think a "H" was easier to write than a "J." In a second her head was mashing the oleander flower in my buttonhole, and I leaned over and—but I didn't.

'"If you don't mind," says I, standing up, "we'll wait for Paisley to come before finishing this. I've never done anything dishonorable yet to our friendship, and this won't be quite fair."

'"Mr Hicks," says Mrs Jessup, looking at me peculiar in the dark, "if it wasn't for but one thing, I'd ask you to hike yourself down the gulch and never disresume your visits to my house."

'"And what is that, ma'am?" I asks.

'"You are too good a friend not to make a good husband," says she.

'In five minutes Paisley was on his side of Mrs Jessup.

'"In Silver City, in the summer of '98," he begins, "I see Jim Bartholomew chew off a Chinaman's ear in the Blue Light Saloon on account of a cross-barred muslin shirt that—what was that noise?"

'I had resumed matters again with Mrs Jessup right where we had left off.

'"Mrs Jessup," says I, "has promised to make it Hicks. And this is another of the same sort."

'Paisley winds his feet around a leg of the bench and kind of groans.

'"Lem," says he, 'we been friends for seven years. Would you mind not kissing Mrs Jessup quite so loud? I'd do the same for you."

'"All right," says I. "The other kind will do as well."

'"This Chinaman," goes on Paisley, "was the one that shot a man named Mullins in the spring of '97, and that was—"

'Paisley interrupted himself again.

'"Lem," says he, "if you was a true friend you wouldn't hug Mrs Jessup quite so hard. I felt the bench shake all over just then. You know you told me you would give me an even chance as long as there was any."

'"Mr Man," says Mrs Jessup turning around to Paisley, "if you was to drop in to the celebration of mine and Mr Hicks's silver wedding, twenty-five years from now, do you think you could get it into that Hubbard squash you call your head that you are *nix cum rous* in this business? I've put up with you a long time because you was Mr Hicks's friend; but it seems to me it's time for you to wear the willow and trot off down the hill."

'"Mrs Jessup," says I, without losing my grasp on the situation as fiancé, "Mr Paisley is my friend, and I offered him a square deal and a equal opportunity as long as there was a chance."

'"A chance!" says she. "Well, he may think he has a chance; but I hope he won't think he's got a cinch, after what he's been next to all the evening."

'Well, a month afterward me and Mrs Jessup was married in the Los Piños Methodist Church; and the whole town closed up to see the performance.

'When we lined up in front, and the preacher was beginning to sing out his rituals and observances, I looks around and misses Paisley. I calls time on the preacher. "Paisley ain't here," says I. "We've got to wait for Paisley. A friend once, a friend always—that's Telemachus Hicks," says I. Mrs Jessup's eyes snapped some; but the preacher holds up the incantations according to instructions.

'In a few minutes Paisley gallops up the aisle, putting on a cuff as he comes. He explains that the only dry-goods store in town was closed for the wedding, and he couldn't get the kind of a boiled shirt that his taste called for until he had broke open the back window of the store and helped himself. Then he ranges up on the other side of the bride, and the wedding goes on. I always imagined that Paisley calculated as a last chance that the preacher might marry him to the widow by mistake.

'After the proceedings was over we had tea and jerked antelope and canned apricots, and then the populace hiked itself away. Last of all Paisley shook me by the hand and told me I'd acted square and on the level with him, and he was proud to call me a friend.

'The preacher had a small house on the side of the street that he'd fixed up to rent; and he allowed me and Mrs Hicks to occupy it till the ten-forty train the next morning, when we was going on a bridal tour to El Paso. His wife had decorated it all up with hollyhocks and poison ivy, and it looked real festal and bowery.

'About ten o'clock that night I sets down in the front door and pulls off my boots a while in the cool breeze, while Mrs Hicks was fixing around in the room. Right soon the light went out inside; and I sat there a while reverberating over old times and scenes. And then I heard Mrs Hicks call out, "Ain't you coming in soon, Lem?"

'"Well, well!" says I, kind of rousing up. "Durn me if I wasn't waiting for old Paisley to—"

'But when I got that far,' concluded Telemachus Hicks, 'I thought somebody had shot this left ear of mine off with a forty-five. But it turned out to be only a lick from a broom-handle in the hands of Mrs Hicks.'

The Circus

by
KATHERINE ANNE PORTER
(1890–1980)

I remember my first time reading "The Circus." After a moment's confusion, I remember saying slowly to myself, "Ah, so that's what she's doing." Seeing a circus through a child's eyes—for the first time—and bringing to life the child's fears and confusion.

T he long planks set on trestles rose one above the other to a monstrous height and stretched dizzyingly in a wide oval ring. They were packed with people—"lak fleas on a dog's ear," said Dicey, holding Miranda's hand firmly and looking about her with disapproval. The white billows of enormous canvas sagged overhead, held up by three poles set evenly apart down the center. The family, when seated, occupied almost a whole section on one level.

On one side of them in a long row sat Father, sister Maria, brother Paul, Grandmother; great-aunt Keziah, cousin Keziah, and second-cousin Keziah, who had just come down from Kentucky on a visit; uncle Charles Breaux, cousin Charles Breaux, and aunt Marie-Anne Breaux. On the other side sat small cousin Lucie Breaux, big cousin Paul Gay, great-aunt Sally Gay (who took snuff and was therefore a disgrace to the family); two strange, extremely handsome young men who might be cousins but who were certainly in love with cousin Miranda Gay; and cousin Miranda Gay herself, a most dashing young lady with crisp silk shirts, a half dozen of them at once, a lovely perfume and wonderful black curly hair above enormous wild gray eyes, "like a colt's," Father said. Miranda hoped to be exactly like her when she grew up. Hanging to Dicey's arm she leaned out and waved to cousin Miranda, who waved back smiling, and the strange young men waved to her also. Miranda was most fearfully excited. It was her first circus; it might also be her last because the whole family had combined to persuade Grandmother to allow her to come with them. "Very well, this once," Grandmother said, "since it's a family reunion."

This once! This once! She could not look hard enough at everything. She even peeped down between the wide crevices of the piled-up plank seats, where she was astonished to see odd-looking, roughly dressed little boys peeping up from the dust below. They were squatted in little heaps, staring up quietly. She looked squarely into the eyes of one, who returned her a look so peculiar she gazed and gazed, trying to understand it. It was a bold grinning stare without any kind of friendliness in it. He was a thin, dirty little boy with a floppy old checkerboard cap pulled over crumpled red ears and dust-colored hair. As she gazed he nudged the little boy next to him, whispered, and the second little boy caught her eye. This was too much. Miranda pulled Dicey's sleeve. "Dicey, what are those little boys doing down there?" "Down where?" asked Dicey, but she seemed to know already, for she bent over and looked through the crevice, drew her knees together and her skirts around her, and said severely: "You jus mind yo' own business and stop throwin' yo' legs around that way. Don't you pay any mind. Plenty o' monkeys right here in the show widout you studyin' dat kind."

An enormous brass band seemed to explode right at Miranda's ear. She jumped, quivered, thrilled blindly and almost forgot to breathe as sound and color and smell rushed together and poured through her skin and hair and beat in her head and hands and feet and pit of her stomach. "Oh," she called out in her panic, closing her eyes and seizing Dicey's hand hard. The flaring lights burned through her lids, a roar of laughter like rage drowned out the steady raging of the drums and horns. She opened her eyes... A creature in a blousy white overall with ruffles at the neck and ankles, with bone-white skull and chalk-white face, with tufted eyebrows far apart in the middle of his forehead, the lids in a black sharp angle, a long scarlet mouth stretching back into sunken cheeks, turned up at the corners in a perpetual bitter grimace of pain, astonishment, not smiling, pranced along a wire stretched down the center of the ring, balancing a long thin pole with little wheels at either end. Miranda thought at first he was walking on air, or flying, and this did not surprise her; but when she saw the wire, she was terrified. High above their heads the inhuman figure pranced, spinning the little wheels. He paused, slipped, the flapping white leg waved in space; he staggered, wobbled, slipped sidewise, plunged, and caught the wire with frantic knee, hanging there upside down, the other leg waving like a feeler above his head; slipped once more, caught by one frenzied heel, and swung back and forth like a scarf... The crowd roared with savage delight, shrieks of dreadful laughter like devils in delicious torment... Miranda shrieked too, with real pain, clutching at her stomach with her knees drawn up... The man on the wire, hanging by his foot, turned his head like a seal from side to side and blew sneering kisses from his cruel mouth. Then Miranda covered her eyes and screamed, the tears pouring over her cheeks and chin.

"Take her home," said her father, "get her out of here at once," but the laughter was not wiped from his face. He merely glanced at her and back to the ring. "Take her away, Dicey," called the Grandmother, from under her half-raised crepe veil. Dicey, rebelliously, very slowly, without taking her gaze from the white figure swaying on the wire, rose, seized the limp, suffering bundle, prodded and lumped her way over knees and feet, through the crowd, down the levels of the scaffolding, across a space of sandy tanbark, out through a flap in the tent. Miranda was crying steadily with an occasional hiccough. A dwarf was standing in the entrance, wearing a little woolly beard, a pointed cap, tight red breeches, long shoes with turned-up toes. He carried a thin white wand. Miranda almost touched him before she saw him, her distorted face with its open mouth and glistening tears almost level with his. He leaned forward and peered at her with kind, not-human golden eyes, like a near-sighted dog: then made a horrid grimace at her, imitating her own face. Miranda struck at him in sheer ill temper, screaming. Dicey drew her away quickly, but not before Miranda had seen in his face, suddenly, a look of haughty, remote displeasure, a true grown-up look. She knew it well. It chilled her with a new kind of fear: she had not believed he was really human.

"Raincheck, get your raincheck!" said a very disagreeable looking fellow as they passed. Dicey turned toward him almost in tears herself. "Mister, caint you see I won't be able to git back? I got this young un to see to... What good dat lil piece of paper goin to do *me*?" All the way home she was cross, and grumbled under her breath: little ole meany...little ole scare-cat...gret big baby...never go nowhere...never see nothin...come on here now, hurry up—always ruinin everything for othah folks...won't let anybody rest a minute, won't let anybody have any good times...come on here now, you wanted to go home and you're going there...snatching Miranda along, vicious but cautious, careful not to cross the line where Miranda could say outright: "Dicey did this or said this to me..." Dicey was allowed a certain freedom up to a point.

The family trooped into the house just before dark and scattered out all over it. From every room came the sound of chatter and laughter. The other children told Miranda what she had missed: wonderful little ponies with plumes and bells on their bridles, ridden by darling little monkeys in velvet jackets and peaked hats...trained white goats that danced...a baby elephant that crossed his front feet and leaned against his cage and opened his mouth to be fed, *such* a baby! ...more clowns, funnier than the first one even...beautiful ladies with bright yellow hair, wearing white silk tights with red satin sashes had performed on white trapezes; they also had hung by their toes, but how gracefully, like flying birds! Huge white horses had lolloped around and round the ring with men and women dancing on their backs! One man had swung by his teeth from the top of the tent and another had put his head in a lion's mouth. Ah, what she had not missed! Everybody had been enjoying themselves while she was missing her first big circus and spoiling the day for Dicey. Poor Dicey. Poor dear Dicey. The other children who hadn't thought of Dicey until that moment, mourned over her with sad mouths, their malicious eyes watching Miranda squirm. Dicey had been looking forward for weeks to this day! And then Miranda must get scared—"Can you imagine being afraid of that funny old clown?" each one asked the other, and then they smiled pityingly on Miranda...

Then too, it had been a very important occasion in another way: it was the first time Grandmother had ever allowed herself to be persuaded to go to the circus. One could not gather, from her rather generalized opinions, whether there had been no circuses when she was young, or there had been and it was not proper to see them. At any rate for her usual sound reasons, Grandmother had never approved of circuses, and though she would not deny she had been amused somewhat, still there had been sights and sounds in this one which she maintained were, to say the least, not particularly edifying to the young. Her son Harry, who came in while the children made an early supper, looked at their illuminated faces, all the brothers and sisters and visiting cousins, and said, "This basket of young doesn't seem to be much damaged." His mother said, "The fruits of their present are in the future so far off, neither of us may live to know whether harm has been done or not. That is the trouble," and she went on ladling out hot milk to pour over their buttered toast. Miranda was sitting silent, her underlip drooping. Her father smiled at her. "You missed it, Baby," he said softly, "and what good did that do you?"

Miranda burst again into tears: had to be taken away at last, and her supper was brought up to her. Dicey was exasperated and silent. Miranda could not eat. She tried, as if she were really remembering them, to think of the beautiful wild beings in white satin and spangles and red sashes who danced and frolicked on the trapezes; of the sweet furry ponies and the lovely pet monkeys in their comical clothes. She fell asleep, and her invented memories gave way before her real ones, the bitter terrified face of the man in blowsy white falling to his death—ah, the cruel joke!—and the terrible grimace of the unsmiling dwarf. She screamed in her sleep and sat up crying for deliverance from her torments.

Dicey came, her cross, sleepy eyes half-closed, her big dark mouth pouted, thumping the floor with her thick bare feet. "I *swear*," she said, in a violent hoarse whisper. "What the matter with you? You need a good spankin, I *swear*. Wakin everybody up like this…"

Miranda was completely subjugated by her fears. She had a way of answering Dicey back. She would say, "Oh, hush up, Dicey." Or she would say, "I don't have to mind you. I don't have to mind anybody but my grandmother," which was pro-vokingly true. And she would say, "You don't know what you're talking about." The day just past had changed all that. Miranda sincerely did not want anybody, not even Dicey, to be cross with her. Ordinarily she did not care how cross she made the harassed adults around her. Now if Dicey must be cross, she still did not really care, if only Dicey might not turn out the lights and leave her to the fathomless terrors of the dark-ness where sleep could overtake her once more. She hugged Dicey with both arms, crying, "Don't, don't leave me. *Don't* be so angry! I c-c-can't b-bear it!"

Dicey lay down beside her with a long moaning sigh, which meant that she was collecting her patience and making up her mind to remember that she was a Christian and must bear her cross. "Now you go to sleep," she said, in her usual warm being-good voice. "Now you jes shut yo eyes and go to sleep. I ain't going to leave you. Dicey ain't mad at nobody…nobody in the whole worl'…"

Why I Stick to the Farm

by
PETER MCARTHUR
(1866–1924)

An ode to the farm: to a sense of place, tradition, stability and hard work; to self-reliance, independence and natural beauty; to things that are often lost in the hurly-burly of everyday life. "Why I Stick to the Farm" goes beyond considerations of cold winters, poor crops and aching backs. It is a story of the seasons, and of the harvest as summer turns once more to autumn.

Why do I stick to the farm?"

You might as well ask a woodchuck why he sticks to his hole.

This comparison has more foundation in fact than you perhaps imagine, for whenever I come home from a little visit to the outer world I always turn into the lane with a joyous chuckle that is much like the chuckle that a woodchuck chuckles when he dives into his tunnel. The farm is a place of peace, a place of refuge, and a home. This is a point on which the woodchuck and I are entirely agreed.

The farm means all these things to me because I was born on it and have learned to realize something of its possibilities. All my memories of childhood and boyhood are bound up with it. To be born on a farm is the greatest good that can befall a human being. To live on a farm and enjoy all that it has to offer is the greatest good that can be attained by a poet or a philosopher.

To make it clear why I harbour these convictions it is necessary to sweep away some mistaken notions about farming. To do this perhaps I cannot do better than explain just how this particular farm came to be hewn from the wilderness. The work of clearing the land and bringing it under cultivation was done by men and women who had only one purpose in life— to establish a home where they and their children might be free. They made their home self-sustaining—winning their food, clothing, and shelter from the land and its products, by the labour of their own hands. The home was their ideal. All the farm work was undertaken to provide for its needs, and when the home was supplied they rested. Their ambition was satisfied.

Brought up in this home I missed learning too young the lessons that destroy so many homes. To begin with I had only the vaguest ideas of personal ownership. The home belonged to all of us and our work went to keep it up and pay expenses. It is true that contact with the world finally educated the children to ideas of personal property and roused our ambitions. Driven by these generally accepted ideas we went our way, but somehow the farm that had been started right stayed in the backs of our minds as home. Although I have lived in far countries and great cities, no place ever was my home except this farm. And in due time I came back to try to carry on the home traditions that had been established by a pioneer father and mother.

I stick to the farm because it is the most satisfactory thing in the world to stick to. It is solid, right down to the centre of the earth. It stays right where it is through depressions, panics, wars, and every other kind of human foolishness. Even an earthquake could only joggle it, and this is not an earthquake region.

Moreover, you can't speed up the farm. It is timed to the sun and the seasons. Airships may pass over it at the rate of one hundred and fifty miles an hour, but the thistledowns that rise from my fields go at the rate of the prevailing wind, just as they did when they rose from the Garden of Eden. You can't hurry the farm and you can't hurry me. The grass grows and the leaves come out when spring comes dawdling back from the south, and not one minute before.

I stick to the farm because it is the only thing I have ever found that is entirely dependable. The seed-time and the harvest come to it every year with easy-going and unworried certainty. They never come twice at exactly the same time nor bring the same bounties, but they never fail to come. They may fail to bring wheat, but if they do they will bring abundant corn:

Cold and dry for wheat and rye,
Wet and warm for Indian corn.

The farm means *safety first* with the safety guaranteed by all-embracing Nature—and the labour of your own hands. It is well not to forget the labour of your own hands.

To get the fullest enjoyment out of the farm you must do things for it with your own hands. A farm is like a friend. The more you do for a friend the better you like him, and the more you do for a farm the dearer it becomes to you.

Although I am friends with all the trees on the farm, the ones I like best are those that I planted myself. The shade trees that I planted myself seem to throw a more generous shade than any other, and no apple tastes as good as one from a tree that I planted, fertilized, pruned, sprayed, and looked after myself. I have planted thousands of trees in the wood-lot, and no artist ever got such a thrill from looking at his finished masterpiece as I get whenever I visit my plantation and see how much the trees have grown since my last visit. To get the most out of a farm you must put yourself into it—do things for it that will be permanent—do them with your own hands.

Of course, farming means hard work. That side of it has been harped on until even a lot of farmers think it means nothing else. That tale has been told since the beginning until it has become exactly what Tennyson has called it:

A tale of little meaning
Although its words are strong.

But even the hardest-working farmer can afford to devote an occasional few minutes to enjoyment—especially at meal-times. Let us give some consideration to this more frivolous side of farming. Let us begin with the spring. When the warm winds and the rain begin to sweep away the snow and to unbind the shackles of frost, just draw a deep breath and realize that you are more alive than anything else on earth. The farmer's work is with the very elements of life, and he should enjoy life to the full. Even the cattle begin to bawl and show an interest in life as soon as the grass shows green beyond the barnyard fence. You do not even have to stop your work to hear the first notes of the song sparrow or the honking of the wild geese passing overhead. The sun is busier than you are, bringing warmth and growth to every seed, bud, and root—to wildflowers and weeds as well as to your precious wheat—and see how serene he is about it all. He can even take time to jocularly burn a blister on the back of your neck on his busiest day.

The tulips and the daffodils in the garden need only a glance to give you their message of beauty, and if you happen to be hurrying through the wood-lot you can surely pause long enough to see the anemones and spring beauties at your feet.

On this particular farm the opening rite of spring is tapping the sugar-bush. But I will not dwell on the joys of making sugar, for all farms are not blessed with sugar-maples.

But my delight in maple syrup is hardly over before I begin paying visits to the asparagus bed. I planted that asparagus myself, and I like to be on hand the first morning that a thick, fat shoot pushes up through the ground. After the asparagus come strawberries, raspberries, new potatoes—a list that becomes more crowded as the seasons pass, until we have picked the last apples and pitted the potatoes in the fall. Spring, summer and autumn are all linked together with beauties and luxuries and delights.

And even the winter has its charms. As the animals are more dependent on us they become more friendly. Horses, cows, sheep, pigs, hens, all greet us in their own characteristic way when we visit them in the morning. And what is more exhilarating than the days spent in the wood-lot, with the snow crunching underfoot and the axe rousing the frosty echoes? The farmer prepares his year's supply of fuel without thought of strikes or soaring prices.

Of course, if you estimate everything in terms of dollars you can never understand why I stick to the farm. Dollars enter very little into the question. If you wish you may quote me a price for the basket of new potatoes I bring in from the garden, but what price can you put on the satisfaction I get from digging potatoes of my own planting and tending? Can you put a price on the joy of turning up a hill of big ones that might have taken the prize at the fall fair and knowing that all this is due to my practical partnership with Nature in producing them? The potatoes themselves may satisfy bodily hunger, but the joy of producing them satisfies the soul's hunger for creation, and it is priceless.

While meditating on this aspect of farm life I went for a ramble in the pasture-field to hunt for mushrooms. For half an hour—while picking up beauties—I canvassed my memory to see if I could remember the price I had got for anything I had ever sold off the farm. Although I have lived on this farm most of my life and have sold all kinds of farm stock and produce, I could not remember the exact price I got for one item. But I remembered how beautiful the apples were the first year we pruned and sprayed the old orchard. I could remember how fine the oats looked the year we had them in the field back of the root-house. I remembered litters of little pigs that were as plump as sausages and as cunning as kittens. I remembered calves that I had fed to admired sleekness and hogs that I had stuffed to fatness, but the prices they fetched I could not remember.

And that was not because I did not need the money—I have always needed the money and sometimes needed it bitterly—but the cash crop was not the crop that satisfied. As I let my memory wander over the past, hunting for prices that had failed to make a record, I remembered climbing the pear tree to get a big pear that had lodged in a fork and had ripened lusciously in the sun. I remembered tramping through a wet pasture gathering mushrooms and how a little moist hand stole into mine because a little maiden was afraid of a cow we were passing. I remembered coasting with a home-made sled on a little bank beside the creek, and also remembered seeing my children coasting on that same bank on sleds of their own making. I could see in the perspective of memory great piles of apples under the trees, shining fields of corn, colts scampering in the pastures, lambs playing king of the castle on anthills—a crowding, joyous film of homely pictures that brought happy tears to my eyes—and there was not a dollar mark on one of them. The dollars are necessary, of course—very necessary— but you can earn dollars digging in a sewer, or get them by sharp practices in business. But where else but on the farm can you get the needful dollars and forget them in the joy of your surroundings?

These are a few of the reasons why I stick to the farm, and I feel sure that the woodchuck would endorse every word I have written.

A
Girl's Story

by
DAVID ARNASON
(1940–   )

This is a cute, comic little piece. I've recorded a couple of stories from David Arnason's The Happiest Man in the World, *and they are all good fun. Arnason has a happy, poking-fun type of voice—coy, satirical, playful, engaging. By the way, this is not really "A Girl's Story" as David Arnason surely knows—it's "A Writer's Story," and a story in which the reader plays a conspiring role.*

You've wondered what it would be like to be a character in a story, to sort of slip out of your ordinary self and into some other character. Well, I'm offering you the opportunity. I've been trying to think of a heroine for this story, and frankly, it hasn't been going too well. A writer's life isn't easy, especially if, like me, he's got a tendency sometimes to drink a little bit too much. Yesterday, I went for a beer with Dennis and Ken (they're real-life friends of mine) and we stayed a little longer than we should have. Then I came home and quickly mixed a drink and started drinking it so my wife would think the liquor on my breath came from the drink I was drinking and not from the drinks I had had earlier. I wasn't going to tell her about those drinks. Anyway, Wayne dropped over in the evening and I had some more drinks, and this morning my head isn't working very well.

To be absolutely frank about it, I always have trouble getting characters, even when I'm stone cold sober. I can think of plots; plots are really easy. If you can't think of one, you just pick up a book, and sure enough, there's a plot. You just move a few things around and nobody knows you stole the idea.

Characters are the problem. It doesn't matter how good the plot is if your characters are dull. You can steal characters too, and put them into different plots. I've done that. I stole Eustacia Vye from Hardy and gave her another name. The problem was that she turned out a lot sulkier than I remembered and the plot I put her in was a light comedy. Now nobody wants to publish the story. I'm still sending it out, though. If you send a story to enough publishers, no matter how bad it is, somebody will ultimately publish it.

For this story I need a beautiful girl. You probably don't think you're beautiful enough, but I can fix that. I can do all kinds of retouching once I've got the basic material, and if I miss anything, Karl (he's my editor) will find it. So I'm going to make you fairly tall, about five-foot eight and a quarter in your stocking feet. I'm going to give you long blonde hair because long blonde hair is sexy and virtuous. Black hair can be sexy too, but it doesn't go with virtue. I've got to deal with a whole literary tradition where black-haired women are basically evil. If I were feeling better I might be able to do it in an ironic way, then black hair would be OK, but I don't think I'm up to it this morning. If you're going to use irony, then you've got to be really careful about tone. I could make you a redhead, but redheads have a way of turning out pixie-ish, and that would wreck my plot.

So you've got long blonde hair and you're this tall slender girl with amazingly blue eyes. Your face is narrow and your nose is straight and thin. I could have turned up the nose a little, but that would have made you cute, and I really need a beautiful girl. I'm going to put a tiny black mole on your cheek. It's traditional. If you want your character to be really beautiful there has to be some minor defect.

Now, I'm going to sit you on the bank of a river. I'm not much for setting. I've read so many things where you get great long descriptions of the setting, and mostly it's just boring. When my last book came out, one of the reviewers suggested that the reason I don't do settings is that I'm not very good at them. That's just silly. I'm writing a different kind of story, not that old realist stuff. If you think I can't do setting, just watch.

There's a curl in the river just below the old dam where the water seems to make a broad sweep. That flatness is deceptive, though. Under the innocent sheen of the mirroring surface, the current is treacherous. The water swirls, stabs, takes sharp angles and dangerous vectors. The trees that lean from the bank shimmer with the multi-hued greenness of elm, oak, maple and aspen. The leaves turn in the gentle breeze, show-ing their paler green undersides. The undergrowth, too, is thick and green, hiding the poison ivy, the poison sumac and the thorns. On a patch of grass that slopes gently to the water, the only clear part of the bank on that side of the river, a girl sits, a girl with long blonde hair. She has slipped a ring from her finger and seems to be holding it toward the light.

You see? I could do a lot more of that, but you wouldn't like it. I slipped a lot of details in there and provided all those hints about strange and dangerous things under the surface. That's called foreshadowing. I put in the ring at the end there so that you'd wonder what was going to happen. That's to cre-ate suspense. You're supposed to ask yourself what the ring means. Obviously it has something to do with love, rings always do, and since she's taken it off, obviously something has gone wrong in the love relationship. Now I just have to hold off answering that question for as long as I can, and I've got my story. I've got a friend who's also a writer who says never tell the buggers anything until they absolutely have to know.

I'm going to have trouble with the feminists about this story. I can see that already. I've got that river that's calm on the sur-face and boiling underneath, and I've got those trees that are gentle and beautiful with poisonous and dangerous under-growth. Obviously, the girl is going to be like that, calm on the surface but passionate underneath. The feminists are going to say that I'm perpetuating stereotypes, that by giving the impression the girl is full of hidden passion I'm encouraging rapists. That's crazy. I'm just using a literary convention. Most of the world's great books are about the conflict between rea-son and passion. If you take that away, what's left to write about?

So I've got you sitting on the riverbank, twirling your ring. I forgot the birds. The trees are full of singing birds. There are meadowlarks and vireos and even Blackburnian warblers. I know a lot about birds but I'm not going to put in too many. You've got to be careful not to overdo things. In a minute I'm going to enter your mind and reveal what you're thinking. I'm going to do this in the third person. Using the first person is sometimes more effective, but I'm always afraid to do a female character in the first person. It seems wrong to me, like putting on a woman's dress.

Your name is Linda. I had to be careful not to give you a biblical name like Judith or Rachel. I don't want any symbolism in this story. Symbolism makes me sick, especially biblical symbolism. You always end up with some crazy moral argument that you don't believe and none of your readers believe. Then you lose control of your characters, because they've got to be like the biblical characters. You've got this terrific episode you'd like to use, but you can't because Rachel or Judith or whoever wouldn't do it. I think of stories with a lot of symbolism in them as sticky.

Here goes.

Linda held the ring up toward the light. The diamond flashed rainbow colours. It was a small diamond, and Linda reflected that it was probably a perfect symbol of her relationship with Gregg. Everything Gregg did was on a small scale. He was careful with his money and just as careful with his emotions. In one week they would have a small wedding and then move into a small apartment. She supposed that she ought to be happy. Gregg was very handsome, and she did love him. Why did it seem that she was walking into a trap?

That sounds kind of distant, but it's supposed to be distant. I'm using indirect quotation because the reader has just met Linda, and we don't want to get too intimate right away. Besides, I've got to get a lot of explaining done quickly, and if you can do it with the character's thoughts, then that's best.

Linda twirled the ring again, then with a suddenness that surprised her, she stood up and threw it into the river. She was immediately struck by a feeling of panic. For a moment she almost decided to dive into the river to try to recover it. Then, suddenly, she felt free. It was now impossible to marry Gregg. He would not forgive her for throwing the ring away. Gregg would say he'd had enough of her theatrics for one lifetime. He always accused her of being a romantic. She'd never had the courage to admit that he was correct, and that she intended to continue being a romantic. She was sitting alone by the river in a long blue dress because it was a romantic pose. Anyway, she thought a little wryly, you're only likely to find romance if you look for it in romantic places and dress for the occasion.

Suddenly, she heard a rustling in the bush, the sound of someone coming down the narrow path from the road above.

I had to do that, you see. I'd used up all the potential in the relationship with Gregg, and the plot would have started to flag if I hadn't introduced a new character. The man who is coming down the path is tall and athletic with wavy brown hair. He has dark brown eyes that crinkle when he smiles, and he looks kind. His skin is tanned, as if he spends a lot of time outdoors, and he moves gracefully. He is smoking a pipe. I don't want to give too many details. I'm not absolutely sure what features women find attractive in men these days, but what I've described seems safe enough. I got all of it from stories written by women, and I assume they must know. I could give him a chiselled jaw, but that's about as far as I'll go.

The man stepped into the clearing. He carried an old-fashioned wicker fishing creel and a telescoped fishing rod. Linda remained sitting on the grass, her blue dress spread out around her. The man noticed her and apologized.

"I'm sorry, I always come here to fish on Saturday afternoons and I've never encountered anyone here before." His voice was low with something of an amused tone in it.

"Don't worry," Linda replied. "I'll only be here for a little while. Go ahead and fish. I won't make any noise." In some way she couldn't understand, the man looked familiar to her. She felt she knew him. She thought she might have seen him on television or in a movie, but of course she knew that movie and television stars do not spend every Saturday afternoon fishing on the banks of small, muddy rivers.

"You can make all the noise you want," he told her. "The fish in this river are almost entirely deaf. Besides, I don't care if I catch any. I only like the act of fishing. If I catch them, then I have to take them home and clean them. Then I've got to cook them and eat them. I don't even like fish that much, and the fish you catch here all taste of mud."

"Why do you bother fishing then?" Linda asked him. "Why don't you just come and sit on the riverbank?"

"It's not that easy," he told her. "A beautiful girl in a blue dress may go and sit on a riverbank any time she wants. But a man can only sit on a riverbank if he has a very good reason. Because I fish, I am a man with a hobby. After a hard week of work, I deserve some relaxation. But if I just came and sat on a riverbank, I would be a romantic fool. People would make fun of me. They would think I was irresponsible, and before long I would be a failure." As he spoke, he attached a lure to his line, untelescoped his fishing pole and cast his line into the water.

You may object that this would not have happened in real life, that the conversation would have been awkward, that Linda would have been a bit frightened by the man. Well, why don't you just run out to the grocery store and buy a bottle of milk and a loaf of bread? The grocer will give you your change without even looking at you. That's what happens in real life, and if that's what you're after, why are you reading a book?

I'm sorry. I shouldn't have got upset. But it's not easy you know. Dialogue is about the hardest stuff to write. You've got all those "he saids" and "she saids" and "he replies." And you've got to remember the quotation marks and whether the comma is inside or outside the quotation marks. Sometimes you can leave out the "he saids" and the "she saids" but then the reader gets confused and can't figure out who's talking. Hemingway is bad for that. Sometimes you can read an entire chapter without figuring out who is on what side.

Anyway, something must have been in the air that afternoon. Linda felt free and open.

Did I mention that it was warm and the sun was shining?

She chattered away, telling the stranger all about her life, what she had done when she was a little girl, the time her dad had taken the whole family to Hawaii and she got such a bad sunburn that she was peeling in February, how she was a better water skier than Gregg and how mad he got when she beat him at tennis. The man, whose name was Michael (you can use biblical names for men as long as you avoid Joshua or Isaac), told her he was a doctor, but had always wanted to be a cowboy. He told her about the time he skinned his knee when he fell off his bicycle and had to spend two weeks in the hospital because of infection. In short, they did what people who are falling in love always do. They unfolded their brightest and happiest memories and gave them to each other as gifts.

Then Michael took a bottle of wine and a Klik sandwich out of his wicker creel and invited Linda to join him in a picnic. He had forgotten his corkscrew and he had to push the cork down into the bottle with his filletting knife. They drank wine and laughed and spat out little pieces of cork. Michael reeled in his line, and to his amazement discovered a diamond ring on his hook. Linda didn't dare tell him where the ring had come from. Then Michael took Linda's hand, and slipped the ring on her finger. In a comic-solemn voice, he asked her to marry him. With the same kind of comic solemnity, she agreed. Then they kissed, a first gentle kiss with their lips barely brushing and without touching each other.

Now I've got to bring this to some kind of ending. You think writers know how stories end before they write them, but that's not true. We're wracked with confusion and guilt about how things are going to end. And just as you're playing the role of Linda in this story, Michael is my alter ego. He even looks a little like me and he smokes the same kind of pipe. We all want this to end happily. If I were going to be realistic about this, I suppose I'd have to let them make love. Then, shaken with guilt and horror, Linda would go back and marry Gregg, and the doctor would go back to his practice. But I'm not going to do that. In the story from which I stole the plot, Michael turned out not to be a doctor at all, but a returned soldier who had always been in love with Linda. She recognized him as they kissed, because they had kissed as children, and even though they had grown up and changed, she recognized the flavour of wintergreen on his breath. That's no good. It brings in too many unexplained facts at the last minute.

I'm going to end it right here at the moment of the kiss. You can do what you want with the rest of it, except you can't make him a returned soldier, and you can't have them make love then separate forever. I've eliminated those options. In fact, I think I'll eliminate all options. This is where the story ends, at the moment of the kiss. It goes on and on forever while cities burn, nations rise and fall, galaxies are born and die, and the universe snuffs out the stars one by one. It goes on, the story, the brush of a kiss.

Oranges

by
ALPHONSE DAUDET
(1840–1897)

Tissue-wrapped oranges on the streets of Paris, scented blossoms in the gardens of Algiers, blood-red oranges by the Corsican shoreline—there's a sense of quietly coloured exoticism, a stillness and calmness about this piece—the scent of the orange trees overhead, date palms reclining in the summer shadows, the blue of the Mediterranean stretching out infinitely from the sand along the shoreline...

I n Paris oranges have the melancholy air of fruit that is dropped from the tree and picked up from the ground. At the time when they arrive, in the cold and rainy midwinter, their high-coloured skins, their excessive perfume in our land of tranquil tastes, give them an exotic aspect a little bohemian. Of a misty night they perambulate the side-walks, heaped in their little handcarts, by the dull light of a red paper lantern. A monotonous and feeble cry escorts them, lost in the roll of carriages and the rattle of omnibuses: "Two sous a Valentia!"

To three-fourths of all Parisians, this fruit gathered afar, monotonous in its roundness, in which the tree has left nothing but a small green twig, seems to belong to confectionery, to sweetmeats. The tissue paper which wraps it, the fêtes it accompanies, contribute to this impression. Toward the last of the year especially, thousands of oranges disseminated through the streets, the peels that lie about in the mud of the gutters, make one think of some gigantic Christmas tree shaking over Paris its branches laden with imitation fruit. Not a corner where we do not find them. In the large show windows selected and arranged; at the door of prisons and hospitals, among packages of biscuit and piles of apples; before the entrances to the Sunday balls and theatres. Their exquisite perfume mingles with the odour of gas, the scraping of fiddles, the dust of the benches in paradise. We have come to forget that oranges grow on orange-trees, for while the fruit arrives from the South in boxes, the trimmed, transformed, disguised tree of the greenhouse where it has passed the winter, makes but a short apparition in our gardens.

To know oranges well, you must see them at home, in the Balearic Isles, in Sardinia, Corsica, Algeria, in the blue, gilded air and the warm atmosphere of the Mediterranean. I remember a little grove of orange-trees at the gates of Blidah; ah! it is there that they are beautiful. Amid the dark, lustrous, varnished foliage the fruits have the splendour of coloured glass; they gild the environing air with the dazzling halo that surrounds a glowing flower. Here and there little clearings through the branches showed the ramparts of the town, the minaret of a mosque, the dome of a saint's tomb, and, towering above them all, the enormous mass of Atlas, green at its base, and crowned with snow like a fleece or a white fur softly fallen.

One night while I was there, I do not know by what phenomenon, unknown for thirty years, that upper zone of wintry hoar-frost shook itself down upon the sleeping town, and Blidah awoke transformed, powdered in white. In that Algerine air, so light, so pure, the snow was like dust of mother-of-pearl. It had all the reflections of a white peacock's plume. Most beautiful of all was the orange grove. The solid leaves held the snow intact, like sherbet on a lacquered dish; and the fruit, all powdered with hoar-frost, had a softened splendour, a discreet glow, like gold veiled lightly in gauze. The scene had vaguely the effect of a church festival, of red cassocks under robes of lace, the golden altars swathed in guipure.

But my best memory of oranges come to me from Barbicaglia, a great garden near Ajaccio, where I went for my siesta in the heat of the day. Here the orange-trees, taller and more spreading than those of Blidah, come down to the main road, from which the garden is separated by only a ditch and an evergreen hedge. Immediately beyond is the sea, the vast blue sea... Oh! what good hours did I pass in that garden! Above my head the orange-trees, in bloom and in fruit, exhaled the perfume of their essence. From time to time a ripe orange, as though weighed down by the heat, fell beside me with a flat, echoless sound on the fecund earth. I had only to put out my hand. The fruit was superb, of a crimson red within. It seemed to me exquisite—and then, the horizon was so beautiful! Between the leaves the sea put azure spaces, dazzling as pieces of broken glass shimmering in the quiver of the air. And with all that, the motion of the waves stirring the atmosphere at a great distance with a cadenced murmur which rocked you like an unseen boat, and the warmth, and the odour of the oranges! Ah! how good it was to sleep in the garden of Barbicaglia!

Sometimes, however, at the pleasantest moment of the siesta, the roll of drums would rouse me with a start. It was those wretched little drummers, practising below on the main-road. Through gaps in the hedge I could see the brass of their instruments and their great white aprons on their red trousers. To shelter themselves a little from the blinding light which the dust of the road reflected pitilessly, the poor young devils would plant themselves at the foot of the garden in the scanty shadow of the hedge. And they drummed! and they were so hot! Then, wrenching myself forcibly from my hypnotism, I amused myself by flinging them some of that beautiful golden-red fruit which hung close to my hand. The drummer first aimed at stopped. There was a moment's hesitation, a look went round to see whence came that splendid orange rolling before him into the ditch; then he picked it up very fast and bit into it with his teeth without peeling off the skin.

I remember also that close to Barbicaglia and separated from it by a low wall, was a queer little garden that I could look into from the height where I lay. 'Twas a small corner of earth laid out in bourgeois fashion. Its paths, yellow with sand and bordered with very green box, and the two cypresses at its entrance gave it the appearance of a Marseillaise surburban villa garden. Not an atom of shade. At the farther end was a building of white stone with cellar windows on a line with the ground. At first, I thought it a country-house; then looking closer, a cross that surmounted it, an inscription cut into the stone that I could see from a distance without distinguishing the letters, made me recognize it as the tomb of a Corsican family. All around Ajaccio, there are many of these mortuary chapels, built in gardens of their own. The family comes on Sunday to pay a visit to its dead. Thus treated, death is less lugubrious than amid the confusion of cemeteries. The feet of friends alone break the silence.

From my station above, I could see a good old man coming and going tranquilly along the paths. Every day he trimmed the trees, he spaded, watered, and picked off the faded flowers with infinite care; then, when the sun was setting, he always entered the little chapel where the dead of his family were sleeping; and he put away his spades and rakes and watering-pots, with the tranquillity, the serenity of a cemetery gardener. And yet, without himself being aware of it, the good man worked with a certain gravity; he subdued all noises and closed the door of the vault discreetly, as if fearing to awaken an inmate. In the great glowing silence the neatness of the little garden was never troubled by even a bird, and its neighbourhood had nothing sad about it. Only, the sea seemed more immense, the heavens higher, and the endless siesta shed around the place, amid a troubled nature oppressive in its strength of life, the feeling of eternal repose.

The Old, Old Story of How Five Men Went Fishing

by
STEPHEN LEACOCK
(1869–1944)

I was going to introduce this story by telling a fishing story of my own, but then remembered the old trap of the one that got away. "The Old, Old Story of How Five Men Went Fishing" takes a typically Leacockian stab at the poor, self-deluded fisherman. I read this story last year at the Leacock festival and was heartened to see how a familiar old chestnut of a story can take on new colours when read in a different time or place. This is a story that has continued to evolve, that has taken on a deeper resonance with the passing of the years.

This is a plain account of a fishing party. It is not a story. There is no plot. Nothing happens in it and nobody is hurt. The only point of this narrative is its peculiar truth. It not only tells what happened to us—the five people concerned in it—but what has happened and is happening to all the other fishing parties that at the season of the year, from Halifax to Idaho, go gliding out on the unruffled surface of our Canadian and American lakes in the still cool of the early summer morning.

We decided to go in the early morning because there is a popular belief that the early morning is the right time for bass fishing. The bass is said to bite in the early morning. Perhaps it does. In fact the thing is almost capable of scientific proof. The bass does *not* bite between eight and twelve. It does *not* bite between twelve and six in the afternoon. Nor does it bite between six o'clock and midnight. All these things are known facts. The inference is that the bass bites furiously at about daybreak.

At any rate our party were unanimous about starting early. "Better make an early start," said the Colonel when the idea of the party was suggested. "Oh, yes," said George Popley, the

Bank Manager, "we want to get right out on the shoal while the fish are biting."

When he said this all our eyes glistened. Everybody's do. There's a thrill in the words. To "get right out on the shoal at daybreak when the fish are biting," is an idea that goes to any man's brain.

If you listen to the men talking in a Pullman car, or a hotel corridor, or better still, at the little tables in a first-class bar, you will not listen long before you hear one say—"Well, we got out early, just after sunrise, right on the shoal." ...And presently, even if you can't hear him you will see him reach out his two hands and hold them about two feet apart for the other men to admire. He is measuring the fish. No, not the fish they caught; this is the big one that they lost. But they had him right up to the top of the water: Oh, yes, he was up to the top of the water all right. The number of huge fish that have been heaved up to the top of the water in our lakes is almost incredible. Or at least it used to be when we still had bar rooms and little tables for serving that vile stuff Scotch whiskey and such foul things as gin Rickeys and John Collinses. It makes one sick to think of it, doesn't it? But there was good fishing in the bars, all winter.

But, as I say, we decided to go early in the morning. Charlie Jones, the railroad man, said that he remembered how when he was a boy, up in Wisconsin, they used to get out at five in the morning—not get up at five but be on the shoal at five. It appears that there is a shoal somewhere in Wisconsin where the bass lie in thousands. Kernin, the lawyer, said that when he was a boy—this was on Lake Rosseau—they used to get out at four. It seems there is a shoal in Lake Rosseau where you can haul up the bass as fast as you can drop your line. The shoal is hard to find—very hard. Kernin can find it, but it is doubtful—so I gather—if any other living man can. The Wisconsin shoal, too, is difficult to find. Once you find it, you are all right; but it's hard to find. Charlie Jones can find it. If you were in Wisconsin right now he'd take you straight to it, but probably no other person now alive could reach that shoal. In the same way Colonel Morse knows of a shoal in

Lake Simcoe where he used to fish years and years ago and which, I understand, he can still find.

I have mentioned that Kernin is a lawyer, and Jones a railroad man and Popley a banker. But I needn't have. Any reader would take it for granted. In any fishing party there is always a lawyer. You can tell him at sight. He is the one of the party that has a landing net and a steel rod in sections with a wheel that is used to wind the fish to the top of the water.

And there is always a banker. You can tell him by his good clothes. Popley, in the bank, wears his banking suit. When he goes fishing he wears his fishing suit. It is much the better of the two, because his banking suit has ink marks on it, and his fishing suit has no fish marks on it.

As for the Railroad Man—quite so, the reader knows it as well as I do—you can tell him because he carries a pole that he cut in the bush himself, with a ten cent line wrapped round the end of it. Jones says he can catch as many fish with this kind of line as Kernin can with his patent rod and wheel. So he can, too. Just the same number.

But Kernin says that with his patent apparatus if you get a fish on you can *play* him. Jones says to Hades with *playing* him: give him a fish on his line and he'll haul him in all right. Kernin says he'd lose him. But Jones says *he* wouldn't. In fact he *guarantees* to haul the fish in. Kernin says that more than once (in Lake Rosseau) he has played a fish for over half an hour. I forget now why he stopped; I think the fish quit playing.

I have heard Kernin and Jones argue this question of their two rods, as to which rod can best pull in the fish, for half an hour. Others may have heard the same question debated. I know no way by which it could be settled.

Our arrangement to go fishing was made at the little golf club of our summer town on the verandah where we sit in the evening. Oh, it's just a little place, nothing pretentious: the links are not much good for *golf*; in fact we don't play much *golf* there, so far as golf goes, and of course, we don't serve meals at the club, it's not like that—and no, we've nothing to drink there because of prohibition. But we go and *sit* there. It's a good place to *sit*, and, after all, what else can you do in the present state of the law?

So it was there that we arranged the party.

The thing somehow seemed to fall into the mood of each of us. Jones said he had been hoping that some of the boys would get up a fishing party. It was apparently the one kind of pleasure that he really cared for. For myself I was delighted to get in with a crowd of regular fishermen like these four, especially as I hadn't been out fishing for nearly ten years: though fishing is a thing I am passionately fond of. I know no pleasure in life like the sensation of getting a four pound bass on the hook and hauling him up to the top of the water, to weigh him. But, as I say, I hadn't been out for ten years: Oh, yes, I live right beside the water every summer, and yes, certainly—I am saying so—I am passionately fond of fishing, but still somehow I hadn't been *out*. Every fisherman knows just how that happens. The years have a way of slipping by. Yet I must say I was surprised to find that so keen a sport as Jones hadn't been out—so it presently appeared—for eight years. I had imagined he practically lived on the water. And Colonel Morse and Kernin—I was amazed to find—hadn't been out for twelve years, not since the day (so it came out in conversation) when they went out together in Lake Rosseau and Kernin landed a perfect monster, a regular corker, five pounds and a half, they said: or no, I don't think he *landed* him. No, I remember he didn't *land* him. He caught him—and he *could* have landed him—he should have landed him—but he *didn't* land him. That was it. Yes, I remember Kernin and Morse had a slight discussion about it—oh, perfectly amicable—as to whether Morse had fumbled with the net—or whether Kernin—the whole argument was perfectly friendly—had made an ass of himself by not "striking" soon enough. Of course the whole thing was so long ago that both of them could look back on it without any bitterness or ill nature. In fact it amused them. Kernin said it was the most laughable thing he ever saw in his life to see poor old Jack (that's Morse's name) shoving away with the landing net wrong side up. And Morse said he'd never forget seeing poor old Kernin yanking his line first this way and then that and not knowing where to try to haul it. It made him laugh to look back at it.

They might have gone on laughing for quite a time but Charlie Jones interrupted by saying that in his opinion a landing net is a piece of darned foolishness. Here Popley agrees with him. Kernin objects that if you don't use a net you'll lose your fish at the side of the boat. Jones says no: give him a hook well through the fish and a stout line in his hand and that fish has *got* to come in. Popley says so too. He says let him have his hook fast through the fish's head with a short stout line, and him (Popley) at the other end of that line and that fish will come in. It's *got* to. Otherwise Popley will know why. That's the alternative. Either the fish must come in or Popley must know why. There's no escape from the logic of it.

But perhaps some of my readers have heard the thing discussed before.

So as I say we decided to go the next morning and to make an early start. All of the boys were at one about that. When I say "boys," I use the word, as it is used in fishing, to mean people from say forty-five to sixty-five. There is something about fishing that keeps men young. If a fellow gets out for a good morning's fishing, forgetting all business worries, once in a while—say once in ten years—it keeps him fresh.

We agree to go in a launch, a large launch—to be exact, the largest in town. We could have gone in row boats, but a row boat is a poor thing to fish from. Kernin said that in a row boat it is impossible properly to "*play*" your fish. The side of the boat is so low that the fish is apt to leap over the side into the boat when half "played." Popley said that there is no *comfort* in a row boat. In a launch a man can reach out his feet, and take it easy. Charlie Jones said that in a launch a man could rest his back against something and Morse said that in a launch a man could rest his neck. Young inexperienced boys, in the small sense of the word, never think of these things. So they go out and after a few hours their necks get tired; whereas a group of expert fishers in a launch can rest their backs and necks and even fall asleep during the pauses when the fish stop biting.

Anyway all the "boys" agreed that the great advantage of a launch would be that we could get a *man* to take us. By that means the man could see to getting the worms, and the man would be sure to have spare lines, and the man would come along to our different places—we were all beside the water—and pick us up. In fact the more we thought about the advantage of having a "man" to take us the better we liked it. As a boy gets old he likes to have a man around to do the work.

Anyway Frank Rolls, the man we decided to get, not only has the biggest launch in town, but what is more, Frank *knows* the lake. We called him up at his boat house over the phone and said we'd give him five dollars to take us out first thing in the morning provided that he knew the shoal. He said he knew it.

I don't know, to be quite candid about it, who mentioned whiskey first. In these days everybody has to be a little careful. I imagine we had all been *thinking* whiskey for some time before anybody said it. But there is a sort of convention that when men go fishing they must have whiskey. Each man makes the pretence that the one thing he needs at six o'clock in the morning is cold raw whiskey. It is spoken of in terms of affection. One man says the first thing you need if you're going fishing is a good "snort" of whiskey: another says that a good "snifter" is the very thing and the others agree, that no man can fish properly without a "horn," or a "bracer" or an "eye-opener." Each man really decides that he himself won't take any. But he feels that in a collective sense, the "boys" need it.

So it was with us. The Colonel said he'd bring along "a bottle of booze." Popley said, no, let *him* bring it; Kernin said let him; and Charlie Jones said no, he'd bring it. It turned out that the Colonel had some very good Scotch at his house that he'd like to bring; oddly enough Popley had some good Scotch in *his* house too; and, queer though it is, each of the boys had Scotch in his house. When the discussion closed we knew that each of the five of us was intending to bring a bottle of whiskey. Each of the five of us expected the others to drink one and a quarter bottles in the course of the morning.

I suppose we must have talked on that verandah till long after one in the morning. It was probably nearer two than one when we broke up. But we agreed that that made no difference. Popley said that for him three hours' sleep, the right kind of sleep, was far more refreshing than ten. Kernin said that a lawyer learns to snatch his sleep when he can, and Jones said that in railroad work a man pretty well cuts out sleep.

So we had no alarms whatever about not being ready by five. Our plan was simplicity itself. Men like ourselves in responsible positions learn to organise things easily. In fact Popley says it is that faculty that has put us where we are. So the plan simply was that Frank Rolls should come along at five o'clock and blow his whistle in front of our places, and at that signal each man would come down to his wharf with his rod and kit and so we'd be off to the shoal without a moment's delay.

The weather was ruled out. It was decided that even if it rained that made no difference. Kernin said that fish bite better in the rain. And everybody agreed that a man with a couple of snorts in him need have no fear of a little rain water.

So we parted, all keen on the enterprise. Nor do I think even now that there was anything faulty or imperfect in that party as we planned it.

I heard Frank Rolls blowing his infernal whistle opposite my summer cottage at some ghastly hour in the morning. Even without getting out of bed, I could see from the window that it was no day for fishing. No, not raining exactly. I don't mean that, but one of those peculiar days—I don't mean *wind*—there was no wind, but a sort of feeling in the air that showed anybody who understands bass fishing that it was a perfectly rotten day for going out. The fish, I seemed to know it, wouldn't bite.

When I was still fretting over the annoyance of the disappointment I heard Frank Rolls blowing his whistle in front of the other cottages. I counted thirty whistles altogether. Then I fell into a light doze—not exactly sleep, but a sort of *doze*—I can find no other word for it. It was clear to me that the other "boys" had thrown the thing over. There was no use in my trying to go out alone. I stayed where I was, my doze lasting till ten o'clock.

When I walked up town later in the morning I couldn't help being struck by the signs in the butchers' shops and the restaurants, FISH, FRESH FISH, FRESH LAKE FISH.

Where in blazes do they get those fish anyway?

True Trash

by
MARGARET ATWOOD
(1939–   )

Margaret Atwood has always had a definite way about her:
quick to the bone, almost malicious, a continually engaging
sense of the wryness of things—and always, always sharp.
From Cat's Eye *and* The Handmaid's Tale *to the wonderful*
Wilderness Tips—*just when you think you've got to know*
her, she takes a different track. "True Trash" is Atwood at
summer camp—a perfect stalking ground for her clear, inci-
sive art and observations.

T he waitresses are basking in the sun like a herd of skinned seals, their pinky-brown bodies shining with oil. They have their bathing suits on because it's the afternoon. In the early dawn and the dusk they sometimes go skinny-dipping, which makes this itchy crouching in the mosquito-infested bushes across from their small private dock a great deal more worthwhile.

Donny has the binoculars, which are not his own but Monty's. Monty's dad gave them to him for bird-watching but Monty isn't interested in birds. He's found a better use for the binoculars: he rents them out to the other boys, five minutes maximum, a nickel a look or else a chocolate bar from the tuck shop, though he prefers the money. He doesn't eat the chocolate bars; he resells them, black market, for twice their original price; but the total supply on the island is limited, so he can get away with it.

Donny has already seen everything worth seeing, but he lingers on with the binoculars anyway, despite the hoarse whispers and the proddings from those next in line. He wants to get his money's worth.

"Would you look at that," he says, in what he hopes is a

tantalizing voice. "Slobber, slobber." There's a stick poking into his stomach, right on a fresh mosquito bite, but he can't move it without taking one hand off the binoculars. He knows about flank attacks.

"Lessee," says Ritchie, tugging at his elbow.

"Piss off," says Donny. He shifts the binoculars, taking in a slippery bared haunch, a red-polka-dotted breast, a long falling strand of bleach-blonde hair: Ronette the tartiest, Ronette the most forbidden. When there are lectures from the masters at St. Jude's during the winter about the danger of consorting with the town girls, it's those like Ronette they have in mind: the ones who stand in line at the town's only movie theatre, chewing gum and wearing their boyfriends' leather jackets, their ruminating mouths glistening and deep red like mushed-up raspberries. If you whistle at them or even look, they stare right through you.

Ronette has everything but the stare. Unlike the others, she has been known to smile. Every day Donny and his friends make bets over whether they will get her at their table. When she leans over to clear the plates, they try to look down the front of her sedate but V-necked uniform. They angle towards her, breathing her in: she smells of hair spray, nail polish, something artificial and too sweet. Cheap, Donny's mother would say. It's an enticing word. Most of the things in his life are expensive, and not very interesting.

Ronette changes position on the dock. Now she's lying on her stomach, chin propped on her hands, her breasts pulled down by gravity. She has a real cleavage, not like some of them. But he can see her collar-bone and some chest ribs, above the top of her suit. Despite the breasts, she's skinny, scrawny; she has little stick arms and a thin, sucked-in face. She has a missing side tooth: you can see it when she smiles, and this bothers him. He knows he's supposed to feel lust for her, but this is not what he feels.

The waitresses know they're being looked at: they can see the bushes jiggling. The boys are only twelve or thirteen, fourteen at most, small fry. If it was counsellors, the waitresses would giggle more, preen more, arch their backs. Or some of them would. As it is, they go on with their afternoon break as if no one is there. They rub oil on one another's backs, toast themselves evenly, turning lazily this way and that and causing Ritchie, who now has the binoculars, to groan in a way that is supposed to madden the other boys, and does. Small punches are dealt out, mutterings of "Jerk" and "Asshole." "Drool, drool," says Ritchie, grinning from ear to ear.

The waitresses are reading out loud. They are taking turns: their voices float across the water, punctuated by occasional snorts and barks of laughter. Donny would like to know what they're reading with such absorption, such relish, but it would be dangerous for him to admit it. It's their bodies that count. Who cares what they read?

"Time's up, shitface," he whispers to Ritchie.

"Shitface yourself," says Ritchie. The bushes thrash.

What the waitresses are reading is a *True Romance* magazine. Tricia has a whole stash of them, stowed under her mattress, and Sandy and Pat have each contributed a couple of others. Every one of these magazines has a woman on the cover, with her dress pulled down over one shoulder or a cigarette in her mouth or some other evidence of a messy life. Usually these women are in tears. Their colours are odd: sleazy, dirt-permeated, like the hand-tinted photos in the five-and-ten. Knee-between-the-leg colours. They have none of the cheerful primaries and clean, toothy smiles of the movie magazines: they are not success stories. True Trash, Hilary calls them. Joanne calls them Moan-o-dramas.

Right now it's Joanne reading. She reads in a serious, histrionic voice, like someone on the radio; she's been in a play, at school. *Our Town.* She's got her sunglasses perched on the end of her nose, like a teacher. For extra hilarity she'd thrown in a fake English accent.

The story is about a girl who lives with her divorced mother in a cramped, run-down apartment above a shoe store. Her name is Marleen. She has a part-time job in the store, after school and on Saturdays, and two of the shoe clerks are chasing around after her. One is dependable and boring and wants them to get married. The other one, whose name is Dirk, rides a motorcycle and has a knowing, audacious grin that turns Marleen's knees to jelly. The mother slaves over Marleen's wardrobe, on her sewing machine—she makes a meagre living doing dressmaking for rich ladies who sneer at her, so the wardrobe comes out all right—and she nags Marleen about choosing the right man and not making a terrible mistake, the way she did. The girl herself has planned to go to trade school and learn hospital management, but lack of money makes this impossible. She is in her last year of high school and her grades are slipping, because she is discouraged and also she can't decide between the two shoe clerks. Now the mother is on her case about the slipping grades as well.

"Oh God," says Hilary. She is doing her nails, with a metal file rather than an emery board. She disapproves of emery boards. "Someone please give her a double Scotch."

"Maybe she should murder the mother, collect the insurance, and get the hell out of there," says Sandy.

"Have you heard one word about any insurance?" says Joanne, peering over the tops of her glasses.

"You could put some in," says Pat.

"Maybe she should try out both of them, to see which one's the best," says Liz brazenly.

"We know which one's the best," says Tricia. "Listen, with a name like *Dirk!* How can you miss?"

"They're both creeps," says Stephanie.

"If she does that, she'll be a Fallen Woman, capital F, capital W," says Joanne. "She'd have to Repent, capital R."

The others hoot. Repentance! The girls in the stories make such fools of themselves. They are so weak. They fall helplessly in love with the wrong men, they give in, they are jilted. Then they cry.

"Wait," says Joanne. "Here comes the big night." She reads on, breathily: *"My mother had gone out to deliver a cocktail dress to one of her customers. I was all alone in our shabby apartment."*

"Pant, pant," says Liz.

"No, that comes later. *I was all alone in our shabby apartment. The evening was hot and stifling. I knew I should be studying, but I could not concentrate. I took a shower to cool off. Then, on impulse, I decided to try on the graduation formal my mother had spent so many late-night hours making for me.*"

"That's right, pour on the guilt," says Hilary with satisfaction. "If it was me I'd axe the mother."

"*It was a dream of pink—*"

"A dream of pink what?" says Tricia.

"A dream of pink, period, and shut up. *I looked at myself in the full-length mirror in my mother's tiny bedroom. The dress was just right for me. It fitted my ripe but slender body to perfection. I looked different in it, older, beautiful, like a girl used to every luxury. Like a princess. I smiled at myself. I was transformed.*

"*I had just undone the hooks at the back, meaning to take the dress off and hang it up again, when I heard footsteps on the stairs. Too late I remembered that I'd forgotten to lock the door on the inside, after my mother's departure. I rushed to the door, holding up my dress—it could be a burglar, or worse! But instead it was Dirk.*"

"Dirk the jerk," says Alex, from underneath her towel.

"Go back to sleep," says Liz.

Joanne drops her voice, does a drawl. "'*Thought I'd come up and keep you company,' he said mischievously. 'I saw your mom go out.' He knew I was alone! I was blushing and shivering. I could hear the blood pounding in my veins. I couldn't speak. Every instinct warned me against him—every instinct but those of my body, and my heart.*"

"So what else is there?" says Sandy. "You can't have a mental instinct."

"You want to read this?" says Joanne. "Then shush. *I held the frothy pink lace in front of me like a shield. 'Hey, you look great in that,' Dirk said. His voice was rough and tender. 'But you'd look even greater out of it.' I was frightened of him. His eyes were burning, determined. He looked like an animal stalking its prey.*"

"Pretty steamy," says Hilary.

"What kind of animal?" says Sandy.

"A weasel," says Stephanie.

"A skunk," says Tricia.

"Shh," says Liz.

"*I backed away from him,*" Joanne reads. "*I had never seen him look that way before. Now I was pressed against the wall and he was crushing me in his arms. I felt the dress slipping down...*"

"So much for all that sewing," says Pat.

"*...and his hand was on my breast, his hard mouth was seeking mine. I knew he was the wrong man for me but I could no longer resist. My whole body was crying out to his.*"

"What did it say?"

"It said, *Hey, body, over here!*"

"Shh."

"*I felt myself lifted. He was carrying me to the sofa. Then I felt the length of his hard, sinewy body pressing against mine. Feebly I tried to push his hands away, but I didn't really want to. And then*—dot dot dot—*we were One*, capital O, exclamation mark."

There was a moment of silence. Then the waitresses laugh. Their laughter is outraged, disbelieving. *One*. Just like that. There has to be more to it.

"The dress is a wreck," says Joanne in her ordinary voice. "Now the mother comes home."

"Not today, she doesn't," says Hilary briskly. "We've only got ten more minutes. I'm going for a swim, get some of this oil off me." She stands up, clips back her honey-blonde hair, stretches her tanned athlete's body, and does a perfect swan-dive off the end of the dock.

"Who's got the soap?" says Stephanie.

Ronette has not said anything during the story. When the others have laughed, she has only smiled. She's smiling now. Hers is an off-centre smile, puzzled, a little apologetic.

"Yeah, but," she says to Joanne, "why is it funny?"

The waitresses stand at their stations around the dining hall, hands clasped in front of them, heads bowed. Their royal-blue uniforms come down almost to the tops of their white socks, worn with white bucks or white-and-black saddle shoes or white sneakers. Over their uniforms they wear plain white aprons. The rustic log sleeping cabins at Camp Adanaqui don't have electric lights, the toilets are outhouses, the boys wash their own clothes, not even in sinks but in the lake; but there are waitresses, with uniforms and aprons. Roughing it builds a boy's character, but only certain kinds of roughing it.

Mr. B. is saying grace. He owns the camp, and is a master at St. Jude's as well, during the winters. He has a leathery, handsome face, the grey, tailored hair of a Bay Street lawyer, and the eyes of a hawk: he sees all, but pounces only sometimes. Today he's wearing a white V-necked tennis sweater. He could be drinking a gin and tonic, but is not.

Behind him on the wall, above his head, there's a weathered plank with a motto painted on it in black Gothic lettering: *As the Twig is Bent.* A piece of bleached driftwood ornaments each end of the plank, and beneath it are two crossed paddles and a gigantic pike's head in profile, its mouth open to show its needle teeth, its one glass eye fixed in a ferocious maniac's glare.

To Mr. B.'s left is the end window, and beyond it is Georgian Bay, blue as amnesia, stretching to infinity. Rising out of it like the backs of whales, like rounded knees, like the calves and thighs of enormous floating women, are several islands of pink rock, scraped and rounded and fissured by glaciers and lapping water and endless weather, a few jack pines clinging to the larger ones, their twisted roots digging into the cracks. It was through these archipelagos that the waitresses were ferried here, twenty miles out from shore, by the same cumbersome mahogany inboard launch that brings the mail and the groceries and everything else to the island. Brings, and takes away. But the waitresses will not be shipped back to the mainland until the end of summer: it's too far for a day off, and they would never be allowed to stay away overnight. So here they are, for the duration. They are the only women on the island, except for Mrs. B. and Miss Fisk, the dietitian. But those two are old and don't count.

There are nine waitresses. There are always nine. Only the names and faces change, thinks Donny, who has been going to this camp ever since he was eight. When he was eight he paid no attention to the waitresses except when he felt homesick. Then he would think of excuses to go past the kitchen window when they were washing the dishes. There they would be, safely aproned, safely behind glass: nine mothers. He does not think of them as mothers any more.

Ronette is doing his table tonight. From between his half-closed eyelids Donny watches her thin averted face. He can see one earring, a little gold hoop. It goes right through her ear. Only Italians and cheap girls have pierced ears, says his mother. It would hurt to have a hole put through your ear. It would take bravery. He wonders what the inside of Ronette's room looks like, what other cheap, intriguing things she's got in there. About someone like Hilary he doesn't have to wonder, because he already knows: the clean bedspread, the rows of shoes in their shoe-trees, the comb and brush and manicure set laid out on the dresser like implements in a surgery.

Behind Ronette's bowed head there's the skin of a rattlesnake, a big one, nailed to the wall. That's what you have to watch out for around here: rattlesnakes. Also poison ivy, thunderstorms, and drowning. A whole war canoe full of kids drowned last year, but they were from another camp. There's been some talk of making everyone wear sissy life-jackets; the mothers want it. Donny would like a rattlesnake skin of his own, to nail up over his bed; but even if he caught the snake himself, strangled it with his bare hands, bit its head off, he'd never be allowed to keep the skin.

Mr. B. winds up the grace and sits down, and the campers begin again their three-times-daily ritual of bread-grabbing, face-stuffing, under-the-table kicking, whispered cursing. Ronette comes from the kitchen with a platter: macaroni and cheese. "There you go, boys," she says, with her good-natured, lopsided smile.

"Thank you kindly, ma'am," says Darce the counsellor, with fraudulent charm. Darce has a reputation as a make-out artist; Donny knows he's after Ronette. This makes him feel sad. Sad, and too young. He would like to get out of his own body for a while; he'd like to be somebody else.

The waitresses are doing the dishes. Two to scrape, one to wash, one to rinse in the scalding-hot rinsing sink, three to dry. The other two sweep the floors and wipe off the tables. Later, the number of dryers will vary because of days off—they'll choose to take their days off in twos, so they can double-date with the counsellors—but today all are here. It's early in the season, things are still fluid, the territories are not yet staked out.

While they work they sing. They're missing the ocean of music in which they float during the winter. Pat and Liz have both brought their portables, though you can't pick up much radio out here, it's too far from shore. There's a record player in the counsellors' rec hall, but the records are out of date. Patti Page, The Singing Rage. "How Much Is That Doggie in the Window." "The Tennessee Waltz." Who waltzes any more?

"'Wake up, little Susie,'" trills Sandy. The Everly Brothers are popular this summer; or they were, on the mainland, when they left.

"'What're we gonna tell your mama, what're we gonna tell your pa,'" sing the others. Joanne can improvise the alto harmony, which makes everything sound less screechy.

Hilary, Stephanie, and Alex don't sing this one. They go to a private school, all girls, and are better at rounds, like "Fire's Burning" and "White Coral Bells." They are good at tennis though, and sailing, skills that have passed the others by.

It's odd that Hilary and the other two are here at all, waitressing at Camp Adanaqui; it's not as if they need the money. (Not like me, thinks Joanne, who haunts the mail desk every noon to see if she got her scholarship.) But it's the doing of their mothers. According to Alex, the three mothers banded together and jumped Mrs. B. at a charity function, and twisted her arm. Naturally Mrs. B. would attend the same functions as the mothers: they've seen her, sunglasses pushed up on her forehead, a tall drink in her hand, entertaining on the veranda of Mr. B.'s white hilltop house, which is well away from the camp proper. They've seen the guests, in their spotless, well-pressed sailing clothes. They've heard the laughter, the voices, husky and casual. Oh God don't tell me. Like Hilary.

"We were kidnapped," says Alex. "They thought it was time we met some boys."

Joanne can see it for Alex, who is chubby and awkward, and for Stephanie, who is built like a boy and walks like one; but Hilary? Hilary is classic. Hilary is like a shampoo ad.

Hilary is perfect. She ought to be sought after. Oddly, here she is not.

Ronette is scraping, and drops a plate. "Shoot," she says. "What a stunned broad." Nobody bawls her out or even teases her as they would anyone else. She is a favourite with them, though it's hard to put your finger on why. It isn't just that she's easygoing: so is Liz, so is Pat. She has some mysterious, extra status. For instance, everyone else has a nickname: Hilary is Hil, Stephanie is Steph, Alex is Al; Joanne is Jo, Tricia is Trish, Sandy is San. Pat and Liz, who cannot be contracted any further, have become Pet and Lizard. Only Ronette has been accorded the dignity of her full, improbable name.

In some ways she is more grown-up than the rest of them. But it isn't because she knows more things. She knows fewer things; she often has trouble making her way through the vocabularies of the others, especially the offhand slang of the private-school trio. "I don't get that," is what she says, and the others take a delight in explaining, as if she's a foreigner, a cherished visitor from some other country. She goes to movies and watches television like the rest of them but she has few opinions about what she has seen. The most she will say is "Crap" or "He's not bad." Though friendly, she is cautious about expressing approval in words. "Fair" is her best compliment. When the others talk about what they've read or what subjects they will take next year at university, she is silent.

But she knows other things, hidden things. Secrets. And these other things are older, and on some level more important. More fundamental. Closer to the bone.

Or so thinks Joanne, who has a bad habit of novelizing.

Outside the window Darce and Perry stroll by, herding a group of campers. Joanne recognizes a few of them: Donny, Monty. It's hard to remember the campers by name. They're just a crowd of indistinguishable, usually grimy young boys who have to be fed three times a day, whose crusts and crumbs and rinds have to be cleaned up afterwards. The counsellors call them Grubbies.

But some stand out. Donny is tall for his age, all elbows and spindly knees, with huge deep-blue eyes; even when he's swearing—they all swear during meals, furtively but also loudly enough so that the waitresses can hear them—it's more like a meditation, or more like a question, as if he's trying the words out, tasting them. Monty on the other hand is like a miniature forty-five-year-old: his shoulders already have a businessman's slump, his paunch is fully formed. He walks with a pompous little strut. Joanne thinks he's hilarious.

Right now he's carrying a broom with five rolls of toilet paper threaded onto the handle. All the boys are: they're on Bog Duty, sweeping out the outhouses, replacing the paper. Joanne wonders what they do with the used sanitary napkins in the brown paper bag in the waitresses' private outhouse. She can imagine the remarks.

"Company...halt!" shouts Darce. The group shambles to a stop in front of the window. "Present . . . arms!" The brooms are raised, the ends of the toilet-paper rolls fluttering in the breeze like flags. The girls laugh and wave.

Monty's salute is half-hearted: this is well beneath his dignity. He may rent out his binoculars—that story is all over camp, by now—but he has no interest in using them himself. He has made that known. *Not on these girls*, he says, implying higher tastes.

Darce himself gives a comic salute, then marches his bunch away. The singing in the kitchen has stopped; the topic among the waitresses is now the counsellors. Darce is the best, the most admired, the most desirable. His teeth are the whitest, his hair the blondest, his grin the sexiest. In the counsellors' rec hall, where they go every night after the dishes are done, after they've changed out of their blue uniforms into their jeans and pullovers, after the campers have been inserted into their beds for the night, he has flirted with each one of them in turn. So who was he really saluting?

"It was me," says Pat, joking. "Don't I wish."

"Dream on," says Liz.

"It was Hil," says Stephanie loyally. But Joanne knows it wasn't. It wasn't her, either. It was Ronette. They all suspect it. None of them says it.

"Perry likes Jo," says Sandy.

"Does not," says Joanne. She has given out that she has a boyfriend already and is therefore exempt from these contests. Half of this is true: she has a boyfriend. This summer he has a job as a salad chef on the Canadian National, running back and forth across the continent. She pictures him standing at the back of the train, on the caboose, smoking a cigarette between bouts of salad-making, watching the country slide away behind him. He writes her letters, in blue ball-point pen, on lined paper. *My first night on the Prairies*, he writes. *It's magnificent—all that land and sky. The sunsets are unbelievable.* Then there's a line across the page and a new date, and he gets to the Rockies. Joanne resents it a little that he raves on about places she's never been. It seems to her a kind of male showing-off: he's footloose. He closes with *Wish you were here* and several X's and O's. This seems too formal, like a letter to your mother. Like a peck on the cheek.

She put the first letter under her pillow, but woke up with blue smears on her face and the pillowcase both. Now she keeps the letters in her suitcase under the bed. She's having trouble remembering what he looks like. An image flits past, his face close up, at night, in the front seat of his father's car. The rustle of cloth. The smell of smoke.

Miss Frisk bumbles into the kitchen. She's short, plump, flustered; what she wears, always, is a hairnet over her grey bun, worn wool slippers—there's something wrong with her toes— and a faded blue knee-length sweater-coat, no matter how hot it is. She thinks of this summer job as her vacation. Occasionally she can be seen bobbing in the water in a droopy-chested bathing suit and a white rubber cap with the earflaps up. She never gets her head wet, so why she wears the cap is anyone's guess.

"Well, girls. Almost done?" She never calls the waitresses by name. To their faces they are *girls*, behind their backs *My girls*. They are her excuse for everything that goes wrong: *One of the girls must have done it*. She also functions as a sort of chaperon: her cabin is on the pathway that leads to theirs, and she has radar ears, like a bat.

I will never be that old, thinks Joanne. I will die before I'm thirty. She knows this absolutely. It's a tragic but satisfactory thought. If necessary, if some wasting disease refuses to carry her off, she'll do it herself, with pills. She is not at all unhappy but she intends to be, later. It seems required.

This is no country for old men, she recites to herself. One of the poems she memorized, though it wasn't on the final exam. Change that to old women.

When they're all in their pyjamas, ready for bed, Joanne offers to read them the rest of the True Trash story. But everyone is too tired, so she reads it herself, with her flashlight, after the one feeble bulb has been switched off. She has a compulsion about getting to the ends of things. Sometimes she reads books backwards.

Needless to say, Marleen gets knocked up and Dirk takes off on his motorcycle when he finds out. *I'm not the settling-down type, baby. See ya round.* Vroom. The mother practically has a nervous breakdown, because she made the same mistake when young and blew her chances and now look at her. Marleen cries and regrets, and even prays. But luckily the other shoe clerk, the boring one, still wants to marry her. So that's what happens. The mother forgives her, and Marleen herself learns the true value of quiet devotion. Her life isn't exciting maybe, but it's a good life, in the trailer park, the three of them. The baby is adorable. They buy a dog. It's an Irish setter, and chases sticks in the twilight while the baby laughs. This is how the story ends, with the dog.

Joanne stuffs the magazine down between her narrow little bed and the wall. She's almost crying. She will never have a dog like that, or a baby either. She doesn't want them, and anyway how would she have time, considering everything she has to get done? She has a long, though vague, agenda. Nevertheless, she feels deprived.

Between two oval hills of pink granite there's a small crescent of beach. The boys, wearing their bathing suits (as they never do on canoe trips but only around the camp where they might be seen by girls), are doing their laundry, standing up to their knees and swabbing their wet T-shirts and underpants with yellow bars of Sunlight soap. This only happens when they run out of clothes, or when the stench of dirty socks in the cabin becomes too overpowering. Darce the counsellor is supervising, stretched out on a rock, taking the sun on his already tanned torso and smoking a fag. It's forbidden to smoke in front of the campers but he knows this bunch won't tell. To be on the safe side he's furtive about it, holding the cigarette down close to the rock and sneaking quick puffs.

Something hits Donny in the side of the head. It's Ritchie's wet underpants, squashed into a ball. Donny throws them back and soon there's an underpants war. Monty refused to join in, so he becomes the common target. "Sod off!" he yells.

"Cut it out, you pinheads," Darce says. But he isn't really paying attention: he's seen something else, a flash of blue uniform, up among the trees. The waitresses aren't supposed to be over here on this side of the island. They're supposed to be on their own dock, having their afternoon break.

Darce is up among the trees now, one arm braced against a trunk. A conversation is going on; there are murmurs. Donny knows it's Ronette, he can tell by the shape, by the colour of the hair. And here he is, with his washboard ribs exposed, his hairless chest, throwing underpants around like a kid. He's disgusted with himself.

Monty, outnumbered but not wanting to admit defeat, says he needs to take a crap and disappears along the path to the outhouse. By now Darce is nowhere in sight. Donny captures Monty's laundry, which is already finished and wrung out and spread neatly on the hot rock to dry. He starts tossing it up into a jack pine, piece by piece. The others, delighted, help him. By the time Monty gets back, the tree is festooned with Monty's underpants and the other boys are innocently rinsing.

They're on one of the pink granite islands, the four of them: Joanne and Ronette, Perry and Darce. It's a double date. The two canoes have been pulled half out of the water and roped to the obligatory jack pines, the fire has done its main burning and is dying down to coals. The western sky is still peach-toned and luminous, the soft ripe juicy moon is rising, the evening air is warm and sweet, the waves wash gently against the rocks. It's the Summer Issue, thinks Joanne. *Lazy Daze. Tanning Tips. Shipboard Romance.*

Joanne is toasting a marshmallow. She has a special way of doing it: she holds it close to the coals but not so close that it catches fire, just close enough so that it swells up like a pillow and browns gently. Then she pulls off the toasted skin and eats it, and toasts the white inside part the same way, peeling it down to the core. She licks marshmallow goo off her fingers and stares pensively into the shifting red glow of the coal bed. All of this is a way of ignoring or pretending to ignore what is really going on.

There ought to be a teardrop, painted and static, on her cheek. There ought to be a caption: *Heartbreak*. On the spread-out groundsheet right behind her, his knee touching her back, is Perry, cheesed off with her because she won't neck with him. Off behind the rocks, out of the dim circle of fire-light, are Ronette and Darce. It's the third week in July and by now they're a couple, everyone knows it. In the rec hall she wears his sweatshirt with the St. Jude's crest; she smiles more these days, and even laughs when the other girls tease her about him. During this teasing Hilary does not join in. Ronette's face seems rounder, healthier, its angles smoothed out as if by a hand. She is less watchful, less diffident. She ought to have a caption too, thinks Joanne. *Was I Too Easy?*

There are rustlings from the darkness, small murmurings, breathing noises. It's like a movie theatre on Saturday night. Group grope. *The young in one another's arms*. Possibly, thinks Joanne, they will disturb a rattlesnake.

Perry puts a hand, tentatively, on her shoulder. "Want me to toast you a marshmallow?" she says to him politely. The frosty freeze. Perry is no consolation prize. He merely irritates her, with his peeling sunburnt skin and begging spaniel's eyes. Her so-called real boyfriend is no help either, whizzing on his train tracks back and forth across the prairies, writing his by-now infrequent inky letters, the image of his face all but obliterated, as if it's been soaked in water.

Nor is it Darce she wants, not really. What she wants is what Ronette has: the power to give herself up, without reservation and without commentary. It's that languor, that leaning back. Voluptuous mindlessness. Everything Joanne herself does is surrounded by quotation marks.

"Marshmallows. Geez," says Perry, in a doleful, cheated voice. All that paddling, and what for? Why the hell did she come along, if not to make out?

Joanne fells guilty of a lapse of manners. Would it hurt so much to kiss him?

Yes. It would.

Donny and Monty are on a canoe trip, somewhere within the tangled bush of the mainland. Camp Adanaqui is known for its tripping. For five days they and the others, twelve boys in all, have been paddling across lake after lake, hauling the gear over wave-rounded boulders or through the suck and stench of the moose-meadows at the portage entrances, grunting uphill with the packs and canoes, slapping the mosquitoes off their legs. Monty has blisters, on both his feet and his hands. Donny isn't too sad about that. He himself has a festering sliver. Maybe he will get blood-poisoning, become delirious, collapse and die on a portage, among the rocks and pine needles. That will serve someone right. Someone ought to be made to pay for the pain he's feeling.

The counsellors are Darce and Perry. During the days they crack the whip; at night they relax, backs against a rock or tree, smoking and supervising while the boys light the fire, carry the water, cook the Kraft Dinners. They both have smooth large muscles which ripple under their tans, they both—by now—have stubbly beards. When everyone goes swimming Donny sneaks covert, envious looks at their groins. They make him feel spindly, and infantile in his own desires.

Right now it's night. Perry and Darce are still up, talking in low voices, poking the embers of the dying fire. The boys are supposed to be asleep. There are tents in case of rain, but nobody's suggested putting them up since the day before yesterday. The smell of grime and sweaty feet and wood smoke is getting too potent at close quarters; the sleeping bags are high as cheese. It's better to be outside, rolled up in the bag, a groundsheet handy in case of a deluge, head under a turned-over canoe.

Monty is the only one who has voted for a tent. The bugs are getting to him; he says he's allergic. He hates canoe trips and makes no secret of it. When he's older, he says, and can finally get his hands on the family boodle, he's going to buy the place from Mr. B. and close it down. "Generations of boys unborn will thank me," he says. "They'll give me a medal." Sometimes Donny almost likes him. He's so blatant about wanting to be filthy rich. No hypocrisy about him, not like some of the other millionaire offshoots, who pretend they want to be scientists or something else that's not paid too much.

Now Monty's twisting around, scratching his bites. "Hey Finley," he whispers.

"Go to sleep," says Donny.

"I bet they've got a flask."

"What?"

"I bet they're drinking. I smelled it on Perry's breath yesterday."

"So?" says Donny.

"So," says Monty. "It's against the rules. Maybe we can get something out of them."

Donny has to hand it to him. He certainly knows the angles. At the very least they might be able to share the wealth.

The two of them inch out of their sleeping bags and circle around the fire, keeping low. Their practice while spying on the waitresses stands them in good stead. They crouch behind a bushy spruce, watching for lifted elbows or the outlines of bottles, their ears straining.

But what they hear isn't about booze. Instead it's about Ronette. Darce is talking about her as if she's a piece of meat. From what he's implying, she lets him do anything he wants. "Summer sausage" is what he calls her. This is an expression Donny has never heard before, and ordinarily he would think it was hilarious.

Monty sniggers under his breath and pokes Donny in the ribs with his elbow. Does he know how much it hurts, is he rubbing it in? *Donny loves Ronette.* The ultimate grade six insult, to be accused of loving someone. Donny feels as if it's he himself who's been smeared with words, who's had his face rubbed in them. He knows Monty will repeat this conversation to the other boys. He will say Darce has been porking Ronette. Right now Donny detests this word, with its conjuring of two heaving pigs, or two dead but animate uncooked Sunday roasts; although just yesterday he used it himself, and found it funny enough.

He can hardly charge out of the bushes and punch Darce in the nose. Not only would he look ridiculous, he'd get flattened.

He does the only thing he can think of. Next morning, when they're breaking camp, he pinches Monty's binoculars and sinks them in the lake.

Monty guesses, and accuses him. Some sort of pride keeps Donny from denying it. Neither can he say why he did it. When they get back to the island there's an unpleasant conversation with Mr. B. in the dining hall. Or not a conversation: Mr. B. talks, Donny is silent. He does not look at Mr. B. but at the pike's head on the wall, with its goggling voyeur's eye.

The next time the mahogany inboard goes back into town, Donny is in it. His parents are not pleased.

It's the end of summer. The campers have already left, though some of the counsellors and all of the waitresses are still here. Tomorrow they'll go down to the main dock, climb into the slow launch, thread their way among the pink islands, heading towards winter.

It's Joanne's half-day off so she isn't in the dining hall, washing the dishes with the others. She's in the cabin, packing up. Her duffle bag is finished, propped like an enormous canvas wiener against her bed; now she's doing her small suitcase. Her paycheque is already tucked inside: two hundred dollars, which is a lot of money.

Ronette comes into the cabin, still in her uniform, shutting the screen door quietly behind her. She sits down on Joanne's bed and lights a cigarette. Joanne is standing there with her folded-up flannelette pyjamas, alert: something's going on. Lately, Ronette has returned to her previous taciturn self; her smiles have become rare. In the counsellors' rec hall, Darce is again playing the field. He's been circling around Hilary, who's pretending—out of consideration for Ronette—not to notice. Maybe, now, Joanne will get to hear what caused the big split. So far Ronette has not said anything about it.

Ronette looks up at Joanne, through her long yellow bangs. Looking up like that makes her seem younger, despite the red lipstick. "I'm in trouble," she says.

"What sort of trouble?" says Joanne. Ronette smiles sadly, blows out smoke. Now she looks old. "You know. Trouble."

"Oh," says Joanne. She sits down beside Ronette, hugging the flannelette pyjamas. She feels cold. It must be Darce. *Caught in that sensual music.* Now he will have to marry her. Or something. "What're you going to do?"

"I don't know," says Ronette. "Don't tell, okay? Don't tell the others."

"Aren't you going to tell *him*?" says Joanne. She can't imagine doing that, herself. She can't imagine any of it.

"Tell who?" Ronette says.

"Darce."

Ronette blows out more smoke. "Darce," she says. "Mr. Chickenshit. It's not *his*."

Joanne is astounded, and relieved. But also annoyed with herself: what's gone past her, what has she missed? "It's not? Then whose is it?"

But Ronette has apparently changed her mind about confiding. "That's for me to know and you to find out," she says, with a small attempt at a laugh.

"Well," says Joanne. Her hands are clammy, as if it's her that's in trouble. She wants to be helpful, but has no idea how. "Maybe you could—I don't know." She doesn't know. An abortion? That is a dark and mysterious word, connected with the States. You have to go away. It costs a lot of money. A home for unwed mothers, followed by adoption? Loss washes through her. She foresees Ronette, bloated beyond recognition, as if she's drowned—a sacrifice, captured by her own body, offered up to it. Truncated in some way, disgraced. Unfree. There is something nunlike about this condition. She is in awe. "I guess you could get rid of it, one way or another," she says; which is not at all what she feels. *Whatever is begotten, born, and dies.*

"Are you kidding?" says Ronette, with something like contempt. "Hell, not me." She throws her cigarette on the floor, grinds it out with her heel. "I'm keeping it. Don't worry, my mom will help me out."

"Yeah," says Joanne. Now she has caught her breath; now she's beginning to wonder why Ronette has dumped all this on her, especially since she isn't willing to tell the whole thing. She's beginning to feel cheated, imposed upon. So who's the guy, so which one of them? She shuffles through the faces of the counsellors, trying to remember hints, traces of guilt, but finds nothing.

"Anyways," says Ronette, "I won't have to go back to school. Thank the Lord for small mercies, like they say."

Joanne hears bravado, and desolation. She reaches out a hand, gives Ronette's arm a small squeeze. "Good luck," she says. It comes out sounding like something you'd say before a race or an exam, or a war. It sounds stupid.

Ronette grins. The gap in her teeth shows, at the side. "Same to you," she says.

Eleven years later Donny is walking along Yorkville Avenue, in Toronto, in the summer heat. He's no longer Donny. At some point, which even he can't remember exactly, he has changed into Don. He's wearing sandals, and a white Indian-style shirt over his cut-off jeans. He has longish hair and a beard. The beard has come out yellow, whereas the hair is brown. He likes the effect: WASP Jesus or Hollywood Viking, depending on his mood. He has a string of wooden beads around his neck.

This is how he dresses on Saturdays, to go to Yorkville; to go there and just hang around, with the crowds of others who are doing the same. Sometimes he gets high, on the pot that circulates freely as cigarettes did once. He thinks he should be enjoying this experience more than he actually does.

During the rest of the week he has a job in his father's law office. He can get away with the beard there, just barely, as long as he balances it with a suit. (But even the older guys are growing their sideburns and wearing coloured shirts, and using words like "creative" more than they used to.) He doesn't tell the people he meets in Yorkville about this job, just as he doesn't tell the law office about his friends' acid trips. He's leading a double life. It feels precarious, and brave.

Suddenly, across the street, he sees Joanne. He hasn't even thought about her for a long time, but it's her all right. She isn't wearing the tie-dyed or flowing-shift uniform of the Yorkville girls; instead she's dressed in a brisk, businesslike white mini-skirt, with matching suit-jacket top. She's swinging a briefcase, striding along as if she has a purpose. This makes her stand out: the accepted walk here is a saunter.

Donny wonders whether he should run across the street, intercept her, reveal what he thinks of as his true but secret identity. Now all he can see is her back. In a minute she'll be gone.

"Joanne," he calls. She doesn't hear him. He dodges between cars, catches up to her, touches her elbow. "Don Finley," he says. He's conscious of himself standing there, grinning like a fool. Luckily and a little disappointingly, she recognizes him at once.

"Donny!" she says. "My God, you're grown!"

"I'm taller than you," he says, like a kid, an idiot.

"You were then," she says, smiling. "I mean you've grown up."

"So have you," says Donny, and they find themselves laughing, almost like equals. Three years, four years between them. It was a large difference, then. Now it's nothing.

So, thinks Joanne, Donny is no longer Donny. That must mean Ritchie is now Richard. As for Monty, he has become initials only, and a millionaire. True, he inherited some of it, but he's used it to advantage; Joanne has tuned in on his exploits now and then, in the business papers. And he got married to Hilary, three years ago. She saw that in the paper too.

They go for coffee and sit drinking it at one of the new, daring, outside tables, under a large, brightly painted wooden parrot. There's an intimacy between them, as if they are old friends. Donny asks Joanne what she's doing. "I live by my wits," she says. "I free-lance." At the moment she's writing ad copy. Her face is thinner, she's lost that adolescent roundness; her once nondescript hair has been shaped into a stylish cap. Good enough legs too. You have to have good legs to wear a mini. So many women look stumpy in them, hams in cloth, their legs bulging out the bottom like loaves of white bread. Joanne's legs are out of sight under the table, but Donny finds himself dwelling on them as he never did when they were clearly visible, all the way up, on the waitresses' dock. He'd skimmed over those legs then, skimmed over Joanne altogether. It was Ronette who had held his attention. He is more of a connoisseur, by now.

"We used to spy on you," he says. "We used to watch you skinny-dipping." In fact they'd never managed to see that much. The girls had held their towels around their bodies until the last minute, and anyway it was dusk. There would be a blur of white, some shrieking and splashing. The great thing would have been pubic hair. Several boys claimed sightings, but Donny had felt they were lying. Or was that just envy?

"Did you?" says Joanne absently. Then, "I know. We could see the bushes waving around. We thought it was so cute."

Donny feels himself blushing. He's glad he has the beard; it conceals things. "It wasn't cute," he says. "Actually we were pretty vicious." He's remembering the word *pork*. "Do you ever see the others?"

"Not any more," says Joanne. "I used to see a few of them, at university. Hilary and Alex. Pat sometimes."

"What about Ronette?" he says, which is the only thing he really wants to ask.

"I used to see Darce," says Joanne, as if she hasn't heard him.

Used to see is an exaggeration. She saw him once.

It was in the winter, a February. He phoned her, at *The*

Varsity office: that was how he knew where to find her, he'd seen her name in the campus paper. By that time Joanne scarcely remembered him. The summer she'd been a waitress was three years, light-years, away. The railroad-chef boyfriend was long gone; nobody so innocent had replaced him. She no longer wore white bucks, no longer sang songs. She wore turtlenecks and drank beer and a lot of coffee, and wrote cynical exposés of such things as campus dining facilities. She'd given up the idea of dying young, however. By this time it seemed overly romantic.

What Darce wanted was to go out with her. Specifically, he wanted her to go to a fraternity party with him. Joanne was so taken aback that she said yes, even though fraternities were in political disfavour among the people she travelled with now. It was something she would have to do on the sly, and she did. She had to borrow a dress from her roommate, however. The thing was a semi-formal, and she had not deigned to go to a semi-formal since high school.

She had last seen Darce with sun-bleached hair and a deep glowing tan. Now, in his winter skin, he looked wan and malnourished. Also, he no longer flirted with everyone. He didn't even flirt with Joanne. Instead he introduced her to a few other couples, danced her perfunctorily around the floor, and proceeded to get very drunk on a mixture of grape juice and straight alcohol that the fraternity brothers called Purple Jesus. He told her he'd been engaged to Hilary for over six months, but she'd just ditched him. She wouldn't even say why. He said he'd asked Joanne out because she was the kind of girl you could talk to, he knew she would understand. After that he threw up a lot of Purple Jesus, first onto her dress, then— when she'd led him outside, to the veranda—onto a snowdrift. The colour scheme was amazing.

Joanne got some coffee into him and hitched a lift back to the residence, where she had to climb up the icy fire escape and in at a window because it was after hours.

Joanne was hurt. All she was for him was a big flapping ear. Also she was irritated. The dress she'd borrowed was pale blue, and the Purple Jesus would not come out with just water. Darce called the next day to apologize—St. Jude's at least taught manners, of a sort—and Joanne stuck him with the cleaning bill. Even so there was a faint residual stain.

While they were dancing, before he started to slur and reel, she said, "Do you ever hear from Ronette?" She still had the narrative habit, she still wanted to know the ends of stories. But he'd looked at her in complete bewilderment.

"Who?" he said. It wasn't a put-down, he really didn't remember. She found this blank in his memory offensive. She herself might forget a name, a face even. But a body? A body that had been so close to your own, that had generated those murmurings, those rustlings in the darkness, that aching pain—it was an affront to bodies, her own included.

After the interview with Mr. B. and the stuffed pike's head, Donny walks down the small beach where they do their laundry. The rest of his cabin is out sailing, but he's free now of camp routine, he'd been discharged. A dishonourable discharge. After seven summers of being under orders here he can do what he wants. He has no idea what this might be.

He sits on a bulge of pink rock, feet on the sand. A lizard goes across the rock, near his hand, not fast. It hasn't spotted him. Its tail is blue and will come off if grabbed. Skinks, they're called. Once he would have taken joy from this knowledge. The waves wash in, wash out, the familiar heartbeat. He closes his eyes and hears only a machine. Possibly he is very angry, or sad. He hardly knows.

Ronette is there without warning. She must have come down the path behind him, through the trees. She's still in her uniform, although it isn't close to dinner. It's only late afternoon, when the waitresses usually leave their dock to go and change.

Ronette sits down beside him, takes out her cigarettes from some hidden pocket under her apron. "Want a cig?" she says.

Donny takes one and says, "Thank you." Not *thanks*, not wordlessly like leather-jacketed men in movies, but "Thank you," like a good boy from St. Jude's, like a suck. He lets her light it. What else can he do? She's got the matches. Gingerly he inhales. He doesn't smoke much really, and is afraid of coughing.

"I heard they kicked you out," Ronette says. "That's really tough."

"It's okay," says Donny. "I don't care." He can't tell her why, how noble he's been. He hopes he won't cry.

"I heard you tossed Monty's binoculars," she says. "In the lake."

Donny can only nod. He glances at her. She's smiling; he can see the heartbreaking space at the side of her mouth: the missing tooth. She thinks he's funny.

"Well, I'm with you," she says. "He's a little creep."

"It wasn't because of him," says Donny, overcome by the need to confess, or to be taken seriously. "It was because of Darce." He turns, and for the first time looks her straight in the eyes. They are so green. Now his hands are shaking. He drops the cigarette in the sand. They'll find the butt tomorrow, after he's gone. After he's gone, leaving Ronette behind, at the mercy of other people's words. "It was because of you. What they were saying about you. Darce was."

Ronette isn't smiling any more. "Such as what?" she says.

"Never mind," says Donny. "You don't want to know."

"I know anyhow," Ronette says. "That shit." She sounds resigned rather than angry. She stands up, puts both her hands behind her back. It takes Donny a moment to realize she's untying her apron. When she's got it off she takes him by the hand, pulls gently. He allows himself to be led around the hill of rock, out of sight of anything but the water. She sits down, lies down, smiles as she reaches up, arranges his hands. Her blue uniform unbuttons down the front. Donny can't believe this is happening, to him, in full daylight. It's like sleepwalking, it's like running too fast, it's like nothing else.

"Want another coffee?" Joanne says. She nods to the waitress. Donny hasn't heard her.

"She was really nice to me," he is saying. "Ronette. You know, when Mr. B. turfed me out. That meant a lot to me at the time." He's feeling guilty, because he never wrote her. He didn't know where she lived, but he didn't take any steps to find out. Also, he couldn't keep himself from thinking: *They're right. She's a slut.* Part of him had been profoundly shocked by what she'd done. He hadn't been ready for it.

Joanne is looking at him with her mouth slightly open, as if he's a talking dog, a talking stone. He fingers his beard nervously, wondering what he's said wrong, or given away.

Joanne has just seen the end of the story, or one end of one story. Or at least a missing piece. So that's why Ronette wouldn't tell: it was Donny. She'd been protecting him; or maybe she'd been protecting herself. A fourteen-year-old boy. Ludicrous.

Ludicrous then, possible now. You can do anything now and it won't cause a shock. Just a shrug. Everything is *cool.* A line has been drawn and on the other side of it is the past, both darker and more brightly intense than the present.

She looks across the line and sees the nine waitresses in their bathing suits, in the clear blazing sunlight, laughing on the dock, herself among them; and off in the shadowy rustling bushes of the shoreline, sex lurking dangerously. It had been dangerous, then. It had been sin. Forbidden, secret, sullying. *Sick with desire.* Three dots had expressed it perfectly, because there had been no ordinary words for it.

On the other hand there had been marriage, which meant wifely checked aprons, playpens, a sugary safety.

But nothing has turned out that way. Sex has been domesticated, stripped of the promised mystery, added to the category of the merely expected. It's just what is done, mundane as hockey. It's celibacy these days that would raise eyebrows.

And what has become of Ronette, after all, left behind in the past, dappled by its chiaroscuro, stained and haloed by it, stuck with other people's adjectives? What is she doing, now that everyone else is following in her footsteps? More practically: did she have the baby, or not? Keep it or not? Donny, sitting sweetly across the table from her, is in all probability the father of a ten-year-old child, and he knows nothing about it at all.

Should she tell him? The melodrama tempts her, the idea of a revelation, a sensation, a neat ending.

But it would not be an ending, it would only be the beginning of something else. In any case, the story itself seems to her outmoded. It's an archaic story, a folktale, a mosaic artefact. It's a story that would never happen now.

The *Mysteries* of *Radio*

by
ROBERT BENCHLEY
(1889–1945)

I slipped this one in when my editor wasn't looking. "The Mysteries of Radio" isn't really a summer story. It's a radio story—but then, I'm a radio person, so that's okay. I remember hearing an old story about Thomas Hardy, the writer, who had a telephone installed in his house for many years but refused to use it. It was there on Mrs. Hardy's insistence, but he would have nothing to do with it. Then one day the phone was ringing and Hardy was the only one home. So he answered it. After that, he was so intrigued by modern technology that he monopolized the telephone for weeks. Anyway, this is a bit of an old-timer's story, for those who remember the days before...well, before almost everything except radio...

I wouldn't be surprised if I knew less about radio than any one in the world, and that is no faint praise. There may be some things, like horseshoeing and putting little ships in bottles, which are closed books to me, but I have a feeling that if someone were to be very patient and explain the principles to me I might be able to get the hang of it. But I don't have any such feeling about radio. A radio expert could come and live with me for two years, and be just as kind and gentle and explicit as a radio expert could be, and yet it would do no good. I simply never could understand it; so there is no good in teasing me to try.

As a matter of fact, I was still wrestling with the principle of the telephone when radio came along, and was still a long way from having mastered it. I knew that I could go to a mouthpiece and say a number into it and get another number, but I was not privy to the means by which this miracle was accomplished. Finally I gave up trying to figure it out, as the telephone company seemed to be getting along all right with it, and it was evident from the condition my own affairs were getting in that there were other things about which I had much better be worrying. And then came radio to confuse me further.

Of course, I know all about the fact that if you toss a stone into a pond it will send out concentric circles which reach to the shores. Everybody pulls that one when you ask them how sound is transmitted through the air. If I have been told about tossing a stone in a pond once I have been told it five hundred times. I have even gone out and done it myself, but I guess that I didn't have the knack, for the concentric circles ran for only about two feet and then disappeared.

But the stone in pond explanation is really no explanation at all, for there you have at least the stone and the pond to work with, whereas in radio you have nothing, absolutely nothing. If people tell me about the stone in the pond once again I shall begin to think that it is a gag worked up by those who don't understand the thing either. They have got to be more explicit if they want me to understand. Perhaps they don't care. I almost think that nobody cares whether I am enlightened or not. (I am sorry if I sound bitter about the thing, but I have stood it just about as long as I can.)

Somebody once did say something which made a great impression on me, but which I can hardly believe. He said that the air had always been full of these sounds, and that all the radio did was to give us some means of catching them. This is a horrible thought. To think that the room in which the Declaration of Independence was signed would have, by the mere installation of radio, been echoing with the strains of something corresponding to "I Kiss Your Hand, Madame," or that Robert and Elizabeth Browning held hands in a chamber which was at that very moment teeming with unheard sylla- bles explaining how to make bran muffins! Reason totters at the thought, and I mention the supposition here only to show how absurd the whole thing is.

But the suggestion is a haunting one, even though you, as I have done, discard it as impractical. If the air has always been full of music and voices which we have only just recently learned to make audible, what else might it not be full of right now which, perhaps in a hundred years, will also be dragged out into the light? If by the installation of a microphone at the other end and a receiving set at my end I learn that my room has all the time been full of noises made by the Little Gypsy Robber Sponge quartet in Newark or a man employed by some slipper concern in Michigan, why isn't it possible that it is also full of things I don't know about, such as the spirits of the men who murdered the little princes in the tower, or perhaps a couple of Borgias? It simply makes a mockery of privacy, that's all it does. A man ought to have some place where he can go and be alone without feeling that he may be breathing in a lot of strangers and what nots.

I will even concede that the air of out of doors may be full of sound waves, but you can't make me believe that they can get through the walls of great big houses. They might get through the walls of a summer hotel, or even come through an open front door and work their way upstairs. I will even go so far as to recognize the possibility of something erected on a roof catching them and bringing them down into the living room to disturb daddy when he is trying to take a nap. But to ask me to believe that a box which has no connection at all with the outside can be carried about a house which is securely locked, and still keep on playing sounds which have pushed their way through stone walls, is just a little too much. For this reason I have refused to turn on my portable radio set which was given to me on my birthday. I will not allow myself to be made a party to any such chicanery.

My biggest argument that the whole thing is a fake is the quality of the stuff that comes out of the air. It is the same thing which makes me distrust spiritualism—the quality of the material offered us from the spirit world. I am really a very simple minded man at heart and will believe most anything as long as the person who tells me has a pleasant face. I might very easily be won over to spiritualism, just as I have in the past been won over to Buddhism, osteopathy, and Swedish bread. But when I go into a darkened room with the expectation of hearing something out of the great unknown which will help clear up this mystery of life and death and find out merely that the uncle of some person in the room is still having that trouble with his hip which he had before he died, or that those old gray gloves which I thought I had lost are in my winter overcoat hanging in the hall closet, it all seems hardly worth the trouble.

It is much the same with radio. Scientists have gone to all the trouble of rigging up apparatus which will pull out of the air sounds which we were never able to hear before, the whole ether is thrown into a turmoil, the south pole is placed in connection with Greenland and modern life is revolutionized by the utilization of these mysterious sound waves. And with what result? We in New York hear Miss Ellen Drangle in Chicago singing "Mighty Lak a Rose." The mountain which brought forth a mouse did a good day's work in comparison.

All of this, however, is probably none of my business. I had better not sit here criticizing others for something which I couldn't possibly do myself. Probably that is what upsets me so—that I don't understand how it works. I have seen other people make it work and that has more or less discouraged me. They get so unpleasant about it. It would seem as if contact with such cosmic natural elements as electricity and sound waves and WJZ would have a tendency to make a man broadminded and gentle, but it doesn't work out that way. It just makes them nasty.

I had a cousin once who built a radio. It seemed to me to be a foolhardy thing to do in the first place, monkeying around with electricity and tubes and things, but I said nothing. He read books on the subject and bought a lot of truck and sat around trying to fit things together for weeks and weeks, not speaking to his family except to tell them to get away from there and, in general, behaving in a very boorish manner.

Finally he got the thing so that it would work and picked up some kind of concert which was being broadcast from a station about half a mile away. The selection was a marimba band playing "Moonlight Waves," and he was tickled to death. Everyone had to come in and listen and congratulate him. "You certainly are a wonder, Ed," they exclaimed, and he said nothing to dispute it. Then he tried another station and broke in on the middle of another marimba band playing "Moonlight Waves." He was so pleased at being able to get another station, however, that he let it finish. That happened to be the end of that program; so he tried what he called "Cleveland, Ohio." Well, it seemed that "Cleveland, Ohio," was specializing that day on marimba band selections of "Moonlight Waves" and Ed got another load of that for half an hour. By this time the rest of the family had tiptoed out of the room.

The upshot of it was that Ed never moved away from that radio set for ten days and nights, always turning little knobs and looking up charts, always hoping against hope, but always getting a marimba band playing "Moonlight Waves." He refused food that was brought to him, but somehow had some whisky smuggled in, which he consumed in great gulps to keep his courage up. Pretty soon this began to tell on him, and he grew emaciated and trembly and nobody dared go near him. His wife got the doctor to come, but he wouldn't let anyone come into the room, simply showing his teeth and growling like an old fox terrier every time the threshold was crossed. And all the time the moaning strains of "Moonlight Waves" dragged through the room, from Detroit, Chicago, Los Angeles, and Boston, until finally his family had to move over to the grandmother's and leave him to his ultimate breakdown, which took the form of crawling into the cabinet himself and singing "Moonlight Waves" until he collapsed and could be carried out.

They never found out quite what had been the matter. Some people said that he had built a gramophone by mistake, and that the marimba band number was a record which kept on playing and playing. Others said that he had stumbled on some new form of sound reproduction and had isolated a certain number of sound waves so that they never could get free. Articles were written about it in scientific journals and he was hailed as an inventor, but it didn't do him any good, as no one would want to buy a lot of sound waves which did nothing but play "Moonlight Waves" over and over again. The whole thing was very tragic.

It only goes to show, however, that even the people who know a lot about radio and electricity really don't know an awful lot, and makes me all the more contented to stick to my old banjo. I don't know many chords on it, but I do know where they come from.

An Adventure on *Island Rock*

by
LUCY MAUD MONTGOMERY
(1874–1942)

*I was at an "Anne of Green Gables" exhibit last summer
where Lucy Maud Montgomery's manuscripts were on display.
When I saw all those thick piles of paper gathered there before
me—pile after pile—I suddenly realize what a tremendously
industrious person Lucy Maud really was. "An Adventure on
Island Rock" is one of Montgomery's lesser-known tales—and
a favourite of mine. It's a simple sort of a boy-and-his-dog
story told in the familiar "Anne of Green Gables" way.*

Who was the man I saw talking to you in the hay-field?" asked Aunt Kate, as Uncle Richard came in to dinner.

"Bob Marks," said Uncle Richard briefly. "I've sold Laddie to him."

Ernest Hughes, the twelve-year old orphan boy whom Uncle "boarded and kept" for the chores he did, suddenly stopped eating.

"Oh, Mr. Lawson, you're not going to sell Laddie?" he cried chokily.

Uncle Richard stared at him. Never before, in the five years that Ernest had lived with him, had the quiet little fellow spoken without being spoken to, much less ventured to protest against anything Uncle Richard might do.

"Certainly I am," answered the latter curtly. "Bob offered me twenty dollars for the dog, and he's coming after him next week."

"Oh, Mr. Lawson," said Ernest, rising to his feet, his small, freckled face crimson. "Oh, don't sell Laddie! *Please*, Mr. Lawson, don't sell him!"

"What nonsense is this?" said Uncle Richard sharply. He was

a man who brooked no opposition from anybody, and who never changed his mind when it was once made up.

"Don't sell Laddie!" pleaded Ernest miserably. "He is the only friend I've got. I can't live if Laddie goes away. Oh, don't sell him, Mr. Lawson!"

"Sit down and hold your tongue," said Uncle Richard sternly. "The dog is mine, and I shall do with him as I think fit. He is sold, and that is all there is about it. Go on with your dinner."

But Ernest for the first time did not obey. He snatched his cap from the back of the chair, dashed it down over his eyes, and ran from the kitchen with a sob choking his breath. Uncle Richard looked angry, but Aunt Kate hastened to soothe him.

"Don't be vexed with the boy, Richard," she said. "You know he is very fond of Laddie. He's had to do with him ever since he was a pup, and no doubt he feels badly at the thought of losing him. I'm rather sorry myself that you have sold the dog."

"Well, he is sold, and there's an end of it. I don't say but that the dog is a good dog. But he is of no use to us, and twenty dollars will come in mighty handy just now. He's worth that to Bob, for he is a good watch dog, so we've both made a fair bargain."

Nothing more was said about Ernest or Laddie. I had taken no part in the discussion, for I felt no great interest in the matter. Laddie was a nice dog; Ernest was a quiet, inoffensive little fellow, five years younger than myself; that was all I thought about either of them.

I was spending my vacation at Uncle Richard's farm on the Nova Scotian Bay of Fundy shore. I was a great favourite with Uncle Richard, partly because he had been much attached to my mother, his only sister, partly because of my strong resemblance to his only son, who had died several years before. Uncle Richard was a stern, undemonstrative man, but I knew that he entertained a deep and real affection for me, and I always enjoyed my vacation sojourns at his place.

"What are you going to do this afternoon, Ned?" he asked, after the disturbance caused by Ernest's outbreak had quieted down.

"I think I'll row out to Island Rock," I replied. "I want to take some views of the shore from it."

Uncle Richard nodded. He was much interested in my new camera.

"If you're on it about four o'clock, you'll get a fine view of the 'Hole in the Wall' when the sun begins to shine on the water through it," he said. "I've often thought it would make a handsome picture."

"After I've finished taking the pictures I think I'll go down shore to Uncle Adam's and stay all night," I said. "Jim's dark room is more convenient than mine, and he has some pictures he is going to develop tonight, too."

I started for the shore about two o'clock. Ernest was sitting on a woodpile as I passed through the yard, with his arms about Laddie's neck and his face buried in Laddie's curly hair. Laddie was a handsome and intelligent black-and-white Newfoundland, with a magnificent coat. He and Ernest were great chums. I felt sorry for the boy who was to lose his pet.

"Don't take it so hard, Ern," I said, trying to comfort him. "Uncle will likely get another pup."

"I don't want any other pup!" Ernest blurted out. "Oh, Ned, won't you try and coax your uncle not to sell him? Perhaps he'd listen to you."

I shook my head. I knew Uncle Richard too well to hope that.

"Not in this case, Ern," I said. "He would say it did not concern me, and you know nothing moves him when he determines on a thing. You'll have to reconcile yourself to losing Laddie, I'm afraid."

Ernest's tow-coloured head went down on Laddie's neck again, and I, deciding that there was no use in saying anything more, proceeded towards the shore, which was about a mile from Uncle Richard's house. The beach along his farm and for several farms along shore was a lonely, untenanted one, for the fisher-folk all lived two miles further down, at Rowley's Cove. About three hundred yards from the shore was the peculiar formation known as Island Rock. This was a large rock that stood abruptly up out of the water. Below, about the usual water-line, it was seamed and fissured, but its summit rose up in a narrow, flat-topped peak. At low tide twenty feet of it was above water, but at high tide it was six feet and often more under water.

I pushed Uncle Richard's small flat down the rough path and rowed out to Island Rock. Arriving there, I thrust the painter deep into a narrow cleft. This was the usual way of mooring it, and no doubt of its safety occurred to me.

I scrambled up the rock and around to the eastern end, where there was a broader space for standing and from which some capital views could be obtained. The sea about the rock was calm, but there was quite a swell on and an off-shore breeze was blowing. There were no boats visible. The tide was low, leaving bare the curious caves and headlands along shore, and I secured a number of excellent snapshots. It was now three o'clock. I must wait another hour yet before I could get the best view of the "Hole in the Wall"—a huge, arch-like opening through a jutting headland to the west of me. I went around to look at it, when I saw a sight that made me stop short in dismay. This was nothing less than the flat, drifting outward around the point. The swell and suction of the water around the rock must have pulled her loose—and I was a prisoner! At first my only feeling was one of annoyance. Then a thought flashed into my mind that made me dizzy with fear. The tide would be high that night. If I could not escape from Island Rock I would inevitably be drowned.

I sat down limply on a ledge and tried to look matters fairly in the face. I could not swim; calls for help could not reach anybody; my only hope lay in the chance of somebody passing down the shore or of some boat appearing.

I looked at my watch. It was a quarter past three. The tide would begin to turn about five, but it would be at least ten before the rock would be covered. I had, then, little more than six hours to live unless rescued.

The flat was by this time out of sight around the point. I hoped that the sight of an empty flat drifting down shore might attract someone's attention and lead to investigation. That seemed to be my only hope. No alarm would be felt at

Uncle Richard's because of my non-appearance. They would suppose I had gone to Uncle Adam's.

I had heard of time seeming long to a person in my predicament, but to me it seemed fairly to fly, for every moment decreased my chance of rescue. I determined I would not give way to cowardly fear, so with a murmured prayer for help, I set myself to the task of waiting for death as bravely as possible. At intervals I shouted as loudly as I could and, when the sun came to the proper angle for the best view of the "Hole in the Wall," I took the picture. It afterwards turned out to be a great success, but I have never been able to look at it without a shudder.

At five the tide began to come in. Very, very slowly the water rose around Island Rock. Up, up, up it came, while I watched it with fascinated eyes, feeling like a rat in a trap. The sun fell lower and lower; at eight o'clock the moon rose large and bright; at nine it was a lovely night, clear, calm, bright as day, and the water was swishing over the highest ledge of the rock. With some difficulty I climbed to the top and sat there to await the end. I had no longer any hope of rescue but, by a great effort, I preserved self-control. If I had to die, I would at least face death staunchly. But when I thought of my mother at home, it tasked all my energies to keep from breaking down utterly.

Suddenly I heard a whistle. Never was sound so sweet. I stood up and peered eagerly shoreward. Coming around the "Hole in the Wall" headland, on top of the cliffs, I saw a boy and a dog. I sent a wild halloo ringing shoreward.

The boy started, stopped and looked out towards Island Rock. The next moment he hailed me. It was Ernest's voice, and it was Laddie who was barking beside him.

"Ernest," I shouted wildly, "run for help—quick! quick! The tide will be over the rock in half an hour! Hurry, or you will be too late!"

Instead of starting off at full speed, as I expected him to do, Ernest stood still for a moment, and then began to pick his steps down a narrow path over the cliff, followed by Laddie.

"Ernest," I shouted frantically, "what are you doing? Why don't you go for help?"

Ernest had by this time reached a narrow ledge of rock just above the water-line. I noticed he was carrying something over his arm.

"It would take too long," he shouted. "By the time I got to the Cove and a boat could row back here, you'd be drowned. Laddie and I will save you. Is there anything there you can tie a rope to? I've a coil of rope here that I think will be long enough to reach you. I've been down to the Cove and Alec Martin sent it up to your uncle."

I looked about me; a smooth, round hole had been worn clean through a thin part of the apex of the rock.

"I could fasten the rope if I had it!" I called. "But how can you get it to me?"

For answer Ernest tied a bit of driftwood to the rope and put it into Laddie's mouth. The next minute the dog was swimming out to me. As soon as he came close I caught the rope. It was just long enough to stretch from shore to rock, allowing for a couple of hitches which Ernest gave around a small boulder on the ledge. I tied my camera case on my head by means of some string I found in my pocket, then I slipped into the water and, holding to the rope, went hand over hand to the shore with Laddie swimming beside me. Ernest held on to the shoreward end of the rope like grim death, a task that was no light one for his small arms. When I finally scrambled up beside him, his face was dripping with perspiration and he trembled like a leaf.

"Ern, you are a brick!" I exclaimed. "You've saved my life!"

"No, it was Laddie," said Ernest, refusing to take any credit at all.

We hurried home and arrived at Uncle Richard's about ten, just as they were going to bed. When Uncle Richard heard what had happened, he turned very pale, and murmured, "Thank God!" Aunt Kate got me out of my wet clothes as quickly as possible, put me away to bed in hot blankets and dosed me with ginger tea. I slept like a top and felt none the worse for my experience the next morning.

At breakfast table Uncle Richard scarcely spoke. But, just as we finished, he said abruptly to Ernest, "I'm not going to sell

Laddie. You and the dog saved Ned's life between you, and no dog who helped do that is ever going to be sold by me. Henceforth he belongs to you. I give him to you for your very own."

"Oh, Mr. Lawson!" said Ernest, with shining eyes.

I never saw a boy look so happy. As for Laddie, who was sitting beside him with his shaggy head on Ernest's knee, I really believe the dog understood, too. The look in his eyes was almost human. Uncle Richard leaned over and patted him.

"Good dog!" he said. "Good dog!"

Casey
at the **Bat**

by
Ernest Thayer
(1863–1940)

A last pitch from the mound. A final swing at bat. An old favourite for many years: it's Casey at the bat…

Casey at the Bat

It looked extremely rocky
  For the Mudville nine that day;
The score stood two to four,
  With but an inning left to play;
So, when Cooney died at second,
  And Burrows did the same,
A pallor wreathed the features
  Of the patrons of the game.

A straggling few got up to go,
  Leaving there the rest,
With that hope which springs eternal
  Within the human breast,
For they thought: "If only Casey
  Could get a whack at that,"
They'd put up even money now,
  With Casey at the bat.

But Flynn preceded Casey,
  And likewise so did Blake,
And the former was a puddin',
  And the latter was a fake;
So on that stricken multitude
  A deathlike silence sat,
For there seemed but little chance
  Of Casey's getting to the bat.

But Flynn let drive a "single,"
   To the wonderment of all,
And the much-despised Blakey
   "Tore the cover off the ball,"
And when the dust had lifted,
   And they saw what had occurred,
There was Blakey safe at second,
   And Flynn a-huggin' third.

Then, from the gladdened multitude
   Went up a joyous yell,
It rumbled in the mountain tops,
   It rattled in the dell;
It struck upon the hillside
   And rebounded on the flat,
For Casey, mighty Casey,
   Was
         advancing
              to the
                  bat.

There was ease in Casey's manner
   As he stepped into his place,
There was pride in Casey's bearing
   And a smile on Casey's face;
And when, responding to the cheers,
   He lightly doffed his hat,
No stranger in the crowd could doubt
   'Twas Casey at the bat.

Ten thousand eyes were on him
  As he rubbed his hands with dirt,
Five thousand tongues applauded
  When he wiped them on his shirt;
Then when the writhing pitcher
  Ground the ball into his hip,
Defiance gleamed in Casey's eye,
  A sneer curled Casey's lip.

And now the leather-covered sphere
Came hurtling through the air,
An' Casey stood a-watchin' it
  In mighty grandeur there;
Close by the sturdy batsman
  The ball, unheeded, sped;
"That ain't my style!" said Casey;
  "Strike one!" the umpire said.

From the benches, black with people,
  There went up a muffled roar
Like the beating of storm waves
  On the stern and distant shore;
"Kill him! Kill the umpire!"
  Shouted someone on the stand;
And it's likely they'd have killed him
  Had not Casey raised his hand.

With the smile of Christian charity
  Great Casey's visage shone;
He stilled the rising tumult,
  He made the game go on;

He signalled to the pitcher,
    And once more the spheroid flew,
But Casey still ignored it,
And the umpire said, "Strike two!"

"Fraud!" cried the maddened thousands,
And the echo answered "Fraud!"
But one scornful look from Casey
    And the audience was awed;
They saw his face grow stern and cold,
    They saw his muscles strain,
And they knew that Casey
    Wouldn't let the ball go by again.

The sneer is gone from Casey's lips,
    His teeth are clenched in hate;
He pounds with cruel vengeance
    His bat upon the plate;
And now the pitcher holds the ball,
    And now he lets it go,
And now the air is shattered
    By the force of Casey's blow

Oh, somewhere in this favored land
    The sun is shining bright,
The band is playing somewhere
    And somewhere hearts are light;
And somewhere men are laughing
    And somewhere children shout,
But there is no joy in Mudville;
    Mighty Casey has struck out.

Copyright Acknowledgments

David Arnason. "A Girl's Story" reprinted with permission from: *The Happiest Man in the World*, © 1989 David Arnason, Talon Books Ltd., Vancouver, Canada.

Margaret Atwood. "True Trash" from *Wilderness Tips* by Margaret Atwood. Used by permission of the Canadian Publishers, McClelland & Stewart, Toronto.

Lesley-Anne Bourne. "Patio Talk" and "Vines" from *Skinny Girls* by Lesley-Anne Bourne. Used by permission of Penumbra Press, Ottawa.

Roch Carrier. "Moon Prayer" from *Prayers of a Very Wise Child* by Roch Carrier. Copyright © Les éditions internationales Alain Stanké, 1988. English translation Copyright © Sheila Fischman, 1991. Reprinted by permission of Penguin Books Canada Limited.

Janice Kulyk Keefer. "Viper's Bugloss" by Janice Kulyk Keefer is reprinted from *The Paris-Napoli Express* by permission of Oberon Press.

W.P. Kinsella. "The Thrill of the Grass" from *The Thrill of the Grass.* Copyright © W.P. Kinsella, 1984. Reprinted by permission of Penguin Books Canada Limited.

John Kooistra. "Shoo-fly Dyck." Copyright © John Kooistra 1990, 1994.

Joyce Marshall. "The Little White Girl" from *Any Time At All* by Joyce Marshall. Used by permission of the Canadian Publishers, McClelland & Stewart, Toronto. "Afterword" by Timothy Findley.

Guy de Maupassant. "Mouche" from *Selected Short Stories* by Guy de Maupassant, translated by Roger Colet (Penguin Classics, 1971) copyright © Roger Colet, 1971.

L.M. Montgomery. "An Adventure on Rock Island" from *Along the Shore* by L.M. Montgomery. Used by permission of the Canadian Publishers, McClelland & Stewart, Toronto.

Alice Munro. "Dulse" from *The Moons of Jupiter* by Alice Munro © 1982. Reprinted by permission of Macmillan Canada.

Katherine A. Porter. "The Circus" from *The Leaning Tower and other stories*, copyright 1935 and renewed 1963 by Katherine Anne Porter, reprinted by permission of Harcourt Brace & Company.

Paul Quarrington. "Poaching with My Old Guy": Copyright Paul Quarrington, August 1992.

Jane Urquhart. "Storm Glass" from *Storm Glass*, copyright © Jane Urquhart, 1987. Used by permission of The Porcupine's Quill, Inc.

Emile Zola. "Shellfish for Monsieur Chabre." © Douglas Parmée 1984. Reprinted from *The Attack on the Mill and Other Stories* by Emile Zola translated by Douglas Parmée (World's Classics 1984) by permission of Oxford University Press.